Between the Acts

Between the Acts

VIRGINIA WOOLF

Annotated and with an introduction
by Melba Cuddy-Keane

Mark Hussey, General Editor

A Harvest Book • Harcourt, Inc.
Orlando Austin New York San Diego London

Requests for permission to make copies of any part of the work should be
submitted online at www.harcourt.com/contact or mailed to the following address:
Permissions Department, Houghton Mifflin Harcourt Publishing Company,
6277 Sea Harbor Drive, Orlando, Florida 32887-6777.

www.HarcourtBooks.com

Library of Congress Cataloging-in-Publication Data
Woolf, Virginia, 882–94 .
Between the acts/Virginia Woolf; annotated and with an introduction
by Melba Cuddy-Keane; Mark Hussey, general editor.—Annotated ed., st ed.
p. cm.—(A Harvest book)
Includes bibliographical references.
. Pageants—Fiction. 2. Country homes—England—Fiction.
3. Psychological fiction. I. Cuddy-Keane, Melba. II. Hussey, Mark, 956 – III. Title.
PR6045.O72B42 2008
823'.9 2 —dc22 2008002970
ISBN 978-0-5-603473-9

Text set in Garamond MT
Designed by Cathy Riggs

Printed in the United States of America

First annotated edition

DOM 10 9 8 7 6 5 4 3

Contents

Between the Acts

Virginia Woolf

VIRGINIA WOOLF was born into what she once described as "a very communicative, literate, letter writing, visiting, articulate, late nineteenth century world." Her parents, Leslie and Julia Stephen, both previously widowed, began their marriage in 1878 with four young children: Laura (1870–1945), the daughter of Leslie Stephen and his first wife, Harriet Thackeray (1840–1875); and George (1868–1934), Gerald (1870–1937), and Stella Duckworth (1869–1897), the children of Julia Prinsep (1846–1895) and Herbert Duckworth (1833–1870). In the first five years of their marriage, the Stephens had four more children. Their third child, Virginia, was born in 1882, the year her father began work on the monumental *Dictionary of National Biography* that would earn him a knighthood in 1902. Virginia, her sister, Vanessa (1879–1961), and brothers, Thoby (1880–1906) and Adrian (1883–1948), all were born in the tall house at 22 Hyde Park Gate in London where the eight children lived with numerous servants, their eminent and irascible father, and their beautiful mother, who, in Woolf's words, was "in the very centre of that great Cathedral space that was childhood."

Woolf's parents knew many of the intellectual luminaries of the late Victorian era well, counting among their close friends novelists such as George Meredith, Thomas Hardy, and Henry James. Woolf's great-aunt Julia Margaret Cameron was a pioneering photographer who made portraits of the poets Alfred

Tennyson and Robert Browning, of the naturalist Charles Darwin, and of the philosopher and historian Thomas Carlyle, among many others. Beginning in the year Woolf was born, the entire Stephen family moved to Talland House in St. Ives, Cornwall, for the summer. There the younger children would spend their days playing cricket in the garden, frolicking on the beach, or taking walks along the coast, from where they could look out across the bay to the Godrevy lighthouse.

The early years of Woolf's life were marred by traumatic events. When she was thirteen, her mother, exhausted by a punishing schedule of charitable visits among the sick and poor, died from a bout of influenza. Woolf's half sister Stella took over the household responsibilities and bore the brunt of their self-pitying father's sorrow until she escaped into marriage in 1897 with Jack Hills, a young man who had been a favorite of Julia's. Within three months, Stella (who was pregnant) was dead, most likely from peritonitis. In this year, which she called "the first really *lived* year of my life," Woolf began a diary. Over the next twelve years, she would record in its pages her voracious reading, her impressions of people and places, feelings about her siblings, and events in the daily life of the large household.[1]

In addition to the premature deaths of her mother and half sister, there were other miseries in Woolf's childhood. In autobiographical writings and letters, Woolf referred to the sexual abuse she suffered at the hands of her two older half brothers, George and Gerald Duckworth. George, in one instance, explained his behavior to a family doctor as his effort to comfort his half sister for the fatal illness of their father. Sir Leslie died

---

[1]Woolf's early diary is published as *A Passionate Apprentice: The Early Journals, 1897–1909,* edited by Mitchell A. Leaska. A 1909 notebook discovered in 2002 has been published as *Carlyle's House and Other Sketches,* edited by David Bradshaw (London: Hesperus, 2003).

from cancer in 1904, and shortly thereafter the four Stephen children—Vanessa, Virginia, Thoby, and Adrian—moved together to the then-unfashionable London neighborhood of Bloomsbury. When Thoby Stephen began to bring his Cambridge University friends to the house on Thursday evenings, what would later become famous as the "Bloomsbury Group" began to form.

In an article marking the centenary of her father's birth, Woolf recalled his "allowing a girl of fifteen the free run of a large and quite unexpurgated library"—an unusual opportunity for a Victorian young woman, and evidence of the high regard Sir Leslie had for his daughter's intellectual talents. In her diary, she recorded the many different kinds of books her father recommended to her—biographies and memoirs, philosophy, history, and poetry. Although he believed that women should be "as well educated as men," Woolf's mother held that "to serve is the fulfilment of women's highest nature." The young Stephen children were first taught at home by their mother and father, with little success. Woolf herself received no formal education beyond some classes in Greek and Latin in the Ladies' Department of King's College in London, beginning in the fall of 1897. In 1899 she began lessons in Greek with Clara Pater, sister of the renowned Victorian critic Walter Pater, and in 1902 she was tutored in the classics by Janet Case (who also later involved her in work for women's suffrage). Such homeschooling was a source of some bitterness later in her life, as she recognized the advantages that derived from the expensive educations her brothers and half brothers received at private schools and university. Yet she also realized that her father's encouragement of her obviously keen intellect had given her an eclectic foundation. In the early years of Bloomsbury, she reveled in the opportunity to discuss ideas with her brother Thoby and his friends, among whom were Lytton Strachey, Clive Bell, and

E. M. Forster. From them, she heard, too, about an intense young man named Leonard Woolf, whom she had met briefly when visiting Thoby at Cambridge, and also in 1904 when he came to dinner at Gordon Square just before leaving for Ceylon (now called Sri Lanka), where he was to administer a far-flung outpost of the British Empire.

Virginia Woolf's first publications were unsigned reviews and essays in an Anglo-Catholic newspaper called the *Guardian,* beginning in December 1904. In the fall of 1906, she and Vanessa went with a family friend, Violet Dickinson, to meet their brothers in Greece. The trip was spoiled by Vanessa's falling ill, and when she returned to London, Virginia found both her brother Thoby—who had returned earlier—and her sister seriously ill. After a misdiagnosis by his doctors, Thoby died from typhoid fever on November 20, leaving Virginia to maintain a cheerful front while her sister and Violet Dickinson recovered from their own illnesses. Two days after Thoby's death, Vanessa agreed to marry his close friend Clive Bell.

While living in Bloomsbury, Woolf had begun to write a novel that would go through many drafts before it was published in 1915 as *The Voyage Out.* In these early years of independence, her social circle widened. She became close to the art critic Roger Fry, organizer of the First Post-Impressionist Exhibition in London in 1910, and also entered the orbit of the famed literary hostess Lady Ottoline Morrell (cruelly caricatured as Hermione Roddice in D. H. Lawrence's 1920 novel *Women in Love*). Her political consciousness also began to emerge. In 1910 she volunteered for the movement for women's suffrage. She also participated that February in a daring hoax that embarrassed the British Navy and led to questions being asked in the House of Commons: She and her brother Adrian, together with some other Cambridge friends, gained access to a secret warship by dressing up and posing as the Emperor of Abyssinia and his retinue. The "Dreadnought Hoax" was front-page news, complete with photographs of the phony Ethiopians with flowing robes, blackened faces, and false beards.

To the British establishment, one of the most embarrassing aspects of the Dreadnought affair was that a woman had taken part in the hoax. Vanessa Bell was concerned at what might have happened to her sister had she been discovered on the ship. She was also increasingly worried about Virginia's erratic health, and by the early summer 1910 had discussed with Dr. George Savage, one of the family's doctors, the debilitating headaches her sister suffered; Dr. Savage prescribed several weeks in a nursing home. Another element in Vanessa's concern was that Virginia was twenty-eight and still unmarried. Clive Bell and Virginia had, in fact, engaged in a hurtful flirtation soon after the birth of Vanessa's first child in 1908. Although she had been proposed to twice in 1909 and once in 1911, Virginia had not taken these offers very seriously.

Dropping by Vanessa's house on a July evening in 1911, Virginia met Leonard Woolf, recently back on leave from Ceylon. Soon after this, Leonard became a lodger at the house Virginia shared with Adrian, the economist John Maynard Keynes, and the painter Duncan Grant. Leonard decided to resign from the Colonial Service, hoping that Virginia would agree to marry him. After some considerable hesitation, she did, and they married in August 1912.

By the end of that year, Woolf was again suffering from the tremendous headaches that afflicted her throughout her life, and in 1913 she was again sent to a nursing home for what was then called a "rest cure." In September of that year, she took an overdose of a sleeping drug and was under care until the following spring. In early 1915 she suffered a severe breakdown and was ill throughout most of the year in which her first novel was published.

Despite this difficult beginning, Virginia and Leonard Woolf's marriage eventually settled into a pattern of immense productivity and mutual support. Leonard worked for a time for the Women's Cooperative Guild, and became increasingly involved with advising the Labour Party and writing on international politics, as well as editing several periodicals. Virginia began to establish herself as an important novelist and influential critic. In 1917 the Woolfs set up their own publishing house, the Hogarth Press, in their home in Richmond. Their first publication was *Two Stories*—Leonard's "Three Jews" and Virginia's experimental "The Mark on the Wall." They had decided to make their livings by writing, and in 1919, a few months before Woolf's second novel, *Night and Day*, was published, they bought a cottage in the village of Rodmell in Sussex. After moving back into London from Richmond in 1923, Woolf would spend summers at Monk's House, returning to the social whirl of the city in the fall.

"The Mark on the Wall" was one of a number of what Woolf called "sketches" that she began to write around the time she and Leonard bought their printing press. *Night and Day* was the last of her books to be published in England by another press. In 1919 Hogarth published her short story *Kew Gardens*, with two woodcuts by Vanessa Bell, and two years later came *Monday or Tuesday*, the only collection of her short fiction published in Woolf's lifetime. Her next novel was *Jacob's Room* (1922), a slim elegy to the generation of 1914, and to her beloved brother Thoby, whose life of great promise had also been cut short so suddenly. Woolf had written to her friend Margaret Llewelyn Davies in 1916 that the Great War, as it was then called, was a "preposterous masculine fiction" that made her "steadily more feminist," and in her fiction and nonfiction she began to articulate and illuminate the connections between the patriarchal status quo, the relatively subordinate position of

women, and war making. Thinking about a novel she was calling "The Hours," Woolf wrote in her diary in 1923 that she
wanted to criticize "the social system." Her inclusion in the
novel of a shell-shocked war veteran named Septimus Warren
Smith would confuse many of the early reviewers of her fourth
novel, *Mrs. Dalloway* (1925), but others recognized that Woolf
was breaking new ground in the way she rendered consciousness and her understanding of human subjectivity.

By the time she wrote *Mrs. Dalloway,* Woolf was also a sought-
after essayist and reviewer who, like many of her celebrated
contemporaries, was staking out her own particular piece of
modernist territory. The Hogarth Press published radical young
writers like Katherine Mansfield, T. S. Eliot, and Gertrude Stein.
Approached by Harriet Shaw Weaver with part of the manuscript of James Joyce's *Ulysses* in 1918, the Woolfs turned it down.
Their own small press could not cope with the long and complex manuscript, nor could Leonard Woolf find a commercial
printer willing to risk prosecution for obscenity by producing it.
In 1924 the Hogarth Press became the official English publisher
of the works of Sigmund Freud, translated by Lytton Strachey's
brother James. Woolf's own literary criticism was collected in a
volume published in 1925, *The Common Reader*—a title signaling
her distrust of academics and love of broad, eclectic reading.

The staggering range of Woolf's reading is reflected in the
more than five hundred essays and reviews she published during her lifetime. Her critical writing is concerned not only with
the canonical works of English literature from Chaucer to her
contemporaries, but also ranges widely through lives of the obscure, memoirs, diaries, letters, and biographies. Models of the
form, her essays comprise a body of work that has only recently
begun to attract the kind of recognition her fiction has received.

In 1922 Woolf met "the lovely and gifted aristocrat" Vita
Sackville-West, already a well-known poet and novelist. Their

close friendship slowly turned into a love affair, glowing most
intensely from about 1925 to 1928, before modulating into
friendship once more in the 1930s. The period of their intimacy
was extremely creative for both writers, Woolf publishing essays
such as "Mr. Bennett and Mrs. Brown" and "Letter to a Young
Poet," as well as three very different novels: *To the Lighthouse*
(1927), which evoked her own childhood and had at its center
the figure of a modernist woman artist, Lily Briscoe; *Orlando*
(1928), a fantastic biography inspired by Vita's own remarkable
family history; and *The Waves* (1931), a mystical and profoundly
meditative work that pushed Woolf's concept of novel form to
its limit. Woolf also published a second *Common Reader* in 1932,
and the "biography" of *Flush,* Elizabeth Barrett Browning's dog
(1933). She went with Sackville-West to Cambridge in the fall of
1928 to deliver the second of the two lectures on which her
great feminist essay *A Room of One's Own* (1929) is based.

As the political situation in Europe in the 1930s moved in-
exorably to its crisis in 1939, Woolf began to collect newspaper
clippings about the relations between the sexes in England,
France, Germany, and Italy. The scrapbooks she made became
the matrix from which developed the perspectives of her penul-
timate novel, *The Years* (1937), and the arguments of her pacifist-
feminist polemic *Three Guineas* (1938). In 1937 Vanessa's eldest
son, Julian Bell, was killed serving as an ambulance driver in the
Spanish Civil War. Woolf later wrote to Vanessa that she had
written *Three Guineas* partly as an argument with Julian. Her
work on *The Years* was grindingly slow and difficult. Ironically,
given Woolf's reputation as a highbrow, it became a bestseller
in the United States, even being published in an Armed Services
edition. While she labored over the novel in 1934, the news
came of the death of Roger Fry, one of her oldest and closest
friends and the former lover of her sister, Vanessa. Reluctantly,

given her distaste for the conventions of biography, Woolf agreed to write his life, which was published in 1940.

In 1939, to relieve the strain of writing Fry's biography, Woolf began to write a memoir, "A Sketch of the Past," which remained unpublished until 1976, when the manuscripts were edited by Jeanne Schulkind for a collection of Woolf's autobiographical writings, *Moments of Being*. Withdrawing with Leonard to Monk's House in Sussex, where they could see the German airplanes flying low overhead on their way to bomb London, Woolf continued to write for peace and correspond with antiwar activists in Europe and the United States. She began to write her last novel, *Between the Acts*, in the spring of 1938, but by early 1941 was dissatisfied with it. Before completing her final revisions, Woolf ended her own life, walking into the River Ouse on the morning of March 28, 1941. To her sister, Vanessa, she wrote, "I can hardly think clearly any more. If I could I would tell you what you and the children have meant to me. I think you know." In her last note to Leonard, she told him he had given her "complete happiness," and asked him to destroy all her papers.

BY THE END of the twentieth century, Virginia Woolf had become an iconic figure, a touchstone for the feminism that revived in the 1960s as well as for the conservative backlash of the 1980s. Hailed by many as a radical writer of genius, she has also been dismissed as a narrowly focused snob. Her image adorns T-shirts, postcards, and even a beer advertisement, while phrases from her writings occur in all kinds of contexts, from peace-march slogans to highbrow book reviews. That Woolf is one of those figures on whom the myriad competing narratives of twentieth- and twenty-first-century Western culture inscribe themselves is testified to by the enormous number of biographical works about her published in the decades since her nephew Quentin Bell broke the ground in 1972 with his two-volume biography of his aunt.

Argument continues about the work and life of Virginia Woolf: about her experience of incest, her madness, her class attitudes, her sexuality, the difficulty of her prose, her politics, her feminism, and her legacy. Perhaps, though, these words from her essay "How Should One Read a Book?" are our best guide: "The only advice, indeed, that one person can give another about reading is to take no advice, to follow your own instincts, to use your own reason, to come to your own conclusions."

—MARK HUSSEY, GENERAL EDITOR

CHRONOLOGY

Information is arranged in this order: 1. Virginia Woolf's family and her works; 2. Cultural and political events; 3. Significant publications and works of art.

1878   Marriage of Woolf's parents, Leslie Stephen (1832–1904) and Julia Prinsep Duckworth (née Jackson) (1846–1895). Leslie Stephen publishes *Samuel Johnson*, first volume in the English Men of Letters series.
England at war in Afghanistan.

1879   Vanessa Stephen (Bell) born (d. 1961). Edward Burne-Jones paints Julia Stephen as the Virgin Mary in *The Annunciation*. Leslie Stephen, *Hours in a Library*, 3rd series.
Somerville and Lady Margaret Hall Colleges for women founded at Oxford University.
Anglo-Zulu war in South Africa.

1880   Thoby Stephen born (d. 1906).
William Gladstone becomes prime minister for second time. First Boer War begins (1880–81). Deaths of Gustave Flaubert (b. 1821) and George Eliot (b. 1819). Lytton Strachey born (d. 1932).
Fyodor Dostoyevsky, *The Brothers Karamazov.*

1881 Leslie Stephen buys lease of Talland House, St. Ives, Cornwall.

Cambridge University Tripos exams opened to women. Henrik Ibsen, *Ghosts;* Henry James, *The Portrait of a Lady, Washington Square;* Christina Rossetti, *A Pageant and Other Poems;* D. G. Rossetti, *Ballads and Sonnets;* Oscar Wilde, *Poems.*

1882 Adeline Virginia Stephen (Virginia Woolf) born January 25. Leslie Stephen begins work as editor of the *Dictionary of National Biography (DNB)*; publishes *The Science of Ethics.* The Stephen family spends its first summer at Talland House.

Married Women's Property Act enables women to buy, sell, and own property and keep their own earnings. Triple Alliance between Germany, Italy, and Austria. Phoenix Park murders of British officials in Dublin, Ireland. James Joyce born (d. 1941). Death of Charles Darwin (b. 1809).

1883 Adrian Leslie Stephen born (d. 1948). Julia Stephen's *Notes from Sick Rooms* published.

Olive Schreiner, *The Story of an African Farm;* Robert Louis Stevenson, *Treasure Island.*

1884 Leslie Stephen delivers the Clark Lectures at Cambridge University.

Third Reform Act extends the franchise in England. Friedrich Engels, *The Origin of the Family, Private Property and the State;* John Ruskin, *The Storm-Cloud of the Nineteenth Century;* Mark Twain, *The Adventures of Huckleberry Finn.*

1885   First volume of Leslie Stephen's *Dictionary of National Biography* published.

Redistribution Act further extends the franchise in England. Ezra Pound born (d. 1972); D. H. Lawrence born (d. 1930).

George Meredith, *Diana of the Crossways;* Émile Zola, *Germinal.*

1887   Queen Victoria's Golden Jubilee.

Arthur Conan Doyle, *A Study in Scarlet;* H. Rider Haggard, *She;* Thomas Hardy, *The Woodlanders.*

1891   Leslie Stephen gives up the *DNB* editorship. Laura Stephen (1870–1945) is placed in an asylum.

William Gladstone elected prime minister of England a fourth time.

Thomas Hardy, *Tess of the D'Urbervilles;* Oscar Wilde, *The Picture of Dorian Gray.*

1895   Death of Julia Stephen.

Armenian Massacres in Turkey. Discovery of X-rays by William Röntgen; Guglielmo Marconi discovers radio; invention of the cinematograph. Trials of Oscar Wilde.

Thomas Hardy, *Jude the Obscure;* H. G. Wells, *The Time Machine;* Oscar Wilde, *The Importance of Being Earnest.*

1896   Vanessa Stephen begins drawing classes three afternoons a week.

Death of William Morris (b. 1834); F. Scott Fitzgerald born (d. 1940).

Anton Chekhov, *The Seagull.*

1897   Woolf attends Greek and history classes at King's College, London, and begins to keep a regular diary. Vanessa, Virginia, and Thoby watch Queen Victoria's Diamond Jubilee procession. Stella Duckworth (b. 1869) marries Jack Hills in April, but dies in July. Gerald Duckworth (1870–1937) establishes a publishing house.
Paul Gauguin, *Where Do We Come From? What Are We? Where Are We Going?;* Bram Stoker, *Dracula.*

1898   Spanish-American War (1898–99). Marie Curie discovers radium. Death of Stéphane Mallarmé (b. 1842).
H. G. Wells, *The War of the Worlds;* Oscar Wilde, *The Ballad of Reading Gaol.*

1899   Woolf begins Latin and Greek lessons with Clara Pater. Thoby Stephen goes up to Trinity College, Cambridge University, entering with Lytton Strachey, Leonard Woolf (1880–1969), and Clive Bell (1881–1964).
The Second Boer War begins (1899–1902) in South Africa. Ernest Hemingway born (d. 1961).

1900   Woolf and Vanessa attend the Trinity College Ball at Cambridge University.
Deaths of Friedrich Nietzsche (b. 1844), John Ruskin (b. 1819), and Oscar Wilde (b. 1854).
Sigmund Freud, *The Interpretation of Dreams.*

1901   Vanessa enters Royal Academy Schools.
Queen Victoria dies January 22. Edward VII becomes king. Marconi sends messages by wireless telegraphy from Cornwall to Newfoundland.

1902   Woolf begins classics lessons with Janet Case. Adrian Stephen enters Trinity College, Cambridge University. Leslie Stephen is knighted.

Joseph Conrad, *Heart of Darkness;* Henry James, *The Wings of the Dove;* William James, *The Varieties of Religious Experience.*

1903   The Wright Brothers fly a biplane 852 feet. Women's Social and Political Union founded in England by Emmeline Pankhurst.

1904   Sir Leslie Stephen dies. George Duckworth (1868– 1934) marries Lady Margaret Herbert. The Stephen children—Vanessa, Virginia, Thoby, and Adrian—move to 46 Gordon Square, in the Bloomsbury district of London. Woolf contributes to F. W. Maitland's biography of her father. Leonard Woolf comes to dine before sailing for Ceylon. Woolf travels in Italy and France. Her first publication is an unsigned review in the *Guardian,* a church weekly.

"Empire Day" inaugurated in London and in Britain's colonies.

Anton Chekhov, *The Cherry Orchard;* Henry James, *The Golden Bowl.*

1905   Woolf begins teaching weekly adult education classes at Morley College. Thoby invites Cambridge friends to their home for "Thursday Evenings"—the beginnings of the Bloomsbury Group. Woolf travels with Adrian to Portugal and Spain. The Stephens visit Cornwall for the first time since their mother's death.

Revolution in Russia.

Albert Einstein, *Special Theory of Relativity;* E. M. Forster, *Where Angels Fear to Tread;* Sigmund Freud, *Essays in the Theory of Sexuality;* Edith Wharton, *The House of Mirth;* Oscar Wilde, *De Profundis.*

1906   The Stephens travel to Greece. Vanessa and Thoby fall ill. Thoby dies November 20; on November 22, Vanessa agrees to marry Clive Bell.
Deaths of Paul Cézanne (b. 1839) and Henrik Ibsen (b. 1828). Samuel Beckett born (d. 1989).

1907   Woolf moves with her brother Adrian to Fitzroy Square. Vanessa marries Clive Bell.
First Cubist exhibition in Paris. W. H. Auden born (d. 1973).
Joseph Conrad, *The Secret Agent;* E. M. Forster, *The Longest Journey;* Edmund Gosse, *Father and Son;* Pablo Picasso, *Demoiselles d'Avignon.*

1908   Birth of Vanessa Bell's first child, Julian. Woolf travels to Italy with Vanessa and Clive Bell.
Herbert Asquith becomes prime minister.
E. M. Forster, *A Room with a View;* Gertrude Stein, *Three Lives.*

1909   Woolf receives a legacy of £2,500 on the death of her Quaker aunt, Caroline Emelia Stephen. Lytton Strachey proposes marriage to Woolf, but they both quickly realize this would be a mistake. Woolf meets Lady Ottoline Morrell for the first time. She travels to the Wagner festival in Bayreuth.
Chancellor of the Exchequer David Lloyd George (1863–1945) introduces a "People's Budget," taxing

wealth to pay for social reforms. A constitutional crisis ensues when the House of Lords rejects it. Death of George Meredith (b. 1828).

Filippo Marinetti, "The Founding and Manifesto of Futurism"; Henri Matisse, *Dance.*

1910 Woolf participates in the Dreadnought Hoax. She volunteers for the cause of women's suffrage. Birth of Vanessa Bell's second child, Quentin (d. 1996).

First Post-Impressionist Exhibition ("Manet and the Post-Impressionists") organized by Roger Fry (1866–1934) at the Grafton Galleries in London. Edward VII dies May 6. George V becomes king. Death of Leo Tolstoy (b. 1828).

E. M. Forster, *Howards End;* Igor Stravinsky, *The Firebird.*

1911 Woolf rents Little Talland House in Sussex. Leonard Woolf returns from Ceylon; in November, he, Adrian Stephen, John Maynard Keynes (1883–1946), Woolf, and Duncan Grant (1885–1978) share a house together at Brunswick Square in London.

Ernest Rutherford makes first model of atomic structure. Rupert Brooke, *Poems;* Joseph Conrad, *Under Western Eyes;* D. H. Lawrence, *The White Peacock;* Katherine Mansfield, *In a German Pension;* Ezra Pound, *Canzoni;* Edith Wharton, *Ethan Frome.*

1912 Woolf leases Asheham House in Sussex. Marries Leonard on August 10; they move to Clifford's Inn, London.

Captain Robert Scott's expedition reaches the South Pole, but he and his companions die on the return journey. The *Titanic* sinks. Second Post-Impression-ist Exhibition, for which Leonard Woolf serves as secretary.

Marcel Duchamp, *Nude Descending a Staircase;* Wassily Kandinsky, *Concerning the Spiritual in Art;* Thomas Mann, *Death in Venice;* George Bernard Shaw, *Pygmalion.*

1913   *The Voyage Out* manuscript delivered to Gerald Duck-worth. Woolf enters a nursing home in July; in Septem-ber, she attempts suicide.

Roger Fry founds the Omega Workshops.

Sigmund Freud, *Totem and Taboo;* D. H. Lawrence, *Sons and Lovers;* Marcel Proust, *Du côté de chez Swann;* Igor Stravinsky, *Le Sacre du printemps.*

1914   Leonard Woolf, *The Wise Virgins;* he reviews Freud's *The Psychopathology of Everyday Life.*

World War I ("The Great War") begins in August. Home Rule Bill for Ireland passed.

Clive Bell, *Art;* James Joyce, *Dubliners;* Wyndham Lewis et al., "Vorticist Manifesto" (in *BLAST*); Gertrude Stein, *Tender Buttons.*

1915   *The Voyage Out,* Woolf's first novel, published by Duck-worth. In April the Woolfs move to Hogarth House in Richmond. Woolf begins again to keep a regular diary. First Zeppelin attack on London. Death of Rupert Brooke (b. 1887).

Joseph Conrad, *Victory;* Ford Madox Ford, *The Good Sol-dier;* D. H. Lawrence, *The Rainbow;* Dorothy Richardson, *Pointed Roofs.*

1916   Woolf discovers Charleston, where her sister, Vanessa
        (no longer living with her husband, Clive), moves in
        October with her sons, Julian and Quentin, and Dun-
        can Grant (with whom she is in love) and David Gar-
        nett (with whom Duncan is in love).
        Easter Rising in Dublin. Death of Henry James (b.
        1843).
        Albert Einstein, *General Theory of Relativity;* James Joyce,
        A Portrait of the Artist as a Young Man; Dorothy Richard-
        son, *Backwater.*

1917   The Hogarth Press established by Leonard and Virginia
        Woolf in Richmond. Their first publication is their
        own *Two Stories,* with woodcuts by Dora Carrington
        (1893–1932).
        Russian Bolshevik Revolution destroys the rule of the
        czar. The United States enters the European war.
        T. S. Eliot, *Prufrock and Other Observations;* Sigmund
        Freud, *Introduction to Psychoanalysis;* Carl Jung, *The Uncon-
        scious;* Dorothy Richardson, *Honeycomb;* W. B. Yeats, *The
        Wild Swans at Coole.*

1918   Woolf meets T. S. Eliot (1888–1965). Harriet Shaw
        Weaver comes to tea with the manuscript of James
        Joyce's *Ulysses.* Vanessa Bell and Duncan Grant's daugh-
        ter, Angelica Garnett, born; her paternity is kept secret
        from all but a very few intimates.
        Armistice signed November 11; Parliamentary Reform
        Act gives votes in Britain to women of thirty and older
        and to all men.
        G. M. Hopkins, *Poems;* James Joyce, *Exiles;* Katherine
        Mansfield, *Prelude* (Hogarth Press); Marcel Proust, *À*

l'ombre des jeunes filles en fleurs; Lytton Strachey, *Eminent Victorians;* Rebecca West, *The Return of the Soldier.*

1919   The Woolfs buy Monk's House in Sussex. Woolf's second novel, *Night and Day,* is published by Duckworth. Her essay "Modern Novels" (republished in 1925 as "Modern Fiction") appears in the *Times Literary Supplement; Kew Gardens* published by Hogarth Press.

Bauhaus founded by Walter Gropius in Weimar. Sex Disqualification (Removal) Act opens many professions and public offices to women. Election of first woman member of Parliament, Nancy Astor. Treaty of Versailles imposes harsh conditions on postwar Germany, opposed by John Maynard Keynes, who writes *The Economic Consequences of the Peace.* League of Nations created. T. S. Eliot, "Tradition and the Individual Talent," *Poems;* Dorothy Richardson, *The Tunnel, Interim;* Robert Wiene, *The Cabinet of Dr. Caligari* (film).

1920   The Memoir Club, comprising thirteen original members of the Bloomsbury Group, meets for the first time. *The Voyage Out* and *Night and Day* are published in the United States by George H. Doran.

Mohandas Gandhi initiates mass passive resistance against British rule in India.

T. S. Eliot, *The Sacred Wood;* Sigmund Freud, *Beyond the Pleasure Principle;* Roger Fry, *Vision and Design;* D. H. Lawrence, *Women in Love;* Katherine Mansfield, *Bliss and Other Stories;* Ezra Pound, *Hugh Selwyn Mauberley;* Marcel Proust, *Le Côté de Guermantes I;* Edith Wharton, *The Age of Innocence.*

1921   Woolf's short story collection *Monday or Tuesday* published by Hogarth Press, which will from this time publish all her books in England. The book is also published in the United States by Harcourt Brace, which from now on is her American publisher.

Aldous Huxley, *Crome Yellow;* Pablo Picasso, *Three Musicians;* Luigi Pirandello, *Six Characters in Search of an Author;* Marcel Proust, *Le Côté de Guermantes II, Sodome et Gomorrhe I;* Dorothy Richardson, *Deadlock;* Lytton Strachey, *Queen Victoria.*

1922   *Jacob's Room* published. Woolf meets Vita Sackville-West (1892–1962) for the first time.

Bonar Law elected prime minister. Mussolini comes to power in Italy. Irish Free State established. British Broadcasting Company (BBC) formed. Discovery of Tutankhamen's tomb in Egypt. Death of Marcel Proust (b. 1871).

T. S. Eliot, *The Waste Land;* James Joyce, *Ulysses;* Katherine Mansfield, *The Garden Party;* Marcel Proust, *Sodome et Gomorrhe II;* Ludwig Wittgenstein, *Tractatus Logico-Philosophicus.*

1923   The Woolfs travel to Spain, stopping in Paris on the way home. Hogarth Press publishes *The Waste Land.*

Stanley Baldwin succeeds Bonar Law as prime minister. Death of Katherine Mansfield (b. 1888).

Mina Loy, *Lunar Baedeker;* Marcel Proust, *La Prisonnière;* Dorothy Richardson, *Revolving Lights;* Rainer Maria Rilke, *Duino Elegies.*

1924   The Woolfs move to Tavistock Square. Woolf lectures on "Character in Fiction" to the Heretics Society at Cambridge University.

The Labour Party takes office for the first time under

the leadership of Ramsay MacDonald but is voted out within the year. Death of Joseph Conrad (b. 1857).
E. M. Forster, *A Passage to India;* Thomas Mann, *The Magic Mountain.*

1925   *Mrs. Dalloway* and *The Common Reader* published. Woolf stays with Vita Sackville-West at her house, Long Barn, for the first time.
Nancy Cunard, *Parallax;* F. Scott Fitzgerald, *The Great Gatsby;* Ernest Hemingway, *In Our Time;* Adolf Hitler, *Mein Kampf;* Franz Kafka, *The Trial;* Alain Locke, ed., *The New Negro;* Marcel Proust, *Albertine disparue;* Dorothy Richardson, *The Trap;* Gertrude Stein, *The Making of Americans.*

1926   Woolf lectures on "How Should One Read a Book?" at Hayes Court School. "Cinema" published in *Arts* (New York), "Impassioned Prose" in *Times Literary Supplement,* and "On Being Ill" in *New Criterion.* Meets Gertrude Stein (1874–1946).
The General Strike in support of mine workers in England lasts nearly two weeks.
Ernest Hemingway, *The Sun Also Rises;* Langston Hughes, *The Weary Blues;* Franz Kafka, *The Castle;* A. A. Milne, *Winnie-the-Pooh.*

1927   *To the Lighthouse,* "The Art of Fiction," "Poetry, Fiction and the Future," and "Street Haunting" published. The Woolfs travel with Vita Sackville-West and her husband, Harold Nicolson, to Yorkshire to see the total eclipse of the sun. They buy their first car.
Charles Lindbergh flies the Atlantic solo.
E. M. Forster, *Aspects of the Novel;* Ernest Hemingway, *Men without Women;* Franz Kafka, *Amerika;* Marcel

Proust, *Le Temps retrouvé;* Gertrude Stein, *Four Saints in Three Acts.*

1928 *Orlando: A Biography* published. In October, Woolf delivers two lectures at Cambridge on which she will base *A Room of One's Own.* Femina-Vie Heureuse prize awarded to *To the Lighthouse.*
The Equal Franchise Act gives the vote to all women over twenty-one. Sound films introduced. Death of Thomas Hardy (b. 1840).
Djuna Barnes, *Ladies Almanack;* Radclyffe Hall, *The Well of Loneliness;* D. H. Lawrence, *Lady Chatterley's Lover;* Evelyn Waugh, *Decline and Fall;* W. B. Yeats, *The Tower.*

1929 *A Room of One's Own* published. "Women and Fiction" in *The Forum* (New York).
Labour Party returned to power under Prime Minister MacDonald. Discovery of penicillin. Museum of Modern Art opens in New York. Wall Street crash.
William Faulkner, *The Sound and the Fury;* Ernest Hemingway, *A Farewell to Arms;* Nella Larsen, *Passing.*

1930 Woolf meets the pioneering composer, writer, and suffragette Ethel Smyth (1858–1944), with whom she forms a close friendship.
Death of D. H. Lawrence (b. 1885).
W. H. Auden, *Poems;* T. S. Eliot, *Ash Wednesday;* William Faulkner, *As I Lay Dying;* Sigmund Freud, *Civilisation and Its Discontents.*

1931 *The Waves* is published. First of six articles by Woolf about London published in *Good Housekeeping;* "Introductory Letter" to *Life As We Have Known It.* Lectures to London branch of National Society for Women's Service on "Professions for Women." Meets John Lehmann (1907–1987), who will become a partner in the Hogarth Press.

Growing financial crisis throughout Europe and beginning of the Great Depression.

1932   *The Common Reader, Second Series* and "Letter to a Young Poet" published. Woolf invited to give the 1933 Clark Lectures at Cambridge, which she declines.
Death of Lytton Strachey (b. 1880).
Aldous Huxley, *Brave New World.*

1933   *Flush: A Biography,* published. The Woolfs travel by car to Italy.
Adolf Hitler becomes chancellor of Germany, establishing the totalitarian dictatorship of his National Socialist (Nazi) Party.
T. S. Eliot, *The Use of Poetry and the Use of Criticism;* George Orwell, *Down and Out in Paris and London;* Gertrude Stein, *The Autobiography of Alice B. Toklas;* Nathanael West, *Miss Lonelyhearts;* W. B. Yeats, *The Collected Poems.*

1934   Woolf meets W. B. Yeats at Ottoline Morrell's house. Writes "Walter Sickert: A Conversation."
George Duckworth dies. Roger Fry dies.
Samuel Beckett, *More Pricks Than Kicks;* Nancy Cunard, ed., *Negro: An Anthology;* F. Scott Fitzgerald, *Tender Is the Night;* Wyndham Lewis, *Men Without Art;* Henry Miller, *Tropic of Cancer;* Ezra Pound, *ABC of Reading;* Evelyn Waugh, *A Handful of Dust.*

1935   The Woolfs travel to Germany, where they accidentally get caught up in a parade for Göring. They return to England via Italy and France.

1936   Woolf reads "Am I a Snob?" to the Memoir Club, and publishes "Why Art Today Follows Politics" in the *Daily Worker*.
Death of George V, who is succeeded by Edward VIII, who then abdicates to marry Wallis Simpson. George VI becomes king. Spanish Civil War (1936–38) begins when General Franco, assisted by Germany and Italy, attacks the Republican government. BBC television begins.
Djuna Barnes, *Nightwood;* Charlie Chaplin, *Modern Times* (film); Aldous Huxley, *Eyeless in Gaza;* J. M. Keynes, *The General Theory of Employment, Interest and Money;* Rose Macaulay, *Personal Pleasures;* Margaret Mitchell, *Gone with the Wind.*

1937   *The Years* published. Woolf's nephew Julian Bell killed in the Spanish Civil War.
Neville Chamberlain becomes prime minister.
Zora Neale Hurston, *Their Eyes Were Watching God;* David Jones, *In Parenthesis;* Pablo Picasso, *Guernica;* John Steinbeck, *Of Mice and Men;* J. R. R. Tolkien, *The Hobbit.*

1938   *Three Guineas* published.
Germany annexes Austria. Chamberlain negotiates the Munich Agreement ("Peace in our time"), ceding Czech territory to Hitler.
Samuel Beckett, *Murphy;* Elizabeth Bowen, *The Death of the Heart;* Jean-Paul Sartre, *La Nausée.*

1939   The Woolfs visit Sigmund Freud, living in exile in London having fled the Nazis. They move to Mecklenburgh Square.

Germany occupies Czechoslovakia; Italy occupies Albania; Russia makes a nonaggression pact with Germany. Germany invades Poland and war is declared by Britain and France on Germany, September 3. Deaths of W. B. Yeats (b. 1865), Sigmund Freud (b. 1856), and Ford Madox Ford (b. 1873).

James Joyce, *Finnegans Wake;* John Steinbeck, *The Grapes of Wrath;* Nathanael West, *The Day of the Locust.*

1940   *Roger Fry: A Biography* published. "Thoughts on Peace in an Air Raid" in the *New Republic.* Woolf lectures on "The Leaning Tower" to the Workers Educational Association in Brighton.

The Battle of Britain leads to German night bombings of English cities. The Woolfs' house at Mecklenburgh Square is severely damaged, as is their former house at Tavistock Square. Hogarth Press is moved out of London.

Ernest Hemingway, *For Whom the Bell Tolls;* Christina Stead, *The Man Who Loved Children.*

1941   Woolf drowns herself, March 28, in the River Ouse in Sussex. *Between the Acts* published in July.

Death of James Joyce (b. 1882).

Rebecca West, *Black Lamb and Grey Falcon.*

INTRODUCTION
BY MELBA CUDDY-KEANE

AN ENGLISH VILLAGE. A country house. A day, likely a Saturday, in June 1939. In the afternoon, the villagers will stage an amateur production on the lawn, depicting imagined scenes from English comedies (not tragedies) in the eras of Queen Elizabeth I, Queen Anne, Queen Victoria, and the present day. The scenario in this novel seems idyllic, until we remember that all this pleasantry occurs under the gathering storm clouds of imminent and cataclysmic war.

Virginia Woolf's last novel, *Between the Acts*, turns on a fundamental incongruity, questioning the relation between everyday life in an English village and momentous events occurring simultaneously on the world's stage. What does it mean, the novel asks, to hold a village festival when the country is on the brink of war? Giles Oliver, a member of the family that owns the country house, can barely repress his irritation with the genteel proceedings, given that Europe is "bristling with guns, poised with planes" across the narrow channel divide (37). The closeness of war further haunts the festivities in scraps of conversation about Jewish refugees (84) and the Germans (103), and at the performance's end the closing speech is interrupted by a formation, presumably of fighter planes, flying low overhead (131). In holding their annual pageant, is the community then in denial? Or are they defending the way of life that war most threatens, forcing us to consider what, out of the destruction, not only could but should survive?

History itself cannot resolve such textual problems, but historical context can offer useful insights into related attitudes at the time. In a scrapbook maintained by a chapter of the Women's Institute for the area around Rodmell, the village where Leonard and Virginia Woolf were living during World War II, someone has pasted a clipping so pertinent to these issues that it's worth quoting in full:[1]

A friend who lived in southern England, describes the behaviour of the villagers when an air raid failed to interrupt the local garden fête in aid of the Red Cross. He writes: "We have two or three air raids most days and we had seven German bombers swoop a few feet over our roofs machine-gunning only six days before our fête — so we know something about the *Blitzkrieg*. But we held our fête on Saturday with stalls, side-shows, dancing on the lawn, and the acting of scenes from *Twelfth Night* under the old mulberry tree, which is a stone's-throw from the path still called Princess Gap because Princess Elizabeth used to walk there when she stayed in our village in the days before she became Shakespeare's Queen Elizabeth.[2] So it was all very much in English order, and we felt quite secure with one foot in the sixteenth and the other in the twentieth century as we listened to the Rector's wife and Tom and Dick and Joyce and Annie transformed under the mulberry tree into Olivia, Malvolio, Sir Toby, Maria. The sun shone from a clear sky and there were 250 of us sitting on the lawn. There were mothers with babies and there were about 20 or 30 children playing about and sometimes getting mixed up with the actors. And then just when the Clown was singing 'Come away, come away, death,' the sirens began to wail. Not a soul moved; the play went on. I thought to myself that at least a mother or two would take her children off to shelter. But not a bit of it; they sat there and watched the children sprawling on the lawn as if Göring and his *Luftwaffe* were as unreal and innocuous as Malvolio."

The clipping is labeled "from the *New Statesman*," and it indeed appears in that periodical's issue of August 31, 1940.[3] The scrapbook moreover contains a photograph of a fête held in the garden of Charmes Cottage, Rodmell, in aid of the Red Cross, and lists a production of *Twelfth Night* as taking place at Charmes Cottage in 1940. Virginia Woolf's diary entry for Monday, August 19 of that year records both German bombers and a "rehearsal," and a letter she wrote to her friend Ethel Smyth dated September 11, 1940, describes a recent village play in strikingly similar terms: "We had a fête: also a village play. The sirens sounded in the middle. All the mothers sat stolid. I also admired that very much" (*Letters* 6: 430). It may not have been Virginia who wrote to the *New Statesman* ("not a bit of it" resembles Leonard's style more than hers), but she clearly attended the performance and shared the letter writer's views. The fête must have taken place on Saturday, August 24, 1940, during the most intense bombing period in the Battle of Britain, and when Woolf had written most of the first draft of *Between the Acts*. The conjunction marks an extraordinary life-art intersection: Woolf witnessed an event that paralleled the storyworld she had recently created, but taking place at a later date, after the outbreak of war. The actual fête cannot explain the fictional one, but it can at least suggest the significance Woolf attributed to such "ordinary" events. In her letter, Woolf's admiration for the villagers is associated with her admiration for two friends (Vita Sackville-West and Rose Macaulay), both of whom were driving ambulances in areas under bombardment at the time. The courage and morale displayed by the Rodmell villagers was for her a similar contribution to the war effort in civilian terms.

The story of the Rodmell fête further reveals the relation between Woolf's subject matter and what recent historians and literary critics term the "quotidian," the everyday. Traditionally, prominence in history has been given to "grand events," famous leaders, and critical turning points in the course of human affairs, but there is another compelling yet frequently unrecorded history concerning the processes of daily life. For Leonard Woolf, this untold story was the "back-stairs of history" (141); for Virginia Woolf, the "Lives of the Obscure,"[4] or perhaps life "between the acts."[5] This approach focuses not only on "ordinary people" but more particularly on the small actions and passing thoughts of daily life. Following the theorist Michel de Certeau, recent criticism has often emphasized the potential empowerment of the quotidian, describing manifestations of resistance or outright subversion as oppositional to the direct power wielded by hegemonic and authoritative regimes. The descriptions of the Rodmell fête construct it as an act of heroic resistance in such terms. The everyday in Woolf's fictional world, however, manifests a conceptual many-sidedness that is disturbingly more complex.

In *Between the Acts,* Woolf uses the surface triviality and circumscribed locality of the everyday to probe deeply into questions of the survival of the human race. The possibility of a positive reading of the festivities remains, but it is tested and subjected to multiple points of view. Cacophonous voices in the novel mix the trivial, the careless, and the nasty, with the yearning, vibrant, and indeed humorous qualities of ordinary life. The narratives of both past and present are infused with pettiness, infidelities, prejudice, greed, and a disturbing undercurrent of violence, yet they are driven as well by inventiveness, sensitivity, creativity, and a longing for meaningful connection. Because Woolf does not idealize her fictional world, the tone of the novel frequently turns satirical. Because she dwells on ordinary life with such precision and intensity, the novel challenges us— whoever and wherever we are—to extend compassion and comprehension, and to take from this world an understanding we might then apply to our own. For just as the pageant at its end turns its mirrors on the audience, so the novel as a whole turns its mirror toward us. "Did you feel," asks old Mrs. Swithin, that "we act different parts but are the same?" "Yes," Isa answers, and then "no." "Yes, yes, yes, the tide rushed out embracing. No, no, no, it contracted" (146). Reading this novel enacts a similar vacillation between difference and similarity, as we alternately cast this fictional community as "them" or as "us." Is this a story of one historically and geographically localizable culture, or is it the story of "ourselves"?

The novel is suffused with such rhythms of alternation, and it continually challenges its readers with the question of what these rhythms mean. Does Woolf present a society on the verge of extinction, with its history a sad tale of loss, both of meaningful relationships with one another and of a meaningful relationship with the land? Or does this spring pageant adumbrate a society revivifying its potentials for renewal and regeneration, trembling on the threshold of a future that could reform and transform its tarnished, yet nevertheless fertile, past? Or is it neither one nor the other of these stark polarities, but rather some third possibility, inhabiting a realm in between? The tide rushes in, then recedes, over and over again, shifting its answers between yes and no. Woolf's skill in placing us on the razor's edge in all our thinking may constitute the greatest power of this rich and haunting work.

History, Writing, and War

THE RODMELL fête reminds us of another historical narrative: the background story of Woolf's writing this work. Her first vague jottings about a new novel date from August 1937, two years before the outbreak of World War II; she completed her last typescript of *Between the Acts* in February 1941, one-and-a-half years after the war began. The events in the novel, however, are set in June 1939, locating us in another razor's-edge world— one of the last moments of peace before Britain and France declared war on Germany in September of that year. In the earliest typed draft of the novel, begun in April 1938, Woolf set the date in July of that year, moving it up to 1939 in her second draft, written in 1940 (a few months after the Rodmell fête), but significantly *not* moving it up, as she might then have done, to a point during the war. By depicting a prewar world for a war-torn audience, Woolf thus wrote a further irony into her work: the disparity between what her villagers suspect but don't know and the outcome her first reading audience would know only too well. Deepening the novel's layers, Woolf used the story-world and the reading world to generate multiple times: Her readers would think about the future the villagers would soon confront; the same readers would also remember their own lives in that earlier, possibly still hopeful, world. We need today to remember that historical audience, since it is through them that we most feel the painful contrast between periods of war and peace.

History is thus a hidden collaborator in the writing of this text, and it plays a role in its final production, too. As Woolf's last novel, *Between the Acts* inevitably suggests a summing up, conclusion, or culmination of her work. But it is, at the same time, a novel she left unfinished, lacking the final revisions she would have made, as always, while seeing a novel into print. It misses, even further, her endorsement of it as a publishable work. Despite her elation on finishing the typescript, she soon expressed concerns about its being "slight and sketchy" (*Letters* 6: 482) or "silly and trivial" (*Letters* 6: 484), and decided to withdraw it from the press. The shift from writing to anticipating critical reaction is difficult, and we might note that Woolf had expressed similar concerns about her previous—and actually well-received—novel *The Years*.[6] In 1941, however, focusing on the everyday was an arguably greater risk. Since she chose not to cast her fictional world heroically, would its concerns not seem trivial in a time of war? And could a work of literature *about* literature be understood as relevant to the annihilation that threatened the European world? Not only do we lack what some editors consider a "definitive text" because it was published after her death; the novel we have is embedded in the uncertainties that Woolf apparently felt. Yet there are details in the process of her writing this work that both reveal her excitement about it and indicate strongly why it mattered to her.

Virginia Woolf produced three different typescripts of this novel, the first two of which were edited by Mitchell Leaska and published in 1983 under the original title, *Pointz Hall.* Leaska named these first versions the Early Typescript, on which she worked until October 1940, and the Later Typescript, which she produced in October and November of that year. Woolf then produced what is known as the Final Typescript, which she completed on February 26, 1941, and it is this typescript, with her many inserted handwritten changes, that Leonard Woolf used when he published the novel after her death. In contrast to the impressively rapid production of the final two versions, the full span of her thinking and writing about the novel extended over some three and a half years. The development of the novel itself makes a fascinating study, but two aspects in particular are relevant here: first, the way the novel took shape in

her mind as a *kind* of writing rather than as a *subject* about which
to write; second, the way this particular kind of writing asserted
for her a different system of values from the mentality that leads
to war.

When Woolf first jotted down ideas for this novel in August
1937, they had nothing to do with plot. Her inspiration was all
about "discourse"—the kind of writing it was to be: "Its to be
dialogue: & poetry: & prose" (*Diary* 5: 105). She wanted to write
a "new criticism" as well. In October of that year, she had a further intuition about form, imagining a story that would present
"the statement of the theme: then the restatement: & so on: repeating the same story: singling out this & then that: until the
central idea is stated" (*Diary* 5: 114). She went on to imagine a
"concentrated small book" that would "contain many varieties
of mood. And possibly criticism" (*Diary* 5: 114–15). We still find
no mention of plot or theme, but her notes turn on two elements that prove crucial in the novel that evolved: the mixture
of genres, and the multiple echoes of a unifying theme. By the
time Woolf began the first typescript in April 1938, she had a
country house setting clearly in mind: Poyntzet Hall (later
Poyntz and finally Pointz Hall). The name suggests a tie to the
colorful Poyntz family (see note to page 25), but more perti-
nently and playfully it juxtaposes *points* and *all*—multiplicity and
totality, the many and the one. For that duality is now, in both
her method and her subject, the articulated theme: " 'I' rejected:
'We' substituted: to whom at the end there shall be an invocation? 'We' . . . composed of many different things . . . we all life,
all art, all waifs & strays—a rambling capricious but somehow
unified whole—the present state of my mind?" (*Diary* 5: 135).
And what persists from her first intuition is the notion of a
loose and hybrid style: The novel is to be "a perpetual variety &
change from intensity to prose. & facts—& notes"; it will be

"random and tentative," allowing her to say "anything that comes into [her] head."

Then, throughout the whole period of the novel's composition, Woolf's diaries and letters offer a most penetrating and moving record of a civilian's experience of war. Numerous biographies describe in detail this portion of her life, but a few key details must at least be noted here. Little more than a week before beginning the first typescript, Woolf recorded her expectation that war would soon be announced (*Diary* 5: 131); by September, she was contemplating the "darkness, strain [and] conceivably death" that war would bring (*Diary* 5: 166). That September was a month of high tension, but a temporary respite seemed offered in the Munich Pact, in which England, France, and Italy ceded to Germany an area in Czechoslovakia called the Sudetenland in return for Hitler's agreement to respect the rest of Europe's borders as they stood (see note to page 10). By the end of 1938, Woolf had written almost the first half of the novel. Then, in March 1939, Germany invaded Czechoslovakia; on September 1, Hitler attacked Poland, and Britain and France declared war. Woolf's progress on the novel went much more slowly in 1939 and the first half of 1940, as she worked on her biography of Roger Fry; yet by August 1940 the novel was close to being finished in its first draft. That fall, Germany launched its most sustained bombing campaign, or blitzkrieg, on England, the famed Battle of Britain, and—as Woolf's diary indicates over and over again, even up to her entry on February 7, 1941—Hitler's invasion of England was expected at any time. Bombs destroyed two houses in London where she had lived, and, in Rodmell, bombs were dropping in the adjoining fields.

Set against such escalating conflict, hostilities, and destruction, writing itself became an act of resistance. On May 15, 1940,

Woolf wrote, "This idea struck me: the army is the body: I am the brain. Thinking is my fighting" (*Diary* 5: 285). In this light, her ideas for her novel constituted the form her "fighting" took: a loose and hybrid mix of genre, the everyday world of a country house, a discussion of literature, a pluralistic communal theme, the freedom to range anywhere and everywhere, repetition with difference and difference with an underlying unity—together all these thoughts articulate a pluralism of style and vision antithetical to the concentrated obsessions of power and aggression at the roots of war. Although Woolf did not specifically relate her objectives in the novel to the war, her diary is filled with relevant remarks. On September 6, 1939, the day of their first air-raid warning, she affirmed writing as her work: "Any idea is more real than any amount of war misery. And what one's made for. And the only contribution one can make" (*Diary* 5: 235). Knowing, with Leonard's Jewishness, their socialist writings, and their membership in the Labour Party, the personal consequences if Hitler should invade, Leonard and Virginia discussed plans for suicide, for which purpose Leonard kept petrol in the garage: "Capitulation will mean all Jews to be given up. Concentration camps. So to our garage" (*Diary* 5: 292–93). Yet even so, in the same entry where she wrote that thinking was her fighting, she declared:

> No, I don't want the garage to see the end of me. I've a wish for 10 years more, & to write my book wh. as usual darts into my brain.... Why am I optimistic? Or rather not either way? because its all bombast, this war. One old lady pinning on her cap has more reality. So if one dies, it'll be a common sense, dull end—not comparable to a days walk, & then an evening reading over the fire. (*Diary* 5: 285)

Ordinary life, and the life of the mind, were in no way pure or faultless, but they marked the location where meaningful struggle must be based. A village pageant, rather than a battlefield, becomes her human stage: "Finished Pointz Hall, the Pageant: the Play—finally Between the Acts this morning" (*Diary* 5: 356).

Narrative

A "CONCENTRATED SMALL BOOK": Virginia Woolf did achieve that aim. *Between the Acts* is a short text with a simple scheme; yet as Lucy Swithin says of the pageant, "The Chinese, you know, put a dagger on the table and that's a battle" (97). Woolf's novel enacts, first of all, an extraordinary time compression: Twenty-four hours from one June evening to the next encapsulates hundreds of years in the pageant's time and thousands of years in Lucy Swithin's *Outline of History*. Time compression then creates space density: The village of Liskeard is also the location of a prehistoric swamp, of Roman occupation, and of numerous phases of English culture. Furthermore, although the physical site is England, references and allusions remind us of England's interconnections with the globe: Europe, of course, but also India, China, Africa, Canada, Persia, Peru. In *Orlando* (1928), Woolf took the life of one person and extended it over three hundred years. In *Between the Acts*, she takes the life of a vast historical and geographical community and compresses it into one day.

The pageant, which mimics the compression of the frame narrative (or, if the audience is framed by the acts, it may be the other way around) must similarly skip, select, hint, suggest, leaving the audience at times so confused that Isa wonders, "Did

the plot matter? . . . The plot was only there to beget emotion,"
and either Isa's thinking or an anonymous voice continues,
"Don't bother about the plot: the plot's nothing" (63). The conflicting emotions that Isa identifies both in the pageant and in
herself, however, love and hate, imply an obsessively repetitive
plot that humanity seems destined to continue: "Surely it was
time someone invented a new plot, or that the author came out
from the bushes" (146). Plot here is more rhythmically cyclical
than sequential and linear, directing our reading equally, if not
more so, to what is surrounding it as opposed to what lies
ahead. In this densely layered text, a variety of textual narrative
elements call for our attention while we read.

Voices

This is a novel of voices. We listen almost as if we are listening
to a documentary recording, almost as if a microphone were set
up in the house, in the barn, on the grass.[7] Voices are multiple
and interacting: pageant and audience; male and female; refined
and simple; "public" and "inner"; human and animal (birds,
sheep, cows, mice); natural and mechanical (telephone, gramophone, and loudspeaker); individual and collective. Voices are
"hollow," "low," "fluty," "loud," "husky," and "primeval"; they
sing and they speak; they are identified, or anonymous, or eerily
"bodiless." Silence is a speaking voice as well. We hear both
conflict and agreement, making us wonder if what we are hearing is *mellay* or *medley*. The novel presents both what the narratologist Mikhail Bakhtin called "polyphony," multiple narrative
voices, and what he called "heteroglossia," multiple discourses
within a society. Then, beyond all the individual voices, there are
two other kinds of voice we hear as well: the voice of the "chorus," and a haunting, mysterious voice "that was no one's voice."

One of the innumerable meanings of "between the acts" is
the chorus, stemming from Greek drama, in which the move-

ment alternates between the chorus's commentary and the represented acts.[8] Throughout the pageant, a group of village players dressed as medieval pilgrims winds in and out of the background trees, chanting a song of the soil; in the Victorian act, another group of players sings "choruses," like the refrains in a Gilbert and Sullivan operetta; and throughout the novel, the audience voices behave like a chorus in a Greek drama, commenting on the action of the play. The traditional heroes and heroines are balanced by the putatively minor figures; observing and doing are given complementary roles. There is yet another voice, however, that escapes registration: "But now that the shower had fallen, it was the other voice speaking, the voice that was no one's voice" (123). It might be the voice of the gramophone, or of the author, or of music, or "Was that voice ourselves?" (128). More important than identifying this voice, perhaps, is the sense of a voice without fixed location, possessing a fluidity that characterizes the narrator's voice as well. For the narrator continually shifts positionality: sometimes an objective, external omniscience; sometimes apparently someone present at the scene; sometimes with the indeterminacy of the technique called free indirect discourse (FID), in which thought shifts almost imperceptibly from the narrator's mind to a character's mind. We are thus not always sure if a thought should be assigned to narrator or a character—an effect that makes it difficult to be too specific about what Woolf or her narrator thinks. But the "other" voice might also suggest the presence of some underlying, unifying common spirit, not transcendent and elsewhere, but—if we could only hear it—immediate and here.

Words and Rhymes

Between the Acts offers a world of words, words that go forward in linear sentences, but words that also leap sidelong in associative fashion, setting up rhythms and patterns, suggestive of underlying connections that network through our lives. Words, in this novel, have a mobile life: "Words this afternoon ceased to lie flat in the sentence. They rose, became menacing and shook their fists at you" (41). They mock our attempts to control reality; they gesture to a deeper reality underneath.

Language becomes a kaleidoscope that resists single relations between signified and signifier. Sometimes the signified holds still, while multiple designators circle around. The person whose name "Lucinda" is never said is Lucy, Cindy, Sindy, Mrs. Swithin, Old Flimsy, Mother Swithin, Batty, and Aunt Lucy. "Isa" is Isabella, Mrs. Giles Oliver, Mrs. Giles, and Mrs. Oliver. Even the cat has a kitchen name (Sunny) and a drawing-room name (Sung-Yen).

Sometimes the signifier remains still, at least in sound, moving through multiple homonyms: the fishy sole, the intangible soul, the crepe soles on the bottom of shoes; a peg on which to hang things, the peg like a nail that holds things down, the peg-top trousers worn in the play. Words leap to their cognates, like *Mrs. Sands* and *sandwiches,* or suggest cockney rhyming words, like *dicky-bird* for *word.* There is the cross that Lucy caresses, crossed daggers on the bottom of a cup, uncrossing of legs, crossings of the terrace or the desert, a crisscross pattern, and, as we shall later discuss, a crisscross letter. Playful, and confusing, language speaks to us of multiple identities. Nothing, nobody, is ever simply and only one thing.

Rhythm and Repetition

Voices and words create patterns or repetitions; repetitions create rhythms. Woolf's description of writing *The Waves* (1931) resonates with the style of *Between the Acts* as well: "I am writing to a rhythm and not to a plot" (*Letters* 4: 204). The systolic/diastolic alternations of rising and falling sound in the novel's fluctuating responses to its questions: "It was Yes, No. Yes, yes, yes, the tide rushed out embracing. No, no, no, it contracted" (146). The play leads Isa to think that "[t]here were only two emotions: love; and hate" (63)—the same two emotions she battles in herself. Two portraits hanging in the dining room set up rhythmic dualities as well: a male-gendered discourse oriented toward talk and possession, vying with a female-gendered discourse leading toward poetry and silence. Gendered dualities motivate the sparring between characters, as, for example, in the conflict between Bart's analytic separations and Lucy's imaginative "one-making" (119), but the double discourse is evident within the characters as well. For it is Lucy who yields the hammer in the barn, Bart who empathetically intuits at the end what Miss La Trobe will need.

In addition to alternating rhythms, there are doubling rhythms of call and response, of sound and echo, and of simultaneous sounds. Bart's clenched hand (13) is echoed in William Dodge's clenched hand (76); the literal blood on Giles's shoes (69) resonates with metaphorical blood on Miss La Trobe's shoes (122); both Mrs. Swithin and Isa forget Dodge's name. In the pageant, such echoes bridge gaps and make transitions: In a moment of peace, "The view repeated in its own way what the tune was saying. . . . The cows, making a step forward, then standing still, were saying the same thing to perfection" (92). A little later, such correspondences save a moment of collapse and emptiness on the stage: "Suddenly the cows stopped; lowered their heads, and began browsing. Simultaneously the audience lowered their heads and read their programmes" (96).

Yet another rhythm is the "triple melody" sounded in the triadic rhyming of the view and the tune and the cows (92). It might be heard in the three notes of the scale, "A.B.C.," which suddenly resolve into the "dog" of "Hark, hark, the dogs do bark" (80); in Isa's "three-folded mirror" that reflects "three separate versions of her rather heavy, yet handsome, face" (10);

or in the triple-sounded conversation between Bart and Lucy about the weather—wet? fine? which?—that Isa hears repeating like the "chime of bells": "As the first peals, you hear the second; as the second peals, you hear the third" (15). Or Isa's two emotions accompanied by a third emotion, an illusive emotion given the coming war, and one that haunts both novel and play: "Peace was the third emotion. Love. Hate. Peace. Three emotions made the ply of human life" (64).

There are the jazz rhythms that, in their syncopation, imply both irreverence and relief: "And not plain. Very up to date, all the same" (124); and the desire to break away from any rhythmic control at all: "*Let's break the rhythm and forget the rhyme*" (127). And then, finally, the multilayered polyphony of the pageant's culminating music, which brings, for one moment, all rhythms into one, as they "crashed; solved; united" (128). Which of all these—or is it all of them—is the rhythm of the human heart?

Mixing Genres

In *Between the Acts,* the multiplicity of voices, of words, and of rhythms is further extended through hybridity of genres. As noted earlier, Woolf first conceived this novel as "dialogue: & poetry: & prose" and possibly criticism as well (*Diary* 5: 105). In the course of its writing, she wrote more poems for Isa than she included in the finished text, and at some point she believed that "Pointz Hall [was] to become in the end a play" (*Diary* 5: 139). In the published version, genres are fully mixed: A play is embedded within a novelistic world; poetry appears as either text or subtext in the language of the pageant, the characters, and the narrator; and the audience's commentary offers an informal critical review. But Woolf, as a literary critic, did not think of drama, poetry, and fiction just as stylistic categories easily identified by their different appearances on the page. Each genre for her was a distinctive mode of thought.

Concepts of genre are pervasive in Woolf's literary essays and reviews, and they are the explicit subject in a talk she published as "Poetry, Fiction, and the Future," which, after her death, Leonard published as "The Narrow Bridge of Art" in the collection titled *Granite & Rainbow* (1958). Characteristically, Woolf argues that different genres respond to different needs. Poetry taps our dreams and imagination; it expresses "the relation of the mind to general ideas and its soliloquy in solitude" (*Essays* 4: 435). The novel is conversational, psychological, representing "people's relation to each other and their activities together" (435). Drama offers "explosive" emotional conflict (438), while theater is the site that brings playwright, actors, and audience collaboratively together. The Elizabethan playhouse—perhaps conceived somewhat idealistically—is a hub inclusive of all classes and ways of life. Each genre thus makes its own contribution, but Woolf's main point is that no single genre is adequate to the modern age. "For it is an age," she writes, "clearly when we are not fast anchored where we are; things are moving round us; we are moving ourselves" (429). Things with no previous connections are now associated together; things that once appeared whole "are now broken up on the threshold" (433). The modern writer thus confronts an extraordinary pressure: to capture innumerable conflicts and yet to encompass them, for forceful impact, with a "shaping power" (430). For this task, Woolf believes, the novel has the greatest potential—not for what it is, but for what it can become. The novel is so flexible, so changeable, and indeed so "cannibalistic" that it can transform into a hybrid genre. And transformation is crucial, for only pluralistic hybridity can express "that queer conglomeration of incongruous things—the modern mind" (436).

The generic hybridity of *Between the Acts* thus crosses another threshold, taking a relatively isolated rural community and locating it within modern flows. For the modern sensibility conceives

no simple, single place: "Modern" is not an urban mentality but
a pervasive sense of life. All genres, all times, all places must thus
conspire together, yet even then complexity escapes: "Life is always and inevitably richer than we who try to express it" (*Essays* 4: 419). Density must then be further thickened through a
multitude of intertexts, so that all writing, all speech, can be revealed as implicated in that queer conglomeration: the modern
collective mind.

Allusions

WHEN THE day's festivities are over and the family is gathered
quietly in the sitting room before retiring for the night, Mrs.
Swithin reads a letter that has arrived for her in the mail. Described as a "criss-cross" (146), the letter employs an old technique for saving on paper or postage: writing the first page in
the normal way and then turning the paper at right angles to
write the second page on top of the first. What Lucy receives is
thus a layered or palimpsestic text—a term deriving from ancient manuscripts on which an earlier and partially effaced writing is still legible under more recent written script. The land
around Pointz Hall is a geographic palimpsest, revealing traces
of Roman civilization beneath the marks of the present day; the
acts of the pageant offer a palimpsestic account of history, with
each era superimposed on a previous era, yet with the outlines
of the old never fully effaced; and in the novel itself, words of
earlier texts are constantly sounding between and underneath
the words that we read. *Between the Acts* may well be Woolf's
most allusive work, with the simplicity, indeed almost slightness
of its plot strikingly thickened and deepened with multiple layers of other texts. The notes in this annotated edition focus
specifically on such intertexts, to reveal, as it were, a vast cultural

root system descending fibrously into the past. But these numerous and lengthy annotations—and they are selective rather than comprehensive—also raise several crucial questions for our critical approach. Many allusions are explicit: when characters, for example, knowingly quote poetry, songs, and nursery rhymes; refer to writers, mythological figures, or historical personages; or question the origin of a common expression or traditional custom. Other allusions are detectable through brief quotations or distinctive images, like "manacled to a rock" (41), the "stricken deer" (59), or "heart of darkness" (148). Still others reverberate in the mind like ghostly echoes, as when, for example, the description of Isa's neck, "broad as a pillar, against an arum lily" (73) stirs associations with the poetry of Edmund Spenser, the paintings of the Pre-Raphaelites, or Stephen Dedalus's pondering ambiguities of spiritual-erotic imagery in James Joyce's *A Portrait of the Artist as a Young Man;* or when the image of the great pear tree (106) taps into a long tradition that links pear trees and the fecundity of the womb. Once we begin allusive reading, however, is there any limit to when we should stop? As a second problem, once we acknowledge the nature of this text as profoundly allusive, does it demand then an educated, sophisticated, and perhaps even British reader to be understood?

The answer to the first question depends on the importance we assign to authorial control and conscious intent. Must we assume that everything we consider an allusion was deliberately and consciously intended by Woolf? If not, how do we distinguish between allusions she intended and allusions that spring from personal associations in the minds of individual readers? In *Practical Criticism* (1929), the modernist critic I. A. Richards deplored the confusion of the poem with the idiosyncratic responses of its readers, and warned in particular of the deleterious effect of "mnemonic irrelevances" that occur when readers project associations from their own pasts onto their interpretations of literary works. Yet the modernist narratologist Mikhail Bakhtin argued that the novel is inherently dialogized by an ever-present heteroglossia, or plurality of social voices ("Discourse in the Novel" [written 1934–1935, translated 1981]); and Roland Barthes, a theorist writing just after the modernist period, came to see the text as a woven network of citations, echoes, and inescapable allusions, engaging the reader in stereophonic play (*Image—Music—Text*). Most approaches today will likely come closer to Bakhtin and Barthes than to Richards, according both voices outside the text and the voices of its readers a collaborative role. Not to abandon Richards entirely, however, we are still likely to see each literary work as creating its own discursive and rhetorical schema, inviting certain kinds of readings and soliciting particular patterns of response. The way allusions work in *Between the Acts* may not be the way they work in all texts. Woolf's novel, however, both explicitly invites allusive thinking and penetrates further to engage the fundamentally allusive nature of words themselves.

Allusion is, of course, the primary mode of Miss La Trobe's pageant, which mixes and merges numerous works of English drama in its plots, and boldly steals from a wide and eclectic range of reading in its script. The pageant also mirrors its own technique in a scene of self-allusion, when the characters combine at the end, "each declaim[ing] some phrase or fragment from their parts" (125). Language that echoes previous texts comes also to echo its own previous utterances of the echoed words. Pageant language furthermore bleeds into "real" language as characters in the audience world think in allusive forms as well. Isa, trying to write her own poetry, is obsessed with images, phrases, and rhythms from past poems, but she is certainly not the only one. Her father-in-law, Bartholomew, quotes Byron (4) and Swinburne (75); Mrs. Manresa quotes *Hamlet* (38) and Oliver

Goldsmith (119); William Dodge completes Isa's quotation from Keats (38) and quotes Racine (141); and anonymous audience voices return to Hamlet's question and recite a Whitman poem (136). Accumulating layers, allusions may refer to texts that are themselves allusive and that frequently involve some question or problem about allusion's role. The name of Bartholomew's dog, Sohrab, for example, recalls not only Matthew Arnold's poem "Sohrab and Rustum," but the controversy over that poem's alleged plagiarism from a Persian tale; the song *"I Never Loved a Dear Gazelle"* in a dizzying cycle echoes James Joyce's citation of Lewis Carroll's parody of Thomas Moore's retelling of another Persian tale; the song furthermore invokes Carroll's accompanying, though facetious, argument that poetry, like music, should dilute its intensity by offering "settings" or arrangements of works we already know. Further thematizing the allusive presence of the past, characters wonder about the origins of the expressions they use (17, 84), and Lucy Swithin, passing a shelf of books, offers what might well be a metacritical comment on a way to understand the novel as a whole: "Here are the poets from whom we descend by way of the mind" (47–48). It is not only poets, or even aspiring poets, who descend from past words; it is language itself. And it is not only poetry that allusively haunts the language; all literature, history, popular culture, folklore, cultural tradition creates, by implication, a global palimpsest, like some gigantic crisscross letter. The characters are always speaking, and we are always reading, through layers of previously sounded words. By constructing a storyworld of proliferating and pervasive allusions, *Between the Acts* releases allusion from any tie to the author's intent; allusion proliferates, and opens itself to proliferation in the reader's mind because citation is inherent in the nature of words themselves.

The idea that no word sounds on its own, that language carries a heavy freight of cumulative use, is a common theme among modernist writers, resonating as well, for example, in the highly allusive works of T. S. Eliot and James Joyce. The preoccupation reflects, to some extent, a modernist sense of belatedness: the difficulty of writing after a great tradition and the need to devise new and creative ways to engage with, to order, or to alter the inheritance of the past. Certainly Isa struggles with the problem of finding a voice in the wake of other voices, and their putative authority may be the source of "abortiveness" in her own efforts to write: "'How am I burdened with what they drew from the earth; memories; possessions. . . . That was the burden,' she mused, 'laid on me in the cradle . . . what we must remember: what we would forget'" (106). Miss La Trobe, however, as the other writer in the text, creates in a way that revels in verbal associations, and in a way that Woolf often celebrates in her literary essays and reviews. Reviewing a production of Shakespeare's *Twelfth Night* in 1933, Woolf writes, "For Shakespeare is writing, it seems, not with the whole of his mind mobilized and under control but with feelers left flying that sort and play with words so that the trail of a chance word is caught and followed recklessly. From the echo of one word is born another word, for which reason, perhaps, the play seems as we read it to tremble perpetually on the brink of music" ("Twelfth Night" 45). Allusion in this view transforms the nature of language, from referential meaning to associative meanings, and in an energizing, not coercive, way.

One of Woolf's last essays, "Craftsmanship," addresses so specifically the echoic nature of words that it suggests the way to read *Between the Acts*. Woolf begins this talk, written for BBC broadcast in 1937, by illustrating her leap from reading instructions in the London Underground to hearing the same words in the poetry of Christina Rossetti, Tennyson, and Keats. Even words used for mundane purposes, she indicates, have the power of triggering associations in our minds. The word *incar-*

nadine, she insists, will always subliminally evoke "multitudinous seas," sounding Macbeth's cry that the blood on his hands from murdering King Duncan will "The multitudinous seas incarnadine, / Making the green one red" (act 2, scene 2). Yet Woolf also distinguishes between "surface" and "sunken" meanings, the former having to do with the specific and conscious communicative message, the latter, with the chaotic unruliness of the unconscious mind's "multitudinous seas." The point is a crucial one, particularly for those of us who seek to be both scholars and readers of Woolf. Annotations, such as this edition provides, isolate and explain individual sources, making them the focus of conscious scrutiny, but as Woolf states, "The moment we single out and emphasize the suggestions as we have done here they become unreal; and we, too, become unreal—specialists, word mongers, phrase finders, not readers" ("Craftsmanship" 202). "In reading," she continues, "we have to allow the sunken meanings to remain sunken, suggested, not stated; lapsing and flowing into each other like reeds on the bed of a river" (202).

In such reading, allusion is not intrusive but ghostly, not isolated but blended and composite in our minds. As Mitchell Leaska writes, "Readers have repeatedly seen that V. W. often tapped multiple literary sources to insinuate a point" (221), or as Gillian Beer notes, "Woolf skeins together words and phrases recognizable from a wide, and multiple, range of poetic contexts" (140 n94). Perhaps it is the Bloomsbury writer David Garnett, however, who most evocatively captures the way Woolf attunes our ears to the whole, when he writes of "her command of language and of all associations which echo in words and can be called out from them like the murmur of the waves evoked for us by the shell clasped to our ear." Through an image anticipating the mirror scene in the pageant's last act, "Craftsmanship" relates such multiplicity to a pluralistic and refracted conception of truth: "The truth [words] try to catch is many-sided, and they convey it by being themselves many-sided, flashing this way, then that" (206). Whereas some modernists (arguably both Eliot and Joyce) use allusion as a way of ordering their texts, Woolf seems more interested in allusion's *dis*ordering potential—or at least in the way simultaneous apprehension of multiple allusions can prevent our settling into any one voice. Her allusions also work to bring past and present meanings collaboratively together, giving precedence neither to the earlier nor to the present text, but rather stimulating the play of interactive meanings in our minds. The deeper community of *Between the Acts* thus resides in the totality of collective thinking: "all life, all art, all waifs & strays—a rambling capricious but somehow unified whole" (*Diary* 5: 135). But what then are the implications for reading, for scholarship, for art?

For today's reader, such pervasive allusion returns us to the vexed question of modernist difficulty: What competency, on the part of the reader, does this text require to be understood? Like much modernist writing, *Between the Acts* itself stages the problematic of cultural memory: How can words enact their subliminal, liberating effects for the reader who lacks the memory that allusions tap? The library, with its bookshelves, stands in Pointz Hall with its many riches, but even the aspiring poet Isa is "book-shy" (14) and the narrative voice laments, "For her generation the newspaper was a book" (14). The problem lies not in reading newspapers, but in the loss of other memories if newspapers or "picture papers" become the only thing we read.

Reading and scholarship thus need to work together. Our scholarly selves can assist in the ongoing task of cultural archaeology, both tracking additional allusions and probing more fully the way that any one annotation works. The goal is not to identify each allusion in order to understand the novel but to acquire a richer feeling for the way citational language works. Then we might look for clusters, patterns, or rhythms in the allusive materials, going beyond identifications of single works. Undercurrents of violence, for example, run throughout this novel, but readers of the annotations here might be struck not only by how overwhelmingly allusions to rape and male violence to women sound in the early section, but also how mixed these are with allusions to pilgrimage and spiritual seeking as well. Allusions seem to become more light and playful in the middle section, returning again to violence at the end. The violence of the later allusions seems more fundamental to human passions and obsessions, yet there are alternations here with allusions to rebirth, resurrections, and seasonal cycles, too. Critical interpretation can thus assist with numerous cross-readings—seeking patterns within the text, within the allusions, and in text and allusions combined.

If scholarship can thus enhance our reading, Woolf's imaging of sunken reading can enhance our scholarship as well. Inevitably, scholarly readings will be partial, leading perhaps to brilliant insights yet constitutionally unable to capture the whole. Summing up, like the Reverend Streatfield's interpretation of the pageant, is necessarily limited and reductive, for the need to express meaning directly must carefully control the indirect and suggestive life of words. There comes a point then, always, when we need to set scholarship aside, when we need to return to unconscious reading, to surrender again to the textual spell. Annotations will achieve their aim only if they return the reader, with greater receptiveness, to the text in between.

Art

IT IS TIME to revisit, in larger terms, the question with which this introduction began: What is literature's significance in a time of war? Or rather, if hostility and conflict are endemic to the human condition, as this novel suggests, what is literature's relevance in our *ordinarily* troubled world? Thematically, *Between the Acts* raises such broadly relevant matters as culture, nation, civilization, ecology, and ethics, but undergirding them all is the novel's self-reflexive questioning of the validity and value of addressing such issues through art. Staging a pageant simultaneously stages an exploration into the nature of aesthetic creation, production, and reception, and the role these processes play in our lives.

In both this novel and its embedded pageant, recollection undergoes a process of radical reconstruction. Language, we have seen, is laden with echoes; the characters are burdened with memories of the personal, the communal, and the geological past. Yet, as we have also noted, a narrative impelled by rhyme and rhythm can alter the anticipated structure, shattering old habits of attention and perception, and stimulating readers to think in new ways. The title of this novel itself enacts a radical reorientation, like a syncopated beat that places the stress a little offside. All conventions of literary criticism place the "acts" at the center; "between the acts" disrupts that concentration with the pull of a space offstage. Our focus reorients itself to highlight what has previously been marginalized, neglected, or ignored.

In this world of shifting perception, however, *between* becomes an unstable and multivalent term. In a literal sense, the novel alternates between pageant and audience, between what is on- and offstage. Yet repetitions and continuities weave throughout all the voices, making it difficult to maintain the binaries of *acts* and *between*. The separation is always tenuous, and then utterly collapsed in the pageant's Present-Time scenes. Traditional realistic drama, performed behind the proscenium, positions the audience as invisible spectators, sheltered behind the equally invisible wall of the stage's four-sided room. Modern experimental theater, in contrast, draws on techniques such as actors directly addressing the audience, or speaking their parts from audience seats, to break what Bertolt Brecht termed the "fourth wall": the illusion of separation between fictional and real worlds. In *Between the Acts*, Woolf's La Trobe radically explodes that illusion by placing her audience fully onstage. In the pageant's scripted ten minutes of silence, all present-time sounds, including any sounds made by the audience, become the aural content of the play. Then, as the stage fills with mirrors, the audience, through their reflections, becomes doubly positioned, located both on and off the stage. The characters *at* the play are also the characters *in* the play, inhabiting a site in between. And, by a domino effect, as the pageant's audience transforms into players, so, too, a responsive reading audience will feel itself shifting position, to become the subject seen as well.

Caught between two worlds, the liminal space is unstable; it is also uncertain terrain. In a positive way, the pageant breaks down barriers of isolation, creating what we might call a participatory community, united not by shared ideologies but in a collaborative act. But the shift—and the audience feels it—is also threatening, for in breaking down barriers of self-protection, the mirrors compel the audience to examine and judge themselves. The "megaphonic, anonymous voice"—ambiguously the voice of mass technology and individual conscience—confronts them with human greed, jealousy, superiority: the knowledge that what *"the gun slayers, bomb droppers"* do *"openly,"* we do *"shyly"* (127). Yet it holds out as well tiny straws of hope—something as small as an impulse of kindness to the cat, or grief for a loved one, or one brave urchin's resistance to being exploited and bought. Playful, performative, and provocative, the pageant strikes out with an ethical challenge, too. But will the audience really look at the reflections? And will the mirrors of self-reflection bring about any change?

When the aim of art is transformative vision, it becomes difficult to gauge its success. When audience members leave asking questions, some part of the pageant's dynamics is carried out into the world. Furthermore, in a scene that "rhymes" with the theatrical mirrors, Lucy Swithin gazes at "reflections" of "ourselves" in the pond (139). In the fish, she sees multiplicity, variety, and beauty; in the lily pads, a broader vision of other continents on the globe. In a small way, she, too, along with bits of other voices, continues part of the pageant's work. Overall, nonetheless, the effect of the day's performance is, like the play itself, a jumbled dispersion of orts and scraps. Transmission and communication are fallible; the materials are too complex, both creation and reception are flawed. Yet disappointments are followed by a series of rebeginnings, enacted on different levels again through rhyming scenes: Miss La Trobe turns to the prospect of another play; Isa and Giles, out of their conflict, may conceive another child; Lucy returns to read once more the story of the beginning of human life. What the pattern means, however, continues to hover in between: An endless, biologically driven cycle compelled by the sex war (imaged in the picture of the cock and the hen in the pub) and the maternal compulsion to give birth (the cow in the stable)? Or the ancient, regenerative ritual of the seasons, celebrating the fertility and fecundity of the land?

In the mind of the artist, at least, the new cycle is initiated through a creative, regenerative act. Out of the land (the mixed violence and vibrancy of the bird-buzzing tree [142]), solitude (ironically aided by La Trobe's own marginalization as an artist and lesbian, and being suspiciously foreign), and human voices (the common talk, excluding but surrounding her, in the pub), a new play begins to form. The outer, conscious world must also, however, leak into the unconscious, a process figured as a descent into the depths of the pool (144). For as Bart Oliver intuits, what La Trobe needs, at the end of the day, is "darkness in the mud; a whisky and soda at the pub; and coarse words descending like maggots through the waters" (138). Just as her pageant was made out of words that have been said before, so the voices of the villagers sink into La Trobe's subconscious—the primeval scene of both struggle and fertility—resting, at the pool's bottom, in the organic mud. The mind, the image implies, is a reservoir, where all that is collectively good and bad, admirable and shameful, all purities and impurities, must be absorbed. As perhaps the most comprehensive of Woolf's novels, *Between the Acts* reaches toward the totality of the human condition, its violence as well as its peace. But then, echoing the conversation's opening controversial image of the cesspool, the mind's "fertile mud" becomes the transformative place out of which new combinations, new creations, might arise (144).

If the novel thus ends with suggestions of art's regenerative possibilities, its readers will inevitably grapple with the questions raised by Woolf's death. After writing such resiliency for her fictional artist, Woolf, shortly after she finished the typescript, made the choice to end her own life. Her reason was the onset of another terrible period of mental and physical illness; and given the expectations still that Hitler might invade at any moment, and the implications of her being possibly incapacitated when he did, we should be wary of making any simple connections between her decision and this work. What should matter most to us now is her enduring, poignant legacy of a work in progress, both literally and in intent. For in both the pageant and the novel, the task of rebuilding civilization's wall (123) is left for those who will survive.

In the final words of the novel, the curtain rises, opening ominously on the act to come. Everything we have been reading—the novel, and by implication, art itself—is placed "between the acts." As participants in the novel, we, too, shift our location once again. In our own palimpsestic layering, we have been the audience for the novel; we have become, like the audience in the pageant, the players self-reflected in its glass; and we are now finally positioned as writers, called on to supply the next words. For after its multiple pathways and trajectories, the novel ends on the need for act and action, leaving us on the point of suspension between the moments "now" and "next." In a later essay, "Thoughts on Peace in an Air Raid" (1940), Woolf looked ahead to the future, to the question of whether peace, rather than conflict, could be the informing condition of our lives. She urged the need to fight with the mind and ideas rather than with arms, but she also made clear the joint task: "Unless we can think peace into existence we—not this one body in this one bed but millions of bodies yet to be born—will lie in the same darkness and hear the same death rattle overhead" (243). To think peace, we must rely on collaborative effort performed by each and every one.

The value of literature, *Between the Acts* asserts, is to stimulate those processes of thinking, but in doing so, literature confronts us with questions that are complex, difficult, and unresolved. Do heterogeneity and hybridity, in this novel, offer a revolutionary alternative to oppositional political and national binaries? Could the competitive and aggressive thinking of warfare be superseded by the ability to think through multiple, contradictory views? Could such in-between consciousness generate an ethics of pluralism and a tolerance of diversity, mixed with an equally important connectivity and multivalent interdependency, too? Such are the large questions that readers and critics of this novel debate, with many more besides. But then, letting us speculate thus broadly, literature, most usefully, returns us to the particular scene. We are concerned, after all, with a twenty-four-hour day in a small community, in England, in 1939. We must focus our attention on a small, localized world of ordinary people, involved in a seemingly simple plot.

NOTES

[1]"A Scrap-book of Rodmell and Southease in the county of Sussex, produced by the Rodmell and Southease Women's Institute, 1950." Compiled by Mrs. Gladys Freeth. According to Mrs. Freeth's records, *Twelfth Night* was also performed in Rodmell in 1931 and 1938. I would like to thank the Rodmell and Southease Women's Institute for permission to cite this scrapbook, and member Madeleine Harvey for her help.

[2]A Web site for St. Peter's Church in Rodmell states that "Henry the Eighth gave Anne Boleyn the manor house of Rodmell and Princess Elizabeth walked here in the gap between the downs that even now is known as Princess Gap." http://yeoldesussexpages.com/churches/suschur/rodmell/rodmell.htm

[3]Critic, "A London Diary," *New Statesman and Nation,* August 31, 1940: 203.

[4]The title of an essay Virginia Woolf published in 1924, and also given to a group of essays published in her *Common Reader* (1925).

[5]One clearly evident meaning of the title, as critics have suggested, is "between the [world] wars." In a similar time out from cultural war, the extraordinary meeting in the mosque between Aziz and Mrs. Moore in chapter 2 of E. M. Forster's *A Passage to India* takes place, as Mrs. Moore explains in the next chapter, when she left the British club "between the acts" of the performance of the play *Cousin Kate* (E. M. Forster, *A Passage to India,* San Diego: Harcourt, 1965).

[6]"I suppose what I expect is that they'll say now that Mrs W. has written a long book about nothing" (*Diary* 5: 58). Woolf writes this criticism, or perhaps limited perception, into an anonymous audience member's response to Miss La Trobe's pageant: "All that fuss about nothing!" (95)

[7]For the connections between Woolf's voices and sound technologies, see my chapter, "Virginia Woolf, Sound Technologies, and the New Aurality," *Virginia Woolf in the Age of Mechanical Reproduction: Music, Cinema, Photography, and Popular Culture.* Edited by Pamela Caughie, 69–96. New York: Garland, 2000.

[8]"In the Attic tragedy, the chorus were 'interested spectators,' sympathizing with the fortunes of the characters, and giving expression, between the 'acts,'

to the moral and religious sentiments evoked by the action of the play" (*Oxford English Dictionary*).

WORKS CITED

Bakhtin, M. M. "Discourse in the Novel." In *The Dialogic Imagination*. Translated by Caryl Emerson and Michael Holquist, 259–422. Austin: University of Texas Press, 1981.

Barthes, Roland. *Image—Music—Text*. Translated by Stephen Heath. New York: Noonday, 1977.

Beer, Gillian. *Between the Acts* by Virginia Woolf. With an introduction and notes by Gillian Beer. London: Penguin, 1992.

Garnett, David. "Virginia Woolf." *New Statesman and Nation*, 12 April 1941: 386.

Leaska, Mitchell A. *Pointz Hall: The Earlier and Later Typescripts of* Between the Acts. New York: University Publications, 1983.

Richards, I. A. *Practical Criticism: A Study of Literary Judgment*. 1929. Reprint, New York: Harcourt, 1956.

Woolf, Leonard S. "The Pageant of History." In *Essays on Literature, History, Politics, Etc.* Freeport, NY: Books for Libraries, 1927.

Woolf, Virginia. "Craftsmanship." In *The Death of the Moth and Other Essays*, 198–207. 1942. Reprint, New York: Harcourt Brace Jovanovich, 1974.

——— "Poetry, Fiction and the Future." In *The Essays of Virginia Woolf*. Vol. 4: 1925–1928. Edited by Andrew McNeillie, 428–41. London: Hogarth Press, 1994.

——— "Twelfth Night at the Old Vic." In *The Death of the Moth and Other Essays*, 45–50. 1942. Reprint, New York: Harcourt Brace Jovanovich, 1974.

Between the Acts

NOTE

The MS. of this book had been completed, but had not been finally revised for the printer, at the time of Virginia Woolf's death. She would not, I believe, have made any large or material alterations in it, though she would probably have made a good many small corrections or revisions before passing the final proofs.

LEONARD WOOLF

IT WAS a summer's night and they were talking, in the big room with the windows open to the garden, about the cesspool. The county council had promised to bring water to the village, but they hadn't.

Mrs. Haines, the wife of the gentleman farmer, a goosefaced woman with eyes protruding as if they saw something to gobble in the gutter, said affectedly: "What a subject to talk about on a night like this!"

Then there was silence; and a cow coughed; and that led her to say how odd it was, as a child, she had never feared cows, only horses. But, then, as a small child in a perambulator, a great cart-horse had brushed within an inch of her face. Her family, she told the old man in the arm-chair, had lived near Liskeard for many centuries. There were the graves in the churchyard to prove it.

A bird chuckled outside. "A nightingale?" asked Mrs. Haines. No, nightingales didn't come so far north. It was a day-light bird, chuckling over the substance and succulence of the day, over worms, snails, grit, even in sleep.

The old man in the arm-chair—Mr. Oliver, of the Indian Civil Service, retired—said that the site they had chosen for the cesspool was, if he had heard aright, on the Roman road. From an aeroplane, he said, you could still see, plainly marked, the scars made by the Britons; by the Romans; by the Elizabethan manor house; and by the plough, when they ploughed the hill to grow wheat in the Napoleonic wars.

"But you don't remember . . ." Mrs. Haines began. No, not that. Still he did remember——— and he was about to tell them what, when there was a sound outside, and Isa, his son's wife, came in with her hair in pigtails; she was wearing a dressing-gown with faded peacocks on it. She came in like a swan swimming its way; then was checked and stopped; was surprised to find people there; and lights burning. She had been sitting with her little boy who wasn't well, she apologized. What had they been saying?

"Discussing the cesspool," said Mr. Oliver.

"What a subject to talk about on a night like this!" Mrs. Haines exclaimed again.

What had *he* said about the cesspool; or indeed about anything? Isa wondered, inclining her head towards the gentleman farmer, Rupert Haines. She had met him at a Bazaar; and at a tennis party. He had handed her a cup and a racquet—that was all. But in his ravaged face she always felt mystery; and in his silence, passion. At the tennis party she had felt this, and at the Bazaar. Now a third time, if anything more strongly, she felt it again.

"I remember," the old man interrupted, "my mother. . . ." Of his mother he remembered that she was very stout; kept her tea-caddy locked; yet had given him in that very room a copy of Byron. It was over sixty years ago, he told them, that his mother had given him the works of Byron in that very room. He paused.

"She walks in beauty like the night," he quoted.

Then again:

"So we'll go no more a-roving by the light of the moon."

Isa raised her head. The words made two rings, perfect rings, that floated them, herself and Haines, like two swans down stream. But his snow-white breast was circled with a tangle of dirty duckweed; and she too, in her webbed feet was entangled, by her husband, the stockbroker. Sitting on her three-cornered chair she swayed, with her dark pigtails hanging, and her body like a bolster in its faded dressing-gown.

Mrs. Haines was aware of the emotion circling them, excluding her. She waited, as one waits for the strain of an organ to die out before leaving church. In the car going home to the red villa in the cornfields, she would destroy it, as a thrush pecks the wings off a butterfly. Allowing ten seconds to intervene, she rose; paused; and then, as if she had heard the last strain die out, offered Mrs. Giles Oliver her hand.

But Isa, though she should have risen at the same moment that Mrs. Haines rose, sat on. Mrs. Haines glared at her out of goose-like eyes, gobbling, "Please, Mrs. Giles Oliver, do me the kindness to recognize my existence. . . ." which she was forced to do, rising at last from her chair, in her faded dressing-gown, with the pigtails falling over each shoulder.

Pointz Hall was seen in the light of an early summer morning to be a middle-sized house. It did not rank among the houses that are mentioned in guide books. It was too homely. But this whitish house with the grey roof, and the wing thrown out at right angles, lying unfortunately low on the meadow with a fringe of trees on the bank above it so that smoke curled up to the nests of the rooks, was a desirable house to live in. Driving past, people said to each other: "I wonder if that'll ever come into the market?" and to the chauffeur: "Who lives there?"

The chauffeur didn't know. The Olivers, who had bought the place something over a century ago, had no connection with the Warings, the Elveys, the Mannerings or the Burnets; the old families who had all intermarried, and lay in their deaths intertwisted, like the ivy roots, beneath the churchyard wall.

Only something over a hundred and twenty years the Olivers had been there. Still, on going up the principal staircase—there was another, a mere ladder at the back for the servants—there was a portrait. A length of yellow brocade was visible half-way up; and, as one reached the top, a small powdered face, a great head-dress slung with pearls, came into view; an ancestress of sorts. Six or seven bedrooms opened out of the corridor. The butler had been a soldier; had married a lady's maid; and, under a glass case there was a watch that had stopped a bullet on the field of Waterloo.

It was early morning. The dew was on the grass. The church clock struck eight times. Mrs. Swithin drew the curtain in her bedroom—the faded white chintz that so agreeably from the outside tinged the window with its green lining. There with her old hands on the hasp, jerking it open, she stood: old Oliver's married sister; a widow. She always meant to set up a house of her own; perhaps in Kensington, perhaps at Kew, so that she could have the benefit of the gardens. But she stayed on all through the summer; and when winter wept its damp upon the panes, and choked the gutters with dead leaves, she said: "Why, Bart, did they build the house in the hollow, facing north?" Her brother said, "Obviously to escape from nature. Weren't four horses needed to drag the family coach through the mud?" Then he told her the famous story of the great eighteenth-century winter; when for a whole month the house had been blocked by snow. And the trees had fallen. So every year, when winter came, Mrs. Swithin retired to Hastings.

But it was summer now. She had been waked by the birds. How they sang! attacking the dawn like so many choir boys attacking an iced cake. Forced to listen, she had stretched for her favourite reading—an Outline of History—and had spent the hours between three and five thinking of rhododendron forests in Piccadilly; when the entire continent, not then, she under-

geological time (handwritten margin note)

stood, divided by a channel, was all one; populated, she understood, by elephant-bodied, seal-necked, heaving, surging, slowly writhing, and, she supposed, barking monsters; the iguanodon, the mammoth, and the mastodon; from whom presumably, she thought, jerking the window open, we descend.

It took her five seconds in actual time, in mind time ever so much longer, to separate Grace herself, with blue china on a tray, from the leather-covered grunting monster who was about, as the door opened, to demolish a whole tree in the green steaming undergrowth of the primeval forest. Naturally, she jumped, as Grace put the tray down and said: "Good morning, Ma'am." "Batty," Grace called her, as she felt on her face the divided glance that was half meant for a beast in a swamp, half for a maid in a print frock and white apron.

"How those birds sing!" said Mrs. Swithin, at a venture. The window was open now; the birds certainly were singing. An obliging thrush hopped across the lawn; a coil of pinkish rubber twisted in its beak. Tempted by the sight to continue her imaginative reconstruction of the past, Mrs. Swithin paused; she was given to increasing the bounds of the moment by flights into past or future; or sidelong down corridors and alleys; but she remembered her mother—her mother in that very room rebuking her. "Don't stand gaping, Lucy, or the wind'll change . . ." How often her mother had rebuked her in that very room—"but in a very different world," as her brother would remind her. So she sat down to morning tea, like any other old lady with a high nose, thin cheeks, a ring on her finger and the usual trappings of rather shabby but gallant old age, which included in her case a cross gleaming gold on her breast.

The nurses after breakfast were trundling the perambulator up and down the terrace; and as they trundled they were talking—not shaping pellets of information or handing ideas from one to another, but rolling words, like sweets on their tongues; which, as they thinned to transparency, gave off pink, green, and sweetness. This morning that sweetness was: "How cook had told 'im off about the asparagus; how when she rang I said: how it was a sweet costume with blouse to match;" and that was leading to something about a feller as they walked up and down the terrace rolling sweets, trundling the perambulator.

It was a pity that the man who had built Pointz Hall had pitched the house in a hollow, when beyond the flower garden and the vegetables there was this stretch of high ground. Nature had provided a site for a house; man had built his house in a hollow. Nature had provided a stretch of turf half a mile in length and level, till it suddenly dipped to the lily pool. The terrace was broad enough to take the entire shadow of one of the great trees laid flat. There you could walk up and down, up and down, under the shade of the trees. Two or three grew close together; then there were gaps. Their roots broke the turf, and among those bones were green waterfalls and cushions of grass in which violets grew in spring or in summer the wild purple orchis.

Amy was saying something about a feller when Mabel, with her hand on the pram, turned sharply, her sweet swallowed. "Leave off grubbing," she said sharply. "Come along, George."

The little boy had lagged and was grouting in the grass. Then the baby, Caro, thrust her fist out over the coverlet and the furry bear was jerked overboard. Amy had to stoop. George grubbed. The flower blazed between the angles of the roots. Membrane after membrane was torn. It blazed a soft yellow, a lambent light under a film of velvet; it filled the caverns behind the eyes with light. All that inner darkness became a hall, leaf smelling, earth smelling, of yellow light. And the tree was beyond the flower; the grass, the flower and the tree were entire. Down on his knees grubbing he held the flower complete. Then there was a roar and a hot breath and a stream of coarse grey hair rushed between him and the flower. Up he leapt, toppling in his fright, and saw coming towards him a terrible peaked eyeless monster moving on legs, brandishing arms.

"Good morning, sir," a hollow voice boomed at him from a beak of paper.

The old man had sprung upon him from his hiding-place behind a tree.

"Say good morning, George; say 'Good morning, Grandpa,'" Mabel urged him, giving him a push towards the man. But George stood gaping. George stood gazing. Then Mr. Oliver crumpled the paper which he had cocked into a snout and appeared in person. A very tall old man, with gleaming eyes, wrinkled cheeks, and a head with no hair on it. He turned.

"Heel!" he bawled, "heel, you brute!" And George turned; and the nurses turned holding the furry bear; they all turned to look at Sohrab the Afghan hound bounding and bouncing among the flowers.

"Heel!" the old man bawled, as if he were commanding a regiment. It was impressive, to the nurses, the way an old boy of his age could still bawl and make a brute like that obey him. Back came the Afghan hound, sidling, apologetic. And as he cringed at the old man's feet, a string was slipped over his collar; the noose that old Oliver always carried with him.

"You wild beast . . . you bad beast," he grumbled, stooping. George looked at the dog only. The hairy flanks were sucked in and out; there was a blob of foam on its nostrils. He burst out crying.

Old Oliver raised himself, his veins swollen, his cheeks flushed; he was angry. His little game with the paper hadn't worked. The boy was a cry-baby. He nodded and sauntered on, smoothing out the crumpled paper and muttering, as he tried to find his line in the column, "A cry-baby—a cry-baby." But the breeze blew the great sheet out; and over the edge he surveyed the landscape—flowing fields, heath and woods. Framed, they became a picture. Had he been a painter, he would have fixed his easel here, where the country, barred by trees, looked like a picture. Then the breeze fell.

"M. Daladier," he read, finding his place in the column, "has been successful in pegging down the franc. . . ."

Mrs. Giles Oliver drew the comb through the thick tangle of hair which, after giving the matter her best attention, she had never had shingled or bobbed; and lifted the heavily embossed silver brush that had been a wedding present and had its uses in impressing chambermaids in hotels. She lifted it and stood in front of the three-folded mirror, so that she could see three separate versions of her rather heavy, yet handsome, face; and also, outside the glass, a slip of terrace, lawn and tree tops.

Inside the glass, in her eyes, she saw what she had felt overnight for the ravaged, the silent, the romantic gentleman farmer. "In love," was in her eyes. But outside, on the washstand, on the dressing-table, among the silver boxes and tooth-brushes, was the other love; love for her husband, the stockbroker—"The father of my children," she added, slipping into the cliché conveniently provided by fiction. Inner love was in the eyes; outer love on the dressing-table. But what feeling was it that stirred in her now when above the looking-glass, out of doors, she saw coming across the lawn the perambulator; two nurses; and her little boy George, lagging behind?

She tapped on the window with her embossed hairbrush. They were too far off to hear. The drone of the trees was in their ears; the chirp of birds; other incidents of garden life, inaudible, invisible to her in the bedroom, absorbed them. Isolated on a green island, hedged about with snowdrops, laid with a counterpane of puckered silk, the innocent island floated under her window. Only George lagged behind.

She returned to her eyes in the looking-glass. "In love," she must be; since the presence of his body in the room last night could so affect her; since the words he said, handing her a teacup, handing her a tennis racquet, could so attach themselves to a certain spot in her; and thus lie between them like a wire, tingling, tangling, vibrating—she groped, in the depths of the looking-glass, for a word to fit the infinitely quick vibrations of the aeroplane propeller that she had seen once at dawn at Croydon. Faster, faster, faster, it whizzed, whirred, buzzed, till all the flails became one flail and up soared the plane away and away. . . .

"Where we know not, where we go not, neither know nor care," she hummed. "Flying, rushing through the ambient, incandescent, summer silent . . ."

The rhyme was "air." She put down her brush. She took up the telephone.

"Three, four, eight, Pyecombe," she said.

"Mrs. Oliver speaking. . . . What fish have you this morning? Cod? Halibut? Sole? Plaice?"

"There to lose what binds us here," she murmured. "Soles. Filleted. In time for lunch please," she said aloud. "With a feather, a blue feather . . . flying mounting through the air . . . there to lose what binds us here . . ." The words weren't worth writing in the book bound like an account book in case Giles suspected. "Abortive," was the word that expressed her. She never came out of a shop, for example, with the clothes she admired; nor did her figure, seen against the dark roll of trousering in a shop window, please her. Thick of waist, large of limb, and, save for her hair, fashionable in the tight modern way, she never looked like Sappho, or one of the beautiful young men whose photographs adorned the weekly papers. She looked what she was: Sir Richard's daughter; and niece of the two old ladies at Wimbledon who were so proud, being O'Neils, of their descent from the Kings of Ireland.

A foolish, flattering lady, pausing on the threshold of what she once called "the heart of the house," the threshold of the library, had once said: "Next to the kitchen, the library's always the nicest room in the house." Then she added, stepping across the threshold: "Books are the mirrors of the soul."

In this case a tarnished, a spotted soul. For as the train took over three hours to reach this remote village in the very heart of England, no one ventured so long a journey without staving off possible mind-hunger, without buying a book on a bookstall. Thus the mirror that reflected the soul sublime, reflected also the soul bored. Nobody could pretend, as they looked at the shuffle of shilling shockers that week-enders had dropped, that the looking-glass always reflected the anguish of a Queen or the heroism of King Harry.

At this early hour of a June morning the library was empty. Mrs. Giles had to visit the kitchen. Mr. Oliver still tramped the terrace. And Mrs. Swithin was of course at church. The light but variable breeze, foretold by the weather expert, flapped the yellow curtain, tossing light, then shadow. The fire greyed, then glowed, and the tortoiseshell butterfly beat on the lower pane of the window; beat, beat, beat; repeating that if no human being ever came, never, never, never, the books would be mouldy, the fire out and the tortoiseshell butterfly dead on the pane.

Heralded by the impetuosity of the Afghan hound, the old man entered. He had read his paper; he was drowsy; and so sank down into the chintz-covered chair with the dog at his feet—the Afghan hound. His nose on his paws, his haunches drawn up, he looked a stone dog, a crusader's dog, guarding even in the realms of death the sleep of his master. But the master was not dead; only dreaming; drowsily, seeing as in a glass, its lustre spotted, himself, a young man helmeted; and a cascade falling. But no water; and the hills, like grey stuff pleated; and in the sand a hoop of ribs; a bullock maggot-eaten in the sun; and in the shadow of the rock, savages; and in his hand a gun. The dream hand clenched; the real hand lay on the chair arm, the veins swollen but only with a brownish fluid now.

The door opened.

"Am I," Isa apologized, "interrupting?"

Of course she was—destroying youth and India. It was his fault, since she had persisted in stretching his thread of life so fine, so far. Indeed he was grateful to her, watching her as she strolled about the room, for continuing.

Many old men had only their India—old men in clubs, old men in rooms off Jermyn Street. She in her striped dress continued him, murmuring, in front of the book cases: "The moor is dark beneath the moon, rapid clouds have drunk the last pale beams of even. . . . I have ordered the fish," she said aloud, turning, "though whether it'll be fresh or not I can't promise. But veal is dear, and everybody in the house is sick of beef and mutton. . . . Sohrab," she said, coming to a standstill in front of them. "What's *he* been doing?"

His tail never wagged. He never admitted the ties of domesticity. Either he cringed or he bit. Now his wild yellow eyes gazed at her, gazed at him. He could outstare them both. Then Oliver remembered:

"Your little boy's a cry-baby," he said scornfully.

"Oh," she sighed, pegged down on a chair arm, like a captive balloon, by a myriad of hair-thin ties into domesticity. "What's been happening?"

"I took the newspaper," he explained, "so . . ."

He took it and crumpled it into a beak over his nose. "So," he had sprung out from behind a tree on to the children.

"And he howled. He's a coward, your boy is."

She frowned. He was not a coward, her boy wasn't. And she loathed the domestic, the possessive; the maternal. And he knew it and did it on purpose to tease her, the old brute, her father-in-law.

She looked away.

"The library's always the nicest room in the house," she quoted, and ran her eyes along the books. "The mirror of the soul" books were. *The Faerie Queene* and Kinglake's *Crimea;* Keats and the *Kreutzer Sonata.* There they were, reflecting. What? What remedy was there for her at her age—the age of the century, thirty-nine—in books? Book-shy she was, like the rest of her generation; and gun-shy too. Yet as a person with a raging tooth runs her eye in a chemist shop over green bottles with gilt scrolls on them lest one of them may contain a cure, she considered: Keats and Shelley; Yeats and Donne. Or perhaps not a poem; a life. The life of Garibaldi. The life of Lord Palmerston. Or perhaps not a person's life; a county's. *The Antiquities of Durham; The Proceedings of the Archaeological Society of Nottingham.* Or not a life at all, but science—Eddington, Darwin, or Jeans.

None of them stopped her toothache. For her generation the newspaper was a book; and, as her father-in-law had dropped the *Times,* she took it and read: "A horse with a green tail . . ." which was fantastic. Next, "The guard at Whitehall . . ." which was romantic and then, building word upon word, she read: "The troopers told her the horse had a green tail; but she found it was just an ordinary horse. And they dragged her up to the barrack room where she was thrown upon a bed. Then one of the troopers removed part of her clothing, and she screamed and hit him about the face. . . ."

That was real; so real that on the mahogany door panels she saw the Arch in Whitehall; through the Arch the barrack room; in the barrack room the bed, and on the bed the girl was screaming and hitting him about the face, when the door (for in fact it was a door) opened and in came Mrs. Swithin carrying a hammer.

She advanced, sidling, as if the floor were fluid under her shabby garden shoes, and, advancing, pursed her lips and smiled, sidelong, at her brother. Not a word passed between them as she went to the cupboard in the corner and replaced the hammer, which she had taken without asking leave; together—she unclosed her fist—with a handful of nails.

"Cindy—Cindy," he growled, as she shut the cupboard door.

Lucy, his sister, was three years younger than he was. The name Cindy, or Sindy, for it could be spelt either way, was short for Lucy. It was by this name that he had called her when they were children; when she had trotted after him as he fished, and had made the meadow flowers into tight little bunches, winding one long grass stalk round and round and round. Once, she remembered, he had made her take the fish off the hook herself. The blood had shocked her—"Oh!" she had cried—for the gills were full of blood. And he had growled: "Cindy!" The ghost of that morning in the meadow was in her mind as she replaced the hammer where it belonged on one shelf; and the nails where they belonged on another; and shut the cupboard about which, for he still kept his fishing tackle there, he was still so very particular.

"I've been nailing the placard on the Barn," she said, giving him a little pat on the shoulder.

The words were like the first peal of a chime of bells. As the first peals, you hear the second; as the second peals, you hear the third. So when Isa heard Mrs. Swithin say: "I've been nailing the placard on the Barn," she knew she would say next:

"For the pageant."

And he would say:

"Today? By Jupiter! I'd forgotten!"

"If it's fine," Mrs. Swithin continued, "they'll act on the terrace . . ."

"And if it's wet," Bartholomew continued, "in the Barn."

"And which will it be?" Mrs. Swithin continued. "Wet or fine?"

Then, for the seventh time in succession, they both looked out of the window.

Every summer, for seven summers now, Isa had heard the same words; about the hammer and the nails; the pageant and the weather. Every year they said, would it be wet or fine; and every year it was—one or the other. The same chime followed the same chime, only this year beneath the chime she heard: "The girl screamed and hit him about the face with a hammer."

"The forecast," said Mr. Oliver, turning the pages till he found it, "says: Variable winds; fair average temperature; rain at times."

He put down the paper, and they all looked at the sky to see whether the sky obeyed the meteorologist. Certainly the weather was variable. It was green in the garden; grey the next. Here came the sun—an illimitable rapture of joy, embracing every flower, every leaf. Then in compassion it withdrew, covering its face, as if it forebore to look on human suffering. There was a fecklessness, a lack of symmetry and order in the clouds, as they thinned and thickened. Was it their own law, or no law, they obeyed? Some were wisps of white hair merely. One, high up, very distant, had hardened to golden alabaster; was made of immortal marble. Beyond that was blue, pure blue, black blue; blue that had never filtered down; that had escaped registration. It never fell as sun, shadow, or rain upon the world, but disregarded the little coloured ball of earth entirely. No flower felt it; no field; no garden.

Mrs. Swithin's eyes glazed as she looked at it. Isa thought her gaze was fixed because she saw God there, God on his throne. But as a shadow fell next moment on the garden Mrs. Swithin loosed and lowered her fixed look and said:

"It's very unsettled. It'll rain, I'm afraid. We can only pray," she added, and fingered her crucifix.

"And provide umbrellas," said her brother.

Lucy flushed. He had struck her faith. When she said "pray," he added "umbrellas." She half covered the cross with her fingers. She shrank; she cowered; but next moment she exclaimed:

"Oh there they are—the darlings!"

The perambulator was passing across the lawn.

Isa looked too. What an angel she was—the old woman! Thus to salute the children; to beat up against those immensities and the old man's irreverences her skinny hands, her laughing eyes! How courageous to defy Bart and the weather!

"He looks blooming," said Mrs. Swithin.

"It's astonishing how they pick up," said Isa.

"He ate his breakfast?" Mrs. Swithin asked.

"Every scrap," said Isa.

"And baby? No sign of measles?"

Isa shook her head. "Touch wood," she added, tapping the table.

"Tell me, Bart," said Mrs. Swithin, turning to her brother, "what's the origin of that? Touch wood . . . Antaeus, didn't he touch earth?"

She would have been, he thought, a very clever woman, had she fixed her gaze. But this led to that; that to the other. What went in at this ear, went out at that. And all were circled, as happens after seventy, by one recurring question. Hers was, should

she live at Kensington or at Kew? But every year, when winter
came, she did neither. She took lodgings at Hastings.

"Touch wood; touch earth; Antaeus," he muttered, bringing
the scattered bits together. Lemprière would settle it; or the Encyclopaedia. But it was not in books the answer to his question—why, in Lucy's skull, shaped so much like his own, there
existed a prayable being? She didn't, he supposed, invest it with
hair, teeth or toenails. It was, he supposed, more of a force or a
radiance, controlling the thrush and the worm; the tulip and the
hound; and himself, too, an old man with swollen veins. It got
her out of bed on a cold morning and sent her down the muddy
path to worship it, whose mouthpiece was Streatfield. A good
fellow, who smoked cigars in the vestry. He needed some sol-
ace, doling out preachments to asthmatic elders, perpetually re-
pairing the perpetually falling steeple, by means of placards
nailed to Barns. The love, he was thinking, that they should give
to flesh and blood they give to the church . . . when Lucy, rap-
ping her fingers on the table, said:

"What's the origin—the origin—of that?"

"Superstition," he said.

She flushed, and the little breath too was audible that she
drew in as once more he struck a blow at her faith. But, brother
and sister, flesh and blood was not a barrier, but a mist. Nothing changed their affection; no argument; no fact; no truth.
What she saw he didn't; what he saw she didn't—and so on, *ad
infinitum.*

"Cindy," he growled. And the quarrel was over.

The Barn to which Lucy had nailed her placard was a great
building in the farmyard. It was as old as the church, and built
of the same stone, but it had no steeple. It was raised on cones
of grey stone at the corners to protect it from rats and damp.
Those who had been to Greece always said it reminded them of

a temple. Those who had never been to Greece—the majority—admired it all the same. The roof was weathered red-orange; and inside it was a hollow hall, sun-shafted, brown, smelling of corn, dark when the doors were shut, but splendidly illuminated when the doors at the end stood open, as they did to let the wagons in—the long low wagons, like ships of the sea, breasting the corn, not the sea, returning in the evening shagged with hay. The lanes caught tufts where the wagons had passed.

Now benches were drawn across the floor of the Barn. If it rained, the actors were to act in the Barn; planks had been laid together at one end to form a stage. Wet or fine, the audience would take tea there. Young men and women—Jim, Iris, David, Jessica—were even now busy with garlands of red and white paper roses left over from the Coronation. The seeds and the dust from the sacks made them sneeze. Iris had a handkerchief bound round her forehead; Jessica wore breeches. The young men worked in shirt sleeves. Pale husks had stuck in their hair, and it was easy to run a splinter of wood into the fingers.

"Old Flimsy" (Mrs. Swithin's nickname) had been nailing another placard on the Barn. The first had been blown down, or the village idiot, who always tore down what had been nailed up, had done it, and was chuckling over the placard under the shade of some hedge. The workers were laughing too, as if old Swithin had left a wake of laughter behind her. The old girl with a wisp of white hair flying, knobbed shoes as if she had claws corned like a canary's, and black stockings wrinkled over the ankles, naturally made David cock his eye and Jessica wink back, as she handed him a length of paper roses. Snobs they were; long enough stationed that is in that one corner of the world to have taken indelibly the print of some three hundred years of customary behaviour. So they laughed; but respected. If she wore pearls, pearls they were.

"Old Flimsy on the hop," said David. She would be in and out twenty times, and finally bring them lemonade in a great jug and a plate of sandwiches. Jessie held the garland; he hammered. A hen strayed in; a file of cows passed the door; then a sheep dog; then the cowman, Bond, who stopped.

He contemplated the young people hanging roses from one rafter to another. He thought very little of anybody, simples or gentry. Leaning, silent, sardonic, against the door he was like a withered willow, bent over a stream, all its leaves shed, and in his eyes the whimsical flow of the waters.

"Hi—huh!" he cried suddenly. It was cow language presumably, for the particoloured cow, who had thrust her head in at the door, lowered her horns, lashed her tail and ambled off. Bond followed after.

"That's the problem," said Mrs. Swithin. While Mr. Oliver consulted the Encyclopaedia, searching under Superstition for the origin of the expression "Touch Wood," she and Isa discussed fish: whether, coming from a distance, it would be fresh.

They were so far from the sea. A hundred miles away, Mrs. Swithin said; no, perhaps a hundred and fifty. "But they do say," she continued, "one can hear the waves on a still night. After a storm, they say, you can hear a wave break. . . . I like that story," she reflected. "Hearing the waves in the middle of the night he saddled a horse and rode to the sea. Who was it, Bart, who rode to the sea?"

He was reading.

"You can't expect it brought to your door in a pail of water," said Mrs. Swithin, "as I remember when we were children, living in a house by the sea. Lobsters, fresh from the lobster pots. How they pinched the stick cook gave them! And salmon. You know if they're fresh because they have lice in their scales."

Bartholomew nodded. A fact that was. He remembered, the house by the sea. And the lobster.

They were bringing up nets full of fish from the sea; but Isa was seeing—the garden, variable as the forecast said, in the light breeze. Again, the children passed, and she tapped on the window and blew them a kiss. In the drone of the garden it went unheeded.

"Are we really," she said, turning round, "a hundred miles from the sea?"

"Thirty-five only," her father-in-law said, as if he had whipped a tape measure from his pocket and measured it exactly.

"It seems more," said Isa. "It seems from the terrace as if the land went on for ever and ever."

"Once there was no sea," said Mrs. Swithin. "No sea at all between us and the continent. I was reading that in a book this morning. There were rhododendrons in the Strand; and mammoths in Piccadilly."

"When we were savages," said Isa.

Then she remembered; her dentist had told her that savages could perform very skilful operations on the brain. Savages had false teeth, he said. False teeth were invented, she thought he said, in the time of the Pharaohs.

"At least so my dentist told me," she concluded.

"Which man d'you go to now?" Mrs. Swithin asked her.

"The same old couple; Batty and Bates in Sloane Street."

"And Mr. Batty told you they had false teeth in the time of the Pharaohs?" Mrs. Swithin pondered.

"Batty? Oh not Batty. Bates," Isa corrected her.

Batty, she recalled, only talked about Royalty. Batty, she told Mrs. Swithin, had a patient a Princess.

"So he kept me waiting well over an hour. And you know, when one's a child, how long that seems."

"Marriages with cousins," said Mrs. Swithin, "can't be good for the teeth."

Bart put his finger inside his mouth and projected the upper row outside his lips. They were false. Yet, he said, the Olivers hadn't married cousins. The Olivers couldn't trace their descent for more than two or three hundred years. But the Swithins could. The Swithins were there before the Conquest.

"The Swithins," Mrs. Swithin began. Then she stopped. Bart would crack another joke about Saints, if she gave him the chance. And she had had two jokes cracked at her already; one about an umbrella; another about superstition.

So she stopped and said, "How did we begin this talk?" She counted on her fingers. "The Pharaohs. Dentists. Fish . . . Oh yes, you were saying, Isa, you'd ordered fish; and you were afraid it wouldn't be fresh. And I said, 'That's the problem. . . .'"

The fish had been delivered. Mitchell's boy, holding them in a crook of his arm, jumped off his motor bike. There was no feeding the pony with lumps of sugar at the kitchen door, nor time for gossip, since his round had been increased. He had to deliver right over the hill at Bickley; also go round by Waythorn, Roddam, and Pyeminster, whose names, like his own, were in Domesday Book. But the cook—Mrs. Sands she was called, but by old friends Trixie—had never in all her fifty years been over the hill, nor wanted to.

He dabbed them down on the kitchen table, the filleted soles, the semi-transparent boneless fish. And before Mrs. Sands had time to peel the paper off, he was gone, giving a slap to the very fine yellow cat who rose majestically from the basket chair and advanced superbly to the table, winding the fish.

Were they a bit whiffy? Mrs. Sands held them to her nose. The cat rubbed itself this way, that way against the table legs, against her legs. She would save a slice for Sunny—his drawing-room name Sung-Yen had undergone a kitchen change into Sunny. She took them, the cat attendant, to the larder, and laid them on a plate in that semi-ecclesiastical apartment. For the house before the Reformation, like so many houses in that neighbourhood, had a chapel; and the chapel had become a larder, changing, like the cat's name, as religion changed. The Master (his drawing-room name; in the kitchen they called him Bartie) would bring gentlemen sometimes to see the larder—often when cook wasn't dressed. Not to see the hams that hung from hooks, or the butter on a blue slate, or the joint for tomorrow's dinner, but to see the cellar that opened out of the larder and its carved arch. If you tapped—one gentleman had a hammer—there was a hollow sound; a reverberation; undoubtedly, he said, a concealed passage where once somebody had hid. So it might be. But Mrs. Sands wished they wouldn't come into her kitchen telling stories with the girls about. It put ideas into their silly heads. They heard dead men rolling barrels. They saw a white lady walking under the trees. No one would cross the terrace after dark. If a cat sneezed, "There's the ghost!"

Sunny had his little bit off the fillet. Then Mrs. Sands took an egg from the brown basket full of eggs; some with yellow fluff sticking to the shells; then a pinch of flour to coat those semi-transparent slips; and a crust from the great earthenware crock full of crusts. Then, returning to the kitchen, she made those quick movements at the oven, cinder raking, stoking, damping, which sent strange echoes through the house, so that in the library, the sitting-room, the dining-room, and the nursery, whatever they were doing, thinking, saying, they knew, they all knew, it was getting on for breakfast, lunch, or dinner.

"The sandwiches . . ." said Mrs. Swithin, coming into the kitchen. She refrained from adding "Sands" to "sandwiches," for Sand and sandwiches clashed. "Never play," her mother used to say, "on people's names." And Trixie was not a name that suited, as Sands did, the thin, acid woman, red-haired sharp and clean, who never dashed off masterpieces, it was true; but then never dropped hairpins in the soup. "What in the name of Thunder?" Bart had said, raising a hairpin in his spoon, in the old days, fifteen years ago, before Sands came, in the time of Jessie Pook.

Mrs. Sands fetched bread; Mrs. Swithin fetched ham. One cut the bread; the other the ham. It was soothing, it was consolidating, this handwork together. The cook's hands cut, cut, cut. Whereas Lucy, holding the loaf, held the knife up. Why's stale bread, she mused, easier to cut than fresh? And so skipped, sidelong, from yeast to alcohol; so to fermentation; so to inebriation; so to Bacchus; and lay under purple lamps in a vineyard in Italy, as she had done, often; while Sands heard the clock tick; saw the cat; noted a fly buzz; and registered, as her lips showed, a grudge she mustn't speak against people making work in the kitchen while they had a high old time hanging paper roses in the Barn.

"Will it be fine?" asked Mrs. Swithin, her knife suspended. In the kitchen they humoured old Mother Swithin's fancies.

"Seems like it," said Mrs. Sands, giving her sharp look-out of the kitchen window.

"It wasn't last year," said Mrs. Swithin. "D'you remember what a rush we had—when the rain came—getting in the chairs?" She cut again. Then she asked about Billy, Mrs. Sands's nephew, apprenticed to the butcher.

"He's been doing," Mrs. Sands said, "what boys shouldn't; cheeking the master."

"That'll be all right," said Mrs. Swithin, half meaning the boy, half meaning the sandwich, as it happened a very neat one, trimmed, triangular.

"Mr. Giles may be late," she added, laying it, complacently, on top of the pile.

For Isa's husband, the stockbroker, was coming from London. And the local train, which met the express train, arrived by no means punctually, even if he caught the early train which was by no means certain. In which case it meant—but what it meant to Mrs. Sands, when people missed their trains, and she, whatever she might want to do, must wait, by the oven, keeping meat hot, no one knew.

"There!" said Mrs. Swithin, surveying the sandwiches, some neat, some not, "I'll take 'em to the Barn." As for the lemonade, she assumed, without a flicker of doubt, that Jane the kitchen-maid would follow after.

Candish paused in the dining-room to move a yellow rose. Yellow, white, carnation red—he placed them. He loved flowers, and arranging them, and placing the green sword or heart-shaped leaf that came, fitly, between them. Queerly, he loved them, considering his gambling and drinking. The yellow rose went there. Now all was ready—silver and white, forks and napkins, and in the middle the splashed bowl of variegated roses. So, with one last look, he left the dining-room.

Two pictures hung opposite the window. In real life they had never met, the long lady and the man holding his horse by the rein. The lady was a picture, bought by Oliver because he liked the picture; the man was an ancestor. He had a name. He held the rein in his hand. He had said to the painter:

"If you want my likeness, dang it sir, take it when the leaves are on the trees." There were leaves on the trees. He had said: "Ain't there room for Colin as well as Buster?" Colin was his famous hound. But there was only room for Buster. It was, he seemed to say, addressing the company not the painter, a damned shame to leave out Colin whom he wished buried at his feet, in the same grave, about 1750; but that skunk the Reverend Whatshisname wouldn't allow it.

He was a talk producer, that ancestor. But the lady was a picture. In her yellow robe, leaning, with a pillar to support her, a silver arrow in her hand, and a feather in her hair, she led the eye up, down, from the curve to the straight, through glades of greenery and shades of silver, dun and rose into silence. The room was empty.

Empty, empty, empty; silent, silent, silent. The room was a shell, singing of what was before time was; a vase stood in the heart of the house, alabaster, smooth, cold, holding the still, distilled essence of emptiness, silence.

Across the hall a door opened. One voice, another voice, a third voice came wimpling and warbling: gruff—Bart's voice; quavering—Lucy's voice; middle-toned—Isa's voice. Their voices impetuously, impatiently, protestingly came across the hall, saying: "The train's late"; saying: "Keep it hot"; saying: "We won't, no, Candish, we won't wait."

Coming out from the library the voices stopped in the hall. They encountered an obstacle evidently; a rock. Utterly impossible was it, even in the heart of the country, to be alone? That was the shock. After that, the rock was raced round, embraced. If it was painful, it was essential. There must be society. Coming out of the library it was painful, but pleasant, to run slap into Mrs. Manresa and an unknown young man with tow-coloured hair and a twisted face. No escape was possible; meeting was inevitable. Uninvited, unexpected, droppers-in, lured off the high road by the very same instinct that caused the sheep and the cows to desire propinquity, they had come. But they had brought a lunch basket. Here it was.

"We couldn't resist when we saw the name on the signpost," Mrs. Manresa began in her rich fluty voice. "And this is a friend—William Dodge. We were going to sit all alone in a field. And I said: 'Why not ask our dear friends,' seeing the signpost, 'to shelter us?' A seat at the table—that's all we want. We have our grub. We have our glasses. We ask nothing but——" society apparently, to be with her kind.

And she waved her hand upon which there was a glove, and under the glove, it seemed, rings, at old Mr. Oliver.

He bowed deep over her hand; a century ago, he would have kissed it. In all this sound of welcome, protestation, apology and again welcome, there was an element of silence, supplied by Isabella, observing the unknown young man. He was of course a gentleman; witness socks and trousers; brainy—tie spotted, waistcoat undone; urban, professional, that is putty coloured, unwholesome; very nervous, exhibiting a twitch at this sudden introduction, and fundamentally infernally conceited, for he deprecated Mrs. Manresa's effusion, yet was her guest.

Isa felt antagonised, yet curious. But when Mrs. Manresa added, to make all shipshape: "He's an artist," and when William Dodge corrected her: "I'm a clerk in an office"—she thought he said Education or Somerset House—she had her finger on the knot which had tied itself so tightly, almost to the extent of squinting, certainly of twitching, in his face.

Then they went in to lunch, and Mrs. Manresa bubbled up, enjoying her own capacity to surmount, without turning a hair, this minor social crisis—this laying of two more places. For had she not complete faith in flesh and blood? and aren't we all flesh and blood? and how silly to make bones of trifles when we're all flesh and blood under the skin—men and women too! But she preferred men—obviously.

"Or what are your rings for, and your nails, and that really adorable little straw hat?" said Isabella, addressing Mrs. Manresa silently and thereby making silence add its unmistakable contribution to talk. Her hat, her rings, her finger nails red as roses, smooth as shells, were there for all to see. But not her life history. That was only scraps and fragments to all of them,

excluding perhaps William Dodge, whom she called "Bill" pub-
licly—a sign perhaps that he knew more than they did. Some
of the things that he knew—that she strolled the garden at
midnight in silk pyjamas, had the loud speaker playing jazz, and
a cocktail bar, of course they knew also. But nothing private; no
strict biographical facts.

She had been born, but it was only gossip said so, in Tasmania: her grandfather had been exported for some hanky-panky
mid-Victorian scandal; malversation of trusts, was it? But the
story got no further the only time Isabella heard it than "exported," for the husband of the communicative lady—Mrs.
Blencowe of the Grange—took exception, pedantically, to "exported," said "expatriated" was more like it, but not the right
word, which he had on the tip of his tongue, but couldn't get at.
And so the story dwindled away. Sometimes she referred to an
uncle, a Bishop. But he was thought to have been a Colonial
Bishop only. They forgot and forgave very easily in the Colonies.
Also it was said her diamonds and rubies had been dug out of
the earth with his own hands by a "husband" who was not Ralph
Manresa. Ralph, a Jew, got up to look the very spit and image of
the landed gentry, supplied from directing City companies—
that was certain—tons of money; and they had no child. But
surely with George the Sixth on the throne it was old fashioned,
dowdy, savoured of moth-eaten furs, bugles, cameos and black-
edged notepaper, to go ferreting into people's pasts?

"All I need," said Mrs. Manresa ogling Candish, as if he were
a real man, not a stuffed man, is a "corkscrew." She had a bottle
of champagne, but no corkscrew.

"Look, Bill," she continued, cocking her thumb—she was
opening the bottle—"at the pictures. Didn't I tell you you'd
have a treat?"

Vulgar she was in her gestures, in her whole person, over-
sexed, over-dressed for a picnic. But what a desirable, at least

valuable, quality it was—for everybody felt, directly she spoke, "She's said it, she's done it, not I," and could take advantage of the breach of decorum, of the fresh air that blew in, to follow like leaping dolphins in the wake of an ice-breaking vessel. Did she not restore to old Bartholomew his spice islands, his youth?

"I told him," she went on, ogling Bart now, "that he wouldn't look at our things" (of which they had heaps and mountains) "after yours. And I promised him you'd show him the— the——" here the champagne fizzed up and she insisted upon filling Bart's glass first. "What is it all you learned gentlemen rave about? An arch? Norman? Saxon? Who's the last from school? Mrs. Giles?"

She ogled Isabella now, conferring youth upon her; but always when she spoke to women, she veiled her eyes, for they, being conspirators, saw through it.

So with blow after blow, with champagne and ogling, she staked out her claim to be a wild child of nature, blowing into this—she did give one secret smile—sheltered harbour; which did make her smile, after London; yet it did, too, challenge London. For on she went to offer them a sample of her life; a few gobbets of gossip; mere trash; but she gave it for what it was worth; how last Tuesday she had been sitting next so and so; and she added, very casually a Christian name; then a nickname; and he'd said—for, as a mere nobody they didn't mind what they said to her—and "in strict confidence, I needn't tell you," she told them. And they all pricked their ears. And then, with a gesture of her hands as if tossing overboard that odious crackling-under-the-pot London life—so—she exclaimed, "There!... And what's the first thing I do when I come down here?" They had only come last night, driving through June lanes, alone with Bill it was understood, leaving London, suddenly become dissolute and dirty, to sit down to dinner. "What do I do? Can I say it aloud? Is it permitted, Mrs. Swithin? Yes,

everything can be said in this house. I take off my stays" (here
she pressed her hands to her sides—she was stout) "and roll in
the grass. Roll—you'll believe that..." She laughed whole-
heartedly. She had given up dealing with her figure and thus
gained freedom.

"That's genuine," Isa thought. Quite genuine. And her love
of the country too. Often when Ralph Manresa had to stay in
town she came down alone; wore an old garden hat; taught the
village women *not* how to pickle and preserve; but how to weave
frivolous baskets out of coloured straw. Pleasure's what they
want, she said. You often heard her, if you called, yodelling
among the hollyhocks "Hoity te doity te ray do..."

A thorough good sort she was. She made old Bart feel
young. Out of the corner of his eye, as he raised his glass, he saw
a flash of white in the garden. Someone passing.

The scullery maid, before the plates came out, was cooling
her cheeks by the lily pond.

There had always been lilies there, self-sown from wind-
dropped seed, floating red and white on the green plates of their
leaves. Water, for hundreds of years, had silted down into the
hollow, and lay there four or five feet deep over a black cushion
of mud. Under the thick plate of green water, glazed in their self-
centred world, fish swam—gold, splashed with white, streaked
with black or silver. Silently they manoeuvred in their water
world, poised in the blue patch made by the sky, or shot silently
to the edge where the grass, trembling, made a fringe of nodding
shadow. On the water-pavement spiders printed their delicate
feet. A grain fell and spiralled down; a petal fell, filled and sank.
At that the fleet of boat-shaped bodies paused; poised; equipped;
mailed; then with a waver of undulation off they flashed.

It was in that deep centre, in that black heart, that the lady
had drowned herself. Ten years since the pool had been dredged

and a thigh bone recovered. Alas, it was a sheep's, not a lady's. And sheep have no ghosts, for sheep have no souls. But, the servants insisted, they must have a ghost; the ghost must be a lady's; who had drowned herself for love. So none of them would walk by the lily pool at night, only now when the sun shone and the gentry still sat at table.

The flower petal sank; the maid returned to the kitchen; Bartholomew sipped his wine. Happy he felt as a boy; yet reckless as an old man; an unusual, an agreeable sensation. Fumbling in his mind for something to say to the adorable lady, he chose the first thing that came handy; the story of the sheep's thigh. "Servants," he said, "must have their ghost." Kitchenmaids must have their drowned lady.

"But so must I!" cried the wild child of nature, Mrs. Manresa. She became, of a sudden, solemn as an owl. She *knew*, she said, pinching a bit of bread to make this emphatic, that Ralph, when he was at the war, couldn't have been killed without her seeing him—"wherever I was, whatever I was doing," she added, waving her hands so that the diamonds flashed in the sun.

"I don't feel that," said Mrs. Swithin, shaking her head.

"No," Mrs. Manresa laughed. "You wouldn't. None of you would. You see I'm on a level with . . ." she waited till Candish had retired, "the servants. I'm nothing like so grown up as you are."

She preened, approving her adolescence. Rightly or wrongly? A spring of feeling bubbled up through her mud. They had laid theirs with blocks of marble. Sheep's bones were sheep's bones to them, not the relics of the drowned Lady Ermyntrude.

"And which camp," said Bartholomew turning to the unknown guest, "d'you belong to? The grown, or the ungrown?"

Isabella opened her mouth, hoping that Dodge would open his, and so enable her to place him. But he sat staring. "I beg

your pardon, sir?" he said. They all looked at him. "I was looking at the pictures."

The picture looked at nobody. The picture drew them down
the paths of silence.

Lucy broke it.

"Mrs. Manresa, I'm going to ask you a favour—If it comes
to a pinch this afternoon, will you sing?"

This afternoon? Mrs. Manresa was aghast. Was it the pageant? She had never dreamt it was this afternoon. They would
never have thrust themselves in—had they known it was this
afternoon. And, of course, once more the chime pealed. Isa
heard the first chime; and the second; and the third—If it was
wet, it would be in the Barn; if it was fine on the terrace. And
which would it be, wet or fine? And they all looked out of the
window. Then the door opened. Candish said Mr. Giles had
come. Mr. Giles would be down in a moment.

Giles had come. He had seen the great silver-plated car at the
door with the initials R. M. twisted so as to look at a distance
like a coronet. Visitors, he had concluded, as he drew up behind;
and had gone to his room to change. The ghost of convention
rose to the surface, as a blush or a tear rises to the surface at the
pressure of emotion; so the car touched his training. He must
change. And he came into the dining-room looking like a cricketer, in flannels, wearing a blue coat with brass buttons; though
he was enraged. Had he not read, in the morning paper, in the
train, that sixteen men had been shot, others prisoned, just over
there, across the gulf, in the flat land which divided them from
the continent? Yet he changed. It was Aunt Lucy, waving her
hand at him as he came in, who made him change. He hung his
grievances on her, as one hangs a coat on a hook, instinctively.
Aunt Lucy, foolish, free; always, since he had chosen, after leaving college, to take a job in the city, expressing her amazement,

her amusement, at men who spent their lives, buying and sell-ing—ploughs? glass beads was it? or stocks and shares?—to savages who wished most oddly—for were they not beautiful naked?—to dress and live like the English? A frivolous, a ma-lignant statement hers was of a problem which, for he had no special gift, no capital, and had been furiously in love with his wife—he nodded to her across the table—had afflicted him for ten years. Given his choice, he would have chosen to farm. But he was not given his choice. So one thing led to another; and the conglomeration of things pressed you flat; held you fast, like a fish in water. So he came for the week-end, and changed.

"How d'you do?" he said all round; nodded to the unknown guest; took against him; and ate his fillet of sole.

He was the very type of all that Mrs. Manresa adored. His hair curled; far from running away, as many chins did, his was firm; the nose straight, if short; the eyes, of course, with that hair, blue; and finally to make the type complete, there was something fierce, untamed, in the expression which incited her, even at forty-five, to furbish up her ancient batteries.

"He is my husband," Isabella thought, as they nodded across the bunch of many-coloured flowers. "The father of my children." It worked, that old cliché; she felt pride; and affec-tion; then pride again in herself, whom he had chosen. It was a shock to find, after the morning's look in the glass, and the arrow of desire shot through her last night by the gentleman farmer, how much she felt when he came in, not a dapper city gent, but a cricketer, of love; and of hate.

They had met first in Scotland, fishing—she from one rock, he from another. Her line had got tangled; she had given over, and had watched him with the stream rushing between his legs, casting, casting—until, like a thick ingot of silver bent in the middle, the salmon had leapt, had been caught, and she had loved him.

Bartholomew too loved him; and noted his anger—about what? But he remembered his guest. The family was not a family in the presence of strangers. He must, rather laboriously, tell them the story of the pictures at which the unknown guest had been looking when Giles came in.

"That," he indicated the man with a horse, "was my ancestor. He had a dog. The dog was famous. The dog has his place in history. He left it on record that he wished his dog to be buried with him."

They looked at the picture.

"I always feel," Lucy broke the silence, "he's saying: 'Paint my dog.'"

"But what about the horse?" said Mrs. Manresa.

"The horse," said Bartholomew, putting on his glasses. He looked at the horse. The hindquarters were not satisfactory.

But William Dodge was still looking at the lady.

"Ah," said Bartholomew who had bought that picture because he liked that picture, "you're an artist."

Dodge denied it, for the second time in half an hour, or so Isa noted.

What for did a good sort like the woman Manresa bring these half-breeds in her trail? Giles asked himself. And his silence made its contribution to talk—Dodge that is, shook his head. "I like that picture." That was all he could bring himself to say.

"And you're right," said Bartholomew. "A man—I forget his name—a man connected with some Institute, a man who goes about giving advice, gratis, to descendants like ourselves, degenerate descendants, said . . . said . . ." He paused. They all looked at the lady. But she looked over their heads, looking at nothing. She led them down green glades into the heart of silence.

"Said it was by Sir Joshua?" Mrs. Manresa broke the silence abruptly.

"No, no," William Dodge said hastily, but under his breath.

"Why's he afraid?" Isabella asked herself. A poor specimen he was; afraid to stick up for his own beliefs—just as she was afraid, of her husband. Didn't she write her poetry in a book bound like an account book lest Giles might suspect? She looked at Giles.

He had finished his fish; he had eaten quickly, not to keep them waiting. Now there was cherry tart. Mrs. Manresa was counting the stones.

"Tinker, tailor, soldier, sailor, apothecary, ploughboy... that's me!" she cried, delighted to have it confirmed by the cherry stones that she was a wild child of nature.

"You believe," said the old gentleman, courteously chaffing her, "in that too?"

"Of course, of course I do!" she cried. Now she was on the rails again. Now she was a thorough good sort again. And they too were delighted; now they could follow in her wake and leave the silver and dun shades that led to the heart of silence.

"I had a father," said Dodge beneath his breath to Isa who sat next him, "who loved pictures."

"Oh, I too!" she exclaimed. Flurriedly, disconnectedly, she explained. She used to stay when she was a child, when she had the whooping cough, with an uncle, a clergyman; who wore a skull cap; and never did anything; didn't even preach; but made up poems, walking in his garden, saying them aloud.

"People thought him mad," she said. "I didn't. . . ."

She stopped.

"Tinker, tailor, soldier, sailor, apothecary, ploughboy. . . . It appears," said old Bartholomew, laying down his spoon, "that I am a thief. Shall we take our coffee in the garden?" He rose.

Isa dragged her chair across the gravel, muttering: "To what dark antre of the unvisited earth, or wind-brushed forest, shall we go now? Or spin from star to star and dance in the maze of the moon? Or. . . ."

She held her deck chair at the wrong angle. The frame with the notches was upside down.

"Songs my uncle taught me?" said William Dodge, hearing her mutter. He unfolded the chair and fixed the bar into the right notch.

She flushed, as if she had spoken in an empty room and someone had stepped out from behind a curtain.

"Don't you, if you're doing something with your hands, talk nonsense?" she stumbled. But what did he do with his hands, the white, the fine, the shapely?

Giles went back to the house and brought more chairs and placed them in a semi-circle, so that the view might be shared, and the shelter of the old wall. For by some lucky chance a wall had been built continuing the house, it might be with the intention of adding another wing, on the raised ground in the sun. But funds were lacking; the plan was abandoned, and the wall remained, nothing but a wall. Later, another generation had planted fruit trees, which in time had spread their arms widely across the red-orange weathered brick. Mrs. Sands called it a good year if she could make six pots of apricot jam from them—the fruit was never sweet enough for dessert. Perhaps three apricots were worth enclosing in muslin bags. But they were so beautiful, naked, with one flushed cheek, one green, that Mrs. Swithin left them naked, and the wasps burrowed holes.

The ground sloped up, so that to quote Figgis's Guide Book (1833), "it commanded a fine view of the surrounding country. . . . The spire of Bolney Minster, Rough Norton woods, and on an eminence rather to the left, Hogben's Folly, so called because...."

The Guide Book still told the truth. 1830 was true in 1939. No house had been built; no town had sprung up. Hogben's Folly was still eminent; the very flat, field-parcelled land had changed only in this—the tractor had to some extent superseded the plough. The horse had gone; but the cow remained. If Figgis were here now, Figgis would have said the same. So they always said when in summer they sat there to drink coffee, if they had guests. When they were alone, they said nothing. They looked at the view; they looked at what they knew, to see if what they knew might perhaps be different today. Most days it was the same.

"That's what makes a view so sad," said Mrs. Swithin, lowering herself into the deck chair which Giles had brought her. "And so beautiful. It'll be there," she nodded at the strip of gauze laid upon the distant fields, "when we're not."

Giles nicked his chair into position with a jerk. Thus only could he show his irritation, his rage with old fogies who sat and looked at views over coffee and cream when the whole of Europe—over there—was bristling like. . . . He had no command of metaphor. Only the ineffective word "hedgehog" illustrated his vision of Europe, bristling with guns, poised with planes. At any moment guns would rake that land into furrows; planes splinter Bolney Minster into smithereens and blast the Folly. He, too, loved the view. And blamed Aunt Lucy, looking at views, instead of—doing what? What she had done was to marry a squire now dead; she had borne two children, one in Canada, the other, married, in Birmingham. His father, whom he loved, he exempted from censure; as for himself, one thing followed another; and so he sat, with old fogies, looking at views.

"Beautiful," said Mrs. Manresa, "beautiful . . ." she mumbled. She was lighting a cigarette. The breeze blew out her

match. Giles hollowed his hand and lit another. She too was exempted—why, he could not say.

"Since you're interested in pictures," said Bartholomew,
turning to the silent guest, "why, tell me, are we, as a race, so
incurious, irresponsive and insensitive"—the champagne had
given him a flow of unusual three-decker words—"to that noble
art, whereas, Mrs. Manresa, if she'll allow me my old man's lib-
erty, has her Shakespeare by heart?"

"Shakespeare by heart!" Mrs. Manresa protested. She struck
an attitude. "To be, or not to be, that is the question. Whether
'tis nobler . . . Go on!" she nudged Giles, who sat next her.

"Fade far away and quite forget what thou amongst the leaves
hast never known . . ." Isa supplied the first words that came into
her head by way of helping her husband out of his difficulty.

"The weariness, the torture, and the fret . . ." William Dodge
added, burying the end of his cigarette in a grave between two
stones.

"There!" Bartholomew exclaimed, cocking his forefinger
aloft. "That proves it! What springs touched, what secret drawer
displays its treasures, if I say"—he raised more fingers—
"Reynolds! Constable! Crome!"

"Why called 'Old'?" Mrs. Manresa thrust in.

"We haven't the words—we haven't the words," Mrs.
Swithin protested. "Behind the eyes; not on the lips; that's all."

"Thoughts without words," her brother mused. "Can that
be?"

"Quite beyond me!" cried Mrs. Manresa, shaking her head.
"Much too clever! May I help myself? I know it's wrong. But
I've reached the age—and the figure—when I do what I like."

She took the little silver cream jug and let the smooth fluid
curl luxuriously into her coffee, to which she added a shovel full
of brown sugar candy. Sensuously, rhythmically, she stirred the
mixture round and round.

"Take what you like! Help yourself!" Bartholomew exclaimed. He felt the champagne withdrawing and hastened, before the last trace of geniality was withdrawn, to make the most of it, as if he cast one last look into a lit-up chamber before going to bed.

The wild child, afloat once more on the tide of the old man's benignity, looked over her coffee cup at Giles, with whom she felt in conspiracy. A thread united them—visible, invisible, like those threads, now seen, now not, that unite trembling grass blades in autumn before the sun rises. She had met him once only, at a cricket match. And then had been spun between them an early morning thread before the twigs and leaves of real friendship emerge. She looked before she drank. Looking was part of drinking. Why waste sensation, she seemed to ask, why waste a single drop that can be pressed out of this ripe, this melting, this adorable world? Then she drank. And the air round her became threaded with sensation. Bartholomew felt it; Giles felt it. Had he been a horse, the thin brown skin would have twitched, as if a fly had settled. Isabella twitched too. Jealousy, anger, pierced her skin.

"And now," said Mrs. Manresa, putting down her cup, "about this entertainment—this pageant, into which we've gone and butted"—she made it, too, seem ripe like the apricot into which the wasps were burrowing—"Tell me, what's it to be?" She turned. "Don't I hear?" She listened. She heard laughter, down among the bushes, where the terrace dipped to the bushes.

Beyond the lily pool the ground sank again, and in that dip of the ground, bushes and brambles had mobbed themselves together. It was always shady; sun-flecked in summer, dark and damp in winter. In the summer there were always butterflies; fritillaries darting through; Red Admirals feasting and floating; cabbage whites, unambitiously fluttering round a bush, like muslin milkmaids, content to spend a life there. Butterfly catching, for generation after generation, began there; for Bartholomew and Lucy; for Giles; for George it had begun only the day before yesterday, when, in his little green net, he had caught a cabbage white.

It was the very place for a dressing-room, just as, obviously, the terrace was the very place for a play.

"The very place!" Miss La Trobe had exclaimed the first time she came to call and was shown the grounds. It was a winter's day. The trees were leafless then.

"That's the place for a pageant, Mr. Oliver!" she had exclaimed. "Winding in and out between the trees. . . ." She waved her hand at the trees standing bare in the clear light of January.

"There the stage; here the audience; and down there among the bushes a perfect dressing-room for the actors."

She was always all agog to get things up. But where did she spring from? With that name she wasn't presumably pure English. From the Channel Islands perhaps? Only her eyes and something about her always made Mrs. Bingham suspect that she had Russian blood in her. "Those deep-set eyes; that very square jaw" reminded her—not that she had been to Russia— of the Tartars. Rumour said that she had kept a tea shop at Winchester; that had failed. She had been an actress. That had failed. She had bought a four-roomed cottage and shared it with an actress. They had quarrelled. Very little was actually known about her. Outwardly she was swarthy, sturdy and thick set; strode about the fields in a smock frock; sometimes with a cigarette in her mouth; often with a whip in her hand; and used rather strong language—perhaps, then, she wasn't altogether a lady? At any rate, she had a passion for getting things up.

The laughter died away.

"Are they going to act?" Mrs. Manresa asked.

"Act; dance; sing; a little bit of everything," said Giles.

"Miss La Trobe is a lady of wonderful energy," said Mrs. Swithin.

"She makes everyone do something," said Isabella.

"Our part," said Bartholomew, "is to be the audience. And a very important part too."

"Also, we provide the tea," said Mrs. Swithin.

"Shan't we go and help?" said Mrs. Manresa. "Cut up bread and butter?"

"No, no," said Mr. Oliver. "We are the audience."

"One year we had *Gammer Gurton's Needle*," said Mrs. Swithin. "One year we wrote the play ourselves. The son of our blacksmith—Tony? Tommy?—had the loveliest voice. And Elsie at the Crossways—how she mimicked! Took us all off. Bart; Giles; Old Flimsy—that's me. People are gifted—very. The question is—how to bring it out? That's where she's so clever—Miss La Trobe. Of course, there's the whole of English literature to choose from. But how can one choose? Often on a wet day I begin counting up; what I've read; what I haven't read."

"And leaving books on the floor," said her brother. "Like the pig in the story; or was it a donkey?"

She laughed, tapping him lightly on the knee.

"The donkey who couldn't choose between hay and turnips and so starved," Isabella explained, interposing—anything—between her aunt and her husband, who hated this kind of talk this afternoon. Books open; no conclusion come to; and he sitting in the audience.

"We remain seated"—"We are the audience." Words this afternoon ceased to lie flat in the sentence. They rose, became menacing and shook their fists at you. This afternoon he wasn't Giles Oliver come to see the villagers act their annual pageant; manacled to a rock he was, and forced passively to behold indescribable horror. His face showed it; and Isa, not knowing what to say, abruptly, half purposely, knocked over a coffee cup.

William Dodge caught it as it fell. He held it for a moment. He turned it. From the faint blue mark, as of crossed daggers, in the glaze at the bottom he knew that it was English, made perhaps at Nottingham; date about 1760. His expression, considering the daggers, coming to this conclusion, gave Giles another peg on which to hang his rage as one hangs a coat on a peg, conveniently. A toady; a lickspittle; not a downright plain man of his senses; but a teaser and twitcher; a fingerer of sensations; picking and choosing; dillying and dallying; not a man to have straightforward love for a woman—his head was close to Isa's head—but simply a —— At this word, which he could not speak in public, he pursed his lips; and the signet-ring on his little finger looked redder, for the flesh next it whitened as he gripped the arm of his chair.

"Oh what fun!" cried Mrs. Manresa in her fluty voice. "A little bit of everything. A song; a dance; then a play acted by the villagers themselves. Only," here she turned with her head on one side to Isabella, "I'm sure *she's* written it. Haven't you, Mrs. Giles?"

Isa flushed and denied it.

"For myself," Mrs. Manresa continued, "speaking plainly, I can't put two words together. I don't know how it is—such a chatterbox as I am with my tongue, once I hold a pen——" She made a face, screwed her fingers as if she held a pen in them. But the pen she held thus on the little table absolutely refused to move.

"And my handwriting—so huge—so clumsy—" She made another face and dropped the invisible pen.

Very delicately William Dodge set the cup in its saucer. "Now *he*," said Mrs. Manresa, as if referring to the delicacy with which he did this, and imputing to him the same skill in writing, "writes beautifully. Every letter perfectly formed."

Again they all looked at him. Instantly he put his hands in his pockets.

Isabella guessed the word that Giles had not spoken. Well, was it wrong if he was that word? Why judge each other? Do we know each other? Not here, not now. But somewhere, this cloud, this crust, this doubt, this dust—— She waited for a rhyme, it failed her; but somewhere surely one sun would shine and all without a doubt, would be clear.

She started. Again, sounds of laughter reached her.

"I think I hear them," she said. "They're getting ready. They're dressing up in the bushes."

Miss La Trobe was pacing to and fro between the leaning birch trees. One hand was deep stuck in her jacket pocket; the other held a foolscap sheet. She was reading what was written there. She had the look of a commander pacing his deck. The leaning graceful trees with black bracelets circling the silver bark were distant about a ship's length.

Wet would it be, or fine? Out came the sun; and, shading her eyes in the attitude proper to an Admiral on his quarter-deck, she decided to risk the engagement out of doors. Doubts were over. All stage properties, she commanded, must be moved from the Barn to the bushes. It was done. And the actors, while she paced, taking all responsibility and plumping for fine, not wet, dressed among the brambles. Hence the laughter.

The clothes were strewn on the grass. Cardboard crowns, swords made of silver paper, turbans that were sixpenny dish cloths, lay on the grass or were flung on the bushes. There were pools of red and purple in the shade; flashes of silver in the sun. The dresses attracted the butterflies. Red and silver, blue and

yellow gave off warmth and sweetness. Red Admirals glut-
tonously absorbed richness from dish cloths, cabbage whites
drank icy coolness from silver paper. Flitting, tasting, returning,
they sampled the colours.

Miss La Trobe stopped her pacing and surveyed the scene.
"It has the makings . . ." she murmured. For another play always
lay behind the play she had just written. Shading her eyes, she
looked. The butterflies circling; the light changing; the children
leaping; the mothers laughing—— "No, I don't get it," she
muttered and resumed her pacing.

"Bossy" they called her privately, just as they called Mrs.
Swithin "Flimsy." Her abrupt manner and stocky figure; her
thick ankles and sturdy shoes; her rapid decisions barked out in
guttural accents—all this "got their goat." No one liked to be
ordered about singly. But in little troops they appealed to her.
Someone must lead. Then too they could put the blame on her.
Suppose it poured?

"Miss La Trobe!" they hailed her now. "What's the idea
about this?"

She stopped. David and Iris each had a hand on the gramophone. It must be hidden; yet must be close enough to the audience to be heard. Well, hadn't she given orders? Where were
the hurdles covered in leaves? Fetch them. Mr. Streatfield had
said he would see to it. Where was Mr. Streatfield? No clergyman was visible. Perhaps he's in the Barn? "Tommy, cut along
and fetch him." "Tommy's wanted in the first scene." "Beryl
then . . ." The mothers disputed. One child had been chosen;
another not. Fair hair was unjustly preferred to dark. Mrs. Ebury
had forbidden Fanny to act because of the nettle-rash. There
was another name in the village for nettle-rash.

Mrs. Ball's cottage was not what you might call clean. In the
last war Mrs. Ball lived with another man while her husband was
in the trenches. All this Miss La Trobe knew, but refused to be

mixed up in it. She splashed into the fine mesh like a great stone into the lily pool. The criss-cross was shattered. Only the roots beneath water were of use to her. Vanity, for example, made them all malleable. The boys wanted the big parts; the girls wanted the fine clothes. Expenses had to be kept down. Ten pounds was the limit. Thus conventions were outraged. Swathed in conventions, they couldn't see, as she could, that a dish cloth wound round a head in the open looked much richer than real silk. So they squabbled; but she kept out of it. Waiting for Mr. Streatfield, she paced between the birch trees.

The other trees were magnificently straight. They were not too regular; but regular enough to suggest columns in a church; in a church without a roof; in an open-air cathedral, a place where swallows darting seemed, by the regularity of the trees, to make a pattern, dancing, like the Russians, only not to music, but to the unheard rhythm of their own wild hearts.

The laughter died away.

"We must possess our souls in patience," said Mrs. Manresa again. "Or could we help?" she suggested, glancing over her shoulder, "with those chairs?"

Candish, a gardener, and a maid were all bringing chairs— for the audience. There was nothing for the audience to do. Mrs. Manresa suppressed a yawn. They were silent. They stared at the view, as if something might happen in one of those fields to relieve them of the intolerable burden of sitting silent, doing nothing, in company. Their minds and bodies were too close, yet not close enough. We aren't free, each one of them felt separately, to feel or think separately, nor yet to fall asleep. We're too close; but not close enough. So they fidgeted.

The heat had increased. The clouds had vanished. All was sun now. The view laid bare by the sun was flattened, silenced, stilled. The cows were motionless; the brick wall, no longer sheltering, beat back grains of heat. Old Mr. Oliver sighed profoundly. His head jerked; his hand fell. It fell within an inch of the dog's head on the grass by his side. Then up he jerked it again on to his knee.

Giles glared. With his hands bound tight round his knees he stared at the flat fields. Staring, glaring, he sat silent.

Isabella felt prisoned. Through the bars of the prison, through the sleep haze that deflected them, blunt arrows bruised her; of love, then of hate. Through other people's bodies she felt neither love nor hate distinctly. Most consciously she felt—she had drunk sweet wine at luncheon—a desire for water. "A beaker of cold water, a beaker of cold water," she repeated, and saw water surrounded by walls of shining glass.

Mrs. Manresa longed to relax and curl in a corner with a cushion, a picture paper, and a bag of sweets.

Mrs. Swithin and William surveyed the view aloofly, and with detachment.

How tempting, how very tempting, to let the view triumph; to reflect its ripple; to let their own minds ripple; to let outlines elongate and pitch over—so—with a sudden jerk.

Mrs. Manresa yielded, pitched, plunged, then pulled herself up.

"What a view!" she exclaimed, pretending to dust the ashes of her cigarette, but in truth concealing her yawn. Then she sighed, pretending to express not her own drowsiness, but something connected with what she felt about views.

Nobody answered her. The flat fields glared green yellow, blue yellow, red yellow, then blue again. The repetition was senseless, hideous, stupefying.

"Then," said Mrs. Swithin, in a low voice, as if the exact moment for speech had come, as if she had promised, and it was time to fulfil her promise, "come, come and I'll show you the house."

She addressed no one in particular. But William Dodge knew she meant him. He rose with a jerk, like a toy suddenly pulled straight by a string.

"What energy!" Mrs. Manresa half sighed, half yawned. "Have I the courage to go too?" Isabella asked herself. They were going; above all things, she desired cold water, a beaker of cold water; but desire petered out, suppressed by the leaden duty she owed to others. She watched them go—Mrs. Swithin tottering yet tripping; and Dodge unfurled and straightened, as he strode beside her along the blazing tiles under the hot wall, till they reached the shade of the house.

A match-box fell—Bartholomew's. His fingers had loosed it; he had dropped it. He gave up the game; he couldn't be bothered. With his head on one side, his hand dangling above the dog's head he slept; he snored.

Mrs. Swithin paused for a moment in the hall among the gilt-clawed tables.

"This," she said, "is the staircase. And now—up we go."

She went up, two stairs ahead of her guest. Lengths of yellow satin unfurled themselves on a cracked canvas as they mounted.

"Not an ancestress," said Mrs. Swithin, as they came level with the head in the picture. "But we claim her because we've known her—O, ever so many years. Who was she?" she gazed. "Who painted her?" She shook her head. She looked lit up, as if for a banquet, with the sun pouring over her.

"But I like her best in the moonlight," Mrs. Swithin reflected, and mounted more stairs.

She panted slightly, going upstairs. Then she ran her hand over the sunk books in the wall on the landing, as if they were pan pipes.

"Here are the poets from whom we descend by way of the

mind, Mr. . . ." she murmured. She had forgotten his name. Yet she had singled him out.

"My brother says, they built the house north for shelter, not south for sun. So they're damp in the winter." She paused. "And now what comes next?"

She stopped. There was a door.

"The morning room." She opened the door. "Where my mother received her guests."

Two chairs faced each other on either side of a fine fluted mantelpiece. He looked over her shoulder.

She shut the door.

"Now up, now up again." Again they mounted. "Up and up they went," she panted, seeing, it seemed, an invisible procession, "up and up to bed."

"A bishop; a traveller;—I've forgotten even their names. I ignore. I forget."

She stopped at a window in the passage and held back the curtain. Beneath was the garden, bathed in sun. The grass was sleek and shining. Three white pigeons were flirting and tiptoeing as ornate as ladies in ball dresses. Their elegant bodies swayed as they minced with tiny steps on their little pink feet upon the grass. Suddenly, up they rose in a flutter, circled, and flew away.

"Now," she said, "for the bedrooms." She tapped twice very distinctly on a door. With her head on one side, she listened.

"One never knows," she murmured, "if there's somebody there." Then she flung open the door.

He half expected to see somebody there, naked, or half dressed, or knelt in prayer. But the room was empty. The room was tidy as pin, not slept in for months, a spare room. Candles stood on the dressing-table. The counterpane was straight. Mrs. Swithin stopped by the bed.

"Here," she said, "yes, here," she tapped the counterpane, "I was born. In this bed."

Her voice died away. She sank down on the edge of the bed. She was tired, no doubt, by the stairs, by the heat.

"But we have other lives, I think, I hope," she murmured. "We live in others, Mr. . . . We live in things."

She spoke simply. She spoke with an effort. She spoke as if she must overcome her tiredness out of charity towards a stranger, a guest. She had forgotten his name. Twice she had said "Mr." and stopped.

The furniture was mid-Victorian, bought at Maples, perhaps, in the forties. The carpet was covered with small purple dots. And a white circle marked the place where the slop pail had stood by the washstand.

Could he say "I'm William"? He wished to. Old and frail she had climbed the stairs. She had spoken her thoughts, ignoring, not caring if he thought her, as he had, inconsequent, sentimental, foolish. She had lent him a hand to help him up a steep place. She had guessed his trouble. Sitting on the bed he heard her sing, swinging her little legs, "Come and see my sea weeds, come and see my sea shells, come and see my dicky bird hop upon its perch"—an old child's nursery rhyme to help a child. Standing by the cupboard in the corner he saw her reflected in the glass. Cut off from their bodies, their eyes smiled, their bodiless eyes, at their eyes in the glass.

Then she slipped off the bed.

"Now," she said, "what comes next?" and pattered down the corridor. A door stood open. Everyone was out in the garden. The room was like a ship deserted by its crew. The children had been playing—there was a spotted horse in the middle of the carpet. The nurse had been sewing—there was a piece of linen on the table. The baby had been in the cot. The cot was empty.

"The nursery," said Mrs. Swithin.

Words raised themselves and became symbolical. "The cradle of our race," she seemed to say.

Dodge crossed to the fireplace and looked at the Newfoundland Dog in the Christmas Annual that was pinned to the wall. The room smelt warm and sweet; of clothes drying; of milk; of biscuits and warm water. "Good Friends" the picture was called. A rushing sound came in through the open door. He turned. The old woman had wandered out into the passage and leant against the window.

He left the door open for the crew to come back to and joined her.

Down in the courtyard beneath the window cars were assembling. Their narrow black roofs were laid together like the blocks of a floor. Chauffeurs were jumping down; here old ladies gingerly advanced black legs with silver-buckled shoes; old men striped trousers. Young men in shorts leapt out on one side; girls with skin-coloured legs on the other. There was a purring and a churning of the yellow gravel. The audience was assembling. But they, looking down from the window, were truants, detached. Together they leant half out of the window.

And then a breeze blew and all the muslin blinds fluttered out, as if some majestic goddess, rising from her throne among her peers, had tossed her amber-coloured raiment, and the other gods, seeing her rise and go, laughed, and their laughter floated her on.

Mrs. Swithin put her hands to her hair, for the breeze had ruffled it.

"Mr. . . ." she began.

"I'm William," he interrupted.

At that she smiled a ravishing girl's smile, as if the wind had warmed the wintry blue in her eyes to amber.

"I took you," she apologized, "away from your friends,

William, because I felt wound tight here. . . ." She touched her bony forehead upon which a blue vein wriggled like a blue worm. But her eyes in their caves of bone were still lambent. He saw her eyes only. And he wished to kneel before her, to kiss her hand, and to say: "At school they held me under a bucket of dirty water, Mrs. Swithin; when I looked up, the world was dirty, Mrs. Swithin; so I married; but my child's not my child, Mrs. Swithin. I'm a half-man, Mrs. Swithin; a flickering, mind-divided little snake in the grass, Mrs. Swithin; as Giles saw; but you've healed me. . . ." So he wished to say; but said nothing; and the breeze went lolloping along the corridors, blowing the blinds out.

Once more he looked and she looked down on to the yellow gravel that made a crescent round the door. Pendant from her chain her cross swung as she leant out and the sun struck it. How could she weight herself down by that sleek symbol? How stamp herself, so volatile, so vagrant, with that image? As he looked at it, they were truants no more. The purring of the wheels became vocal. "Hurry, hurry, hurry," it seemed to say, "or you'll be late. Hurry, hurry, hurry, or the best seats'll be taken."

"O," cried Mrs. Swithin, "there's Mr. Streatfield!" And they saw a clergyman, a strapping clergyman, carrying a hurdle, a leafy hurdle. He was striding through the cars with the air of a person of authority, who is awaited, expected, and now comes.

"Is it time," said Mrs. Swithin, "to go and join——" She left the sentence unfinished, as if she were of two minds, and they fluttered to right and to left, like pigeons rising from the grass.

The audience was assembling. They came streaming along the paths and spreading across the lawn. Some were old; some were in the prime of life. There were children among them. Among them, as Mr. Figgis might have observed, were representatives of our most respected families—the Dyces of Denton; the Wickhams of Owlswick; and so on. Some had been there for centuries, never selling an acre. On the other hand there were new-comers, the Manresas, bringing the old houses up to date, adding bathrooms. And a scatter of odds and ends, like Cobbet of Cobbs Corner, retired, it was understood, on a pension from a tea plantation. Not an asset. He did his own housework and dug in his garden. The building of a car factory and of an aerodrome in the neighbourhood had attracted a number of unattached floating residents. Also there was Mr. Page, the reporter, representing the local paper. Roughly speaking, however, had Figgis been there in person and called a roll call, half the ladies and gentlemen present would have said: "*Adsum;* I'm here, in place of my grandfather or great-grandfather," as the case might be. At this very moment, half-past three on a June day in 1939 they greeted each other, and as they took their seats, finding if possible a seat next one another, they said: "That hideous new house at Pyes Corner! What an eyesore! And those bungalows!—have you seen 'em?"

Again, had Figgis called the names of the villagers, they too would have answered. Mrs. Sands was born Iliffe; Candish's mother was one of the Perrys. The green mounds in the church-yard had been cast up by their molings, which for centuries had made the earth friable. True, there were absentees when Mr. Streatfield called his roll call in the church. The motor bike, the motor bus, and the movies—when Mr. Streatfield called his roll call, he laid the blame on them.

Rows of chairs, deck chairs, gilt chairs, hired cane chairs, and indigenous garden seats had been drawn up on the terrace. There were plenty of seats for everybody. But some preferred to sit on the ground. Certainly Miss La Trobe had spoken the truth when she said: "The very place for a pageant!" The lawn was as flat as the floor of a theatre. The terrace, rising, made a natural stage. The trees barred the stage like pillars. And the human figure was seen to great advantage against a background of sky. As for the weather, it was turning out, against all expectation, a very fine day. A perfect summer afternoon.

"What luck!" Mrs. Carter was saying. "Last year..." Then the play began. Was it, or was it not, the play? Chuff, chuff, chuff sounded from the bushes. It was the noise a machine makes when something has gone wrong. Some sat down hastily; others stopped talking guiltily. All looked at the bushes. For the stage was empty. Chuff, chuff, chuff the machine buzzed in the bushes. While they looked apprehensively and some finished their sentences, a small girl, like a rosebud in pink, advanced; took her stand on a mat, behind a conch hung with leaves, and piped:

Gentles and simples, I address you all...

So it was the play then. Or was it the prologue?

Come hither for our festival (she continued)
This is a pageant, all may see
Drawn from our island history.
    England am I....

"She's England," they whispered. "It's begun." "The prologue," they added, looking down at the programme.

"*England am I*," she piped again; and stopped.

She had forgotten her lines.

"Hear! Hear!" said an old man in a white waistcoat briskly. "Bravo! Bravo!"

"Blast 'em!" cursed Miss La Trobe, hidden behind the tree. She looked along the front row. They glared as if they were exposed to a frost that nipped them and fixed them all at the same level. Only Bond the cowman looked fluid and natural.

"Music!" she signalled. "Music!" But the machine continued: Chuff, chuff, chuff.

"*A child new born...*" she prompted.

"A child new born," Phyllis Jones continued,
Sprung from the sea
Whose billows blown by mighty storm
Cut off from France and Germany
    This isle.

She glanced back over her shoulder. Chuff, chuff, chuff, the machine buzzed. A long line of villagers in shirts made of sacking began passing in and out in single file behind her between the trees. They were singing, but not a word reached the audience.

England am I, Phyllis Jones continued, facing the audience,
Now weak and small
A child, as all may see . . .

Her words peppered the audience as with a shower of hard little stones. Mrs. Manresa in the very centre smiled; but she felt as if her skin cracked when she smiled. There was a vast vacancy between her, the singing villagers and the piping child.

Chuff, chuff, chuff, went the machine like a corn-cutter on a hot day.

The villagers were singing, but half their words were blown away.

Cutting the roads . . . up to the hill top . . . we climbed. Down in the valley . . . sow, wild boar, hog, rhinoceros, reindeer . . . Dug ourselves in to the hill top . . . Ground roots between stones . . . Ground corn . . . till we too . . . lay under g—r—o—u—n—d . . .

The words petered away. Chuff, chuff, chuff, the machine ticked. Then at last the machine ground out a tune!

Armed against fate
The valiant Rhoderick
Armed and valiant

Bold and blatant
Firm elatant
See the warriors—here they come . . .

The pompous popular tune brayed and blared. Miss La Trobe watched from behind the tree. Muscles loosened; ice cracked. The stout lady in the middle began to beat time with her hand on her chair. Mrs. Manresa was humming:

> My home is at Windsor, close to the Inn.
> Royal George is the name of the pub.
> And boys you'll believe me,
> I don't want no asking . . .

She was afloat on the stream of the melody. Radiating royalty, complacency, good humour, the wild child was Queen of the festival. The play had begun.

But there was an interruption. "O," Miss La Trobe growled behind her tree, "the torture of these interruptions!"

"Sorry I'm so late," said Mrs. Swithin. She pushed her way through the chairs to a seat beside her brother.

"What's it all about? I've missed the prologue. England? That little girl? Now she's gone . . ."

Phyllis had slipped off her mat.

"And who's this?" asked Mrs. Swithin.

It was Hilda, the carpenter's daughter. She now stood where England had stood.

"*O, England's grown . . .*" Miss La Trobe prompted her.

"*O, England's grown a girl now,*" Hilda sang out
("What a lovely voice!" someone exclaimed)
With roses in her hair,
Wild roses, red roses,
She roams the lanes and chooses
A garland for her hair.

"A cushion? Thank you so much," said Mrs. Swithin, stuffing the cushion behind her back. Then she leant forward.

"That's England in the time of Chaucer, I take it. She's been maying, nutting. She has flowers in her hair . . . But those passing behind her——" she pointed. "The Canterbury pilgrims? Look!"

All the time the villagers were passing in and out between the trees. They were singing; but only a word or two was audible " . . . *wore ruts in the grass . . . built the house in the lane . . .*" The wind blew away the connecting words of their chant, and then, as they reached the tree at the end they sang:

> "*To the shrine of the Saint . . . to the tomb . . . lovers . . . believers . . . we come . . .*"

They grouped themselves together.

Then there was a rustle and an interruption. Chairs were drawn back. Isa looked behind her. Mr. and Mrs. Rupert Haines, detained by a breakdown on the road, had arrived. He was sitting to the right, several rows back, the man in grey.

Meanwhile the pilgrims, having done their homage to the tomb, were, it appeared, tossing hay on their rakes.

> *I kissed a girl and let her go,*
> *Another did I tumble,*
> *In the straw and in the hay . . .*

—that was what they were singing, as they scooped and tossed the invisible hay, when she looked round again.

"Scenes from English history," Mrs. Manresa explained to Mrs. Swithin. She spoke in a loud cheerful voice, as if the old lady were deaf. "Merry England."

She clapped energetically.

The singers scampered away into the bushes. The tune stopped. Chuff, chuff, chuff the machine ticked. Mrs. Manresa looked at her programme. It would take till midnight unless they skipped. Early Briton; Plantagenets; Tudors; Stuarts—she ticked them off, but probably she had forgotten a reign or two.

"Ambitious, ain't it?" she said to Bartholomew, while they waited. Chuff, chuff, chuff went the machine. Could they talk? Could they move? No, for the play was going on. Yet the stage was empty; only the cows moved in the meadows; only the tick of the gramophone needle was heard. The tick, tick, tick seemed to hold them together, tranced. Nothing whatsoever appeared on the stage.

"I'd no notion we looked so nice," Mrs. Swithin whispered to William. Hadn't she? The children; the pilgrims; behind the pilgrims the trees, and behind them the fields—the beauty of the visible world took his breath away. Tick, tick, tick the machine continued.

"Marking time," said old Oliver beneath his breath.

"Which don't exist for us," Lucy murmured. "We've only the present."

"Isn't that enough?" William asked himself. Beauty—isn't that enough? But here Isa fidgeted. Her bare brown arms went nervously to her head. She half turned in her seat. "No, not for us, who've the future," she seemed to say. The future disturbing our present. Who was she looking for? William, turning, following her eyes, saw only a man in grey.

The ticking stopped. A dance tune was put on the machine. In time to it, Isa hummed: "What do I ask? To fly away, from night and day, and issue where—no partings are—but eye meets eye—and . . . O," she cried aloud: "Look at her!"

Everyone was clapping and laughing. From behind the bushes issued Queen Elizabeth—Eliza Clark, licensed to sell tobacco. Could she be Mrs. Clark of the village shop? She was splendidly made up. Her head, pearl-hung, rose from a vast ruff. Shiny satins draped her. Sixpenny brooches glared like cats' eyes and tigers' eyes; pearls looked down; her cape was made of cloth of silver—in fact swabs used to scour saucepans. She looked the age in person. And when she mounted the soap box in the centre, representing perhaps a rock in the ocean, her size made her appear gigantic. She could reach a flitch of bacon or haul a tub of oil with one sweep of her arm in the shop. For a moment she stood there, eminent, dominant, on the soap box with the blue and sailing clouds behind her. The breeze had risen.

The Queen of this great land . . .

—those were the first words that could be heard above the roar of laughter and applause.

Mistress of ships and bearded men (she bawled)
Hawkins, Frobisher, Drake,
Tumbling their oranges, ingots of silver,
Cargoes of diamonds, ducats of gold,
Down on the jetty, there in the west land—
(she pointed her fist at the blazing blue sky)
Mistress of pinnacles, spires and palaces—
(her arm swept towards the house)
For me Shakespeare sang—
(a cow mooed. A bird twittered)
The throstle, the mavis (she continued)
In the green wood, the wild wood,
Carolled and sang, praising England, the Queen,
Then there was heard too
On granite and cobble
From Windsor to Oxford
Loud laughter, low laughter
Of warrior and lover,
The fighter, the singer.
The ashen haired babe

(she stretched out her swarthy, muscular arm)
Stretched his arm in contentment
As home from the Isles came
The sea faring men. . . .

Here the wind gave a tug at her head dress. Loops of pearls made it top-heavy. She had to steady the ruffle which threatened to blow away.

"Laughter, loud laughter," Giles muttered. The tune on the gramophone reeled from side to side as if drunk with merriment. Mrs. Manresa began beating her foot and humming in time to it.

"Bravo! Bravo!" she cried. "There's life in the old dog yet!" And she trolloped out the words of the song with an abandonment which, if vulgar, was a great help to the Elizabethan age. For the ruff had become unpinned and Great Eliza had forgotten her lines. But the audience laughed so loud that it did not matter.

"I fear I am not in my perfect mind," Giles muttered to the same tune. Words came to the surface—he remembered "a stricken deer in whose lean flank the world's harsh scorn has struck its thorn. . . . Exiled from its festival, the music turned ironical. . . . A churchyard haunter at whom the owl hoots and the ivy mocks tap-tap-tapping on the pane. . . . For they are dead, and I . . . I . . . I," he repeated, forgetting the words, and glaring at his Aunt Lucy who sat craned forward, her mouth gaping, and her bony little hands clapping.

What were they laughing at?

At Albert, the village idiot, apparently. There was no need to dress him up. There he came, acting his part to perfection. He came ambling across the grass, mopping and mowing.

I know where the tit nests, he began
In the hedgerow. I know, I know—
What don't I know?

All your secrets, ladies,
And yours too, gentlemen . . .

He skipped along the front row of the audience, leering at each in turn. Now he was picking and plucking at Great Eliza's skirts. She cuffed him on the ear. He tweaked her back. He was enjoying himself immensely.

"Albert having the time of his life," Bartholomew muttered.

"Hope he don't have a fit," Lucy murmured.

"*I know . . . I know . . .*" Albert tittered, skipping round the soap box.

"The village idiot," whispered a stout black lady—Mrs. Elmhurst—who came from a village ten miles distant where they, too, had an idiot. It wasn't nice. Suppose he suddenly did something dreadful? There he was pinching the Queen's skirts. She half covered her eyes, in case he did do—something dreadful.

Hoppety, jiggety, Albert resumed
In at the window, out at the door,
What does the little bird hear? (he whistled on his fingers)
And see! There's a mouse. . . .
(he made as if chasing it through the grass)
Now the clock strikes!
(he stood erect, puffing out his cheeks as if he were
blowing a dandelion clock)
One, two, three, four. . . .

And off he skipped, as if his turn was over.

"Glad that's over," said Mrs. Elmhurst, uncovering her face. "Now what comes next? A tableau . . . ?"

For helpers, issuing swiftly from the bushes, carrying hurdles, had enclosed the Queen's throne with screens papered to represent walls. They had strewn the ground with rushes. And the pilgrims who had continued their march and their chant in the background, now gathered round the figure of Eliza on her soap box as if to form the audience at a play.

Were they about to act a play in the presence of Queen Elizabeth? Was this, perhaps, the Globe theatre?

"What does the programme say?" Mrs. Herbert Winthrop asked, raising her lorgnette.

She mumbled through the blurred carbon sheet. Yes; it was a scene from a play.

"About a false Duke; and a Princess disguised as a boy; then the long lost heir turns out to be the beggar, because of a mole on his cheek; and Ferdinando and Carinthia—that's the Duke's daughter, only she's been lost in a cave—falls in love with Ferdinando who had been put into a basket as a baby by an aged crone. And they marry. That's I think what happens," she said, looking up from the programme.

"Play out the play," Great Eliza commanded. An aged crone tottered forward.

("Mrs. Otter of the End House," someone murmured.)

She sat herself on a packing case, and made motions, plucking her dishevelled locks and rocking herself from side to side as if she were an aged beldame in a chimney corner.

("The crone, who saved the rightful heir," Mrs. Winthrop explained.)

'Twas a winter's night (she croaked out)
I mind me that, I to whom all's one now, summer or winter.
You say the sun shines? I believe you, Sir.
'Oh but it's winter, and the fog's abroad.'
All's one to Elsbeth, summer or winter,
By the fireside, in the chimney corner, telling her beads.

I've cause to tell 'em.
Each bead (she held a bead between thumb and finger)
A crime!
'Twas a winter's night, before cockcrow,
Yet the cock did crow ere he left me—
The man with a hood on his face, and the bloody hands
And the babe in the basket.
'Tee hee,' he mewed, as who should say, 'I want my toy.'
Poor witling!
"Tee hee, tee hee!" I could not slay him!
For that, Mary in Heaven forgive me
The sins I've sinned before cockcrow!
Down to the creek i' the dawn I slipped
Where the gull haunts and the heron stands
Like a stake on the edge of the marshes . . .
Who's here?
(Three young men swaggered on to the stage and
       accosted her)
—Are you come to torture me, Sirs?
There is little blood in this arm,
(she extended her skinny forearm from her ragged shift)
Saints in Heaven preserve me!

She bawled. They bawled. All together they bawled, and so
loud that it was difficult to make out what they were saying: apparently it was: *Did she remember concealing a child in a cradle among
the rushes some twenty years previously? A babe in a basket, crone! A
babe in a basket?* they bawled. *The wind howls and the bittern shrieks,*
she replied.

"There is little blood in my arm," Isabella repeated.
That was all she heard. There was such a medley of things
going on, what with the beldame's deafness, the bawling of the

youths, and the confusion of the plot that she could make nothing of it.

Did the plot matter? She shifted and looked over her right shoulder. The plot was only there to beget emotion. There were only two emotions: love; and hate. There was no need to puzzle out the plot. Perhaps Miss La Trobe meant that when she cut this knot in the centre?

Don't bother about the plot: the plot's nothing.

But what was happening? The Prince had come.

Plucking up his sleeve, the beldame recognized the mole; and, staggering back in her chair, shrieked:

My child! My child!

Recognition followed. The young Prince (Albert Perry) was almost smothered in the withered arms of the beldame. Then suddenly he started apart.

Look where she comes! he cried.

They all looked where she came—Sylvia Edwards in white satin.

Who came? Isa looked. The nightingale's song? The pearl in night's black ear? Love embodied.

All arms were raised; all faces stared.

Hail, sweet Carinthia! said the Prince, sweeping his hat off. And she to him, raising her eyes:

My love! My lord!

"It was enough. Enough. Enough," Isa repeated.

All else was verbiage, repetition.

The beldame meanwhile, because that was enough, had sunk back on her chair, the beads dangling from her fingers.

Look to the beldame there—old Elsbeth's sick!
(They crowded round her)
Dead, Sirs!

She fell back lifeless. The crowd drew away. Peace, let her pass. She to whom all's one now, summer or winter.

Peace was the third emotion. Love. Hate. Peace. Three emotions made the ply of human life. Now the priest, whose cotton wool moustache confused his utterance, stepped forward and pronounced benediction.

From the distaff of life's tangled skein, unloose her hands.
(They unloosed her hands)
Of her frailty, let nothing now remembered be.
Call for the robin redbreast and the wren.
And roses fall your crimson pall.
(Petals were strewn from wicker baskets)
Cover the corpse. Sleep well.
(They covered the corpse)
On you, fair Sirs (he turned to the happy couple)
Let Heaven rain benediction!
Haste ere the envying sun
Night's curtain hath undone. Let music sound
And the free air of Heaven waft you to your slumber!
Lead on the dance!

The gramophone blared. Dukes, priests, shepherds, pilgrims and serving men took hands and danced. The idiot scampered in and out. Hands joined, heads knocking, they danced round the majestic figure of the Elizabethan age personified by Mrs. Clark, licensed to sell tobacco, on her soap box.

It was a mellay; a medley; an entrancing spectacle (to William) of dappled light and shade on half clothed, fantastically coloured, leaping, jerking, swinging legs and arms. He clapped till his palms stung.

Mrs. Manresa applauded loudly. Somehow she was the Queen; and he (Giles) was the surly hero.

"Bravo! Bravo!" she cried, and her enthusiasm made the surly hero squirm on his seat. Then the great lady in the bath chair, the lady whose marriage with the local peer had obliterated in his trashy title a name that had been a name when there were brambles and briars where the Church now stood—so indigenous was she that even her body, crippled by arthritis, resembled an uncouth, nocturnal animal, now nearly extinct—clapped and laughed loud—the sudden laughter of a startled jay.

"Ha, ha, ha!" she laughed and clutched the arms of her chair with ungloved twisted hands.

A-maying, a-maying, they bawled. *In and out and round about, a-maying, a-maying.* . . .

It didn't matter what the words were; or who sang what. Round and round they whirled, intoxicated by the music. Then, at a sign from Miss La Trobe behind the tree, the dance stopped. A procession formed. Great Eliza descended from her soap box. Taking her skirts in her hand, striding with long strides, surrounded by Dukes and Princes, followed by the lovers arm in arm, with Albert the idiot playing in and out, and the corpse on its bier concluding the procession, the Elizabethan age passed from the scene.

"Curse! Blast! Damn 'em!" Miss La Trobe in her rage stubbed her toe against a root. Here was her downfall; here was the Interval. Writing this skimble-skamble stuff in her cottage, she had agreed to cut the play here; a slave to her audience—to Mrs. Sands' grumble—about tea; about dinner—she had gashed the scene here. Just as she had brewed emotion, she spilt it. So she signalled: Phyllis! And, summoned, Phyllis popped up on the mat again in the middle.

> *Gentles and simples, I address you all* (she piped)
> *Our act is done, our scene is over.*
> *Past is the day of crone and lover.*
> *The bud has flowered; the flower has fallen.*
> *But soon will rise another dawning,*
> *For time whose children small we be*
> *Hath in his keeping, you shall see,*
> *You shall see. . . .*

Her voice petered out. No one was listening. Heads bent, they read "Interval" on the programme. And, cutting short her words, the megaphone announced in plain English: "An interval." Half an hour's interval, for tea. Then the gramophone blared out:

> *Armed against fate,*
> *The valiant Rhoderick,*
> *Bold and blatant,*
> *Firm, elatant, etc., etc.*

At that, the audience stirred. Some rose briskly; others stooped, retrieving walking-sticks, hats, bags. And then, as they raised themselves and turned about, the music modulated. The music chanted: *Dispersed are we.* It moaned: *Dispersed are we.* It lamented: *Dispersed are we,* as they streamed, spotting the grass with colour, across the lawns, and down the paths: *Dispersed are we.*

Mrs. Manresa took up the strain. *Dispersed are we.* "Freely, boldly, fearing no one" (she pushed a deck chair out of her way). "Youths and maidens" (she glanced behind her; but Giles had his back turned). "Follow, follow, follow me. . . . Oh Mr. Parker, what a pleasure to see *you* here! I'm for tea!"

"Dispersed are we," Isabella followed her, humming. "All is over. The wave has broken. Left us stranded, high and dry. Single, separate on the shingle. Broken is the three-fold ply . . . Now I follow" (she pushed her chair back . . . The man in grey was lost in the crowd by the ilex) "that old strumpet" (she invoked Mrs. Manresa's tight, flowered figure in front of her) "to have tea."

Dodge remained behind. "Shall I," he murmured, "go or stay? Slip out some other way? Or follow, follow, follow the dispersing company?"

Dispersed are we, the music wailed; *dispersed are we.* Giles remained like a stake in the tide of the flowing company.

"Follow?" He kicked his chair back. "Whom? Where?" He stubbed his light tennis shoes on the wood. "Nowhere. Anywhere." Stark still he stood.

Here Cobbet of Cobbs Corner, alone under the monkey puzzle tree, rose and muttered: "What was in her mind, eh? What idea lay behind, eh? What made her indue the antique with this glamour—this sham lure, and set 'em climbing, climbing, climbing up the monkey puzzle tree?"

Dispersed are we, the music wailed. *Dispersed are we.* He turned and sauntered slowly after the retreating company.

Now Lucy, retrieving her bag from beneath the seat, chirruped to her brother:

"Bart, my dear, come with me. . . . D'you remember, when we were children, the play we acted in the nursery?"

He remembered. Red Indians the game was; a reed with a note wrapped up in a pebble.

"But for us, my old Cindy"—he picked up his hat—"the game's over." The glare and the stare and the beat of the tom-tom, he meant. He gave her his arm. Off they strolled. And

Mr. Page, the reporter, noted, "Mrs. Swithin; Mr. B. Oliver," then turning, added further "Lady Haslip, of Haslip Manor," as he spied that old lady wheeled in her chair by her footman winding up the procession.

To the valediction of the gramophone hid in the bushes the audience departed. *Dispersed,* it wailed, *Dispersed are we.*

Now Miss La Trobe stepped from her hiding. Flowing, and streaming, on the grass, on the gravel, still for one moment she held them together—the dispersing company. Hadn't she, for twenty-five minutes, made them see? A vision imparted was relief from agony . . . for one moment . . . one moment. Then the music petered out on the last word *we.* She heard the breeze rustle in the branches. She saw Giles Oliver with his back to the audience. Also Cobbet of Cobbs Corner. She hadn't made them see. It was a failure, another damned failure! As usual. Her vision escaped her. And turning, she strode to the actors, undressing, down in the hollow, where butterflies feasted upon swords or silver paper; where the dish cloths in the shadow made pools of yellow.

Cobbet had out his watch. Three hours till seven, he noted; then water the plants. He turned.

Giles, nicking his chair into its notch, turned too, in the other direction. He took the short cut by the fields to the Barn. This dry summer the path was hard as brick across the fields. This dry summer the path was strewn with stones. He kicked— a flinty yellow stone, a sharp stone, edged as if cut by a savage for an arrow. A barbaric stone; a pre-historic. Stone-kicking was a child's game. He remembered the rules. By the rules of the game, one stone, the same stone, must be kicked to the goal. Say a gate, or a tree. He played it alone. The gate was a goal; to be reached in ten. The first kick was Manresa (lust). The second, Dodge (perversion). The third, himself (coward). And the fourth and the fifth and all the others were the same.

He reached it in ten. There, couched in the grass, curled in an olive green ring, was a snake. Dead? No, choked with a toad in its mouth. The snake was unable to swallow; the toad was unable to die. A spasm made the ribs contract; blood oozed. It was birth the wrong way round—a monstrous inversion. So, raising his foot, he stamped on them. The mass crushed and slithered. The white canvas on his tennis shoes was bloodstained and sticky. But it was action. Action relieved him. He strode to the Barn, with blood on his shoes.

The Barn, the Noble Barn, the barn that had been built over seven hundred years ago and reminded some people of a Greek temple, others of the middle ages, most people of an age before their own, scarcely anybody of the present moment, was empty.

The great doors stood open. A shaft of light like a yellow banner sloped from roof to floor. Festoons of paper roses, left over from the Coronation, drooped from the rafters. A long table, on which stood an urn, plates and cups, cakes and bread and butter, stretched across one end. The Barn was empty. Mice slid in and out of holes or stood upright, nibbling. Swallows were busy with straw in pockets of earth in the rafters. Countless beetles and insects of various sorts burrowed in the dry wood. A stray bitch had made the dark corner where the sacks stood a lying-in ground for her puppies. All these eyes, expanding and narrowing, some adapted to light, others to darkness, looked from different angles and edges. Minute nibblings and rustlings broke the silence. Whiffs of sweetness and richness veined the air. A blue-bottle had settled on the cake and stabbed its yellow rock with its short drill. A butterfly sunned itself sensuously on a sunlit yellow plate.

But Mrs. Sands was approaching. She was pushing her way through the crowd. She had turned the corner. She could see the great open door. But butterflies she never saw; mice were only black pellets in kitchen drawers; moths she bundled in her hands and put out of the window. Bitches suggested only servant girls misbehaving. Had there been a cat she would have seen it—any cat, a starved cat with a patch of mange on its rump opened the flood gates of her childless heart. But there was no cat. The Barn was empty. And so running, panting, set upon reaching the Barn and taking up her station behind the tea urn before the company came, she reached the Barn. And the butterfly rose and the blue-bottle.

Following her in a scud came the servants and helpers—David, John, Irene, Lois. Water boiled. Steam issued. Cake was sliced. Swallows swooped from rafter to rafter. And the company entered.

"This fine old Barn..." said Mrs. Manresa, stopping in the doorway. It was not for her to press ahead of the villagers. It was for her, moved by the beauty of the Barn, to stand still; to draw aside; to gaze; to let other people come first.

"We have one, much like it, at Lathom," said Mrs. Parker, stopping, for the same reasons. "Perhaps," she added, "not quite so large."

The villagers hung back. Then, hesitating, dribbled past.

"And the decorations..." said Mrs. Manresa, looking round for someone to congratulate. She stood smiling, waiting. Then old Mrs. Swithin came in. She was gazing up too, but not at the decorations. At the swallows apparently.

"They come every year," she said, "the same birds." Mrs. Manresa smiled benevolently, humouring the old lady's whimsy. It was unlikely, she thought, that the birds were the same.

"The decorations, I suppose, are left over from the Coronation," said Mrs. Parker. "We kept ours too. We built a village hall."

Mrs. Manresa laughed. She remembered. An anecdote was on the tip of her tongue, about a public lavatory built to celebrate the same occasion, and how the Mayor... Could she tell it? No. The old lady, gazing at the swallows, looked too refined.

"Refeened"—Mrs. Manresa qualified the word to her own advantage, thus confirming her approval of the wild child she was, whose nature was somehow "just human nature." Somehow she could span the old lady's "refeenment," also the boy's fun—Where was that nice fellow Giles? She couldn't see him; nor Bill either. The villagers still hung back. They must have someone to start the ball rolling.

"Well, I'm dying for my tea!" she said in her public voice; and strode forward. She laid hold of a thick china mug. Mrs. Sands giving precedence, of course, to one of the gentry, filled it at once. David gave her cake. She was the first to drink, the first to bite. The villagers still hung back. "It's all my eye about democracy," she concluded. So did Mrs. Parker, taking her mug too. The people looked to them. They led; the rest followed.

"What delicious tea!" each exclaimed, disgusting though it was, like rust boiled in water, and the cake fly-blown. But they had a duty to society.

"They come every year," said Mrs. Swithin, ignoring the fact that she spoke to the empty air. "From Africa." As they had come, she supposed, when the Barn was a swamp.

The Barn filled. Fumes rose. China clattered; voices chattered. Isa pressed her way to the table.

"Dispersed are we," she murmured. And held her cup out to be filled. She took it. "Let me turn away," she murmured, turning, "from the array"—she looked desolately round her—"of china faces, glazed and hard. Down the ride, that leads under the nut tree and the may tree, away, till I come to the wishing well, where the washer-woman's little boy—" she dropped sugar, two lumps, into her tea, "dropped a pin. He got his horse, so they say. But what wish should I drop into the well?" She looked round. She could not see the man in grey, the gentleman farmer; nor anyone known to her. "That the waters should cover me," she added, "of the wishing well."

The noise of china and chatter drowned her murmur. "Sugar for you?" they were saying. "Just a spot of milk? And you?" "Tea without milk or sugar. That's the way I like it." "A bit too strong? Let me add water."

"That's what I wished," Isa added, "when I dropped my pin. Water. Water . . ."

"I must say," the voice said behind her, "it's brave of the King and Queen. They're said to be going to India. She looks such a dear. Someone I know said his hair. . . ."

"There," Isa mused, "would the dead leaf fall, when the leaves fall, on the water. Should I mind not again to see may tree or nut tree? Not again to hear on the trembling spray the thrush sing, or to see, dipping and diving as if he skimmed waves in the air, the yellow woodpecker?"

She was looking at the canary yellow festoons left over from the Coronation.

"I thought they said Canada, not India," the voice said behind her back. To which the other voice answered: "D'you believe what the papers say? For instance, about the Duke of Windsor. He landed on the south coast. Queen Mary met him. She'd been buying furniture—that's a fact. And the papers say she met him . . ."

"Alone, under a tree, the withered tree that keeps all day murmuring of the sea, and hears the Rider gallop . . ."

Isa filled in the phrase. Then she started. William Dodge was by her side.

He smiled. She smiled. They were conspirators; each murmuring some song my uncle taught me.

"It's the play," she said. "The play keeps running in my head."

"Hail, sweet Carinthia. My love. My life," he quoted.

"My lord, my liege," she bowed ironically.

She was handsome. He wanted to see her, not against the tea urn, but with her glass green eyes and thick body, the neck was broad as a pillar, against an arum lily or a vine. He wished she would say: "Come along. I'll show you the greenhouse, the pig sty, or the stable." But she said nothing, and they stood there holding their cups, remembering the play. Then he saw her face change, as if she had got out of one dress and put on another. A small boy battled his way through the crowd, striking against skirts and trousers as if he were swimming blindly.

"Here!" she cried, raising her arm.

He made a bee-line for her. He was her little boy, apparently, her son, her George. She gave him cake; then a mug of milk. Then Nurse came up. Then again she changed her dress. This time, from the expression in her eyes it was apparently something in the nature of a strait waistcoat. Hirsute, handsome, virile, the young man in blue jacket and brass buttons, standing in a beam of dusty light, was her husband. And she his wife. Their relations, as he had noted at lunch, were as people say in novels "strained." As he had noted at the play, her bare arm had raised itself nervously to her shoulder when she turned—looking for whom? But here he was; and the muscular, the hirsute, the virile plunged him into emotions in which the mind had no share. He forgot how she would have looked against vine leaf in a greenhouse. Only at Giles he looked; and looked and looked. Of whom was he thinking as he stood with his face turned? Not of Isa. Of Mrs. Manresa?

Mrs. Manresa half-way down the Barn had gulped her cup of tea. How can I rid myself, she asked, of Mrs. Parker? If they were of her own class, how they bored her—her own sex! Not the class below—cooks, shopkeepers, farmers' wives; nor the class above—peeresses, countesses; it was the women of her own class that bored her. So she left Mrs. Parker, abruptly.

"Oh Mrs. Moore," she hailed the keeper's wife. "What did you think of it? And what did baby think of it?" Here she pinched baby. "I thought it every bit as good as anything I'd seen in London.... But we mustn't be outdone. We'll have a play of our own. In *our* Barn. We'll show 'em" (here she winked obliquely at the table; so many bought cakes, so few made at home) "how *we* do it."

Then cracking her jokes, she turned; saw Giles; caught his eye; and swept him in, beckoning. He came. And what—she looked down—had he done with his shoes? They were blood-stained. Vaguely some sense that he had proved his valour for her admiration flattered her. If vague it was sweet. Taking him in tow, she felt: I am the Queen, he my hero, my sulky hero.

"That's Mrs. Neale!" she exclaimed. "A perfect marvel of a woman, aren't you, Mrs. Neale! She runs our post office, Mrs. Neale. She can do sums in her head, can't you, Mrs. Neale? Twenty-five halfpenny stamps, two packets of stamped envelopes and a packet of postcards—how much does that come to, Mrs. Neale?"

Mrs. Neale laughed; Mrs. Manresa laughed; Giles too smiled, and looked down at his shoes.

She drew him down the Barn, in and out, from one to another. She knew 'em all. Every one was a thorough good sort. No, she wouldn't allow it, not for a moment—Pinsent's bad leg. "No, no. We're not going to take that for an excuse, Pinsent." If he couldn't bowl, he could bat. Giles agreed. A fish on a line meant the same to him and Pinsent; also jays and magpies. Pinsent stayed on the land; Giles went to an office. That was all. And she was a thorough good sort, making him feel less of an audience, more of an actor, going round the Barn in her wake.

Then, at the end by the door, they came upon the old couple, Lucy and Bartholomew, sitting on their Windsor chairs.

Chairs had been reserved for them. Mrs. Sands had sent them tea. It would have caused more bother than it was worth—

asserting the democratic principle; standing in the crowd at the table.

"Swallows," said Lucy, holding her cup, looking at the birds. Excited by the company they were flitting from rafter to rafter. Across Africa, across France they had come to nest here. Year after year they came. Before there was a channel, when the earth, upon which the Windsor chair was planted, was a riot of rhododendrons, and humming birds quivered at the mouths of scarlet trumpets, as she had read that morning in her Outline of History, they had come . . . Here Bart rose from his chair.

But Mrs. Manresa absolutely refused to take his seat. "Go on sitting, go on sitting," she pressed him down again. "I'll squat on the floor." She squatted. The surly knight remained in attendance.

"And what did you think of the play?" she asked.

Bartholomew looked at his son. His son remained silent.

"And you Mrs. Swithin?" Mrs. Manresa pressed the old lady.

Lucy mumbled, looking at the swallows.

"I was hoping you'd tell me," said Mrs. Manresa. "Was it an old play? Was it a new play?"

No one answered.

"Look!" Lucy exclaimed.

"The birds?" said Mrs. Manresa, looking up.

There was a bird with a straw in its beak; and the straw dropped.

Lucy clapped her hands. Giles turned away. She was mocking him as usual, laughing.

"Going?" said Bartholomew. "Time for the next act?"

And he heaved himself up from his chair. Regardless of Mrs. Manresa and of Lucy, off he strolled too.

"Swallow, my sister, O sister swallow," he muttered, feeling for his cigar case, following his son.

Mrs. Manresa was nettled. What for had she squatted on the floor then? Were her charms fading? Both were gone. But, woman of action as she was, deserted by the male sex, she was not going to suffer tortures of boredom from the refeened old lady. Up she scrambled, putting her hands to hair as if it were high time that she went too, though it was nothing of the kind and her hair was perfectly tidy. Cobbet in his corner saw through her little game. He had known human nature in the East. It was the same in the West. Plants remained—the carnation, the zinnia, and the geranium. Automatically he consulted his watch; noted time to water at seven; and observed the little game of the woman following the man to the table in the West as in the East.

William at the table, now attached to Mrs. Parker and Isa, watched him approach. Armed and valiant, bold and blatant, firm elatant—the popular march tune rang in his head. And the fingers of William's left hand closed firmly, surreptitiously, as the hero approached.

Mrs. Parker was deploring to Isa in a low voice the village idiot.

"Oh that idiot!" she was saying. But Isa was immobile, watching her husband. She could feel the Manresa in his wake. She could hear in the dusk in their bedroom the usual explanation. It made no difference; his infidelity—but hers did.

"The idiot?" William answered Mrs. Parker for her. "He's in the tradition."

"But surely," said Mrs. Parker, and told Giles how creepy the idiot—"We have one in our village"—had made her feel. "Surely, Mr. Oliver, we're more civilized?"

"*We?*" said Giles. "*We?*" He looked, once, at William. He knew not his name; but what his left hand was doing. It was a bit of luck—that he could despise him, not himself. Also Mrs. Parker. But not Isa—not his wife. She had not spoken to him, not one word. Nor looked at him either.

"Surely," said Mrs. Parker, looking from one to the other. "Surely we are?"

Giles then did what to Isa was his little trick; shut his lips; frowned; and took up the pose of one who bears the burden of the world's woe, making money for her to spend.

"No," said Isa, as plainly as words could say it. "I don't admire you," and looked, not at his face, but at his feet. "Silly little boy, with blood on his boots."

Giles shifted his feet. Whom then did she admire? Not Dodge. That he could take for certain. Who else? Some man he knew. Some man, he was sure, in the Barn. Which man? He looked round him.

Then Mr. Streatfield, the clergyman, interrupted. He was carrying cups.

"So I shake hands with my heart!" he exclaimed, nodding his handsome, grizzled head and depositing his burden safely.

Mrs. Parker took the tribute to herself.

"Mr. Streatfield!" she exclaimed. "Doing all the work! While we stand gossiping!"

"Like to see the greenhouse?" said Isa suddenly, turning to William Dodge.

O not now, he could have cried. But had to follow, leaving Giles to welcome the approaching Manresa, who had him in thrall.

The path was narrow. Isa went ahead. And she was broad; she fairly filled the path, swaying slightly as she walked, and plucking a leaf here and there from the hedge.

"Fly then, follow," she hummed, "the dappled herds in the cedar grove, who, sporting, play, the red with the roe, the stag with the doe. Fly, away. I grieving stay. Alone I linger, I pluck the bitter herb by the ruined wall, the churchyard wall, and press its sour, its sweet, its sour, long grey leaf, so, twixt thumb and finger. . . ."

She threw away the shred of Old Man's Beard that she had

picked in passing and kicked open the greenhouse door. Dodge had lagged behind. She waited. She picked up a knife from the plank. He saw her standing against the green glass, the fig tree, and the blue hydrangea, knife in hand.

"She spake," Isa murmured. "And from her bosom's snowy antre drew the gleaming blade. 'Plunge blade!' she said. And struck. 'Faithless!' she cried. Knife, too! It broke. So too my heart," she said.

She was smiling ironically as he came up.

"I wish the play didn't run in my head," she said. Then she sat down on a plank under the vine. And he sat beside her. The little grapes above them were green buds; the leaves thin and yellow as the web between birds' claws.

"Still the play?" he asked. She nodded. "That was your son," he said, "in the Barn?"

She had a daughter too, she told him, in the cradle.

"And you—married?" she asked. From her tone he knew she guessed, as women always guessed, everything. They knew at once they had nothing to fear, nothing to hope. At first they resented—serving as statues in a greenhouse. Then they liked it. For then they could say—as she did—whatever came into their heads. And hand him, as she handed him, a flower.

"There's something for your buttonhole Mr. . . ." she said, handing him a sprig of scented geranium.

"I'm William," he said, taking the furry leaf and pressing it between thumb and finger.

"I'm Isa," she answered. Then they talked as if they had known each other all their lives; which was odd, she said, as they always did, considering she'd known him perhaps one hour. Weren't they, though, conspirators, seekers after hidden faces? That confessed, she paused and wondered, as they always did, why they could speak so plainly to each other. And added: "Perhaps because we've never met before, and never shall again."

"The doom of sudden death hanging over us," he said. "There's no retreating and advancing"—he was thinking of the old lady showing him the house—"for us as for them."

The future shadowed their present, like the sun coming through the many-veined transparent vine leaf; a criss-cross of lines making no pattern.

They had left the greenhouse door open, and now music came through it. A.B.C., A.B.C., A.B.C.—someone was practising scales. C.A.T. C.A.T. C.A.T. ... Then the separate letters made one word "Cat." Other words followed. It was a simple tune, like a nursery rhyme——

> The King is in his counting house
> Counting out his money,
> The Queen is in her parlour
> Eating bread and honey.

They listened. Another voice, a third voice, was saying something simple. And they sat on in the greenhouse, on the plank with the vine over them, listening to Miss La Trobe or whoever it was, practising her scales.

He could not find his son. He had lost him in the crowd. So old Bartholomew left the Barn, and went to his own room, holding his cheroot and murmuring:

> "O sister swallow, O sister swallow,
> How can thy heart be full of the spring?"

"How can my heart be full of the spring?" he said aloud, standing in front of the book case. Books: the treasured life-blood of immortal spirits. Poets; the legislators of mankind. Doubtless, it was so. But Giles was unhappy. "How can my heart, how can my heart," he repeated, puffing at his cheroot. "Condemned in life's infernal mine, condemned in solitude to pine . . ." Arms akimbo, he stood in front of his country gentleman's library. Garibaldi; Wellington; Irrigation Officers' Reports; and Hibbert on the Diseases of the Horse. A great harvest the mind had reaped; but for all this, compared with his son, he did not care one damn.

"What's the use, what's the use," he sank down into his chair muttering, "O sister swallow, O sister swallow, of singing your song?" The dog, who had followed him, flopped down on to the floor at his feet. Flanks sucked in and out, the long nose resting on his paws, a fleck of foam on the nostril, there he was, his familiar spirit, his Afghan hound.

The door trembled and stood half open. That was Lucy's way of coming in—as if she did not know what she would find. Really! It was her brother! And his dog! She seemed to see them for the first time. Was it that she had no body? Up in the clouds, like an air ball, her mind touched ground now and then with a shock of surprise. There was nothing in her to weight a man like Giles to the earth.

She perched on the edge of a chair like a bird on a telegraph wire before starting for Africa.

"Swallow, my sister, O sister swallow . . ." he murmured.

From the garden—the window was open—came the sound of someone practising scales. A.B.C. A.B.C. A.B.C. Then the separate letters formed one word "Dog." Then a phrase. It was a simple tune, another voice speaking.

> "Hark, hark, the dogs do bark,
> The beggars are coming to town . . ."

Then it languished and lengthened, and became a waltz. As they listened and looked—out into the garden—the trees tossing and the birds swirling seemed called out of their private lives, out of their separate avocations, and made to take part.

> The lamp of love burns high, over the dark cedar
>   groves,
> The lamp of love shines clear, clear as a star in the
>   sky. . . .

Old Bartholomew tapped his fingers on his knee in time to the tune.

> Leave your casement and come, lady,
>   I love till I die,

He looked sardonically at Lucy, perched on her chair. How, he wondered, had she ever borne children?

> For all are dancing, retreating and advancing,
>   The moth and the dragon fly. . . .

She was thinking, he supposed, God is peace. God is love. For she belonged to the unifiers; he to the separatists.

Then the tune with its feet always on the same spot, became sugared, insipid; bored a hole with its perpetual invocation to perpetual adoration. Had it—he was ignorant of musical terms—gone into the minor key?

> For this day and this dance and this merry, merry May
> Will be over (he tapped his forefinger on his knee)
> With the cutting of the clover this retreating and
>   advancing—the swifts seemed to have shot beyond
>   their orbits—
> Will be over, over, over,

And the ice will dart its splinter, and the winter,
O the winter, will fill the grate with ashes,
And there'll be no glow, no glow on the log.

He knocked the ash off his cheroot and rose.

"So we must," said Lucy; as if he had said aloud, "It's time to go."

The audience was assembling. The music was summoning them. Down the paths, across the lawns they were streaming again. There was Mrs. Manresa, with Giles at her side, heading the procession. In taut plump curves her scarf blew round her shoulders. The breeze was rising. She looked, as she crossed the lawn to the strains of the gramophone, goddess-like, buoyant, abundant, her cornucopia running over. Bartholomew, following, blessed the power of the human body to make the earth fruitful. Giles would keep his orbit so long as she weighted him to the earth. She stirred the stagnant pool of his old heart even—where bones lay buried, but the dragon flies shot and the grass trembled as Mrs. Manresa advanced across the lawn to the strains of the gramophone.

Feet crunched the gravel. Voices chattered. The inner voice, the other voice was saying: How can we deny that this brave music, wafted from the bushes, is expressive of some inner harmony? "When we wake" (some were thinking) "the day breaks us with its hard mallet blows." "The office" (some were thinking) "compels disparity. Scattered, shattered, hither thither summoned by the bell. 'Ping-ping-ping' that's the phone. 'Forward!' 'Serving!'—that's the shop." So we answer to the infernal, age-long and eternal order issued from on high. And obey. "Working, serving, pushing, striving, earning wages—to be spent—here? Oh dear no. Now? No, by and by. When ears are deaf and the heart is dry."

Here Cobbet of Cobbs Corner who had stooped—there was a flower—was pressed on by people pushing from behind.

For I hear music, they were saying. Music wakes us. Music makes us see the hidden, join the broken. Look and listen. See the flowers, how they ray their redness, whiteness, silverness and blue. And the trees with their many-tongued much syllabling, their green and yellow leaves hustle us and shuffle us, and bid us, like the starlings, and the rooks, come together, crowd together, to chatter and make merry while the red cow moves forward and the black cow stands still.

The audience had reached their seats. Some sat down; others stood a moment, turned, and looked at the view. The stage was empty; the actors were still dressing up among the bushes. The audience turned to one another and began to talk. Scraps and fragments reached Miss La Trobe where she stood, script in hand, behind the tree.

"They're not ready . . . I hear 'em laughing" (they were saying). ". . . Dressing up. That's the great thing, dressing up. And it's pleasant now, the sun's not so hot . . . That's one good the war brought us—longer days . . . Where did we leave off? D'you remember? The Elizabethans . . . Perhaps she'll reach the present, if she skips. . . . D'you think people change? Their clothes, of course. . . . But I meant ourselves . . . Clearing out a cupboard, I found my father's old top hat. . . . But ourselves—do we change?"

"No, I don't go by politicians. I've a friend who's been to Russia. He says . . . And my daughter, just back from Rome, she says the common people, in the cafés, hate Dictators. . . . Well, different people say different things. . . ."

"Did you see it in the papers—the case about the dog? D'you believe dogs can't have puppies? . . . And Queen Mary and the Duke of Windsor on the south coast? . . . D'you believe what's in the papers? I ask the butcher or the grocer . . . That's

Mr. Streatfield, carrying a hurdle. . . . The good clergyman, I say, does more work for less pay than all the lot . . . It's the wives that make the trouble. . . ."

"And what about the Jews? The refugees . . . the Jews . . . People like ourselves, beginning life again . . . But it's always been the same. . . . My old mother, who's over eighty, can remember . . . Yes, she still reads without glasses. . . . How amazing! Well, don't they say, after eighty . . . Now they're coming . . . No, that's nothing. . . . I'd make it penal, leaving litter. But then, who's, my husband says, to collect the fines? . . . Ah there she is, Miss La Trobe, over there, behind that tree . . ."

Over there behind the tree Miss La Trobe gnashed her teeth. She crushed her manuscript. The actors delayed. Every moment the audience slipped the noose; split up into scraps and fragments.

"Music!" she signalled. "Music!"

"What's the origin," said a voice, "of the expression 'with a flea in his ear'?"

Down came her hand peremptorily. "Music, music," she signalled.

And the gramophone began A.B.C., A.B.C.

> *The King is in his counting house*
> *Counting out his money,*
> *The Queen is in her parlour*
> *Eating bread and honey. . . .*

Miss La Trobe watched them sink down peacefully into the nursery rhyme. She watched them fold their hands and compose their faces. Then she beckoned. And at last, with a final touch to her head dress, which had been giving trouble, Mabel Hopkins strode from the bushes, and took her place on the raised ground facing the audience.

Eyes fed on her as fish rise to a crumb of bread on the water. Who was she? What did she represent? She was beautiful—very. Her cheeks had been powdered; her colour glowed smooth and clear underneath. Her grey satin robe (a bedspread), pinned in stone-like folds, gave her the majesty of a statue. She carried a sceptre and a little round orb. England was she? Queen Anne was she? Who was she? She spoke too low at first; all they heard was

... reason holds sway.

Old Bartholomew applauded.
"Hear! Hear!" he cried. "Bravo! Bravo!"
Thus encouraged Reason spoke out.

Time, leaning on his sickle, stands amazed. While Commerce from her Cornucopia pours the mingled tribute of her different ores. In distant mines the savage sweats; and from the reluctant earth the painted pot is shaped. At my behest, the armed warrior lays his shield aside; the heathen leaves the Altar steaming with unholy sacrifice. The violet and the eglantine over the riven earth their flowers entwine. No longer fears the unwary wanderer the poisoned snake. And in the helmet, yellow bees their honey make.

She paused. A long line of villagers in sacking were passing in and out of the trees behind her.

Digging and delving, ploughing and sowing they were singing, but the wind blew their words away.

Beneath the shelter of my flowing robe (she resumed, extending her arms) *the arts arise. Music for me unfolds her heavenly harmony. At my behest the miser leaves his hoard untouched; at peace the mother sees her children play.... Her children play* ... she repeated, and, waving her sceptre, figures advanced from the bushes.

Let swains and nymphs lead on the play, while Zephyr sleeps, and the unruly tribes of Heaven confess my sway.

A merry little old tune was played on the gramophone. Old Bartholomew joined his finger tips; Mrs. Manresa smoothed her skirts about her knees.

> *Young Damon said to Cynthia,*
> *Come out now with the dawn*
> *And don your azure tippet*
> *And cast your cares adown*
> *For peace has come to England,*
> *And reason now holds sway.*
> *What pleasure lies in dreaming*
> *When blue and green's the day?*
> *Now cast your cares behind you.*
> *Night passes: here is Day.*

Digging and delving, the villagers sang passing in single file in and out between the trees, *for the earth is always the same, summer and winter and spring; and spring and winter again; ploughing and sowing, eating and growing; time passes. . . .*

The wind blew the words away.

The dance stopped. The nymphs and swains withdrew. Reason held the centre of the stage alone. Her arms extended, her robes flowing, holding orb and sceptre, Mabel Hopkins stood sublimely looking over the heads of the audience. The audience gazed at her. She ignored the audience. Then while she gazed, helpers from the bushes arranged round her what appeared to be the three sides of a room. In the middle they stood a table. On the table they placed a china tea service. Reason surveyed this domestic scene from her lofty eminence unmoved. There was a pause.

"Another scene from another play, I suppose," said Mrs. Elmhurst, referring to her programme. She read out for the benefit of her husband, who was deaf: "*Where there's a Will there's a Way*. That's the name of the play. And the characters. . . ." She read out: "Lady Harpy Harraden, in love with Sir Spaniel Lilyliver. Deb, her maid. Flavinda, her niece, in love with Valentine. Sir Spaniel Lilyliver, in love with Flavinda. Sir Smirking Peace-be-with-you-all, a clergyman. Lord and Lady Fribble. Valentine, in love with Flavinda. What names for real people! But look—here they come!"

Out they came from the bushes—men in flowered waistcoats, white waistcoats and buckled shoes; women wearing brocades tucked up, hooped and draped; glass stars, blue ribands and imitation pearls made them look the very image of Lords and Ladies.

"The first scene," Mrs. Elmhurst whispered into her husband's ear, "is Lady Harraden's dressing-room. . . . That's her. . . ." She pointed. "Mrs. Otter, I think, from the End House; but she's wonderfully made up. And that's Deb her maid. Who she is, I don't know."

"Hush, hush, hush," someone protested.

Mrs. Elmhurst dropped her programme. The play had begun.

Lady Harpy Harraden entered her dressing-room, followed by Deb her maid.

LADY H. H. . . . *Give me the pounce-box. Then the patch. Hand me the mirror, girl. So. Now my wig. . . . A pox on the girl—she's dreaming!*

DEB . . . *I was thinking, my lady, what the gentleman said when he saw you in the Park.*

LADY H. H. (gazing in the glass). *So, so—what was it? Some silly trash! Cupid's dart—hah, hah! lighting his taper—tush—at my eyes. . . . pooh! That was in milord's time, twenty years since. . . . But now—what'll he say of me now?* (She looks in the mirror.) *Sir Spaniel*

Lilyliver, I mean . . . (a rap at the door). *Hark! That's his chaise at the door. Run child. Don't stand gaping.*

DEB . . . (going to the door). *Say? He'll rattle his tongue as a gambler rattles dice in a box. He'll find no words to fit you. He'll stand like a pig in a poke. . . . Your servant, Sir Spaniel.*

Enter Sir Spaniel.

SIR S. L. . . . *Hail, my fair Saint! What, out o' bed so early? Methought, as I came along the Mall the air was something brighter than usual. Here's the reason. . . . Venus, Aphrodite, upon my word a very galaxy, a constellation! As I'm a sinner, a very Aurora Borealis!*

(He sweeps his hat off.)

LADY H. H. *Oh flatterer, flatterer! I know your ways. But come. Sit down. . . . A glass of Aqua Vitae. Take this seat, Sir Spaniel. I've something very private and particular to say to you. . . . You had my letter, Sir?*

SIR S. L. . . . *Pinned to my heart!*

(He strikes his breast.)

LADY H. H. . . . *I have a favour to ask of you, Sir.*

SIR S. L. . . . (singing). *What favour could fair Chloe ask that Damon would not get her? . . . A done with rhymes. Rhymes are still-a-bed. Let's speak prose. What can Asphodilla ask of her plain servant Lilyliver? Speak out, Madam. An ape with a ring in his nose, or a strong young jackanapes to tell tales of us when we're no longer here to tell truth about ourselves?*

LADY H. H. (flirting her fan). *Fie, fie, Sir Spaniel. You make me blush—you do indeed. But come closer.* (She shifts her seat nearer to him.) *We don't want the whole world to hear us.*

SIR S. L. (aside). *Come closer? A pox on my life! The old hag stinks like a red herring that's been stood over head in a tar barrel!* (Aloud.) *Your meaning, Madam? You were saying?*

LADY H. H. *I have a niece, Sir Spaniel, Flavinda by name.*

Sir S. L. (aside). *Why that's the girl I love, to be sure!* (Aloud.) *You have a niece, Madam? I seem to remember hearing so. An only child, left by your brother, so I've heard, in your Ladyship's charge—him that perished at sea.*

Lady H. H. *The very same Sir. She's of age now and marriageable. I've kept her close as a weevil, Sir Spaniel, wrapped in the sere cloths of her virginity. Only maids about her, never a man to my knowledge, save Clout the serving man, who has a wart on his nose and a face like a nutgrater. Yet some fool has caught her fancy. Some gilded fly—some Harry, Dick; call him what you will.*

Sir S. L. (aside). *That's young Valentine, I warrant. I caught 'em at the play together.* (Aloud.) *Say you so, Madam?*

Lady H. H. *She's not so ill favoured, Sir Spaniel—there's beauty in our line—but that a gentleman of taste and breeding like yourself now might take pity on her.*

Sir S. L. *Saving your presence, Madam. Eyes that have seen the sun are not so easily dazzled by the lesser lights—the Cassiopeias, Aldebarans, Great Bears and so on—A fig for them when the sun's up!*

Lady H. H. (ogling him). *You praise my hairdresser, Sir, or my ear-rings.* (She shakes her head.)

Sir S. L. (aside). *She jingles like a she-ass at a fair! She's rigged like a barber's pole of a May Day.* (Aloud.) *Your commands, Madam?*

Lady H. H. *Well Sir, 'twas this way Sir. Brother Bob, for my father was a plain country gentleman and would have none of the fancy names the foreigners brought with 'em—Asphodilla I call myself, but my Christian name's plain Sue—Brother Bob, as I was telling you, ran away to sea; and, so they say, became Emperor of the Indies; where the very stones are emeralds and the sheep-crop rubies. Which, for a tenderer-hearted man never lived, he would have brought back with him, Sir, to mend the family fortunes, Sir. But the brig, frigate or what they call it, for I've no head for sea terms, never crossed a ditch without saying the Lord's Prayer backwards, struck a rock. The Whale had him. But the cradle was by the bounty of Heaven washed ashore. With the girl in it; Flavinda here.*

What's more to the point, with the Will in it; safe and sound; wrapped in parchment. Brother Bob's Will. Deb there! Deb I say! Deb!

(She holloas for Deb.)

Sir S. L. (aside). *Ah hah! I smell a rat! A will, quotha! Where there's a Will there's a Way.*

Lady H. H. (bawling). *The Will, Deb! The Will! In the ebony box by the right hand of the escritoire opposite the window. . . . A pox on the girl! She's dreaming. It's these romances, Sir Spaniel—these romances. Can't see a candle gutter but it's her heart that's melting, or snuff a wick without reciting all the names in Cupid's Calendar . . .*

(Enter Deb carrying a parchment.)

Lady H. H. *So . . . Give it here. The Will. Brother Bob's Will.* (She mumbles over the Will.)

Lady H. H. *To cut the matter short, Sir, for these lawyers even at the Antipodes are a long-winded race——*

Sir S. L. *To match their ears, Ma'am——*

Lady H. H. *Very true, very true. To cut the matter short, Sir, my Brother Bob left all he died possessed of to his only child Flavinda; with this proviso, mark ye. That she marry to her Aunt's liking. Her Aunt; that's me. Otherwise, mark ye, all—to wit ten bushels of diamonds; item of rubies; item two hundred square miles of fertile territory bounding the River Amazon to the Nor-Nor-East; item his snuff box; item his flageo-let—he was always one to love a tune, Sir, Brother Bob; item six Macaws and as many Concubines as he had with him at the time of his decease—all this with other trifles needless to specify he left, mark ye, should she fail to marry to her Aunt's liking—that's me—to found a Chapel, Sir Spaniel, where six poor Virgins should sing hymns in perpetuity for the repose of his soul—which, to speak the truth, Sir Spaniel, poor Brother Bob stands in need of, perambulating the Gulf Stream as he is and con-sorting with Syrens. But take it; read the Will yourself, Sir.*

SIR S. L. (reading). *"Must marry to her Aunt's liking."* That's plain enough.

LADY H. H. *Her Aunt, Sir. That's me. That's plain enough.*

SIR S. L. (aside). *She speaks the truth there!* (Aloud.) *You would have me understand, Madam. . . . ?*

LADY H. H. *Hist! Come closer. Let me whisper in your ear . . . You and I have long entertained a high opinion of one another, Sir Spaniel. Played at ball together. Bound our wrists with daisy chains together. If I mind aright, you called me little bride—'tis fifty years since. We might have made a match of it, Sir Spaniel, had fortune favoured. . . . You take my meaning, Sir?*

SIR S. L. *Had it been written in letters of gold, fifty feet high, visible from Paul's Churchyard to the Goat and Compasses at Peckham, it could have been no plainer. . . . Hist, I'll whisper it. I, Sir Spaniel Lilyliver, do hereby bind myself to take thee—what's the name of the green girl that was cast up in a lobster pot covered with seaweed? Flavinda, eh? Flavinda, so—to be my wedded wife . . . O for a lawyer to have it all in writing!*

LADY H. H. *On condition, Sir Spaniel.*

SIR S. L. *On condition, Asphodilla.*

(Both speak together.)

That the money is shared between us.

LADY H. H. *We want no lawyer to certify that! Your hand on it, Sir Spaniel!*

SIR S. L. *Your lips, Madam!*

(They embrace.)

SIR S. L. *Pah! She stinks!*

"Ha! Ha! Ha!" laughed the indigenous old lady in her bathchair.

"Reason, begad! Reason!" exclaimed old Bartholomew, and looked at his son as if exhorting him to give over these woman-ish vapours and be a man, Sir.

Giles sat straight as a dart, his feet tucked under him.

Mrs. Manresa had out her mirror and lipstick and attended to her lips and nose.

The gramophone, while the scene was removed, gently stated certain facts which everybody knows to be perfectly true. The tune said, more or less, how Eve, gathering her robes about her, stands reluctant still to let her dewy mantle fall. The herded flocks, the tune continued, in peace repose. The poor man to his cot returns, and, to the eager ears of wife and child, the simple story of his toil relates: what yield the furrow bears; and how the team the plover on the nest has spared; while Wat her courses ran; and speckled eggs in the warm hollow lay. Meanwhile the good wife on the table spreads her simple fare; and to the shepherd's flute, from toil released, the nymphs and swains join hands and foot it on the green. Then Eve lets down her sombre tresses brown and spreads her lucent veil o'er ham-let, spire, and mead, etc., etc. And the tune repeated itself once more.

The view repeated in its own way what the tune was saying. The sun was sinking; the colours were merging; and the view was saying how after toil men rest from their labours; how cool-ness comes; reason prevails; and having unharnessed the team from the plough, neighbours dig in cottage gardens and lean over cottage gates.

The cows, making a step forward, then standing still, were saying the same thing to perfection.

Folded in this triple melody, the audience sat gazing; and be-held gently and approvingly without interrogation, for it seemed inevitable, a box tree in a green tub take the place of the ladies' dressing-room; while on what seemed to be a wall, was hung a great clock face; the hands pointing to three minutes to the hour; which was seven.

Mrs. Elmhurst roused herself from her reverie; and looked at her programme.

"Scene Two. The Mall," she read out. "Time; early morning. Enter Flavinda. Here she comes!"

Here came Millie Loder (shop assistant at Messrs. Hunt and Dicksons, drapery emporium), in sprigged satin, representing Flavinda.

FLAV. *Seven he said, and there's the clock's word for it. But Valentine—where's Valentine? La! How my heart beats! Yet it's not the time o' day, for I'm often afoot before the sun's up in the meadows . . . See— the fine folk passing! All a-tiptoeing like peacocks with spread tails! And I in my petticoat that looked so fine by my Aunt's cracked mirror. Why, here it's a dish clout . . . And they heap their hair up like a birthday cake stuck about with candles. . . . That's a diamond—that's a ruby . . . Where's Valentine? The Orange Tree in the Mall, he said. The tree— there. Valentine—nowhere. That's a courtier, I'll warrant, that old fox with his tail between his legs. That's a serving wench out without her master's knowledge. That's a man with a broom to sweep paths for the fine ladies' flounces . . . La! the red in their cheeks! They never got that in the fields, I warrant! O faithless, cruel, hard-hearted Valentine. Valentine! Valentine!*

(She wrings her hands, turning from side to side.)

Didn't I leave my bed a-tiptoe and steal like a mouse in the wainscot for fear of waking Aunt? And lard my hair from her powder box? And scrub my cheeks to make 'em shine? And lie awake watching the stars climb the chimney pots? And give my gold guinea that Godfather hid behind the mistletoe last Twelfth Night to Deb so she shouldn't tell on me? And grease the key in the lock so that Aunt shouldn't wake and shriek Flavvy! Flavvy! Val, I say Val———That's him coming. . . . No, I could tell him

a mile off the way he strides the waves like what d'you call him in the pic-
ture book. . . . That's not Val. . . . That's a cit; that's a fop; raising his
glass, prithee, to have his fill of me . . . I'll be home then . . . No, I
won't . . . That's to play the green girl again and sew samplers . . . I'm of
age, ain't I, come Michaelmas? Only three turns of the moon and I in-
herit . . . Didn't I read it in the Will the day the ball bounced on top of
the old chest where Aunt keeps her furbelows, and the lid opened? . . . "All
I die possessed of to my Daughter . . ." So far I'd read when the old lady
came tapping down the passage like a blind man in an alley. . . . I'm no
castaway, I'd have you know, Sir; no fish-tailed mermaid with a robe of
sea weed, at your mercy. I'm a match for any of 'em — the chits you dally
with, and bid me meet you at the Orange Tree when you're drowsing the
night off spent in their arms. . . . Fie upon you, Sir, making sport with a
poor girl so. . . . I'll not cry, I swear I won't. I'll not brew a drop of the
salt liquid for a man who's served me so. . . . Yet to think on't — how we
hid in the dairy the day the cat jumped. And read romances under the
holly tree. La! how I cried when the Duke left poor Polly. . . . And my
Aunt found me with eyes like red jellies. "What stung, niece?" says she.
And cried "Quick Deb, the blue bag." I told ye . . . La, to think I read
it all in a book and cried for another! . . . Hist, what's there among the
trees? It's come — it's gone. The breeze is it? In the shade now — in the
sun now. . . . Valentine on my life! It's he! Quick, I'll hide. Let the tree
conceal me!

(Flavinda hides behind the tree.)

He's here . . . He turns . . . He casts about . . . He's lost the scent . . . He
gazes — this way, that way. . . . Let him feast his eyes on the fine faces —
taste 'em, sample 'em, say: "That's the fine lady I danced with . . . that I
lay with . . . that I kissed under the mistletoe . . ." Ha! How he spews 'em
out! Brave Valentine! How he casts his eyes upon the ground! How his
frowns become him! "Where's Flavinda?" he sighs. "She I love like the
heart in my breast." See him pull his watch out! "O faithless wretch!" he
sighs. See how he stamps the earth! Now turns on his heel. . . . He sees

me—no, the sun's in his eyes. Tears fill 'em ... Lord, how he fingers his sword! He'll run it through his breast like the Duke in the story book! ... Stop, Sir, stop!

(She reveals herself.)

VALENTINE. ... *O Flavinda, O!*
FLAVINDA. ... *O Valentine, O!*

(They embrace.)

The clock strikes nine.

"All that fuss about nothing!" a voice exclaimed. People laughed. The voice stopped. But the voice had seen; the voice had heard. For a moment Miss La Trobe behind her tree glowed with glory. The next, turning to the villagers who were passing in and out between the trees, she barked:
"Louder! Louder!"
For the stage was empty; the emotion must be continued; the only thing to continue the emotion was the song; and the words were inaudible.
"Louder! Louder!" She threatened them with her clenched fists.

Digging and delving (they sang), *hedging and ditching, we pass. ... Summer and winter, autumn and spring return ... All passes but we, all changes ... but we remain forever the same ...* (The breeze blew gaps between their words.)

"Louder, louder!" Miss La Trobe vociferated.

Palaces tumble down (they resumed), *Babylon, Nineveh, Troy ... And Caesar's great house ... all fallen they lie ... Where the plover nests was the arch ... through which the Romans trod ... Digging and delving*

we break with the share of the plough the clod . . . Where Clytemnestra
watched for her Lord . . . saw the beacons blaze on the hills . . . we see only
the clod . . . Digging and delving we pass. . . . and the Queen and the
Watch Tower fall . . . for Agamemnon has ridden away. . . . Clytemnestra
is nothing but. . . .

The words died away. Only a few great names—Babylon,
Nineveh, Clytemnestra, Agamemnon, Troy—floated across the
open space. Then the wind rose, and in the rustle of the leaves
even the great words became inaudible; and the audience sat staring at the villagers, whose mouths opened, but no sound came.

And the stage was empty. Miss La Trobe leant against the
tree, paralyzed. Her power had left her. Beads of perspiration
broke on her forehead. Illusion had failed. "This is death," she
murmured, "death."

Then suddenly, as the illusion petered out, the cows took up
the burden. One had lost her calf. In the very nick of time she
lifted her great moon-eyed head and bellowed. All the great
moon-eyed heads laid themselves back. From cow after cow
came the same yearning bellow. The whole world was filled with
dumb yearning. It was the primeval voice sounding loud in the
ear of the present moment. Then the whole herd caught the infection. Lashing their tails, blobbed like pokers, they tossed their
heads high, plunged and bellowed, as if Eros had planted his
dart in their flanks and goaded them to fury. The cows annihi-
lated the gap; bridged the distance; filled the emptiness and continued the emotion.

Miss La Trobe waved her hand ecstatically at the cows.

"Thank Heaven!" she exclaimed.

Suddenly the cows stopped; lowered their heads, and began
browsing. Simultaneously the audience lowered their heads and
read their programmes.

"The producer," Mrs. Elmhurst read out for her husband's

benefit, "craves the indulgence of the audience. Owing to lack of time a scene has been omitted; and she begs the audience to imagine that in the interval Sir Spaniel Lilyliver has contracted an engagement with Flavinda; who had been about to plight her troth; when Valentine, hidden inside the grandfather's clock, steps forward; claims Flavinda as his bride; reveals the plot to rob her of her inheritance; and, during the confusion that ensues, the lovers fly together, leaving Lady Harpy and Sir Spaniel alone together."

"We're asked to imagine all that," she said, putting down her glasses.

"That's very wise of her," said Mrs. Manresa, addressing Mrs. Swithin. "If she'd put it all in, we should have been here till midnight. So we've got to imagine, Mrs. Swithin." She patted the old lady on the knee.

"Imagine?" said Mrs. Swithin. "How right! Actors show us too much. The Chinese, you know, put a dagger on the table and that's a battle. And so Racine . . ."

"Yes, they bore one stiff," Mrs. Manresa interrupted, scenting culture, resenting the snub to the jolly human heart. "T'other day I took my nephew—such a jolly boy at Sandhurst—to *Pop Goes the Weasel.* Seen it?" She turned to Giles.

"Up and down the City Road," he hummed by way of an answer.

"Did your Nanny sing that!" Mrs. Manresa exclaimed. "Mine did. And when she said 'Pop' she made a noise like a cork being drawn from a ginger-beer bottle. Pop!"

She made the noise.

"Hush, hush," someone whispered.

"Now I'm being naughty and shocking your aunt," she said. "We must be good and attend. This is Scene Three. Lady Harpy Harraden's Closet. The sound of horses' hooves is heard in the distance."

The sound of horses' hooves, energetically represented by Albert the idiot with a wooden spoon on a tray, died away.

LADY H. H. *Half-way to Gretna Green already. O my deceitful niece! You that I rescued from the brine and stood on the hearthstone dripping! O that the whale had swallowed you whole! Perfidious porpoise, O! Didn't the Horn book teach you Honour thy Great Aunt? How have you misread it and misspelt it, learnt thieving and cheating and reading of wills in old boxes and hiding of rascals in honest time-pieces that have never missed a second since King Charles's day! O Flavinda! O porpoise, O!*

SIR S. L. (trying to pull on his jack boots). *Old—old—old. He called me "old"—"To your bed, old fool, and drink hot posset!"*

LADY H. H. *And she, stopping at the door and pointing the finger of scorn at me said "old," Sir—"woman" Sir—I that am in the prime of life and a lady!*

SIR S. L. (tugging at his boots). *But I'll be even with him. I'll have the law on 'em! I'll run 'em to earth . . .*

> (He hobbles up and down, one boot on, one boot off.)

LADY H. H. (laying her hand on his arm). *Have mercy on your gout, Sir Spaniel. Bethink you, Sir—let's not run mad, we that are on the sunny side of fifty. What's this youth they prate on? Nothing but a goose feather blown on a north wind. Sit you down, Sir Spaniel. Rest your leg—so——*

> (She pushes a cushion under his leg.)

SIR S. L. *"Old" he called me . . . jumping from the clock like a jack-in-the-box . . . And she, making mock of me, points to my leg and cries "Cupid's darts, Sir Spaniel, Cupid's darts." O that I could braise 'em in a mortar and serve 'em up smoking hot on the altar of—O my gout, O my gout!*

LADY H. H. *This talk, Sir, ill befits a man of sense. Bethink you, Sir, only t'other day you were invoking—ahem—the Constellations. Cassiopeia, Aldebaran; the Aurora Borealis . . . It's not to be denied that one of 'em has left her sphere, has shot, has eloped, to put it plainly, with the entrails of a time-piece, the mere pendulum of a grandfather's clock. But, Sir Spaniel, there are some stars that—ahem—stay fixed; that shine, to put it in a nutshell, never so bright as by a sea-coal fire on a brisk morning.*

SIR S. L. *O that I were five and twenty with a sharp sword at my side!*

LADY H. H. (bridling). *I take your meaning, Sir. Tee hee—To be sure, I regret it as you do. But youth's not all. To let you into a secret, I've passed the meridian myself. Am on t'other side of the Equator too. Sleep sound o' nights without turning. The dog days are over. . . . But bethink you, Sir. Where there's a will there's a way.*

SIR S. L. *God's truth Ma'am . . . ah my foot's like a burning, burning horseshoe on the devil's anvil ah!—What's your meaning?*

LADY H. H. *My meaning, Sir? Must I disrupt my modesty and un-quilt that which has been laid in lavender since my lord, peace be to his name—'tis twenty years since—was lapped in lead? In plain words, Sir, Flavinda's flown. The cage is empty. But we that have bound our wrists with cowslips might join 'em with a stouter chain. To have done with fal-lals and figures. Here am I, Asphodilla—but my plain name Sue. No matter what my name is—Asphodilla or Sue—here am I, hale and hearty, at your service. Now that the plot's out, Brother Bob's bounty must go to the virgins. That's plain. Here's Lawyer Quill's word for it. "Vir-gins . . . in perpetuity . . . sing for his soul." And I warrant you, he has need of it . . . But no matter. Though we have thrown that to the fishes that might have wrapped us in lamb's-wool, I'm no beggar. There's mes-suages; tenements; napery; cattle; my dowry; an inventory. I'll show you; engrossed on parchment; enough I'll warrant you to keep us handsomely, for what's to run of our time, as husband and wife.*

SIR S. L. *Husband and wife! So that's the plain truth of it! Why, Madam, I'd rather lash myself to a tar barrel, be bound to a thorn tree in a winter's gale. Faugh!*

LADY H. H. . . . *A tar barrel, quotha! A thorn tree—quotha! You that were harping on galaxies and milky ways! You that were swearing I outshone 'em all! A pox on you—you faithless! You shark, you! You serpent in jack boots, you! So you won't have me? Reject my hand do you?*

(She proffers her hand; he strikes it from him.)

SIR S. L. . . . *Hide your chalk stones in a woollen mit! pah! I'll none of 'em! Were they diamond, pure diamond, and half the habitable globe and all its concubines strung in string round your throat I'd none of it . . . none of it. Unhand me, scritch owl, witch, vampire! Let me go!*

LADY H. H. . . . *So all your fine words were tinsel wrapped round a Christmas cracker!*

SIR S. L. . . . *Bells hung on an ass's neck! Paper roses on a barber's pole . . . O my foot, my foot . . . Cupid's darts, she mocked me . . . Old, old, he called me old . . .*

(He hobbles away.)

LADY H. H. (left alone). *All gone. Following the wind. He's gone; she's gone; and the old clock that the rascal made himself into a pendulum for is the only one of 'em all to stop. A pox on 'em—turning an honest woman's house into a brothel. I that was Aurora Borealis am shrunk to a tar barrel. I that was Cassiopeia am turned to a she-ass. My head turns. There's no trusting man nor woman; nor fine speeches; nor fine looks. Off comes the sheep's skin; out creeps the serpent. Get ye to Gretna Green; couch on the wet grass and breed vipers. My head spins . . . Tar barrels, quotha. Cassiopeia . . . Chalk stones . . . Andromeda . . . Thorn trees. . . . Deb, I say, Deb.* (She holloas.) *Unlace me. I'm fit to burst . . . Bring me my green baize table and set the cards. . . . And my fur lined slippers, Deb. And a dish of chocolate. . . . I'll be even with 'em . . . I'll outlive 'em all . . . Deb, I say! Deb! A pox on the girl! Can't she hear me? Deb, I say, you gipsy's spawn that I snatched from the hedge and taught to sew samplers! Deb! Deb!*

(She throws open the door leading to the maid's closet.)

Empty! She's gone too!... Hist, what's that on the dresser?

(She picks up a scrap of paper and reads.)

"What care I for your goose-feather bed? I'm off with the raggle-taggle gipsies, O! Signed; Deborah, one time your maid." So! She that I fed on apple parings and crusts from my own table, she that I taught to play cribbage and sew chemises ... she's gone too. O ingratitude, thy name is Deborah! Who's to wash the dishes now; who's to bring me my posset now, suffer my temper and unlace my stays? ... All gone. I'm alone then. Sans niece, sans lover; and sans maid.

> *And so to end the play, the moral is,*
> *The God of love is full of tricks;*
> *Into the foot his dart he sticks,*
> *But the way of the will is plain to see;*
> *Let holy virgins hymn perpetually:*
> *"Where there's a will there's a way."*
> *Good people all, farewell.*

(Dropping a curtsey, Lady H. H. withdrew.)

The scene ended. Reason descended from her plinth. Gathering her robes about her, serenely acknowledging the applause of the audience, she passed across the stage; while Lords and Ladies in stars and garters followed after; Sir Spaniel limping escorted Lady Harraden smirking; and Valentine and Flavinda arm in arm bowed and curtsied.

"God's truth!" cried Bartholomew, catching the infection of the language. "There's a moral for you!"

He threw himself back in his chair and laughed, like a horse whinnying.

A moral. What? Giles supposed it was: Where there's a Will there's a Way. The words rose and pointed a finger of scorn at him. Off to Gretna Green with his girl; the deed done. Damn the consequences.

"Like to see the greenhouse?" he said abruptly, turning to Mrs. Manresa.

"Love to!" she exclaimed, and rose.

Was there an interval? Yes, the programme said so. The machine in the bushes went chuff, chuff, chuff. And the next scene?

"The Victorian Age," Mrs. Elmhurst read out. Presumably there was time then for a stroll round the gardens, even for a look over the house. Yet somehow they felt—how could one put it—a little not quite here or there. As if the play had jerked the ball out of the cup; as if what I call myself was still floating unattached, and didn't settle. Not quite themselves, they felt. Or was it simply that they felt clothes conscious? Skimpy out-of-date voile dresses; flannel trousers; panama hats; hats wreathed with raspberry-coloured net in the style of the Royal Duchess's hat at Ascot seemed flimsy somehow.

"How lovely the clothes were," said someone, casting a last look at Flavinda disappearing. "Most becoming. I wish . . ."

Chuff, chuff, chuff went the machine in the bushes, accurately, insistently.

Clouds were passing across the sky. The weather looked a little unsettled. Hogben's Folly was for a moment ashen white. Then the sun struck the gilt vane of Bolney Minster.

"Looks a little unsettled," said someone.

"Up you get . . . Let's stretch our legs," said another voice. Soon the lawns were floating with little moving islands of coloured dresses. Yet some of the audience remained seated.

"Major and Mrs. Mayhew," Page the reporter noted, licking his pencil. As for the play, he would collar Miss Whatshername and ask for a synopsis. But Miss La Trobe had vanished.

Down among the bushes she worked like a nigger. Flavinda was in her petticoats. Reason had thrown her mantle on a holly hedge. Sir Spaniel was tugging at his jack boots. Miss La Trobe was scattering and foraging.

"The Victorian mantle with the bead fringe ... Where is the damned thing? Chuck it here ... Now the whiskers ..."

Ducking up and down she cast her quick bird's eye over the bushes at the audience. The audience was on the move. The audience was strolling up and down. They kept their distance from the dressing-room; they respected the conventions. But if they wandered too far, if they began exploring the grounds, going over the house, then.... Chuff, chuff, chuff went the machine. Time was passing. How long would time hold them together? It was a gamble; a risk.... And she laid about her energetically, flinging clothes on the grass.

Over the tops of the bushes came stray voices, voices without bodies, symbolical voices they seemed to her, half hearing, seeing nothing, but still, over the bushes, feeling invisible threads connecting the bodiless voices.

"It all looks very black."

"No one wants it—save those damned Germans."

There was a pause.

"I'd cut down those trees ..."

"How they get their roses to grow!"

"They say there's been a garden here for five hundred years ..."

"Why, even old Gladstone, to do him justice ..."

Then there was silence. The voices passed the bushes. The trees rustled. Many eyes, Miss La Trobe knew, for every cell in her body was absorbent, looked at the view. Out of the corner of her eye she could see Hogben's Folly; then the vane flashed.

"The glass is falling," said a voice.

She could feel them slipping through her fingers, looking at the view.

"Where's that damned woman, Mrs. Rogers? Who's seen Mrs. Rogers?" she cried, snatching up a Victorian mantle.

Then, ignoring the conventions, a head popped up between the trembling sprays: Mrs. Swithin's.

"Oh Miss La Trobe!" she exclaimed; and stopped. Then she began again: "Oh Miss La Trobe, I do congratulate you!"

She hesitated. "You've given me..." She skipped, then alighted— "Ever since I was a child I've felt..." A film fell over her eyes, shutting off the present. She tried to recall her childhood; then gave it up; and, with a little wave of her hand, as if asking Miss La Trobe to help her out, continued: "This daily round; this going up and down stairs; this saying 'What am I going for? My specs? I have 'em on my nose.' ..."

She gazed at Miss La Trobe with a cloudless old-aged stare. Their eyes met in a common effort to bring a common meaning to birth. They failed; and Mrs. Swithin, laying hold desperately of a fraction of her meaning, said: "What a small part I've had to play! But you've made me feel I could have played .. Cleopatra!"

She nodded between the trembling bushes and ambled off.

The villagers winked. "Batty" was the word for Old Flimsy, breaking through the bushes.

"I might have been—Cleopatra," Miss La Trobe repeated. "You've stirred in me my unacted part," she meant.

"Now for the skirt, Mrs. Rogers," she said.

Mrs. Rogers stood grotesque in her black stockings. Miss La Trobe pulled the voluminous flounces of the Victorian age over her head. She tied the tapes. "You've twitched the invisible strings," was what the old lady meant; and revealed—of all people—Cleopatra! Glory possessed her. Ah, but she was not merely a twitcher of individual strings; she was one who seethes wandering bodies and floating voices in a cauldron, and makes rise up from its amorphous mass a re-created world. Her moment was on her—her glory.

"There!" she said, tying the black ribbons under Mrs. Rogers' chin. "That's done it! Now for the gentleman. Hammond!"

She beckoned Hammond. Sheepishly he came forward, and submitted to the application of black side whiskers. With his eyes half shut, his head leant back, he looked, Miss La Trobe thought, like King Arthur—noble, knightly, thin.

"Where's the Major's old frock coat?" she asked, trusting to the effect of that to transform him.

Tick, tick, tick, the machine continued. Time was passing. The audience was wandering, dispersing. Only the tick, tick of the gramophone held them together. There, sauntering solitary far away by the flower beds was Mrs. Giles escaping.

"The tune!" Miss La Trobe commanded. "Hurry up! The tune! The next tune! Number Ten!"

"Now may I pluck," Isa murmured, picking a rose, "my single flower. The white or the pink? And press it so, twixt thumb and finger. . . ."

She looked among the passing faces for the face of the man in grey. There he was for one second; but surrounded, inaccessible. And now vanished.

She dropped her flower. What single, separate leaf could she press? None. Nor stray by the beds alone. She must go on; and she turned in the direction of the stable.

"Where do I wander?" she mused. "Down what draughty tunnels? Where the eyeless wind blows? And there grows nothing for the eye. No rose. To issue where? In some harvestless dim field where no evening lets fall her mantle; nor sun rises. All's equal there. Unblowing, ungrowing are the roses there. Change is not; nor the mutable and lovable; nor greetings nor partings; nor furtive findings and feelings, where hand seeks hand and eye seeks shelter from the eye."

She had come into the stable yard where the dogs were chained; where the buckets stood; where the great pear tree spread its ladder of branches against the wall. The tree, whose roots went beneath the flags, was weighted with hard green pears. Fingering one of them she murmured: "How am I burdened with what they drew from the earth; memories; possessions. This is the burden that the past laid on me, last little donkey in the long caravanserai crossing the desert. 'Kneel down,' said the past. 'Fill your pannier from our tree. Rise up, donkey. Go your way till your heels blister and your hoofs crack.'"

The pear was hard as stone. She looked down at the cracked flags beneath which the roots spread. "That was the burden," she mused, "laid on me in the cradle; murmured by waves; breathed by restless elm trees; crooned by singing women; what we must remember: what we would forget."

She looked up. The gilt hands of the stable clock pointed inflexibly at two minutes to the hour. The clock was about to strike.

"Now comes the lightning," she muttered, "from the stone blue sky. The thongs are burst that the dead tied. Loosed are our possessions."

Voices interrupted. People passed the stable yard, talking.

"It's a good day, some say, the day we are stripped naked. Others, it's the end of the day. They see the Inn and the Inn's keeper. But none speaks with a single voice. None with a voice free from the old vibrations. Always I hear corrupt murmurs; the chink of gold and metal. Mad music...."

More voices sounded. The audience was streaming back to the terrace. She roused herself. She encouraged herself. "On, little donkey, patiently stumble. Hear not the frantic cries of the leaders who in that they seek to lead desert us. Nor the chatter of china faces glazed and hard. Hear rather the shepherd, coughing by the farmyard wall; the withered tree that sighs when the Rider gallops; the brawl in the barrack room when they stripped her naked; or the cry which in London when I thrust the window open someone cries . . ." She had come out on to the path that led past the greenhouse. The door was kicked open. Out came Mrs. Manresa and Giles. Unseen, Isa followed them across the lawns to the front row of seats.

The chuff, chuff, chuff of the machine in the bushes had stopped. In obedience to Miss La Trobe's command, another tune had been put on the gramophone. Number Ten. London street cries it was called. "A Pot Pourri."

"Lavender, sweet lavender, who'll buy my sweet lavender," the tune trilled and tinkled, ineffectively shepherding the audience. Some ignored it. Some still wandered. Others stopped, but stood upright. Some, like Colonel and Mrs. Mayhew, who had never left their seats, brooded over the blurred carbon sheet which had been issued for their information.

"The Nineteenth Century." Colonel Mayhew did not dispute the producer's right to skip two hundred years in less than fifteen minutes. But the choice of scenes baffled him.

"Why leave out the British Army? What's history without the Army, eh?" he mused. Inclining her head, Mrs. Mayhew protested after all one mustn't ask too much. Besides, very likely there would be a Grand Ensemble, round the Union Jack, to end with. Meanwhile, there was the view. They looked at the view.

"Sweet lavender . . . sweet lavender. . . ." Humming the tune old Mrs. Lynn Jones (of the Mount) pushed a chair forward.

"Here, Etty," she said, and plumped down, with Etty Springett, with whom, since both were widows now, she shared a house.

"I remember..." she nodded in time to the tune. "You remember too—how they used to cry it down the streets." They remembered—the curtains blowing, and the men crying: "All a blowing, all a growing," as they came with geraniums, sweet william, in pots, down the street.

"A harp, I remember, and a hansom and a growler. So quiet the street was then. Two for a hansom, was it? One for a growler? And Ellen, in cap and apron, whistling in the street? D'you remember? And the runners, my dear, who followed, all the way from the station, if one had a box."

The tune changed. "Any old iron, any old iron to sell?" "D'you remember? That was what the men shouted in the fog. Seven Dials they came from. Men with red handkerchiefs. Garrotters, did they call them? You couldn't walk—Oh, dear me, no—home from the play. Regent Street. Piccadilly. Hyde Park Corner. The loose women ... And everywhere loaves of bread in the gutter. The Irish you know round Covent Garden ... Coming back from a Ball, past the clock at Hyde Park Corner, d'you remember the feel of white gloves? ... My father remembered the old Duke in the Park. Two fingers like that—he'd touch his hat ... I've got my mother's album. A lake and two lovers. She'd copied out Byron, I suppose, in what was called then the Italian hand...."

"What's that? 'Knocked 'em in the Old Kent Road.' I remember the bootboy whistled it. Oh, my dear, the servants ... Old Ellen ... Sixteen pound a year wages ... And the cans of hot water! And the crinolines! And the stays! D'you remember the Crystal Palace, and the fireworks, and how Mira's slipper got lost in the mud?"

"That's young Mrs. Giles ... I remember her mother. She died in India ... We wore, I suppose, a great many petticoats then. Unhygienic? I dare say ... Well, look at my daughter. To the right, just behind you. Forty, but slim as a wand. Each flat has its refrigerator ... It took my mother half the morning to order dinner. ... We were eleven. Counting servants, eighteen in family. ... Now they simply ring up the Stores ... That's Giles coming, with Mrs. Manresa. She's a type I don't myself fancy. I may be wrong ... And Colonel Mayhew, as spruce as ever ... And Mr. Cobbet of Cobbs Corner, there, under the monkey puzzle tree. One don't see him often ... That's what's so nice— it brings people together. These days, when we're all so busy, that's what one wants ... The programme? Have you got it? Let's see what comes next ... The Nineteenth Century ... Look, there's the chorus, the villagers, coming on now, between the trees. First, there's a prologue. ..."

A great box, draped in red baize festooned with heavy gold tassels, had been moved into the middle of the stage. There was a swish of dresses, a stir of chairs. The audience seated themselves, hastily, guiltily. Miss La Trobe's eye was on them. She gave them ten seconds to settle their faces. Then she flicked her hand. A pompous march tune brayed. "Firm, elatant, bold and blatant," etc. ... And once more a huge symbolical figure emerged from the bushes. It was Budge the publican; but so disguised that even cronies who drank with him nightly failed to recognize him; and a little titter of enquiry as to his identity ran about among the villagers. He wore a long black many-caped cloak; waterproof; shiny; of the substance of a statue in Parliament Square; a helmet which suggested a policeman; a row of medals crossed his breast; and in his right hand he held extended a special constable's baton (loaned by Mr. Willert of the Hall). It was his voice, husky and rusty, issuing from a thick black cotton-wool beard that gave him away.

"Budge, Budge. That's Mr. Budge," the audience whispered. Budge extended his truncheon and spoke:

It ain't an easy job, directing the traffic at 'Yde Park Corner. Buses and 'ansom cabs. All a-clatter on the cobbles. Keep to the right, can't you? Hi there, Stop!

(He waved his truncheon.)

There she goes, the old party with the umbrella right under the 'orse's nose.

(The truncheon pointed markedly at Mrs. Swithin.)

She raised her skinny hand as if in truth she had fluttered off the pavement on the impulse of the moment to the just rage of authority. Got her, Giles thought, taking sides with authority against his aunt.

Fog or fine weather, I does my duty (Budge continued). *At Piccadilly Circus; at 'Yde Park Corner, directing the traffic of 'Er Majesty's Empire. The Shah of Persia; Sultan of Morocco; or it may be 'Er Majesty in person; or Cook's tourists; black men; white men; sailors, soldiers; crossing the ocean; to proclaim her Empire; all of 'em Obey the Rule of my truncheon.*

(He flourished it magnificently from right to left.)

But my job don't end there. I take under my protection and direction the purity and security of all Her Majesty's minions; in all parts of her dominions; insist that they obey the laws of God and Man.

The laws of God and Man (he repeated and made as if to consult a Statute; engrossed on a sheet of parchment which with great deliberation he now produced from his trouser pocket.)

Go to Church on Sunday; on Monday, nine sharp, catch the City Bus. On Tuesday it may be, attend a meeting at the Mansion House for the redemption of the sinner; at dinner on Wednesday attend another—turtle soup. Some bother it may be in Ireland; Famine. Fenians. What not. On Thursday it's the natives of Peru require protection and correction; we give 'em what's due. But mark you, our rule don't end there. It's a Christian country, our Empire; under the White Queen Victoria. Over thought and religion; drink; dress; manners; marriage too, I wield my truncheon. Prosperity and respectability always go, as we know, 'and in 'and. The ruler of an Empire must keep his eye on the cot; spy too in the kitchen; drawing-room; library; wherever one or two, me and you, come together. Purity our watchword; prosperity and respectability. If not, why, let 'em fester in . . .

(He paused—no, he had not forgotten his words.)

Cripplegate; St. Giles's; Whitechapel; the Minories. Let 'em sweat at the mines; cough at the looms; rightly endure their lot. That's the price of Empire; that's the white man's burden. And, I can tell you, to direct the traffic orderly, at 'Yde Park Corner, Piccadilly Circus, is a whole-time, white man's job.

He paused, eminent, dominant, glaring from his pedestal. A very fine figure of a man he was, everyone agreed, his truncheon extended; his waterproof pendant. It only wanted a shower of rain, a flight of pigeons round his head, and the pealing bells of St. Paul's and the Abbey to transform him into the very spit and image of a Victorian constable; and to transport them to a foggy London afternoon, with the muffin bells ringing and the church bells pealing at the very height of Victorian prosperity.

There was a pause. The voices of the pilgrims singing, as they wound in and out between the trees, could be heard; but the words were inaudible. The audience sat waiting.

"Tut-tut-tut," Mrs. Lynn Jones expostulated. "There were grand men among them . . ." Why she did not know, yet somehow she felt that a sneer had been aimed at her father; therefore at herself.

Etty Springett tutted too. Yet, children did draw trucks in mines; there was the basement; yet Papa read Walter Scott aloud after dinner; and divorced ladies were not received at Court. How difficult to come to any conclusion! She wished they would hurry on with the next scene. She liked to leave a theatre knowing exactly what was meant. Of course this was only a village play. . . . They were setting another scene, round the red baize box. She read out from her programme:

"The Picnic Party. About 1860. Scene: A Lake. Characters——"

She stopped. A sheet had been spread on the Terrace. It was a lake apparently. Roughly painted ripples represented water. Those green stakes were bulrushes. Rather prettily, real swallows darted across the sheet.

"Look, Minnie!" she exclaimed. "Those are real swallows!"

"Hush, hush," she was admonished. For the scene had begun. A young man in peg-top trousers and side whiskers carrying a spiked stick appeared by the lake.

EDGAR T. . . . *Let me help you, Miss Hardcastle! There!*

(He helps Miss Eleanor Hardcastle, a young lady in crinoline and mushroom hat, to the top. They stand for a moment panting slightly, looking at the view.)

ELEANOR. *How small the Church looks down among the trees!*

EDGAR. . . . *So this is Wanderer's Well, the trysting place.*

ELEANOR. . . . *Please Mr. Thorold, finish what you were saying before the others come. You were saying, "Our aim in life . . ."*

EDGAR. . . . *Should be to help our fellow men.*

ELEANOR (sighing deeply). *How true—how profoundly true!*

EDGAR. . . . *Why sigh, Miss Hardcastle?—You have nothing to reproach yourself with—you whose whole life is spent in the service of others. It was of myself that I was thinking. I am no longer young. At twenty-four the best days of life are over. My life has passed* (he throws a pebble on to the lake) *like a ripple in water.*

ELEANOR. *Oh Mr. Thorold, you do not know me. I am not what I seem. I too*——

EDGAR. *. . . Do not tell me, Miss Hardcastle—no, I cannot believe it— You have doubted?*

ELEANOR. *Thank Heaven not that, not that . . . But safe and sheltered as I am, always at home, protected as you see me, as you think me. O what am I saying? But yes, I will speak the truth, before Mama comes. I too have longed to convert the heathen!*

EDGAR. *. . . Miss Hardcastle . . . Eleanor . . . You tempt me! Dare I ask you? No—so young, so fair, so innocent. Think, I implore you, before you answer.*

ELEANOR. *. . . I have thought—on my knees!*

EDGAR (taking a ring from his pocket). *Then. . . . My mother with her last breath charged me to give this ring only to one to whom a lifetime in the African desert among the heathens would be*——

ELEANOR (taking the ring). *Perfect happiness! But hist!* (She slips the ring into her pocket.) *Here's Mama!* (They start asunder.)

(Enter Mrs. Hardcastle, a stout lady in black bombazine, upon a donkey, escorted by an elderly gentleman in a deer-stalker's cap.)

MRS. H. *. . . So you stole a march upon us, young people. There was a time, Sir John, when you and I were always first on top, Now . . .*

(He helps her to alight. Children, young men, young women, some carrying hampers, others butterfly nets, others spy-glasses, others tin botanical cases, arrive. A rug is thrown by the lake and Mrs. H. and Sir John seat themselves on camp stools.)

MRS. H. *. . . Now who'll fill the kettles? Who'll gather the sticks? Alfred* (to a small boy), *don't run about chasing butterflies or you'll*

make yourself sick ... Sir John and I will unpack the hampers, here
where the grass is burnt, where we had the picnic last year.

(The young people scatter off in different directions.
Mrs. H. and Sir John begin to unpack the hamper.)

MRS. H. ... *Last year poor dear Mr. Beach was with us. It was a*
blessed release. (She takes out a black-bordered handkerchief and
wipes her eyes.) *Every year one of us is missing. That's the ham ...*
That's the grouse ... There in that packet are the game pasties ... (She
spreads the eatables on the grass.) *As I was saying poor dear Mr.*
Beach ... I do hope the cream hasn't curdled. Mr. Hardcastle is bringing
the claret. I always leave that to him. Only when Mr. Hardcastle gets talk-
ing with Mr. Pigott about the Romans ... last year they quite came to
words. ... But it's nice for gentlemen to have a hobby, though they do gather
the dust—those skulls and things. ... But I was saying—— poor dear
Mr. Beach. ... I wanted to ask you (she drops her voice) *as a friend*
of the family, about the new clergyman—they can't hear us, can they? No,
they're picking up sticks. ... Last year, such a disappointment. Just got the
things out ... down came the rain. But I wanted to ask you, about the new
clergyman, the one who's come in place of dear Mr. Beach. I'm told the
name's Sibthorp. To be sure, I hope I'm right, for I had a cousin who mar-
ried a girl of that name, and as a friend of the family, we don't stand on
ceremony ... And when one has daughters—I'm sure I quite envy you,
with only one daughter, Sir John, and I have four! So I was asking you to
tell me in confidence, about this young—if that's-his-name—Sibthorp, for
I must tell you the day before yesterday our Mrs. Potts happened to say, as
she passed the Rectory, bringing our laundry, they were unpacking the fur-
niture; and what did she see on top of the wardrobe? A tea cosy! But of
course she might be mistaken ... But it occurred to me to ask you, as a
friend of the family, in confidence, has Mr. Sibthorp a wife?

Here a chorus composed of villagers in Victorian mantles,
side whiskers and top hats sang in concert:

O has Mr. Sibthorp a wife? O has Mr. Sibthorp a wife? That is the hornet, the bee in the bonnet, the screw in the cork and the drill; that whirling and twirling are for ever unfurling the folds of the motherly heart; for a mother must ask, if daughters she has, begot in the feathery billowy fourposter family bed, O did he unpack, with his prayer book and bands; his gown and his cane; his rod and his line; and the family album and gun; did he also display the connubial respectable tea-table token, a cosy with honeysuckle embossed. Has Mr. Sibthorp a wife? O has Mr. Sibthorp a wife?

While the chorus was sung, the picnickers assembled. Corks popped. Grouse, ham, chickens were sliced. Lips munched. Glasses were drained. Nothing was heard but the chump of jaws and the chink of glasses.

"They did eat," Mrs. Lynn Jones whispered to Mrs. Springett. "That's true. More than was good for them, I dare say."

MR. HARDCASTLE . . . (brushing flakes of meat from his whiskers). *Now . . .*

"Now what?" whispered Mrs. Springett, anticipating further travesty.

Now that we have gratified the inner man, let us gratify the desire of the spirit. I call upon one of the young ladies for a song.
CHORUS OF YOUNG LADIES . . . *O not me . . . not me . . . I really couldn't . . . No, you cruel thing, you know I've lost my voice . . . I can't sing without the instrument . . . etc., etc.*
CHORUS OF YOUNG MEN. *O bosh! Let's have "The Last Rose of Summer." Let's have "I Never Loved a Dear Gazelle."*
MRS. H. (authoritatively). *Eleanor and Mildred will now sing "I'd be a Butterfly."*

(Eleanor and Mildred rise obediently and sing a duet: "I'd be a Butterfly.")

MRS. H. *Thank you very much, my dears. And now gentlemen, Our Country!*

(Arthur and Edgar sing "Rule, Britannia.")

MRS. H. . . . *Thank you very much. Mr. Hardcastle——*

MR. HARDCASTLE (rising to his feet, clasping his fossil). *Let us pray.*

(The whole company rise to their feet.)

"This is too much, too much," Mrs. Springett protested.

MR. H. . . . *Almighty God, giver of all good things, we thank Thee: for our food and drink; for the beauties of Nature; for the understanding with which Thou hast enlightened us* (he fumbled with his fossil). *And for thy great gift of Peace. Grant us to be thy servants on earth; grant us to spread the light of thy . . .*

Here the hindquarters of the donkey, represented by Albert the idiot, became active. Intentional was it, or accidental? "Look at the donkey! Look at the donkey!" A titter drowned Mr. Hardcastle's prayer; and then he was heard saying:

. . . a happy homecoming with bodies refreshed by thy bounty, and minds inspired by thy wisdom. Amen.

Holding his fossil in front of him, Mr. Hardcastle marched off. The donkey was captured; hampers were loaded; and forming into a procession, the picnickers began to disappear over the hill.

EDGAR (winding up the procession with Eleanor). *To convert the heathen!*

ELEANOR. *To help our fellow men!*

(The actors disappeared into the bushes.)

BUDGE.... *It's time, gentlemen, time ladies, time to pack up and be gone. From where I stand, truncheon in hand, guarding respectability, and prosperity, and the purity of Victoria's land, I see before me*—(he pointed: there was Pointz Hall; the rooks cawing; the smoke rising)—

'Ome, Sweet 'Ome.

The gramophone took up the strain: *Through pleasures and palaces, etc. There's no place like Home.*

BUDGE.... *Home, gentlemen; home, ladies, it's time to pack up and go home. Don't I see the fire* (he pointed: one window blazed red) *blazing ever higher? In kitchen; and nursery; drawing-room and library? That's the fire of 'Ome. And see! Our Jane has brought the tea. Now children where's the toys? Mama, your knitting, quick. For here* (he swept his truncheon at Cobbet of Cobbs Corner) *comes the bread-winner, home from the city, home from the counter, home from the shop. "Mama, a cup o' tea." "Children, gather round my knee. I will read aloud. Which shall it be? Sindbad the sailor? Or some simple tale from the Scriptures? And show you the pictures? What none of 'em? Then out with the bricks. Let's build: A conservatory? A laboratory? A mechanics' institute? Or shall it be a tower; with our flag on top; where our widowed Queen, after tea, calls the Royal orphans round her knee? For it's 'Ome, ladies, 'Ome, gentlemen. Be it never so humble, there's no place like 'Ome."*

The gramophone warbled Home, Sweet Home, and Budge, swaying slightly, descended from his box and followed the procession off the stage.

There was an interval.

"Oh but it was beautiful," Mrs. Lynn Jones protested. Home she meant; the lamplit room; the ruby curtains; and Papa reading aloud.

They were rolling up the lake and uprooting the bulrushes.

Real swallows were skimming over real grass. But she still saw the home.

"It was . . ." she repeated, referring to the home.

"Cheap and nasty, I call it," snapped Etty Springett, referring to the play, and shot a vicious glance at Dodge's green trousers, yellow spotted tie, and unbuttoned waistcoat.

But Mrs. Lynn Jones still saw the home. Was there, she mused, as Budge's red baize pediment was rolled off, something—not impure, that wasn't the word—but perhaps "unhygienic" about the home? Like a bit of meat gone sour, with whiskers, as the servants called it? Or why had it perished? Time went on and on like the hands of the kitchen clock. (The machine chuffed in the bushes.) If they had met with no resistance, she mused, nothing wrong, they'd still be going round and round and round. The Home would have remained; and Papa's beard, she thought, would have grown and grown; and Mama's knitting—what did she do with all her knitting?—Change had to come, she said to herself, or there'd have been yards and yards of Papa's beard, of Mama's knitting. Nowadays her son-in-law was clean shaven. Her daughter had a refrigerator. . . . Dear, how my mind wanders, she checked herself. What she meant was, change had to come, unless things were perfect; in which case she supposed they resisted Time. Heaven was changeless.

"Were they like that?" Isa asked abruptly. She looked at Mrs. Swithin as if she had been a dinosaur or a very diminutive mammoth. Extinct she must be, since she had lived in the reign of Queen Victoria.

Tick, tick, tick, went the machine in the bushes.

"The Victorians," Mrs. Swithin mused. "I don't believe," she said with her odd little smile, "that there ever were such people. Only you and me and William dressed differently."

"You don't believe in history," said William.

The stage remained empty. The cows moved in the field. The shadows were deeper under the trees.

Mrs. Swithin caressed her cross. She gazed vaguely at the view. She was off, they guessed, on a circular tour of the imagination—one-making. Sheep, cows, grass, trees, ourselves—all are one. If discordant, producing harmony—if not to us, to a gigantic ear attached to a gigantic head. And thus—she was smiling benignly—the agony of the particular sheep, cow, or human being is necessary; and so—she was beaming seraphically at the gilt vane in the distance—we reach the conclusion that *all* is harmony, could we hear it. And we shall. Her eyes now rested on the white summit of a cloud. Well, if the thought gave her comfort, William and Isa smiled across her, let her think it.

Tick, tick, tick the machine reiterated.

"D'you get her meaning?" said Mrs. Swithin alighting suddenly. "Miss La Trobe's?"

Isa, whose eyes had been wandering, shook her head.

"But you might say the same of Shakespeare," said Mrs. Swithin.

"Shakespeare and the musical glasses!" Mrs. Manresa intervened. "Dear, what a barbarian you all make me feel!"

She turned to Giles. She invoked his help against this attack upon the jolly human heart.

"Tosh," Giles muttered.

Nothing whatever appeared on the stage.

Darts of red and green light flashed from the rings on Mrs. Manresa's fingers. He looked from them at Aunt Lucy. From her to William Dodge. From him to Isa. She refused to meet his eyes. And he looked down at his blood-stained tennis shoes.

He said (without words), "I'm damnably unhappy."

"So am I," Dodge echoed.

"And I too," Isa thought.

They were all caught and caged; prisoners; watching a spectacle. Nothing happened. The tick of the machine was maddening.

"On, little donkey," Isa murmured, "crossing the desert . . . bearing your burden . . ."

She felt Dodge's eye upon her as her lips moved. Always some cold eye crawled over the surface like a winter blue-bottle! She flicked him off.

"What a time they take!" she exclaimed irritably.

"Another interval," Dodge read out, looking at the programme.

"And after that, what?" asked Lucy.

"Present Time. Ourselves," he read.

"Let's hope to God that's the end," said Giles gruffly.

"Now you're being naughty," Mrs. Manresa reproved her little boy, her surly hero.

No one moved. There they sat, facing the empty stage, the cows, the meadows and the view, while the machine ticked in the bushes.

"What's the object," said Bartholomew, suddenly rousing himself, "of this entertainment?"

"The profits," Isa read out from her blurred carbon copy, "are to go to a fund for installing electric light in the Church."

"All our village festivals," Mr. Oliver snorted turning to Mrs. Manresa, "end with a demand for money."

"Of course, of course," she murmured, deprecating his severity, and the coins in her bead bag jingled.

"Nothing's done for nothing in England," the old man continued. Mrs. Manresa protested. It might be true, perhaps, of the Victorians; but surely not of ourselves? Did she really believe that we were disinterested? Mr. Oliver demanded.

"Oh you don't know my husband!" the wild child exclaimed, striking an attitude.

Admirable woman! You could trust her to crow when the

hour struck like an alarm clock; to stop like an old bus horse when the bell rang. Oliver said nothing. Mrs. Manresa had out her mirror and attended to her face.

All their nerves were on edge. They sat exposed. The machine ticked. There was no music. The horns of cars on the high road were heard. And the swish of trees. They were neither one thing nor the other; neither Victorians nor themselves. They were suspended, without being, in limbo. Tick, tick, tick went the machine.

Isa fidgeted; glancing to right and to left over her shoulder.

"Four and twenty blackbirds, strung upon a string," she muttered.

"Down came an Ostrich, an eagle, an executioner,
'Which of you is ripe,' he said, 'to bake in my pie?
Which of you is ripe, which of you is ready,
Come my pretty gentleman,
Come my pretty lady.' . . ."

How long was she going to keep them waiting? "The Present Time. Ourselves." They read it on the programme. Then they read what came next: "The profits are to go to a fund for installing electric light in the Church." Where was the Church? Over there. You could see the spire among the trees.

"Ourselves. . . ." They returned to the programme. But what could she know about ourselves? The Elizabethans, yes; the Victorians, perhaps; but ourselves; sitting here on a June day in 1939—it was ridiculous. "Myself"—it was impossible. Other people, perhaps . . . Cobbet of Cobbs Corner; the Major; old Bartholomew; Mrs. Swithin—them, perhaps. But she won't get me—no, not me. The audience fidgeted. Sounds of laughter came from the bushes. But nothing whatsoever appeared on the stage.

"What's she keeping us waiting for?" Colonel Mayhew asked irritably. "They don't need to dress up if it's present time."

Mrs. Mayhew agreed. Unless of course she was going to end with a Grand Ensemble. Army; Navy; Union Jack; and behind them perhaps—Mrs. Mayhew sketched what she would have done had it been her pageant—the Church. In cardboard. One window, looking east, brilliantly illuminated to symbolize—she could work that out when the time came.

"There she is, behind the tree," she whispered, pointing at Miss La Trobe.

Miss La Trobe stood there with her eye on her script. "After Vic.," she had written, "try ten mins. of present time. Swallows, cows, etc." She wanted to expose them, as it were, to douche them, with present-time reality. But something was going wrong with the experiment. "Reality too strong," she muttered. "Curse 'em!" She felt everything they felt. Audiences were the devil. O to write a play without an audience—*the* play. But here she was fronting her audience. Every second they were slipping the noose. Her little game had gone wrong. If only she'd a back-cloth to hang between the trees—to shut out cows, swallows, present time! But she had nothing. She had forbidden music. Grating her fingers in the bark, she damned the audience. Panic seized her. Blood seemed to pour from her shoes. This is death, death, death, she noted in the margin of her mind; when illusion fails. Unable to lift her hand, she stood facing the audience.

And then the shower fell, sudden, profuse.

No one had seen the cloud coming. There it was, black, swollen, on top of them. Down it poured like all the people in the world weeping. Tears. Tears. Tears.

"O that our human pain could here have ending!" Isa murmured. Looking up she received two great blots of rain full in her face. They trickled down her cheeks as if they were her own tears. But they were all people's tears, weeping for all people. Hands were raised. Here and there a parasol opened. The rain was sudden and universal. Then it stopped. From the grass rose a fresh earthy smell.

"That's done it," sighed Miss La Trobe, wiping away the drops on her cheeks. Nature once more had taken her part. The risk she had run acting in the open air was justified. She brandished her script. Music began—A.B.C.—A.B.C. The tune was as simple as could be. But now that the shower had fallen, it was the other voice speaking, the voice that was no one's voice. And the voice that wept for human pain unending said:

> *The King is in his counting house*
> *Counting out his money,*
> *The Queen is in her parlour . . .*

"O that my life could here have ending," Isa murmured (taking care not to move her lips). Readily would she endow this voice with all her treasure if so be tears could be ended. The little twist of sound could have the whole of her. On the altar of the rain-soaked earth she laid down her sacrifice. . . .

"O look!" she cried aloud.

That was a ladder. And that (a cloth roughly painted) was a wall. And that a man with a hod on his back. Mr. Page the reporter, licking his pencil, noted: "With the very limited means at her disposal, Miss La Trobe conveyed to the audience Civilization (the wall) in ruins; rebuilt (witness man with hod) by human effort; witness also woman handing bricks. Any fool could grasp that. Now issued black man in fuzzy wig; coffee-coloured ditto in silver turban; they signify presumably the League of . . ."

A burst of applause greeted this flattering tribute to ourselves. Crude of course. But then she had to keep expenses down. A painted cloth must convey—what the *Times* and *Telegraph* both said in their leaders that very morning.

The tune hummed:

> *The King is in his counting house*
> *Counting out his money,*
> *The Queen is in her parlour*
> *Eating . . .*

Suddenly the tune stopped. The tune changed. A waltz, was it? Something half known, half not. The swallows danced it. Round and round, in and out they skimmed. Real swallows. Retreating and advancing. And the trees, O the trees, how gravely and sedately like senators in council, or the spaced pillars of some cathedral church. . . . Yes, they barred the music, and massed and hoarded; and prevented what was fluid from overflowing. The swallows—or martins were they?—The temple-haunting martins who come, have always come . . . Yes, perched on the wall, they seemed to foretell what after all the *Times* was saying yesterday. Homes will be built. Each flat with its refrigerator, in the crannied wall. Each of us a free man; plates washed by machinery; not an aeroplane to vex us; all liberated; made whole. . . .

The tune changed; snapped; broke; jagged. Fox-trot, was it? Jazz? Anyhow the rhythm kicked, reared, snapped short. What a jangle and a jingle! Well, with the means at her disposal, you can't ask too much. What a cackle, a cacophony! Nothing ended. So abrupt. And corrupt. Such an outrage; such an insult; And not plain. Very up to date, all the same. What is her game? To disrupt? Jog and trot? Jerk and smirk? Put the finger to the nose? Squint and pry? Peak and spy? O the irreverence of the generation which is only momentarily—thanks be—"the young." The young, who can't make, but only break; shiver into splinters the old vision; smash to atoms what was whole. What a cackle, what a rattle, what a yaffle—as they call the woodpecker, the laughing bird that flits from tree to tree.

Look! Out they come, from the bushes—the riff-raff. Children? Imps—elves—demons. Holding what? Tin cans? Bedroom candlesticks? Old jars? My dear, that's the cheval glass from the Rectory! And the mirror—that I lent her. My mother's. Cracked. What's the notion? Anything that's bright enough to reflect, presumably, ourselves?

Ourselves! Ourselves!

Out they leapt, jerked, skipped. Flashing, dazzling, dancing, jumping. Now old Bart . . . he was caught. Now Manresa. Here a nose . . . There a skirt . . . Then trousers only . . . Now perhaps a face. . . . Ourselves? But that's cruel. To snap us as we are, before we've had time to assume . . . And only, too, in parts. . . . That's what's so distorting and upsetting and utterly unfair.

Mopping, mowing, whisking, frisking, the looking-glasses darted, flashed, exposed. People in the back rows stood up to see the fun. Down they sat, caught themselves . . . What an awful show-up! Even for the old who, one might suppose, hadn't any longer any care about their faces. . . . And Lord! the jangle and the din! The very cows joined in. Walloping, tail lashing, the reticence of nature was undone, and the barriers which should divide Man the Master from the Brute were dissolved. Then the dogs joined in. Excited by the uproar, scurrying and worrying, here they came! Look at them! And the hound, the Afghan hound . . . look at him!

Then once more, in the uproar which by this time has passed quite beyond control, behold Miss Whatshername behind the tree summoned from the bushes—or was it *they* who broke away—Queen Bess; Queen Anne; and the girl in the Mall; and the Age of Reason; and Budge the policeman. Here they came. And the Pilgrims. And the lovers. And the grandfather's clock. And the old man with a beard. They all appeared. What's more, each declaimed some phrase or fragment from their parts. . . . *I am not* (said one) *in my perfect mind* . . . Another,

Reason am I . . . And I? I'm the old top hat. . . . Home is the hunter,
home from the hill . . . Home? Where the miner sweats, and the maiden
faith is rudely strumpeted. . . . Sweet and low; sweet and low, wind of the
western sea . . . Is that a dagger that I see before me? . . . The owl hoots
and the ivy mocks tap-tap-tapping on the pane. . . . Lady I love till I die,
leave thy chamber and come . . . Where the worm weaves its winding
sheet . . . I'd be a butterfly. I'd be a butterfly. . . . In thy will is our
peace. . . . Here, Papa, take your book and read aloud. . . . Hark, hark,
the dogs do bark and the beggars . . .

It was the cheval glass that proved too heavy. Young Bon-
thorp for all his muscle couldn't lug the damned thing about any
longer. He stopped. So did they all—hand glasses, tin cans,
scraps of scullery glass, harness room glass, and heavily embossed silver mirrors—all stopped. And the audience saw
themselves, not whole by any means, but at any rate sitting still.

The hands of the clock had stopped at the present moment.
It was now. Ourselves.

So that was her little game! To show us up, as we are, here
and how. All shifted, preened, minced; hands were raised, legs
shifted. Even Bart, even Lucy, turned away. All evaded or
shaded themselves—save Mrs. Manresa who, facing herself in
the glass, used it as a glass; had out her mirror; powdered her
nose; and moved one curl, disturbed by the breeze, to its place.

"Magnificent!" cried old Bartholomew. Alone she preserved
unashamed her identity, and faced without blinking herself.
Calmly she reddened her lips.

The mirror bearers squatted; malicious; observant; expec-
tant; expository.

"That's them," the back rows were tittering. "Must we sub-
mit passively to this malignant indignity?" the front row demanded. Each turned ostensibly to say—O whatever came
handy—to his neighbour. Each tried to shift an inch or two beyond the inquisitive insulting eye. Some made as if to go.

"The play's over, I take it," muttered Colonel Mayhew, retrieving his hat. "It's time..."

But before they had come to any common conclusion, a voice asserted itself. Whose voice it was no one knew. It came from the bushes—a megaphonic, anonymous, loud-speaking affirmation. The voice said:

Before we part, ladies and gentlemen, before we go... (Those who had risen sat down) *... let's talk in words of one syllable, without larding, stuffing or cant. Let's break the rhythm and forget the rhyme. And calmly consider ourselves. Ourselves. Some bony. Some fat.* (The glasses confirmed this.) *Liars most of us. Thieves too.* (The glasses made no comment on that.) *The poor are as bad as the rich are. Perhaps worse. Don't hide among rags. Or let our cloth protect us. Or for the matter of that book learning; or skilful practice on pianos; or laying on of paint. Or presume there's innocency in childhood. Consider the sheep. Or faith in love. Consider the dogs. Or virtue in those that have grown white hairs. Consider the gun slayers, bomb droppers here or there. They do openly what we do slyly. Take for example* (here the megaphone adopted a colloquial, conversational tone) *Mr. M's bungalow. A view spoilt for ever. That's murder.... Or Mrs. E's lipstick and blood-red nails.... A tyrant, remember, is half a slave. Item the vanity of Mr. H. the writer, scraping in the dunghill for sixpenny fame... Then there's the amiable condescension of the lady of the manor—the upper class manner. And buying shares in the market to sell 'em.... O we're all the same. Take myself now. Do I escape my own reprobation, simulating indignation, in the bush, among the leaves? There's a rhyme, to suggest, in spite of protestation and the desire for immolation, I too have had some, what's called, education... Look at ourselves, ladies and gentlemen! Then at the wall; and ask how's this wall, the great wall, which we call, perhaps miscall, civilization, to be built by* (here the mirrors flicked and flashed) *orts, scraps and fragments like ourselves?*

All the same here I change (by way of the rhyme mark ye) to a loftier strain—there's something to be said: for our kindness to the cat; note too in today's paper "Dearly loved by his wife"; and the impulse which leads us—mark you, when no one's looking—to the window at midnight to smell the bean. Or the resolute refusal of some pimpled dirty little scrub in sandals to sell his soul. There is such a thing—you can't deny it. What? You can't descry it? All you can see of yourselves is scraps, orts and fragments? Well then listen to the gramophone affirming. . . .

A hitch occurred here. The records had been mixed. Foxtrot, Sweet Lavender, Home Sweet Home, Rule Britannia—sweating profusely, Jimmy, who had charge of the music, threw them aside and fitted the right one—was it Bach, Handel, Beethoven, Mozart or nobody famous, but merely a traditional tune? Anyhow, thank heaven, it was somebody speaking after the anonymous bray of the infernal megaphone.

Like quicksilver sliding, filings magnetized, the distracted united. The tune began; the first note meant a second; the second a third. Then down beneath a force was born in opposition; then another. On different levels they diverged. On different levels ourselves went forward; flower gathering some on the surface; others descending to wrestle with the meaning; but all comprehending; all enlisted. The whole population of the mind's immeasurable profundity came flocking; from the unprotected, the unskinned; and dawn rose; and azure; from chaos and cacophony measure; but not the melody of surface sound alone controlled it; but also the warring battle-plumed warriors straining asunder: To part? No. Compelled from the ends of the horizon; recalled from the edge of appalling crevasses; they crashed; solved; united. And some relaxed their fingers; and other uncrossed their legs.

Was that voice ourselves? Scraps, orts and fragments, are we, also, that? The voice died away.

As waves withdrawing uncover; as mist uplifting reveals; so, raising their eyes (Mrs. Manresa's were wet; for an instant tears ravaged her powder) they saw, as waters withdrawing leave vis-

ible a tramp's old boot, a man in a clergyman's collar surreptitiously mounting a soap-box.

"The Rev. G. W. Streatfield," the reporter licked his pencil
and noted, "then spoke . . ."

All gazed. What an intolerable constriction, contraction,
and reduction to simplified absurdity he was to be sure! Of all
incongruous sights a clergyman in the livery of his servitude to
the summing up was the most grotesque and entire. He opened
his mouth. O Lord, protect and preserve us from words the de-
filers, from words the impure! What need have we of words to
remind us? Must I be Thomas, you Jane?

As if a rook had hopped unseen to a prominent bald
branch, he touched his collar and hemmed his preliminary
croak. One fact mitigated the horror; his forefinger, raised in
the customary manner, was stained with tobacco juice. He
wasn't such a bad fellow; the Rev. G. W. Streatfield; a piece of
traditional church furniture; a corner cupboard; or the top beam
of a gate, fashioned by generations of village carpenters after
some lost-in-the-mists-of-antiquity model.

He looked at the audience; then up at the sky. The whole
lot of them, gentles and simples, felt embarrassed, for him, for
themselves. There he stood their representative spokesman;
their symbol; themselves; a butt, a clod, laughed at by looking-
glasses; ignored by the cows, condemned by the clouds which
continued their majestic rearrangement of the celestial landscape; an irrelevant forked stake in the flow and majesty of the
summer silent world.

His first words (the breeze had risen; the leaves were
rustling) were lost. Then he was heard saying: "What." To that
word he added another "Message"; and at last a whole sentence
emerged; not comprehensible; say rather audible. "What message," it seemed he was asking, "was our pageant meant to
convey?"

They folded their hands in the traditional manner as if they were seated in church.

"I have been asking myself"—the words were repeated—"what meaning, or message, this pageant was meant to convey?"

If he didn't know, calling himself Reverend, also M.A., who after all could?

"As one of the audience," he continued (words now put on meaning), "I will offer, very humbly, for I am not a critic"—and he touched the white gate that enclosed his neck with a yellow forefinger—"my interpretation. No, that is too bold a word. The gifted lady . . ." He looked round. La Trobe was invisible. He continued: "Speaking merely as one of the audience, I confess I was puzzled. For what reason, I asked, were we shown these scenes? Briefly, it is true. The means at our disposal this afternoon were limited. Still we were shown different groups. We were shown, unless I mistake, the effort renewed. A few were chosen; the many passed in the background. That surely we were shown. But again, were we not given to understand—am I too presumptuous? Am I treading, like angels, where as a fool I should absent myself? To me at least it was indicated that we are members one of another. Each is part of the whole. Yes, that occurred to me, sitting among you in the audience. Did I not perceive Mr. Hardcastle here" (he pointed) "at one time a Viking? And in Lady Harridan—excuse me, if I get the names wrong—a Canterbury pilgrim? We act different parts; but are the same. That I leave to you. Then again, as the play or pageant proceeded, my attention was distracted. Perhaps that too was part of the producer's intention? I thought I perceived that nature takes her part. Dare we, I asked myself, limit life to ourselves? May we not hold that there is a spirit that inspires, pervades . . ." (The swallows were sweeping round him. They seemed cognizant of his meaning. Then they swept out of sight.) "I leave that to you. I am not here to explain. That role has not been assigned me. I speak only as one of the audience, one of ourselves. I caught myself too reflected, as it happened in my own mirror . . ." (Laughter) "Scraps, orts and fragments! Surely, we should unite?"

"But" ("but" marked a new paragraph) "I speak also in another capacity. As Treasurer of the Fund. In which capacity" (he consulted a sheet of paper) "I am glad to be able to tell you that a sum of thirty-six pounds ten shillings and eightpence has been raised by this afternoon's entertainment towards our object: the illumination of our dear old church."

"Applause," the reporter reported.

Mr. Streatfield paused. He listened. Did he hear some distant music?

He continued: "But there is still a deficit" (he consulted his paper) "of one hundred and seventy-five pounds odd. So that each of us who has enjoyed this pageant has still an opp . . ." The word was cut in two. A zoom severed it. Twelve aeroplanes in perfect formation like a flight of wild duck came overhead. *That* was the music. The audience gaped; the audience gazed. Then zoom became drone. The planes had passed.

". . . portunity," Mr. Streatfield continued, "to make a contribution." He signalled. Instantly collecting boxes were in operation. Hidden behind glasses they emerged. Coppers rattled. Silver jingled. But O what a pity—how creepy it made one feel! Here came Albert, the idiot, jingling his collecting box—an aluminium saucepan without a lid. You couldn't very well deny him, poor fellow. Shillings were dropped. He rattled and sniggered; chattered and jibbered. As Mrs. Parker made her contribution— half a crown as it happened—she appealed to Mr. Streatfield to exorcise this evil, to extend the protection of his cloth.

The good man contemplated the idiot benignly. His faith had room, he indicated, for him too. He too, Mr. Streatfield appeared to be saying, is part of ourselves. But not a part we like to recognize, Mrs. Springett added silently, dropping her sixpence.

Contemplating the idiot, Mr. Streatfield had lost the thread of his discourse. His command over words seemed gone. He twiddled the cross on his watchchain. Then his hand sought his trouser pocket. Surreptitiously he extracted a small silver box. It was plain to all that the natural desire of the natural man was overcoming him. He had no further use for words.

"And now," he resumed, cuddling the pipe lighter in the palm of his hand, "for the pleasantest part of my duty. To propose a vote of thanks to the gifted lady . . ." He looked round for an object corresponding to this description. None such was visible. ". . . who wishes it seems to remain anonymous." He paused. "And so . . ." He paused again.

It was an awkward moment. How to make an end? Whom to thank? Every sound in nature was painfully audible; the swish of the trees; the gulp of a cow; even the skim of the swallows over the grass could be heard. But no one spoke. Whom could they make responsible? Whom could they thank for their entertainment? Was there no one?

Then there was a scuffle behind the bush; a preliminary premonitory scratching. A needle scraped a disc; chuff, chuff, chuff; then having found the rut, there was a roll and a flutter which portended *God* . . . (they all rose to their feet) *Save the King.*

Standing, the audience faced the actors; who also stood with their collecting boxes quiescent, their looking-glasses hidden, and the robes of their various parts hanging stiff.

> *Happy and glorious,*
> *Long to reign over us,*
> *God save the King*

The notes died away.

Was that the end? The actors were reluctant to go. They

lingered; they mingled. There was Budge the policeman talking to old Queen Bess. And the Age of Reason hobnobbed with the foreparts of the donkey. And Mrs. Hardcastle patted out the folds of her crinoline. And little England, still a child, sucked a peppermint drop out of a bag. Each still acted the un-acted part conferred on them by their clothes. Beauty was on them. Beauty revealed them. Was it the light that did it?—the tender, the fading, the uninquisitive but searching light of evening that reveals depths in water and makes even the red brick bungalow radiant?

"Look," the audience whispered, "O look, look, look—" And once more they applauded; and the actors joined hands and bowed.

Old Mrs. Lynn Jones, fumbling for her bag, sighed, "What a pity—must they change?"

But it was time to pack up and be off.

"Home, gentlemen; home ladies; it's time to pack up and be off," the reporter whistled, snapping the band round his note-book. And Mrs. Parker was stooping.

"I'm afraid I've dropped my glove. I'm so sorry to trouble you. Down there, between the seats. . . ."

The gramophone was affirming in tones there was no deny-ing, triumphant yet valedictory: *Dispersed are we; who have come to-gether. But,* the gramophone asserted, *let us retain whatever made that harmony.*

O let us, the audience echoed (stooping, peering, fumbling), keep together. For there is joy, sweet joy, in company.

Dispersed are we, the gramophone repeated.

And the audience turning saw the flaming windows, each daubed with golden sun; and murmured: "Home, gentlemen; sweet . . ." yet delayed a moment, seeing through the golden glory perhaps a crack in the boiler; perhaps a hole in the carpet; and hearing, perhaps, the daily drop of the daily bill.

Dispersed are we, the gramophone informed them. And dismissed them. So, straightening themselves for the last time, each grasping, it might be a hat, or a stick or a pair of suède gloves, for the last time they applauded Budge and Queen Bess; the trees; the white road; Bolney Minster; and the Folly. One hailed another, and they dispersed, across lawns, down paths, past the house to the gravel-strewn crescent, where cars, push bikes and cycles were crowded together.

Friends hailed each other in passing.

"I do think," someone was saying, "Miss Whatshername should have come forward and not left it to the rector . . . After all, she wrote it. . . . I thought it brilliantly clever . . . O my dear, I thought it utter bosh. Did *you* understand the meaning? Well, he said she meant we all act all parts. . . . He said, too, if I caught his meaning, Nature takes part. . . . Then there was the idiot. . . . Also, why leave out the Army, as my husband was saying, if it's history? And if one spirit animates the whole, what about the aeroplanes? . . . Ah, but you're being too exacting. After all, remember, it was only a village play. . . . For my part, I think they should have passed a vote of thanks to the owners. When we had our pageant, the grass didn't recover till autumn . . . Then we had tents. . . . That's the man, Cobbet of Cobbs Corner, who wins all the prizes at all the shows. I don't myself admire prize flowers, nor yet prize dogs . . ."

Dispersed are we, the gramophone triumphed, yet lamented, *Dispersed are we. . . .*

"But you must remember," the old cronies chatted, "they had to do it on the cheap. You can't get people, at this time o' year, to rehearse. There's the hay, let alone the movies. . . . What we need is a centre. Something to bring us all together . . . The Brookes have gone to Italy, in spite of everything. Rather rash? . . . If the worst should come—let's hope it won't— they'd hire an aeroplane, so they said. . . . What amused me was old Streatfield, feeling for his pouch. I like a man to be natural, not always on a perch.... Then those voices from the bushes.... Oracles? You're referring to the Greeks? Were the oracles, if I'm not being irreverent, a foretaste of our own religion? Which is what?... Crepe soles? That's so sensible... They last much longer and protect the feet.... But I was saying: can the Christian faith adapt itself? In times like these... At Larting no one goes to church... There's the dogs, there's the pictures.... It's odd that science, so they tell me, is making things (so to speak) more spiritual... The very latest notion, so I'm told is, nothing's solid... There, you can get a glimpse of the church through the trees....

"Mr. Umphelby! How nice to see you! Do come and dine... No, alas, we're going back to town. The House is sitting... I was telling them, the Brookes have gone to Italy. They've seen the volcano. Most impressive, so they say—they were lucky—in eruption. I agree—things look worse than ever on the continent. And what's the channel, come to think of it, if they mean to invade us? The aeroplanes, I didn't like to say it, made one think.... No, I thought it much too scrappy. Take the idiot. Did she mean, so to speak, something hidden, the unconscious as they call it? But why always drag in sex.... It's true, there's a sense in which we all, I admit, are savages still. Those women with red nails. And dressing up—what's that? The old savage, I suppose.... That's the bell. Ding dong. Ding... Rather a cracked old bell... And the mirrors! Reflecting us... I called that cruel. One feels such a fool, caught unprotected... There's Mr. Streatfield, going, I suppose to take the evening service. He'll have to hurry, or he won't have time to change.... He said she meant we all act. Yes, but whose play? Ah, that's the question! And if we're left asking questions, isn't it a failure, as a play? I must say I like to feel sure if I go to the theatre, that I've grasped the meaning... Or was that, perhaps, what she meant? . . . Ding dong. Ding . . . that if we don't jump to conclusions, if you think, and I think, perhaps one day, thinking differently, we shall think the same?

"There's dear old Mr. Carfax . . . Can't we give you a lift, if you don't mind playing bodkin? We were asking questions, Mr. Carfax, about the play. The looking-glasses now—did they mean the reflection is the dream; and the tune—was it Bach, Handel, or no one in particular—is the truth? Or was it t'other way about?

"Bless my soul, what a dither! Nobody seems to know one car from another. That's why I have a mascot, a monkey . . . But I can't see it . . . While we're waiting, tell me, did you feel when the shower fell, someone wept for us all? There's a poem, *Tears, tears tears,* it begins. And goes on, *O then the unloosened ocean . . .* but I can't remember the rest.

"Then when Mr. Streatfield said: One spirit animates the whole—the aeroplanes interrupted. That's the worst of playing out of doors. . . . Unless of course she meant that very thing . . . Dear me, the parking arrangements are not what you might call adequate . . . I shouldn't have expected either so many Hispano-Suizas . . . That's a Rolls . . . That's a Bentley . . . That's the new type of Ford. . . . To return to the meaning—Are machines the devil, or do they introduce a discord . . . Ding dong, ding . . . by means of which we reach the final . . . Ding dong. . . . Here's the car with the monkey . . . Hop in . . . And good-bye, Mrs. Parker . . . Ring us up. Next time we're down don't forget . . . Next time . . . Next time . . ."

The wheels scurred on the gravel. The cars drove off.

The gramophone gurgled *Unity—Dispersity.* It gurgled *Un . . dis . . .* And ceased.

The little company who had come together at luncheon were left standing on the terrace. The pilgrims had bruised a lane on the grass. Also, the lawn would need a deal of clearing up. Tomorrow the telephone would ring: "Did I leave my hand-bag? . . . A pair of spectacles in a red leather case? . . . A little old brooch of no value to anyone but me?" Tomorrow the telephone would ring.

Now Mr. Oliver said: "Dear lady," and, taking Mrs. Manresa's gloved hand in his, pressed it, as if to say: "You have given me what you now take from me." He would have liked to hold on for a moment longer to the emeralds and rubies dug up, so people said, by thin Ralph Manresa in his ragamuffin days. But alas, sunset light was unsympathetic to her make-up; plated it looked, not deeply interfused. And he dropped her hand; and she gave him an arch roguish twinkle, as if to say—but the end of that sentence was cut short. For she turned, and Giles stepped forward; and the light breeze which the meteorologist had foretold fluttered her skirts; and she went, like a goddess, buoyant, abundant, with flower-chained captives following in her wake.

All were retreating, withdrawing and dispersing; and he was left with the ash grown cold and no glow, no glow on the log. What word expressed the sag at his heart, the effusion in his veins, as the retreating Manresa, with Giles attendant, admirable woman, all sensation, ripped the rag doll and let the sawdust stream from his heart?

The old man made a guttural sound, and turned to the right. On with the hobble, on with the limp, since the dance was over. He strolled alone past the trees. It was here, early that very morning, that he had destroyed the little boy's world. He had popped out with his newspaper; the child had cried.

Down in the dell, past the lily pool, the actors were undress-ing. He could see them among the brambles. In vests and trousers; unhooking; buttoning up: on all fours; stuffing clothes into cheap attaché cases; with silver swords, beards and emeralds on the grass. Miss La Trobe in coat and skirt—too short, for her legs were stout—battled with the billows of a crinoline. He must respect the conventions. So he stopped, by the pool. The water was opaque over the mud.

Then, coming up behind him, "Oughtn't we to thank her?" Lucy asked him. She gave him a light pat on the arm.

How imperceptive her religion made her! The fumes of that incense obscured the human heart. Skimming the surface, she ignored the battle in the mud. After La Trobe had been excruciated by the Rector's interpretation, by the maulings and the manglings of the actors ... "She don't want our thanks, Lucy," he said gruffly. What she wanted, like that carp (something moved in the water) was darkness in the mud; a whisky and soda at the pub; and coarse words descending like maggots through the waters.

"Thank the actors, not the author," he said. "Or ourselves, the audience."

He looked over his shoulder. The old lady, the indigenous, the prehistoric, was being wheeled away by a footman. He rolled her through the arch. Now the lawn was empty. The line of the roof, the upright chimneys, rose hard and red against the blue of the evening. The house emerged; the house that had been obliterated. He was damned glad it was over—the scurry and the scuffle, the rouge and the rings. He stooped and raised a peony that had shed its petals. Solitude had come again. And reason and the lamplit paper. . . . But where was his dog? Chained in a kennel? The little veins swelled with rage on his temples. He whistled. And here, released by Candish, racing across the lawn with a fleck of foam on the nostril, came his dog.

Lucy still gazed at the lily pool. "All gone," she murmured, "under the leaves." Scared by shadows passing, the fish had withdrawn. She gazed at the water. Perfunctorily she caressed her cross. But her eyes went water searching, looking for fish.

The lilies were shutting; the red lily, the white lily, each on its plate of leaf. Above, the air rushed; beneath was water. She stood between two fluidities, caressing her cross. Faith required hours of kneeling in the early morning. Often the delight of the roaming eye seduced her—a sunbeam, a shadow. Now the jagged leaf at the corner suggested, by its contours, Europe. There were other leaves. She fluttered her eye over the surface, naming leaves India, Africa, America. Islands of security, glossy and thick.

"Bart . . ." She spoke to him. She had meant to ask him about the dragon-fly—couldn't the blue thread settle, if we destroyed it here, then there? But he had gone into the house.

Then something moved in the water; her favorite fantail. The golden orfe followed. Then she had a glimpse of silver— the great carp himself, who came to the surface so very seldom. They slid on, in and out between the stalks, silver; pink; gold; splashed; streaked; pied.

"Ourselves," she murmured. And retrieving some glint of faith from the grey waters, hopefully, without much help from reason, she followed the fish; the speckled, streaked, and blotched; seeing in that vision beauty, power, and glory in ourselves.

Fish had faith, she reasoned. They trust us because we've never caught 'em. But her brother would reply: "That's greed." "Their beauty!" she protested. "Sex," he would say. "Who makes sex susceptible to beauty?" she would argue. He shrugged who? Why? Silenced, she returned to her private vision; of beauty which is goodness; the sea on which we float. Mostly impervious, but surely every boat sometimes leaks?

He would carry the torch of reason till it went out in the darkness of the cave. For herself, every morning, kneeling, she protected her vision. Every night she opened the window and looked at leaves against the sky. Then slept. Then the random ribbons of birds' voices woke her.

The fish had come to the surface. She had nothing to give them—not a crumb of bread. "Wait, my darlings," she addressed them. She would trot into the house and ask Mrs. Sands for a biscuit. Then a shadow fell. Off they flashed. How vexatious! Who was it? Dear me, the young man whose name she had forgotten; not Jones! nor Hodge . . .

Dodge had left Mrs. Manresa abruptly. All over the garden he had been searching for Mrs. Swithin. Now he found her; and she had forgotten his name.

"I'm William," he said. At that she revived, like a girl in a garden in white, among roses, who came running to meet him—an unacted part.

"I was going to get a biscuit—no, to thank the actors," she stumbled, virginal, blushing. Then she remembered her brother. "My brother," she added, "says one mustn't thank the author, Miss La Trobe."

It was always "my brother . . . my brother" who rose from the depths of her lily pool.

As for the actors, Hammond had detached his whiskers and was now buttoning up his coat. When the chain was inserted between the buttons he was off.

Only Miss La Trobe remained, bending over something in the grass.

"The play's over," he said. "The actors have departed."

"And we mustn't, my brother says, thank the author," Mrs. Swithin repeated, looking in the direction of Miss La Trobe.

"So I thank you," he said. He took her hand and pressed it. Putting one thing with another, it was unlikely that they would ever meet again.

The church bells always stopped, leaving you to ask: Won't there be another note? Isa, half-way across the lawn, listened. . . . Ding, dong, ding . . . There was not going to be another note.

The congregation was assembled, on their knees, in the church. The service was beginning. The play was over; swallows skimmed the grass that had been the stage.

There was Dodge, the lip reader, her semblable, her conspirator, a seeker like her after hidden faces. He was hurrying to rejoin Mrs. Manresa who had gone in front with Giles—"the father of my children," she muttered. The flesh poured over her, the hot, nerve wired, now lit up, now dark as the grave physical body. By way of healing the rusty fester of the poisoned dart she sought the face that all day long she had been seeking. Preening and peering, between backs, over shoulders, she had sought the man in grey. He had given her a cup of tea at a tennis party; handed her, once, a racquet. That was all. But, she was crying, had we met before the salmon leapt like a bar of silver . . . had we met, she was crying. And when her little boy came battling through the bodies in the Barn "Had he been his son," she had muttered . . . In passing she stripped the bitter leaf that grew, as it happened, outside the nursery window. Old Man's Beard. Shrivelling the shreds in lieu of words, for no words grow there, nor roses either, she swept past her conspirator, her semblable, the seeker after vanished faces "like Venus" he thought, making a rough translation, "to her prey . . ." and followed after.

Turning the corner, there was Giles attached to Mrs. Manresa. She was standing at the door of her car. Giles had his foot on the edge of the running board. Did they perceive the arrows about to strike them?

"Jump in, Bill," Mrs. Manresa chaffed him.

And the wheels scurred on the gravel, and the car drove off.

At last, Miss La Trobe could raise herself from her stooping position. It had been prolonged to avoid attention. The bells had stopped; the audience had gone; also the actors. She could straighten her back. She could open her arms. She could say to the world, You have taken my gift! Glory possessed her—for one moment. But what had she given? A cloud that melted into the other clouds on the horizon. It was in the giving that the triumph was. And the triumph faded. Her gift meant nothing. If they had understood her meaning; if they had known their parts; if the pearls had been real and the funds illimitable—it would have been a better gift. Now it had gone to join the others.

"A failure," she groaned, and stooped to put away the records.

Then suddenly the starlings attacked the tree behind which she had hidden. In one flock they pelted it like so many winged stones. The whole tree hummed with the whizz they made, as if each bird plucked a wire. A whizz, a buzz rose from the bird-buzzing, bird-vibrant, bird-blackened tree. The tree became a rhapsody, a quivering cacophony, a whizz and vibrant rapture, branches, leaves, birds syllabling discordantly life, life, life, without measure, without stop devouring the tree. Then up! Then off!

What interrupted? It was old Mrs. Chalmers, creeping through the grass with a bunch of flowers—pinks apparently—to fill the vase that stood on her husband's grave. In winter it was holly, or ivy. In summer, a flower. It was she who had scared the starlings. Now she passed.

Miss La Trobe nicked the lock and hoisted the heavy case of gramophone records to her shoulder. She crossed the terrace and stopped by the tree where the starlings had gathered. It was here that she had suffered triumph, humiliation, ecstasy, despair—for nothing. Her heels had ground a hole in the grass.

It was growing dark. Since there were no clouds to trouble the sky, the blue was bluer, the green greener. There was no longer a view—no Folly, no spire of Bolney Minster. It was land merely, no land in particular. She put down her case and stood looking at the land. Then something rose to the surface.

"I should group them," she murmured, "here." It would be midnight; there would be two figures, half concealed by a rock. The curtain would rise. What would the first words be? The words escaped her.

Again she lifted the heavy suit case to her shoulder. She strode off across the lawn. The house was dormant; one thread of smoke thickened against the trees. It was strange that the earth, with all those flowers incandescent—the lilies, the roses, and clumps of white flowers and bushes of burning green—should still be hard. From the earth green waters seemed to rise over her. She took her voyage away from the shore, and, raising her hand, fumbled for the latch of the iron entrance gate.

She would drop her suit case in at the kitchen window, and then go on up to the Inn. Since the row with the actress who had shared her bed and her purse the need of drink had grown on her. And the horror and the terror of being alone. One of these days she would break—which of the village laws? Sobriety? Chastity? Or take something that did not properly belong to her?

At the corner she ran into old Mrs. Chalmers returning from the grave. The old woman looked down at the dead flowers she was carrying and cut her. The women in the cottages with the red geraniums always did that. She was an outcast. Nature had somehow set her apart from her kind. Yet she had scribbled in the margin of her manuscript: "I am the slave of my audience."

She thrust her suit case in at the scullery window and walked on, till at the corner she saw the red curtain at the bar window. There would be shelter; voices; oblivion. She turned the handle of the public house door. The acrid smell of stale beer saluted her; and voices talking. They stopped. They had been talking about Bossy as they called her—it didn't matter. She took her chair and looked through the smoke at a crude glass painting of a cow in a stable; also at a cock and a hen. She raised her glass to her lips. And drank. And listened. Words of one syllable sank down into the mud. She drowsed; she nodded. The mud became fertile. Words rose above the intolerably laden dumb oxen plodding through the mud. Words without meaning—wonderful words.

The cheap clock ticked; smoke obscured the pictures. Smoke became tart on the roof of her mouth. Smoke obscured the earth-coloured jackets. She no longer saw them, yet they upheld her, sitting arms akimbo with her glass before her. There was the high ground at midnight; there the rock; and two scarcely perceptible figures. Suddenly the tree was pelted with starlings. She set down her glass. She heard the first words.

Down in the hollow, at Pointz Hall, beneath the trees, the table was cleared in the dining room. Candish, with his curved brush had swept the crumbs; had spared the petals and finally left the family to dessert. The play was over, the strangers gone, and they were alone—the family.

Still the play hung in the sky of the mind—moving, diminishing, but still there. Dipping her raspberry in sugar, Mrs. Swithin looked at the play. She said, popping the berry into her mouth, "What did it mean?" and added: "The peasants; the kings; the fool and" (she swallowed) "ourselves?"

They all looked at the play; Isa, Giles and Mr. Oliver. Each of course saw something different. In another moment it would be beneath the horizon, gone to join the other plays. Mr. Oliver, holding out his cheroot said: "Too ambitious." And, lighting his cheroot he added: "Considering her means."

It was drifting away to join the other clouds: becoming invisible. Through the smoke Isa saw not the play but the audience dispersing. Some drove; others cycled. A gate swung open.

A car swept up the drive to the red villa in the cornfields. Low hanging boughs of acacia brushed the roof. Acacia petalled the car arrived.

"The looking-glasses and the voices in the bushes," she murmured. "What did she mean?"

"When Mr. Streatfield asked her to explain, she wouldn't," said Mrs. Swithin.

Here, with its sheaf sliced in four, exposing a white cone, Giles offered his wife a banana. She refused it. He stubbed his match on the plate. Out it went with a little fizz in the raspberry juice.

"We should be thankful," said Mrs. Swithin, folding her napkin, "for the weather, which was perfect, save for one shower."

Here she rose, Isa followed her across the hall to the big room.

They never pulled the curtains till it was too dark to see, nor shut the windows till it was too cold. Why shut out the day before it was over? The flowers were still bright; the birds chirped. You could see more in the evening often when nothing interrupted, when there was no fish to order, no telephone to answer. Mrs. Swithin stopped by the great picture of Venice—school of Canaletto. Possibly in the hood of the gondola there was a little figure—a woman, veiled; or a man?

Isa, sweeping her sewing from the table, sank, her knee doubled, into the chair by the window. Within the shell of the room she overlooked the summer night. Lucy returned from her voyage into the picture and stood silent. The sun made each pane of her glasses shine red. Silver sparkled on her black shawl. For a moment she looked like a tragic figure from another play.

Then she spoke in her usual voice. "We made more this year than last, he said. But then last year it rained."

"This year, last year, next year, never..." Isa murmured. Her hand burnt in the sun on the window sill. Mrs. Swithin took her knitting from the table.

"Did you feel," she asked, "what he said: we act different parts but are the same?"

"Yes," Isa answered. "No," she added. It was Yes, No. Yes, yes, yes, the tide rushed out embracing. No, no, no, it contracted. The old boot appeared on the shingle.

"Orts, scraps and fragments," she quoted what she remembered of the vanishing play.

Lucy had just opened her lips to reply, and had laid her hand on her cross caressingly, when the gentlemen came in. She made her little chirruping sound of welcome. She shuffled her feet to clear a space. But in fact there was more space than was needed, and great hooded chairs.

They sat down, ennobled both of them by the setting sun. Both had changed. Giles now wore the black coat and white tie of the professional classes, which needed—Isa looked down at his feet—patent leather pumps. "Our representative, our spokesman," she sneered. Yet he was extraordinarily handsome. "The father of my children, whom I love and hate." Love and hate—how they tore her asunder! Surely it was time someone invented a new plot, or that the author came out from the bushes ...

Here Candish came in. He brought the second post on a silver salver. There were letters; bills; and the morning paper—the paper that obliterated the day before. Like a fish rising to a crumb of biscuit, Bartholomew snapped at the paper. Giles slit the flap of an apparently business document. Lucy read a crisscross from an old friend at Scarborough. Isa had only bills.

The usual sounds reverberated through the shell; Sands making up the fire; Candish stoking the boiler. Isa had done with her bills. Sitting in the shell of the room she watched the pageant fade. The flowers flashed before they faded. She watched them flash.

The paper crackled. The second hand jerked on. M. Daladier had pegged down the franc. The girl had gone skylarking with the troopers. She had screamed. She had hit him. . . . What then?

When Isa looked at the flowers again, the flowers had faded.

Bartholomew flicked on the reading lamp. The circle of the readers, attached to white papers, was lit up. There in that hollow of the sun-baked field were congregated the grasshopper, the ant, and the beetle, rolling pebbles of sun-baked earth through the glistening stubble. In that rosy corner of the sun-baked field Bartholomew, Giles and Lucy polished and nibbled and broke off crumbs. Isa watched them.

Then the newspaper dropped.

"Finished?" said Giles, taking it from his father.

The old man relinquished his paper. He basked. One hand caressing the dog rippled folds of skin towards the collar.

The clock ticked. The house gave little cracks as if it were very brittle, very dry. Isa's hand on the window felt suddenly cold. Shadow had obliterated the garden. Roses had withdrawn for the night.

Mrs. Swithin folding her letter murmured to Isa: "I looked in and saw the babies, sound asleep, under the paper roses."

"Left over from the Coronation," Bartholomew muttered, half asleep.

"But we needn't have been to all that trouble with the decorations," Lucy added, "for it didn't rain this year."

"This year, last year, next year, never," Isa murmured.

"Tinker, tailor, soldier, sailor," Bartholomew echoed. He was talking in his sleep.

Lucy slipped her letter into its envelope. It was time to read now, her Outline of History. But she had lost her place. She turned the pages looking at pictures—mammoths, mastodons, prehistoric birds. Then she found the page where she had stopped.

The darkness increased. The breeze swept round the room. With a little shiver Mrs. Swithin drew her sequin shawl about her shoulders. She was too deep in the story to ask for the window to be shut. "England," she was reading, "was then a swamp. Thick forests covered the land. On the top of their matted branches birds sang . . ."

The great square of the open window showed only sky now. It was drained of light, severe, stone cold. Shadows fell. Shadows crept over Bartholomew's high forehead; over his great nose. He looked leafless, spectral, and his chair monumental. As a dog shudders its skin, his skin shuddered. He rose, shook himself, glared at nothing, and stalked from the room. They heard the dog's paws padding on the carpet behind him.

Lucy turned the page, quickly, guiltily, like a child who will be told to go to bed before the end of the chapter.

"Prehistoric man," she read, "half-human, half-ape, roused himself from his semi-crouching position and raised great stones."

She slipped the letter from Scarborough between the pages to mark the end of the chapter, rose, smiled, and tiptoed silently out of the room.

The old people had gone up to bed. Giles crumpled the newspaper and turned out the light. Left alone together for the first time that day, they were silent. Alone, enmity was bared; also love. Before they slept, they must fight; after they had fought, they would embrace. From that embrace another life might be born. But first they must fight, as the dog fox fights with the vixen, in the heart of darkness, in the fields of night.

Isa let her sewing drop. The great hooded chairs had become enormous. And Giles too. And Isa too against the window. The window was all sky without colour. The house had lost its shelter. It was night before roads were made, or houses. It was the night that dwellers in caves had watched from some high place among rocks.

Then the curtain rose. They spoke.

A Note on the Text

The text of this edition follows the first U.S. edition of the novel, with the following variations: The phrase "and 'in strict confidence, I needn't tell you' on page 29 had an erroneous repetition of "in" that was not present in the first British edition and so has been corrected here; and the typographical error "We're the oracles" has been corrected to "Were the oracles" on page 135.

Notes to *Between the Acts*

The following abbreviations are used below: *PH (Pointz Hall: The Earlier and Later Typescripts of* Between the Acts. Edited by Mitchell A. Leaska. New York: University Publications, 1983); SH (Virginia Woolf, *Between the Acts*. Edited by Susan Dick and Mary S. Millar. Oxford: Shakespeare Head Press, 2002). Details of other sources cited will be found either in the list of works cited in the introduction, in the suggestions for further reading, or within specific notes. In annotating this rich and complex novel, I am deeply indebted to its previous annotators, Mitchell Leaska (*PH*), Susan Dick and Mary S. Millar (SH), Gillian Beer (Penguin, 1992), and Mark Hussey (Cambridge University Press, 2008). I would not have been able to identify so many allusions and echoes if it had not been for their previous work. I would also like to thank John Baird and Brian Corman for helpful suggestions, Bob Johnson of Bacchus Antiques for information on champagne openers, and Tania Botticella, Kimberly Fairbrother Canton, Glenn Clifton, Rohanna Green, Adam Hammond, and Daniel Harney for their help with some of the materials and with the electronic files.

cesspool [3]   A cesspool is a tank or well for processing raw sewage; "to bring water to the village" would mean to introduce indoor plumbing. The Woolfs lived for years with an earth closet—a "cane chair over a bucket"—at Rodmell and, at the time when Virginia Woolf was beginning this novel, they were engaged in fighting the district council over a proposal to erect a sewage pump in the adjoining field (*Diary* 5: 341; 162–63).

What a subject to talk about [3]   Mrs. Haines's response epitomizes
the still-lingering taboos against discussing bodily wastes and
fluids in polite, middle-class, mixed society. See E. M. Forster's
preface to Mulk Raj Anand's novel *Untouchable* (1935), whose
central character is a cleaner of latrines in India: "We have been
trained from childhood to think excretion shameful, and grave
evils have resulted, both physical and psychological, with which
modern education is just beginning to cope" (London: Penguin, 1940, vi). Virginia Woolf considered the liberation of
Bloomsbury dated from the moment when the word *semen* was
said aloud, in mixed company ("Old Bloomsbury," *Moments of
Being* 200).

Liskeard [3]   An ancient market town in Cornwall, recorded in the
Domesday Book. Some of the details, however, suggest the location of this village is in the north or the midlands, whereas references, such as to the village of Pyecombe [11], would place the
village in Sussex where the Woolfs were living during the war.
The setting is a composite place. (See SH xxiii–iv.)

nightingale [3]   The first of many specific birds to be named in this
novel; the nightingale, because of its melodious song, is associated with the lyric poetic voice.

Indian Civil Service [3]   Bartholomew's occupation implicates him
in England's imperial project, although in a milder fashion than
E. M. Forster's Ronny Heaslop in *A Passage to India* (1924). In
Imperialism and Civilization, Leonard Woolf indicted the British
government of India for "debarr[ing] Indians, however able and
educated, from all the higher administrative posts" (London:
Hogarth Press, 1928, 56).

Roman road [3]   Woolf associated the Roman road, because of
its precise straightness, with sequential logic and administrative
efficiencies: "Insiders are the glory of the 19th century. They do

a great service like Roman roads. But they avoid the forests & the will o the wisps" (*Diary* 5: 333). In *The Waves,* Bernard describes the traditional "biographic style" as "phrases laid like Roman roads across the tumult of our lives" (Orlando: Harcourt, 2006: 192).

Romans [4]   The traces of Roman roads visible from the air mark the period of the Roman conquest from A.D. 43 to 420, when "Britannia," as the Romans named the island, was itself subject to an imperial invader. In Joseph Conrad's *Heart of Darkness* (1902), Marlow similarly begins his narrative by imagining the invasion of England by imperial Rome.

faded peacocks [4]   The peacock names yet another bird, but Isa's dressing gown (or kimono) also implies a lingering fin de siècle aestheticism, with its passion for Japanese style and design. See Aubrey Beardsley's famous illustration *The Peacock Skirt* (1893), itself influenced by James McNeill Whistler's decoration of the Peacock Room in Frederick Leyland's London house (1877).

She walks in beauty . . . So we'll go no more a-roving [4]   Poems by George Gordon Byron, aka Lord Byron (1788–1824), the second of which echoes the old Scots ballad "And we'll gang nae mair a-roving" (David Herd, *Ancient and Modern Scots Songs,* 1776), and which in turn is echoed in the chorus of "An Old Song" by the poet Edward Thomas (1878–1917): "I'll go no more a-roving." Although Woolf disdained the masculinist orientation of Byron's letters and his poem *Don Juan* ("Indiscretions," *Essays* 3: 461), she nevertheless singled out *Don Juan* as pointing the way to a new flexibility in poetry ("Poetry, Fiction, and the Future," *Essays* 4: 435); note that Bartholomew recalls not the proud, rebellious Byron, beloved of Stephen Dedalus in James Joyce's *A Portrait of the Artist as a Young Man* (1916; reprint, New York: Penguin, 1993), but the gentler, musical Byron of the short lyrics.

duckweed [5]   Small green plants that float on the surface of sheltered water. For Woolf, there may be further personal negative
associations here with a play on *Duckworth,* the surname of her
half brothers George and Gerald, both of whom exploited her
sexually in her youth (see "A Sketch of the Past" in *Moments of
Being*).

Waterloo [6]   The Battle of Waterloo, fought on June 18, 1815, in
which Napoléon was decisively defeated by the British and Al-
lied armies led by the Duke of Wellington.

Outline of History [6]   The history Lucy is reading conflates (and, at
least in her mind, compresses) H. G. Wells's *The Outline of History: Being a Plain History of Life and Mankind* (Cassell, 1920) and
G. M. Trevelyan's *History of England* (Longmans, Green, 1926).
Wells's evolutionary history devotes six chapters to history before the appearance of humanlike forms, marking the transition
with "The Age of Mammals culminated in ice and hardship and
man." See also the note to page 147.

when the entire continent . . . was all one [6–7]   The idea, first posed
by eighteenth-century geologists, is in Wells (above), but there
may also be an echo of Matthew Arnold's 1852 poem "To
Marguerite—Continued" ("For surely once, they feel, we
were / Parts of a single continent!"), especially given the
poem's modern theme of isolation in a crowd and longings for
an imagined communal past. Recent scientific research further
evidences the existence of a prehistoric land bridge uniting
England and the European continent, later destroyed by cataclysmic floods.

nurses [7]   Nursemaids, employed to care for children.

feller [8]   The word *feller* (i.e., fellow) indicates a blending between
the narrator's voice and the voices of the nursemaids.

you [8]   The pronoun *you* suggests a narrator who is here a character in the story world.

Caro [8]   A variant of Caroline; also, in Italian, the masculine form of *dear.*

the flower complete [8]   Woolf records a similar experience of unified perception as one of her most powerful childhood experiences: "I was looking at the flower bed by the front door; 'That is the whole,' I said. I was looking at a plant with a spread of leaves; and it seemed suddenly plain that the flower itself was a part of the earth; that a ring enclosed what was the flower; and that was the real flower; part earth; part flower" ("A Sketch of the Past," *Moments of Being* 71).

Sohrab [9]   See Matthew Arnold's poem "Sohrab and Rustum" (1853), based on the tenth-century Persian epic, the *Shahnameh.* The story concerns a father who realizes he has slain the son whose existence has been hidden from him, only when the dying son reveals a seal that his mother has placed on his arm. Also relevant may be Arnold's defense of his poem against one reader's charge of plagiarism: In the second edition of his poems, along with excerpts from his sources, Arnold included a note distinguishing between plagiarism and reinvention ("*re-manier et réinventer à sa manière*"): "I hope that it will not in the future be supposed, if I am silent as to the sources from which a poem is derived, that I am trying to conceal obligations, or to claim an absolute originality for all parts of it. . . . The use of the tradition, above everything else, gives to a work that *naiveté,* that flavour of reality and truth, which is the very life of poetry" (*Poems.* 2nd ed. London: Longman, Brown, Green, and Longmans, 1854: 58–59).

Daladier [10]   Édouard Daladier (1884–1970) was the French prime minister and minister of national defense. His participation, along with the British prime minister Neville Chamberlain, and Italy's Benito Mussolini, in the Munich Pact in September 1938 was initially hailed as a peace-making effort but, after Germany's invasion of Czechoslovakia in March 1939, the Munich Pact was increasingly condemned as an appeasement of, and hence capitulation to, Hitler.

pegging down [10]   To tie a monetary currency to a standard, as opposed to letting the value float. France finally abandoned the gold standard in 1936 but, on May 5, 1938, in an effort to restore a measure of economic stability and address its escalating economic crisis, France pegged the franc to the British pound sterling. While stabilizing the currency by setting the rate of 175 francs to the pound, with a maximum of F179/£, France also significantly undervalued the franc to give its government an advantage in borrowing money. Forced hastily to agree, the government of Great Britain considered France had failed to honor its commitment to international consultation under the Tripartite Agreement signed by France, Great Britain, and the United States in 1936.

Pyecombe [11]   A village in Sussex. See note to page 3, "Liskeard."

Sappho [11]   Ancient Greek poet (7th–6th century B.C.) born on the isle of Lesbos, from which the word *lesbian* derives.

mirrors of the soul [12]   See Lecture 5, "The Hero as Man of Letters," in Thomas Carlyle's *On Heroes, Hero-Worship, and the Heroic in History* (1841): "In Books lies the *soul* of the whole Past Time." By adding the image of a mirror, Woolf gives more emphasis to the reader's active, self-reflexive role. Woolf generally mocks Carlyle's approach to history as the "Biographies of Great Men"—the topic of an essay assigned to Jacob Flanders in her novel *Jacob's Room* (1922) and a recurrent subject of Stephen

Dedalus's reading in Joyce's *Portrait of the Artist* (New York: Penguin, 1993: 55). However, Carlyle's Lecture 5 presents a view very similar to one Woolf was herself developing in a concurrently planned book on the history of readers and reading: that the advent of the printed book superseded the authority of the university and democratized knowledge by making it available to all. See "'Anon' and 'The Reader': Virginia Woolf's Last Essays." Edited by Brenda Silver. *Twentieth Century Literature* 25 (1979): 356–441.

shilling shockers [12]   Also called "railway novels," shilling shockers were a genre of cheap paperback fiction, typically with sensational and sometimes science-fictional plots, which sold for a shilling in railway station bookstalls in the nineteenth century. In comparison, when the Victorian three-decker novel finally became available in one-volume editions, the retail price was six shillings. By 1939, prices had changed, but the distinction between light and serious reading, and their relative costs, still obtained.

anguish of a Queen or the heroism of King Harry [12]   The subject matter, for example, of Shakespearean drama, King Harry being Henry V.

But no water . . . the shadow of the rock [13]   Striking images from the first section of T. S. Eliot's *The Waste Land* (1922).

youth and India [13]   For a recent documentation of the lives of retired members of the Indian Civil Service in England, their work as paternalistic despots, and yet the loneliness of their later lives as exiles from India, see David Gilmour, *The Ruling Caste: Imperial Lives in the Victorian Raj* (New York: Farrar, Straus and Giroux, 2006).

The moor is dark [13]   Isa is quoting, almost exactly, the first two lines of Percy Bysshe Shelley's "Stanzas—April 1814," concerning the withdrawal back into solitude of a repudiated (and guilty) lover: "Away! the moor is dark beneath the moon, / Rapid clouds have drank the last pale beam of even."

pegged down [13]   Literally "held down" but also a rhyming pun with "pegging down the franc" (10). See also "another peg on which to hang his rage" (42) and "peg-top trousers" (112).

The Faerie Queene *and Kinglake's* Crimea; *Keats and the* Kreutzer Sonata [14]   Books offering a choice of widely varied reading: a richly allegorical Elizabethan poem by Edmund Spenser, a nineteenth-century history of the Crimean War, a volume of Romantic poetry, and a Russian novel that concerns sexual conflict within a marriage, and in which the jealous husband kills his wife with a dagger. Together, these books mix themes of love and war. The other books named as being in the library further extend the range of genre: poetry (Shelley, Yeats, Donne); biography (Giuseppe Garibaldi, Lord Palmerston); county archival records (*The Antiquities*); science (the astronomer Arthur Eddington [1882–1944], the naturalist Charles Darwin [1809–1882], and the physicist Sir James Jeans [1877–1946]).

A horse with a green tail [14]   The detail accurately reflects a rape case reported in the London *Times* in June 1938, which ended in the conviction of the soldiers; the following month, the *Times* carried a report on the trial of the doctor who had performed a compassionate abortion on the teenage victim. The doctor was acquitted. See S. N. Clarke, "The Horse with a Green Tail," *Virginia Woolf Miscellany* 34 (1990): 3–4.

Cindy, or Sindy . . . was short for Lucy [15]   In effect, three different variations of Mrs. Swithin's Christian name, Lucinda, which itself suggests a combination of Lucida (Latin) meaning "shining, bright, and clear," and Lucina, an older title for Juno (sometimes called Juno Lucina), the feminine principle of celestial light, and thus associated as well with Diana, the moon goddess.

Touch wood . . . Antaeus [17]   Touch wood, like "knock on wood," invokes an old belief that touching the wood of sacred trees (later, the wood of the Cross) would bring protection or ward off evil; Antaeus, in Greek mythology the son of Gaia (Earth), was a giant wrestler whose strength was dependent on his remaining in contact with his mother, that is, on his touching the earth.

Lemprière . . . the Encyclopaedia [18]   Standard reference books: John Lemprière, *Bibliotheca Classica* or, *A Classical Dictionary* (1788) and the *Encyclopaedia Britannica.*

red and white paper roses [19]   Recalling the Wars of the Roses (1455–1487) between the feuding houses of Lancaster and York, which ended with the death of Richard III (of York) and the victory of Henry VII (of the Lancastrian force). Henry VII united the red and white roses in the Tudor rose, but the memory of the conflict lived on, as witness the division of schoolboys into teams of Lancaster and York in Joyce's *Portrait of the Artist.*

the Coronation [19]   After Edward VIII abdicated to marry Wallis Warfield Simpson, his younger brother Albert ascended to the throne as King George VI. The coronation took place on May 12, 1937, and was marked by celebrations throughout the countryside.

knobbed shoes [19]   Rounded toes (shaped like a knob) would indicate unfashionable, "old lady's" shoes in the 1930s, but there may be also an echo of the anticlerical, antiauthoritarian medieval poem, *Pierce the Ploughmans Crede:* "His hod was full of holes & his heer oute, / With his knopped schon clouted full thykke"

(Edited by Rev. Walter W. Skeat, Early English Text Society, 1867: lines 423–24). At the end of the poem, the narrator states that just as he has amended the words of the Ploughman, so he beseeches men after him to amend his own words. Thus, according to Helen Barr, at the end of the poem, "The voices of Peres, narrator and poet all merge" into a single "I" (*Signes and Sothe: Language in the Piers Plowman Tradition* [Cambridge: D. S. Brewer, 1994]).

simples [20]   From the meaning of *simple* as humble, unpretentious, and so signifying people of low rank, the common people, as opposed to the gentry, or the people in the rank immediately below the nobility.

false teeth . . . in the time of the Pharaohs [21]   *Encyclopaedia Britannica* (11th edition, 1910–1911) points to evidence that the Egyptians and the Hindus had developed a method for replacing lost teeth with wood or ivory substitutes attached to adjacent sound teeth with threads or wires (SH).

before the Conquest [22]   In 1066, William, Duke of Normandy (known in history as William the Conquerer), defeated the English army at the Battle of Hastings and established Norman rule.

another joke about Saints [22]   St. Swithin was a Bishop of Winchester in the ninth century, whose shrine was a popular place of pilgrimage until its destruction in the Reformation. Perhaps originating in his request to be buried out of doors so that the rain would fall on his grave, a popular superstition arose about his feast day (July 15), as expressed in the following rhyme: "St. Swithin's day if thou dost rain / For forty days it will remain / St. Swithin's day if thou be fair / For forty days 'twill rain nae mair" (*Catholic Encyclopedia*).

Domesday Book [22]   The grand survey, made in 1086, of English land, buildings, occupants, animals, and property, commissioned by William the Conqueror for potential taxation purposes. It acquired its popular name in the twelfth century from Domesday as the day of Last Judgment, suggesting it was the book by which all men would be judged.

Sung-Yen [23]   The name may derive from Sung Yun, an early Chinese traveler who made a pilgrimage, in the early sixth century, on the Silk Road to the Peshawar region of India in quest of Buddhist scriptures. In 1942, two members of extended Bloomsbury, Arthur Waley (translator) with Duncan Grant (illustrator), published *Monkey,* an abridged version of *Journey to the West,* a sixteenth-century novel by Wu Cheng'en about the seventh-century travels of Xuan Zang (Hsüan Tsang), perhaps the most famous of the early Chinese Buddhist pilgrims to India. Among his sources, Waley cites Herbert Allen Giles's *History of Chinese Literature* (Heinemann, 1901), which references Sung Yün [*sic*], but Waley, a prolific translator, most certainly would have known Samuel Beal's 1869 translation, *Travels of Fah-Hian and Sung-Yun: Buddhist pilgrims, from China to India (400 A.D. and 518 A.D.).*

before the Reformation [23]   The period of the Reformation in England began when King Henry VIII rejected the pope as the supreme spiritual (and political) authority; what followed was a repression of the Roman Catholic Church in England, involving the destruction of monasteries, chantries, religious icons, and pilgrimage shrines.

in the name of Thunder [24]   Popular expression referring to the god of thunder, Thor (in Norse mythology), from which the name Thursday is derived.

Bacchus [24]   Roman name of Dionysus, the god of wine.

cheeking the master [24]   Standing up to the master, challenging the master's authority.

the man holding his horse by the rein [25]   Although there are numerous portraits of men with their horses, notably Thomas Gainsborough's *George, Prince of Wales, Later George IV* (1782), the implied facial expression here has more in common with Gainsborough's painting *William Poyntz* (1762), who, although depicted with his dog not his horse, bears a name that resonates with the present novel as well.

The lady was a picture [25]   As has been noted, the description bears some resemblance to Thomas Gainsborough's painting *Georgiana, Duchess of Devonshire* (1783), depicting the duchess in a long yellow gown, with a pillar behind her back (SH); however, there are features in the description strikingly missing in Gainsborough's portrait but present in Joshua Reynolds's painting of the same name (1775–1776). Not only does Reynolds's duchess have feathers in her hair and lean forward to rest her weight on a stone balustrade, but, more significantly, the background to the left of the figure leads the eye down a leafy allée to an opening of distant sky. The further detail of the silver arrow implies that the sitter in Woolf's fictional portrait was posing as Cynthia or Diana, huntress and goddess of the moon, and there is indeed a portrait known as *The Duchess of Devonshire as Cynthia*, painted by Maria Cosway. Although it lacks physical resemblance to Woolf's description, Cosway's painting supplies the iconography, which Cosway emphasized with an accompanying quotation, in the Royal Academy exhibition catalog, from Spenser's *The Faerie Queene*. To further complicate the allusion, yet another Gainsborough painting of the duchess was the subject of a notorious theft, when it was stolen from the premises of an art dealer in 1875. Missing for over twenty-five years, until the thief finally agreed to arrangements for its return in 1901, it acquired a legendary status as the "Lost Duchess" and became the subject of innumerable reproductions. The portrait hanging in Pointz Hall is thus enriched through a palimpsest of multiple, syncretic allusions, while still remaining a portrait of an unidentified subject painted by an obscure artist—features which for Woolf (who celebrated the "Lives of the Obscure") had positive implications. (In 1940, reviewing a collection of letters by the duchess's daughter, Woolf significantly turned her subject about to focus on the daughter's governess, Selina Trimmer.) The legendary duchess (an ancestor on the paternal side in the Spencer family and thus of Lady Diana Spencer, "Princess Di") was further known to the British public through the triangulation of her unconventional sexual life, which involved a ménage à trois in which her dearest and closest female friend was also her husband's mistress. She is further entangled in this text as a descendant, on the maternal side, of the Poyntz family, reminding us that Woolf's earliest titles for this novel were Poyntzet Hall (*Diary* 5: 135) and Poyntz Hall (*Diary* 5: 141).

the still, distilled essence of emptiness, silence [26] The cold alabaster vase, with its resonances of the silence and stasis of eternity, recalls John Keats's "Ode on a Grecian Urn" (1819; 1820), a poem itself based not on a single urn but on a composite of memories. The sense of movement in stasis suggests an echo, too, of a passage from T. S. Eliot's "Burnt Norton" (1936): "Words, after speech, reach / Into silence. Only by the form, the pattern, / Can words or music reach / The stillness, as a Chinese jar still / Moves perpetually in its stillness." Whereas both Keats and Eliot focus on the shape and form of the container, however, Woolf's image draws our attention in to the hollow inside the vase, and her complex, off-center syllabic repetitions convey a pattern that is both fluid and resonant: *still*/[de]*still*[ed]; *e*[ssence]/*e*[mptiness; [ess]*ence*/[sil]*ence*.

Manresa [26]   The name Manresa is both a London street and a Spanish town noted for its Dominican monastery, but if there are connections between Mrs. Manresa and Katherine Mansfield (see the note to page 28, "Tasmania"), then Woolf may be thinking of the puns on sexual proclivities in both names.

Somerset House [27]   In 1939, this major government building housed the offices of Internal Revenue, Probate Registry, and the Registry for Births, Marriages, and Deaths.

Tasmania [28]   An island-state of Australia, noted for its unspoiled natural environment, it was separated from the Australian continent 10,000 years ago by the sea. In the early nineteenth century, settlement consisted mainly of transported convicts, although Katherine Mansfield's grandfather had been drawn there, as a prospector, by the goldfields.

not the right word [28]   Presumably the right word is *deported* or *transported* (see above); Mr. Blencowe has been seeking the rhyme in the wrong syllable.

spit and image [28]   The colloquial expression (meaning exact likeness), usually rendered as *spitting image* in American English, indicates that the voice here is that of village gossip, and that it is this same voice that singles out Ralph Manresa as a Jew, and his money as new money (made in business) rather than the more respectable old money (from the landed gentry).

stuffed man [28]   Recalling the lines from T. S. Eliot's "The Hollow Men," "We are the hollow men / We are the stuffed men," which in turn allude to Guy Fawkes, a Roman Catholic zealot who, in 1605, attempted to blow up the Houses of Parliament, and whose stuffed effigies are traditionally burned in England on Guy Fawkes night.

corkscrew [28]   The more accurate term would be champagne opener, an instrument shaped like a pair of pliers with a curved gripping surface that would go around the cork, enabling it to be twisted open. This not-uncommon misnomer may derive from confusion with a champagne tap, which *is* like a corkscrew, but since the tap was used to draw out only a small amount of champagne, it would not accord with Mrs. Manresa's "cocking her thumb" to uncork the champagne herself, or with her subsequent exuberance in filling the glasses. Manresa's misusage then leads to an off-color pun, although it is probably unintentional: Given that she considers herself unconventional in saying the word *stays* out loud in this company (a rather old-fashioned word at the time, when *corset* or *girdle* would be the more usual term), it is unlikely that she consciously implies a double entendre with the word *screw*, despite some evidence that *cork* was a slang term for butler (SH). But the subsequent reaction of the company, "She's said it, she's done it, not I," would suggest that at least some of them pick up on a welcome vulgarity in her speech as well as in her behavior. The novel's concern throughout with puns, and with what can and cannot be said in "polite" company, suggests that the malapropism is intended as Mrs. Manresa's, and is not Woolf's own.

Norman? Saxon? [29]   History is thus written into the architecture of the house, recalling the Saxon (ca. 900–1066) or the Norman (post-1066) past.

lily pond [30]   Pools are frequent images in Woolf's writing for the mind as a reservoir of both conscious and unconscious memories. See Woolf's sketch "The Fascination of the Pool" (*Complete*

Shorter Fiction) for a description of voices contained in a pool, including that of a girl who had drowned herself.

He must change. [32]   Giles follows proper etiquette by changing out of his business suit, but with the implication, too, of changing roles or identities.

some Institute [34]   Possibly the Courtauld Institute of Art, but for Woolf's opinion of institutional judgments of art, see her essay "The Royal Academy," which ends with her fleeing the horrors of institutional values: "Honour, patriotism, chastity, wealth, success, importance, position, patronage, power" (*Essays* 3: 93).

Sir Joshua [35]   The painter, Sir Joshua Reynolds (1723–1792) (see also note to page 25).

Tinker, tailor [35]   An old counting rhyme, often played by children with the number of stones or pits left in their bowls of fruit, and used to predict the future. Dating back to the seventeenth century, it appears in many versions; Mrs. Manresa's version is quoted in George Meredith's *Evan Harrington* (book 2, chapter 8), but a slightly different version, which includes the word *gentleman* after *sailor*, appears in both Anthony Trollope's *The Three Clerks* (chapter 4) and in the Rev. Walter W. Skeat's annotations to *The Complete Works of Geoffrey Chaucer* (1894–1897), where it is described as "our common saying" (I.481–82).

Figgis's Guide Book [36]   A fictional title but a common type of book, pointing to another kind of source text for the recording of history.

To be, or not to be [38]   Hamlet's famous soliloquy (III.i.56 ff.), which, at the time, most children would have memorized in school. Concerning the specific question of whether Hamlet's best course of action would be to commit suicide, it also poses the larger question of whether thinking can inhibit action. Compare

Prufrock's "overwhelming question" in T. S. Eliot's "The Love Song of J. Alfred Prufrock" and "Between the idea / And the reality . . . / Falls the Shadow" in Eliot's "The Hollow Men."

Fade far away [38]   Isa and Dodge make an associative leap from Shakespeare to Keats's "Ode to a Nightingale," reciting lines, albeit somewhat inexactly, that also concern an ambivalent wish for death as a release from suffering: "Fade far away, dissolve, and quite forget / What thou among the leaves hast never known, / The weariness, the fever, and the fret."

Reynolds! Constable! Crome! [38]   Like Joshua Reynolds, John Constable (1776–1837) and John Crome (1768–1821) were eminent English painters, all recognized members of the Royal Academy.

Why called 'Old'? [38]   John Crome was commonly called Old Crome, to distinguish him from his son, John Bernay Crome (1794–1842), who was also a painter.

Gammer Gurton's Needle [41]   One of the earliest English comedies, dating from the sixteenth century, of uncertain authorship, and full of fun and scatological humor: Gammer (Old Lady) Gurton loses her needle, which, after much "horseplay," is finally found in the seat of a young man's pants. Woolf reviewed the play in 1920 and claimed that in its simplicity and directness, and its approach to "indecency" in a way that is "wholesome and natural," the play is "pure English" (*Essays* 3: 237).

The donkey [41]   The story of Buridan's ass, named after the fourteenth-century French philosopher Jean Buridan, and depicting a classic predicament of indecision (not unlike Hamlet's) caused by being placed between equally compelling alternatives.

manacled to a rock [41]   In Greek mythology, Prometheus was the son of a Titan who offended Zeus by sympathetically giving fire to humans and bringing the arts and civilization to earth. As punishment, Zeus caused Prometheus to be chained to a rock, where each day an eagle tore out his liver, which—since Prometheus was immortal—reconstituted itself every night. Prometheus is a prominent figure throughout the history of sculpture, painting, and literature, but particularly in the Romantic period (in the works of Byron, Shelley, and Mary Shelley), where he epitomizes the defiant or heroic endurance of undeserved suffering. Although seeming perhaps to trivialize Promethean suffering, Woolf used similar imagery to describe the tortures of her own caged experience when restricted during an illness from walking and writing: "Here I am chained to my rock. . . . Still if one is Prometheus, if the rock is hard and the gadflies pungent, gratitude, affection, none of the nobler feelings hold sway" (*Diary* 2: 133). It also crops up in her account of suffering the oppressive presence of in-laws: "But there I am pinned down, as firmly as Prometheus on his rock, to have my day, Friday 26th of September 1930, picked to pieces" (*Diary* 3: 321). It should be noted, however, that neither passage is without self-criticism.

this word, which he could not speak in public [42]   Although he has changed out of his business suit and stockbroker identity, Giles is still conventional both in clothes and manner, censoring the words *sodomite* or *bugger* as being beyond the bounds of respectability to which he adheres.

nettle-rash [44]   The medical name is urticaria, but a common name is hives.

unheard rhythm [45]   Yet another echo of Keats's "Ode on a Grecian Urn": "Heard melodies are sweet, but those unheard / Are sweeter."

A beaker of cold water [46]   Isa echoes but reverses the speaker's longing for "a beaker full of the warm South" in Keats's "Ode to a Nightingale."

picture paper [46]   Illustrated newspapers (or newsmagazines) rose to great popularity in the nineteenth century, especially among less educated readers, and the twentieth century saw an upsurge in illustrated magazines designed specifically for women. In Woolf's *Jacob's Room*, a novel that distinguishes among characters according to their reading materials, it is Mrs. Pascoe, a cottager living in a Cornish village, who reads the "picture papers." Mrs. Manresa is likely reading a slightly more upscale magazine like *Vogue* or the *Tatler* (a twentieth-century magazine that took its name from the famous eighteenth-century periodical), both of which offered news, society pages, fiction, and photography, and both of which Woolf knew.

pan pipes [47]   In Greek mythology, Pan, the goat-footed shepherd god, pursued the nymph Syrinx, a worshipper of Diana, until she escaped by metamorphosing into a cluster of reeds growing in a marshy river. Out of these reeds, Pan fashioned the "pan pipes" with which Pan challenged Apollo, whose instrument was the lyre, to a contest, which Apollo wins (the only dissenting vote being that of King Midas, whom Apollo punished by giving ass's ears). In two companionate poems written for Mary Shelley's play *Midas*, Percy Bysshe Shelley articulates the conflict as one between two musical and poetic genres: Apollo representing the Olympian, serene, and divinely ordered aesthetic, and Pan, the pastoral, human, and heterogeneous. Pan as nature god is a frequent motif in modernist writing, particularly in the fiction of E. M. Forster: In *The Longest Journey*, the semiautobiographical character's collection of short stories is entitled "Pan Pipes" (see chapters 15 and 35).

Newfoundland Dog [50]   Most likely a reproduction of a painting by
    Sir Edwin Henry Landseer (1802–1873) a popular Victorian En-
    glish painter noted for his sentimentalized paintings of dogs.
    The Landseer variety of Newfoundland dog derives its name
    from his paintings.

snake in the grass [51]   A hidden enemy, or concealed danger, deriv-
    ing from the incident, in Greek mythology, related by Virgil, in
    which Orpheus's wife, Eurydice, attempting to flee an un-
    wanted seducer, steps on a snake in the grass (*anguis in herba*) and
    is fatally bitten (*Eclogues III* 93). In *Jacob's Room,* it is sex itself that
    is the hidden snake in the grass (81). In Cockney rhyming slang,
    the phrase means "looking glass."

of two minds [51]   A common figurative expression meaning inde-
    cisive, but it also suggests literally that Lucy is hovering between
    two different modes of thought, the rational and the intuitive,
    the practical and the mystical.

a tea plantation [52]   Another indication that the tentacles of impe-
    rialism reach far down into the lives of ordinary people. Cobbet
    himself is a simple man connected with nature, but since there
    was not a single tea plantation in the United Kingdom until the
    twenty-first century, his work would have been in one of the
    colonies, most likely in India or Ceylon.

Adsum [52]   The traditional response, in Latin, to a roll call,
    meaning "Here! Present!" In the calling up to Holy Orders, it
    has the connotation as well of "I am ready to serve." In the last
    chapter of *The Newcomes* (1855) by William Makepeace Thack-
    eray, in a chapter titled "In which the Colonel says 'Adsum'
    when his Name is called," Thomas Newcome pronounces this
    word on his deathbed, thus both returning to roll call at his (un-
    doubtedly privileged) boys' school and revealing humility before
    his Maker.

a June day in 1939 [52]   Given that the pageant is likely being held on a Saturday, the date of the pageant would be either June 3, 10, or 17. By June 24, the king and queen would no longer be in Canada, since they returned to Britain on June 22 and participated in a royal procession to Guildhall on June 23.

sacking [54]   Coarse material, the wearing of which, in the medieval period, signified self-humbling and repentance, and thus appropriately the garb of pilgrims journeying to a shrine.

Rhoderick [54]   The martial opening might stir associations with Roderick, the last Visigoth king of Spain, and a heroic figure in Sir Walter Scott's "The Vision of Don Roderick" (1811), Walter Savage Landor's *Count Julian* (1812), Robert Southey's *Roderick, the Last of the Goths* (1814), and Byron's *Childe Harold's Pilgrimage* (1812; canto 1). According to legend, Roderick's rape of Florinda, daughter of Count Julian of the Visigoths, led to Julian's inciting the Moors to invade, and to Roderick's defeat in 711. In the context of English history, however, the more relevant Roderick would be Roderick Dhu, 39th chieftain of the McNeil Clan and a Catholic Jacobite, who was fatally wounded in his battle against the Protestant king James V. Roderick is a heroic figure in Sir Walter Scott's poem "The Lady of the Lake," a story replete with star-crossed young lovers, disguised identity, a talisman (a signet ring) enabling a recognition scene, and a marriage that reconciles warring factions.

maying, nutting [56]   The celebration of spring, or "going a-maying," is a frequent motif in Elizabethan poetry and can be traced back, through Geoffrey Chaucer's "The Knight's Tale," to the troubadour or trouvère lyrics of twelfth- and thirteenth-century France, and the medieval French poem the *Roman de la Rose*. "Nutting" has associations with the nursery rhyme "Here we come gathering nuts in May," in which "nuts" is probably a corruption of "knots" or blossoms, gathered to decorate the maypole.

Canterbury pilgrims [56]   The villagers' serpentine weaving through the trees suggests the progress of Chaucer's Canterbury pilgrims, wending their way from London to Canterbury in a pilgrimage to the shrine of St. Thomas à Becket, murdered by four knights believing that they were following the wishes of King Henry II.

Merry England [56]   Dating from the Middle Ages, the phrase invokes a positive, utopian view of England, poetically expressed in images of spring and spring festivals and politically grounded in the ideal of an egalitarian, communal society. William Wordsworth responded to later cynicism about this ideal in sonnet III of "Poems Composed or Suggested During a Tour in the Summer of 1833": "Can, I ask, / This face of rural beauty be a mask / For discontent, and poverty, and crime; / These spreading towns a cloak for lawless will? / Forbid it, Heaven!—and MERRY ENGLAND still / Shall be thy rightful name, in prose and rhyme!" (lines 9–14).

Hawkins, Frobisher, Drake [58]   Sir John Hawkins (1532–1595), Sir Martin Frobisher (ca. 1535–1594), and Sir Francis Drake (ca. 1540–1596) were naval commanders and explorers during the reign of Queen Elizabeth I, 1558–1603. Woolf both celebrated glories of the Elizabethan age and perceived that its riches (of both objects and images) depended on imperialist plunder. See "Traffics and Discoveries," her 1906 review of Professor Walter Raleigh's *The English Voyages of the Sixteenth Century* (*Essays* 1: 120–24).

throstle, the mavis [58]   Old dialect terms for the song thrush (*Turdus philomelos*), a bird that characteristically repeats its melodic phrases. See "The throstle with his note so true" (Shakespeare,

Midsummer Night's Dream) and "The thrush replyes, the Mavis descant playes" (Edmund Spenser, "Epithalamion").

I fear I am not in my perfect mind [59]   King Lear's words when, recovering from his madness, he begins to recognize his daughter Cordelia: "Pray, do not mock me: / . . . / I fear I am not in my perfect mind" (*King Lear,* IV.vii.59; 63).

a stricken deer [59]   The image comes from William Cowper's poem, *The Task* (Book III: "The Garden," 108), in which the poet casts himself as a stricken deer pierced by the world's arrows. The speaker's overpowering sense of loneliness and alienation, and his withdrawal into rural life as an escape from the corrupt commercial world of London, make the poem an apt one for Giles to recall. There are ironies in Giles's recourse to Cowper, however, given Giles's homophobia and speculations that the source of Cowper's profound melancholy was bodily and possibly sexual. Woolf joked about one particular and now discredited rumor when, referring to male and female parts of car engines, she declared their secondhand car "to be hermaphrodite, like the poet Cowper" (*Letters* 3: 463), but her published view of Cowper's sensibilities was that "he was a man singularly without thought of sex" ("Cowper and Lady Austen," *The Second Common Reader,* 145 [Orlando: Harcourt, 1986]). Woolf valued Cowper highly as a writer, finding lines and phrases in his poetry that burned with a "white fire," and that conveyed a "central transparency" (*Letters* 3: 333), yet oddly, and perhaps self-defensively, she lacked sympathy for his mental afflictions, judged his melancholia as self-absorption, and did not pursue the possibility that Cowper's domestic, putatively feminine identifications challenged prevailing stereotypes of gendered masculinity. She most likely also distanced herself from the poem's resolution in submission to the will of God.

mopping and mowing [59]   Making facial expressions like grimacing and pouting. Albert's performance recalls Tom o'Bedlam's description of the fiend "Flibbertigibbet, of mopping and mowing, who since possesses chambermaids and waiting-women" (*King Lear,* IV.i), a description later echoed in Christina Rossetti's "Goblin Market": "Mopping and mowing, / Full of airs and graces, / Pulling wry faces" (lines 336–38).

Hoppety, jiggety [60]   A phrase akin to the reduplicative compound words characteristic of nursery rhymes, such as "Higgledy piggledy, / My black hen." Other nursery rhymes folded into Albert's lines are "In and out the windows" and "Hickory, dickory, dock."

dandelion clock [60]   A game explained in the story "Dandelion Clock" by Juliana Horatia Ewing (1841–1885), one of England's most popular writers of children's literature: "You blow till the seed is all blown away, and you count each of the puffs—an hour to a puff." The story concerns a little boy who wonders why such "fairy clocks" tell different times for different people.

a scene from a play [61]   Perhaps anticipating Tom Stoppard's riotous fifteen-minute and then two-minute *Hamlet* (*Dogg's Hamlet,* 1979), Miss La Trobe offers a condensation of all Shakespeare and Elizabethan drama in the space of approximately half an hour. A false Duke (who turns against his brother) can be found in both *As You Like It* and *The Tempest;* a girl disguised as a boy figures in the plots of *As You Like It, Twelfth Night,* and *Cymbeline;* in *Twelfth Night,* a brother and sister identify themselves to each other by divulging that each had a father with a mole on his brow, and in *Cymbeline* the king's daughter hides for safety in a cave and the identity of her long-lost brother, stolen in infancy, is at the end proven by a mole on his neck; the aged crone recalls both Juliet's nurse and the "aged beldame" in

Keats's "The Eve of St. Agnes," a poem much patterned on *Romeo and Juliet*, but with a happier ending for the lovers. A hilarious pastiche, this scene in the pageant nevertheless encompasses most of the standard plot elements in comedy and romance, with traces of the histories and tragedies, as evident in the quotations below.

Play out the play [61]   Falstaff's line in *Henry IV*, part 1, challenging Prince Hal to follow through to the end of an argument (II.iv). The figurative meaning is to carry on in the face of all odds, as notably (combined with a near-quotation from *Macbeth*), in Byron's *Don Juan:* "Life's a poor player,"—then "play out the play, / Ye villains!" (canto 11, stanza 86, lines 684–85).

Yet the cock did crow ere he left me— [62]   In act I, scene i of *Hamlet*, the apparition of Hamlet's father is about to speak when the cock crows, causing the ghost to disappear. Horatio and Marcellus discuss the belief that the crowing of the cock, the "bird of dawning," nullifies the power of fairies, witches, and spirits. In Eliot's *The Waste Land*, a cock crows, "Co co rico co co rico," just before a promising "gust / Bringing rain" (lines 392–95). Associations of guilt with the moment before dawn stem from Peter's thrice-uttered denial of Christ (Matthew 26:34).

There is little blood in this arm [62]   The bloody hands above, and the guilty scene, prompt associations with Lady Macbeth's "Who would have thought the old man to have had so much blood in him?" (*Macbeth*, V.i)

The plot was only there to beget emotion [63]   In "On Re-Reading Novels," Woolf rejects Percy Lubbock's formalist approach to the structure of a novel, arguing that a work of literature "is not form which you see, but emotion which you feel," and that the accumulation of detail, in building up impressions, leads the reader to moments of emotional understanding (*Essays* 3: 340).

Look where she comes! [63]   "Lo where she comes .. ∕ . . Clad all in white, that seems a virgin best" (Spenser, "Epithalamion").

pearl in night's black ear [63]   Romeo's response on first sight of Juliet: "It seems she hangs upon the cheek of night / As a rich jewel in an Ethiop's ear" (Shakespeare, *Romeo and Juliet*, I.v).

Peace, let her pass [64]   Echoing Kent's words on the death of King Lear: "O, let him pass! He hates him / That would upon the rack of this tough world / Stretch him out longer" (*Lear*, V.iii).

Love. Hate. Peace. Three emotions [64]   Earlier versions of the novel show Woolf experimenting with different configurations of these emotions: love, hate, fear (*PH* 103); love, sorrow, fear (*PH* 104); love, hate, anguish (*PH* 329); and sometimes with four emotions: love, hate, fear, sorrow (*PH* 105), and love, hate, anguish, peace (*PH* 330). The implication is that more important than the specific emotions named is her plan to isolate a few basic emotions to suggest a pervasive and continuous rhythm underlying all life. Her final choice of the "three-fold ply" of emotion finds an echo in the frequent repetition of three words ("chuff, chuff, chuff"; "tapping, tapping, tapping"). In similar rhythmic fashion, Sir Thomas Browne's *The Garden of Cyrus* (1658)—a work Woolf knew well—traces occurrences of quincuncial patterns (patterns of five) in gardens and nature to evidence the universe's underlying pattern.

Of her frailty, let nothing now remembered be [64]   Having killed Lord Henry Percy (Hotspur) in battle, Prince Hal absolves him of his guilt: "Adieu, and take thy praise with thee to heaven! / Thy ignominy sleep with thee in the grave, / But not remembered in thy epitaph" (*Henry IV,* part 1, V.iv).

Call for the robin redbreast and the wren [64]   The dirge Cornelia distractedly sings (in close parallel with Ophelia) for her dead son, Marcello, in John Webster's tragedy *The White Devil* (1612; V.iv). The robin and the wren are called on to bring leaves and flowers to cover the grave; the song continues: "But keep the wolf far thence, that's foe to men, / For with his nails he'll dig them up again" (lines 110–1). Compare lines 74–75 in T. S. Eliot's *The Waste Land.*

Cover the corpse [64]   Recalling words spoken over the dead body of the duchess in John Webster's tragedy *The Duchess of Malfi:* "Cover her face. Mine eyes dazzle" (IV.ii.253).

waft you to your slumber [64]   Horatio's words over Hamlet's dead body: "Good night, sweet prince, / And flights of angels sing thee to thy rest" *(Hamlet,* V.ii.351).

Lead on the dance! [64]   The traditional ending of a comedy.

a mellay; a medley [64]   The shift in connotation from mellay or mêlée (suggesting confusion, chaos, and conflict) to medley (indicative of multiplicity, heterogeneity, and interrelation) identifies a crux of the pageant, of the novel, of life. Do the mixed styles and diversity of sources and voices create a muddle or a new hybrid form? A similar dilemma is posed by another likely intertext, Alfred Lord Tennyson's poem "The Princess, A Medley."

skimble-skamble [65]   A reduplicative compound (like "Hoppety, jiggety"), derived from *scamble,* meaning rambling or foolish. The first recorded use is Hotspur's railing against fancy and superstition in *Henry IV,* part 1: "such a deal of skimble-skamble stuff" (III.i.153). In the same month that Woolf began the first typescript of this novel, she referred to her own "rather skimble skamble works" *(Diary* 5: 134).

Follow, follow, follow [67]   Repetitions of *follow* occur in many folk
songs, but Woolf's continuing emphasis on three associates the
phrase most specifically with a three-part round, or "catch," by
the seventeenth-century poet John Hilton. Catches were notable
for off-color double entendres or for bitter satire, so that during the nineteenth century most were revised to be more suit-
able for children's singing. By Woolf's time, the most common
words for Hilton's round were: part 1, "Come, follow, follow,
follow, / Follow, follow, follow me"; part 2, "Whither shall I fol-
low, follow, follow, / Whither shall I follow, follow thee?"; part
3, "To the greenwood, to the greenwood, / To the greenwood,
greenwood tree." The original lines for part 3, however, were
"To the gallow, gallow tree."

Red Indians the game was [67]   Allusions in these mystifying comments have not been identified. The oddity of "a note wrapped
up in a pebble" may be explained by the usage of *pebble* as a
short form for pebble-leather—leather with a mottled appearance produced by pebbling. But if there are specific allusions
here, they are again likely multiple and syncretic; holograph versions of this passage include the details of "the beat of the tom-
tom in India" and "the reed with the message . . . rolled round
a pebble, shot over the fort" (*PH* 335; 484–85).

made them see [68]   A number of writers have articulated their task
in this way, emphasizing, too, the active role the reader/viewer
performs in seeing. Robert Browning grouped artists into three
different gradations of imparted vision: "For the worst of us to
say they so have seen; / For the better, what it was they saw; the
best / Impart the gift of seeing to the rest" (*Sordello* 3.866–68).
In his preface to *The Nigger of the "Narcissus,"* Joseph Conrad
similarly claimed that his task was "to make you hear, to make
you feel . . . before all, to make you *see*!" And in a fictionalized
conversation between two writers in Virginia Woolf's essay

"Walter Sickert," one of the writers says, "The novelist after all wants to make us see" (*The Captain's Death Bed and Other Essays* [New York: Harcourt, 1950], 198). The complexities of this task for the modernist writer, when both seeing and the seen are fraught with uncertainty, belie the seeming simplicity of the statement.

a snake . . . choked with a toad in its mouth [69]   This haunting image has been linked to an incident Woolf described on September 4, 1935: "We saw a snake eating a toad: it had half the toad in, half out; gave a suck now & then. The toad slowly disappearing. L. poked its tail; the snake was sick of the crushed toad" (*Diary* 4: 338). The entry, which proceeds to Woolf's dreaming of men committing suicide, also records intense political discussion of Mussolini's threatened invasion of Abyssinia (Ethiopia)—a concern Woolf wrote was disrupting her sleep (*Letters* 5: 428). The League of Nations' inability to avert this crisis was a major factor in the downfall of the League and of the escalation of tensions leading to a European war. Some knowledge of Woolf's thoughts seems implicit in Vita Sackville-West's column in the *New Statesman and Nation*, "Country Notes," for July 20, 1940, which comments on the "permanence and recurrence" of nature as a "calming and reassuring thought" in wartime, and yet draws attention to nature's cruelty as well. Sackville-West describes a "small horrifying sight": an injured frog on the garden path and, issuing from a hole in the wall, "a beautiful snake full of venom, that drew the frog towards him, terrified and fascinated by the superior power." Sackville-West continues, "The frog remained frozen as a bas-relief, his body flattened in terror against the wall. The snake put out his dangerous, his fanged head, alive, spiteful, menacing. He did not dare to send out the length of his lithe body because of my presence there." Stories of snake-frog encounters are relatively common, but what is striking in these descriptions is the powerful symbolic read-ing—"a psychological effect," Sackville-West posits, "of war-time" (62).

Lathom [70]   A village in Lancashire, England, notable for the vast lands of the Manor of Lathom recorded in the Domesday Book.

They come every year . . . From Africa [70–71]   The migration of swal-lows to southern Europe and Africa is a persistent theme in Gilbert White's *The Natural History and Antiquities of Selborne, in the County of Southampton* (1789), a work that Woolf reviewed in 1939. Like Cowper, White is notable for his intense focus on nature and on a small rural community, yet White's fascination with migratory patterns imparts a global dimension to his otherwise intensely local history. Woolf also notes White's sensitivity to "unsought memories that come of their own accord" and his propensity for making the same comments every year ("White's 'Selborne,'" *The Captain's Death Bed and Other Essays* [New York: Harcourt, 1950], 18).

the wishing well, where the washer-woman's little boy . . . dropped a pin [71]   An ancient custom, spread throughout Ireland, Great Britain, and Europe, of dropping pins into holy wells (or inserting pins or nails into sacred trees) to achieve the granting of some prayer or wish. The origins of the practice are buried in early folklore, but the ritual implies an offering to a god or presiding spirit.

Canada, not India [72]   In 1939, both countries were asserting in-creasing independence from England, although the situation in India was more turbulent and antagonistic. The visit of King George VI and his consort, Queen Elizabeth, to Canada and the United States was intended, from the British side, to consolidate support in the anticipated European war, but as the *New States-man and Nation* warned, the more immediate result was to reinforce developing ideas of Canadian identity, since the domestic focus was on loyalty to the king of Canada, rather than to the British Empire ("A London Diary," June 17, 1939: 927). In any event, Canada followed closely on the heels of Britain in declaring war.

the Duke of Windsor [72]   Determined to marry Mrs. Wallis Simpson, a twice-divorced American with two previous husbands still living, Edward VIII abdicated on December 11, 1936, before the official coronation could take place, and was given the title Duke of Windsor. Enjoying the gossip, and perhaps the affront to respectability, Woolf joked, "If you ask me would I rather meet Einstein or the Prince of Wales [as he had been known], I plump for the Prince without hesitation" ("Am I a Snob?," *Moments of Being* 208).

the neck was broad as a pillar, against an arum lily [72–73]   Isa's appearance continues to link her with nineteenth-century aestheticism: A swanlike, or pillarlike, neck is a characteristic feature in the Pre-Raphaelite painting of Dante Gabriel Rossetti, whose ideal of female beauty, typified in Jane Morris, contrasted strongly with the blond, fragile, corseted female form made desirable by Victorian convention. Rossetti also used the lily as a sexual/sacred symbol connected with the Virgin Mary, and the arum lily, though properly not a lily, is a symbol of purity, while highly sexual (and hermaphrodite) in appearance. The phrase *Tower of Ivory* perplexes the young Stephen Dedalus with similarly mixed connotations, as an epithet applied to the Virgin Mary (and deriving from the Song of Solomon), but which for Stephen attaches as well to his emerging fascination with the female body. The sexual/sacred overtones are united in Spenser's "Epithalamion," in which a litany of the bride's beauties includes "Her snowie neck lyke to a marble towre" (177).

the greenhouse, the pig sty, or the stable [73]   Book III of Cowper's "The Task" includes a long passage on the greenhouse ("Who loves a garden loves a greenhouse too"), following what must be the first extended poetic description of a manure pile, a composting "hotbed" used to generate heat for growing cucumbers in cold weather ("The stable yields a stercoraceous heap"). Cowper implies the interrelatedness of functions—a theme pertinent to *Between the Acts.*

Swallow, my sister, O sister swallow [75]   Bart quotes, and continues to quote, from Algernon Charles Swinburne's poem "Itylus," thus weaving together the repeated references to swallows and nightingales and the pervasive theme of rape. According to the Greek myth as told by Ovid in his *Metamorphoses,* Tereus, King of Thrace, raped his wife's sister, Philomela, and to ensure her silence cut out her tongue. But Philomela wove her story into a tapestry to let her sister, Procne, know the truth. In revenge, Procne killed her son, Itylus, and fed him to the unsuspecting Tereus and the two sisters were then transformed into birds— Procne into a swallow and Philomela into a nightingale—to enable their escape. Swinburne's poem is Philomela's elegiac lament—a contrast to the sister swallow's ability to follow the natural cycle by welcoming the spring and later migrating south. The myth has supplied the subject or an informing trope for numerous works of literature, painting, and music—perhaps most notably among the modernists, in T. S. Eliot's "Sweeney among the Nightingales" and *The Waste Land.*

The idiot? . . . in the tradition [76]   A reference to the humble fool of folk festivals or mummer's plays, not to the jester or court fool, from whom Shakespeare's fools derive. The spring festival plays are understood to be reenactments of the death and rebirth of the year, and the fool, who may wear a hood with ass's ears, suggesting an animal disguise, is often killed and then resurrected.

what his left hand was doing [76]   Presumably either stimulating himself or trying to control an erection. Left-handedness has traditionally been associated with what falls outside the norm.

Old Man's Beard [77]   The description of a bitter herb with pungent leaves indicates the plant is actually southernwood or old man (a variety of wormwood) rather than old man's beard (a wild clematis, with mildly almond-scented flowers). Both plants occur in poems by Edward Thomas (1878–1917), but it is his poem "Old Man" (rather than "Lob," which mentions old man's beard) that most connects with Isa's mood. The poet muses on the double and seemingly paradoxical names of the herb—"Old Man, or Lad's-love"—both perhaps deriving from the folkloric belief that it could heighten male virility, or that rubbing it on the face could promote the growth of a beard. The herb's scent tantalizes the poem's speaker with elusive but powerful memories: "I, too, [like his daughter] often shrivel the grey shreds, / Sniff them and think and sniff again and try / Once more to think what it is I am remembering, / . . . / I have mislaid the key" (26–28, 230). The botanical name for southernwood, *Artemisia abrotanum,* indicates it belongs to the genus *Artemisia*—named for Artemis, the Greek goddess whose name, in Roman myth, is Cynthia or Diana.

Books: the treasured life-blood of immortal spirits. Poets; the legislators of mankind [79]   Bart is thinking of two of the most memorable testimonies to the value of the written word: John Milton's *Areopagitica* (1644), with its arguments against censorship: "Who kills a man kills a reasonable creature, God's image; but he who destroys a good book, kills reason itself, kills the image of God, as it were, in the eye. . . . a good book is the precious life-blood of a master spirit"; and P. B. Shelley's "A Defence of Poetry" (1821), which ends, "Poets are the unacknowledged legislators of the world."

I love till I die [81]   From a lute song by Thomas Ford (ca. 1580–1648): "There is a lady sweet and kind, / Was never face so pleased my mind, / I did but see her passing by, / And yet I love her till I die."

Music makes us see the hidden, join the broken [83]   In Robert Browning's poem "Abt Vogler," the speaker, an organist improvising at his instrument, conveys his idea of earthly music as an intuition of the heavenly through a similar image: "On the earth the broken arcs; in the heaven, a perfect round" (73).

what about the Jews [84]   In early 1939, the British public generally knew less about Hitler's persecution of Jews than the American public did, largely because Prime Minister Neville Chamberlain's policy was to censor news of atrocities in his efforts to avert a European war. The British public was well aware, however, of the arrival of Jewish children as refugees: An item in the *New Statesman and Nation* on June 10, 1939, for example, drew attention to their plight, giving the name of the agency (in Bloomsbury) that people could contact if they were willing to serve as foster parents. The Woolfs, with their tour of Germany in 1935, their meeting with Sigmund Freud after his escape from Nazi-occupied Austria in 1938, and their political contacts, were well informed about Nazi atrocities. "Jews persecuted, only just over the Channel" Woolf wrote on May 15, 1940, and, as Hitler's invasion of England threatened as an imminent possibility, she reflected increasingly on the implications for Leonard and herself (given his Jewishness and their Labour affiliations): "we in concentration camps, or taking sleeping draughts" (*Diary* 5: 186, 292).

with a flea in his ear [84]   An old saying, dating from medieval times, and used in various ways. In England, it would refer to something annoying or irritating, such as receiving a rebuke. See, for example, *Love's Cure: Or, the Martial Maid,* an early seventeenth-century comedy, attributed to the combined authorship of John Fletcher, Francis Beaumont, and Philip Massinger: "He went away with a Flea in's Ear, / Like a poor Cur, clapping his trundle Tail / Betwixt his Legs" (III.iii). In French, the expression means to have a bee in the bonnet—that is, having an obsessive idea or a suspicion. In François Rabelais' sixteenth-century satiric and—for Mikhail Bakhtin (see introduction xlvi)—carnivalesque novel *Gargantua and Pantagruel,* the inveterate trickster Panurge makes literal play with the image by having his ear pierced so that he can wear a dangling gold earring in which he has encased a flea, claiming then that he has a flea in his ear and a mind to marry (book 3, chapter 7). The saying also provides the title for Georges Feydeau's highly popular bedroom farce, *La Puce à l'oreille* (1907), in which the hilarious convoluted absurdist plot is instigated by a woman's suspicions about her husband's infidelity.

reason holds sway [85]   The period from the mid-seventeenth century up to the late eighteenth century and the beginning of the Romantic era used to be called, after Thomas Paine (1737–1809), the Age of Reason. The pageant is beginning to imply a historical pattern that imitates the cyclical process of seasonal change, like that proposed in Oswald Spengler's *The Decline of the West* (1918). For Spengler, the eighteenth century was the high-autumn turning point, marking the shift from the Dionysian (or Faustian) to the Apollonian (or Euclidian)—a reorientation from creativity to rationalism that begins a culture's inevitable decline. The play that follows, however, and the allusions to eighteenth-century poets of sentiment like Oliver Goldsmith and William Cowper, suggest that rationalism has not entirely "won."

Time, leaning on his sickle [85]   This image combines Chronos or time, depicted in modern times with a scythe, with Cronus, the Titan god of the harvest who castrated his father with a sickle (a precursor of the scythe), thus heralding the destruction of the old crop to make room for the new crop in the spring. The blend is traditional: See Thomas Dekker, "For all Times sickle has gone ouer you, you are Orlando still" (*The Honest Whore*, 1604).

While Commerce from her Cornucopia [85]   The following passage is a pastiche or an echo chamber of allusions, all evoking a world beyond strife and warfare: The peaceful empire ushered in by commerce recalls "Thy cities shall with commerce shine" from James Thomson's "Rule Britannia" (1740; line 20); the stranger fearful of the snake appears in Oliver Goldsmith's "The Deserted Village" (1770; line 354), a poem about the disappearing calm of rural life; violets and eglantines image an idyllic, longed-for imaginative realm in John Keats's "Ode to a Nightingale" (1819; lines 46–47), later echoed in George Meredith's "Love in the Valley" (1878; lines 101–2); and the image of the bees conflates "His helmet now shall make a hive for bees" from George Peele's "A Farewell to Arms" (*Polyhymnia*, 1590; line 7) with "The yellow bees i' the ivy bloom," in a passage describing the poet's visionary dream in P. B. Shelley's *Prometheus Unbound* (1820; I.745).

while Zephyr sleeps [85]   The Greek god of the west wind, and thus the harbinger of spring and, in Chaucer's *The Canterbury Tales*, of the call to pilgrimage: "When Zephyrus eek with his sweete breeth / Inspired hath in every holt and heeth / The tendre croppes" (lines 4–6).

Damon [86]   A poetic shepherd in Virgil's eighth *Eclogue*, Damon occurs frequently as a name in the English pastoral tradition— in poems, for example, by Andrew Marvell, Edmund Spenser, John Milton, Anne Finch, Mary Leapor, and Alexander Pope. Pope's "Spring: The First Pastoral or Damon" is notable for shifting the pastoral scene from Arcadia or Arcady (the mythical "green world" in Greek and Sicilian pastoral poetry) to the banks of the Thames: "Damon: First in these Fields I try the Sylvan Strains, / Nor blush to sport on Windsor's blissful Plains: / Fair Thames flow gently from thy sacred Spring, / While on thy Banks Sicilian Muses sing" (lines 1–3). Line 3 echoes Spenser's "Prothalamion," which is later famously echoed in T. S. Eliot's *The Waste Land* (lines 183–84). For Cynthia, see the notes to pages 25, "the lady was a picture," and 77, "Old Man's Beard."

Where there's a Will there's a Way [87]   The eighteenth-century act of the pageant encapsulates the stock situations and characters in Restoration comedy, although it owes most to William Congreve's *Love for Love* (1695) and *The Way of the World* (1700). In the latter, Millamant inherits her fortune only if she marries in a way that pleases her aunt Lady Wishfort; in the former, Angelica tricks her suitor Valentine's father, Sir Sampson Legend, into proposing marriage, so that she can acquire and destroy a paper that would sign Valentine's inheritance away. Money and love are Restoration comedy's characteristic twin themes.

Give me the pounce-box [87]   Much fun was made in Restoration comedy of older women trying to recover youth through cosmetics and aromatics. A pounce or pouncet box held either powder for drying ink or perfume; small black patches on the face were used as beauty marks and also to hide blemishes or smallpox scars.

A pox [87]   A mild oath, referring to venereal disease.

lighting his taper [87]   A double entendre for a bit of bawdy wordplay.

a pig in a poke [88]   While the most common meaning of "a pig in a poke" is "a pig in a bag," an expression that generally refers to buying something sight unseen, here "poke" refers to a yoke or halter placed around an animal's neck with a pole inserted,

pointing or poking forward, to prevent the animal from breaking through or jumping over a fence (*OED*, from Webster 1828).
Deb's speech is typical of the verbal dexterity valued in Restoration comedy, in which wit was often displayed in rapid and in-
ventive strings of similes, frequently with sexual innuendo.

Asphodilla [88]   Asphodel is a plant belonging to the lily family,
associated by poets with the narcissus and thought to be an immortal flower covering the Elysian fields: "Others in Elysian
valleys dwell, / Resting weary limbs at last on beds of asphodel." Alfred Lord Tennyson, "The Lotos-Eaters" (line 170).

jackanapes [88]   A pet monkey, or a young man who acts like one.
Much sexual flattery is implied in Sir Spaniel's speech.

Emperor of the Indies [89]   The West Indies. Like Rachel Vin-
race, the heroine of Woolf's first novel, *The Voyage Out* (1915),
Flavinda has a father whose fortune derives from South America, exposing the reliance of British wealth on colonial plunder.

Where there's a Will there's a Way [90]   The phrase returns with
a punning humor characteristic of Restoration comedy.

To match their ears [90]   Implying ass's ears, like those of King
Midas, and making a stock joke about lawyers.

The poor man to his cot returns [92]   The tune returns us to the calm
simplicities of ordinary life, evoked in images resembling those
in Thomas Gray's "Elegy Written in a Country Churchyard"
(1751) and Robert Burns's "The Cotter's Saturday Night" (1785),
and standing in marked contrast to the machinations of the
aristocracy.

with his tail between his legs [93]   Flavinda's observations upon
high-society amours place her closer to the more worldly heroine
of Restoration comedy than to the innocent heroine in the senti-

mental comedies that began to appear in the Augustan age of
Queen Anne. See also the note to page 84, "with a flea in his ear."

a cit . . . a fop [94]   Words for *citizen* and *dandy*, both implying
decadent life in the city.

What stung . . . the blue bag [94] The blue bag used in the laundry
to prevent the yellowing of white linens was also, when wetted
and applied to the wound, an old remedy for bee sting.

Palaces tumble down [95]   The destruction of Babylon, Nineveh,
Troy, and Rome image the fall of civilizations, again suggesting
the end of historical cycles. Compare T. S. Eliot's lines, "Falling
towers / Jerusalem Athens Alexandria / Vienna London / Unreal" in *The Waste Land* (V.374–77).

The Chinese, you know, put a dagger on the table [97]   Mrs. Swithin is
thinking of traditional Chinese theater, most likely Peking opera
(*jingju* or *jingxi*), as opposed to the realistic spoken drama
(*huaju*) that developed in the twentieth century. Combining ac-
robatics, mime, speech, song, and dance, Peking opera uses a
bare stage and a minimum of props, relying on gesture and symbol to delineate setting and to convey emotion in a highly styl-
ized and rigorously compressed way. Peking opera would have
been known in England in the 1930s as a result of the widely
publicized tours of the legendary Mei Lanfang and his troupe to
the United States in 1930 and to the Soviet Union in 1935, where
Mei's performance greatly impressed Bertolt Brecht. A translation and adaptation, by Hsuing Shi-i, of *Lady Precious Stream*, a
story taken from Peking opera, played for an extraordinarily
successful long run in London from 1934–1936, although it only
loosely represented the traditional style.

And so Racine [97]   Woolf's close friend (Giles) Lytton Strachey
(1880–1932), an authority on the French dramatist Jean Racine

(1639–1699), wrote that unlike the English dramatist, Racine employed "the art of subtle suggestion," with a daring that was "not the daring of adventure but of intensity." Whereas the Elizabethan tragedians "traced, with elaborate and abounding detail, the rise, the growth, the decline, and the ruin of great causes," Racine focused on the crisis alone, and thus seized "the very heart of his subject ... in a single stroke" (Lytton Strachey, "Racine" [1908], *Books and Characters: French and English,* 5–27. London: Chatto & Windus, 1922).

Pop Goes the Weasel [97]   An old popular song with its basis in Victorian working-class poverty, using *pop* as slang for *pawn.* A friend of popular culture as opposed to the classics, Mrs. Manresa most likely took her nephew to a music hall show, or perhaps a film. The Three Stooges produced two shorts in the 1930s using the tune "Pop Goes the Weasel" as a theme: *Punch Drunks* (1934) and *Pop Goes the Easel* (1935). Surviving theater contracts from the famous music-hall theater the Argyle, in Birkenhead, show the Three Stooges booked for live performances there in August 1940, just before the theater's destruction in a bombing raid in September of that year; they may have appeared there earlier, but most contracts from the 1930s are missing, possibly destroyed in the fire. Since the Argyle also broadcast its performances on radio, there are several possibilities for Woolf having the Stooges' slapstick routines in mind. In any case, the song provides another opportunity for Mrs. Manresa to be linked to a popping cork.

Gretna Green [98]   A village just over the border in Scotland, where young couples, unable to marry in England, could be married under Scottish law.

the Horn book [98]   A child's lesson book, generally a page mounted on a wooden paddle and covered with a protective laminate made from cow's horn.

my foot's like a burning, burning horseshoe [99]   Sir Spaniel's gout links him to P. B. Shelley's *Oedipus Tyrannus; or, Swellfoot the Tyrant,* an earthy, parodic comedy that satirically represents its characters as pigs. Suppressed in Shelley's time, the play was inspired by the rowdy, carnivalesque behavior of a crowd in Italy on St. Bartholomew's Day. Bartholomew Fair, one of the most raucous of public festivals, was abolished in England in 1855. *Oedipus* means "swollen foot," referring to his being maimed in the foot as an infant, and possibly connecting him to the Fisher King, whose sexual wound functions as a motif of sterility in T. S. Eliot's *The Waste Land.*

chalk stones [100]   Common name for deposits formed in gouty joints; the practice of relieving the pain by keeping the hands warm links Lady Harpy with the audience's "indigenous" old lady in the bath (wheel) chair, "crippled by arthritis," with her "ungloved twisted hands."

O ingratitude, thy name is Deborah! [101] Lady Harpy appears to combine Hamlet's "Frailty, thy name is woman!" (I.ii) and King Lear's "Ingratitude! . . . More hideous when thou show'st thee in a child / Than the sea-monster" (I.iv).

Sans niece, sans lover; and sans maid [101]   Lady Harpy Harraden echoes two previous expressions of fatalistic resignation: Jacques' famous speech in Shakespeare's *As You Like It,* beginning "All the world's a stage" and ending with a depiction of old age as "second childishness and mere oblivion, / Sans teeth, sans eyes, sans taste, sans everything" (II.vii), and the similar sentiments expressed in Edward FitzGerald's nineteenth-century translation of the great Persian poem, his "Rubáiyát of Omar Khayyám of Naishápúr": "Ah, make the most of what we yet may spend, / Before we too into the Dust descend; / Dust into Dust, and under Dust to lie / Sans Wine, sans Song, sans Singer, and—sans End!" (lines 93–96).

what I call myself [102]   The narrator's voice, situated here in the audience, signals the difference between a person's name, which implies a single entity, and the conflicting, multitudinous, conscious, and unconscious voices that make up a complex subjectivity. The notion of the discontinuous self, usually associated with postmodernism, is evident throughout Woolf's work.

worked like a nigger [103]   An expression originating in the United States, meaning to work exceptionally hard. It was generally used to denote praise or at least grudging admiration, with little or no consciousness of its racist implications. A 1949 article in *American Speech* labeled *nigger* a "powder-keg word," noting increasing public awareness of its derogatory connotations in the United States, yet claiming that racial tension, and hence awareness of racial prejudice, was significantly less in England. Dictionaries in the 1930s, including the supplement to the *Oxford English Dictionary* (1933), were beginning to identify the word *nigger* as a word of contempt, but the *American College Dictionary* of 1947 was the first to label the word "offensive." (See Rossell Hope Robbins, "Social Awareness and Semantic Change," *American Speech* 24.2 [1949]: 156–58.) In a letter written in 1939, Woolf described her own hard work in these terms (*Letters* 6: 362), but in *Between the Acts,* these words seem to be reported by an observer at the scene. It is unclear whether Woolf herself slips into unconscious racial stereotyping or whether she is exposing such stereotyping in the supposedly "innocent" language of the time.

No one wants it [103]   No one in England wants a war.

Gladstone [103]   William Ewart Gladstone (four times British Liberal prime minister between 1868 and 1894) was not a pacifist and, in the 1880s, he used force, however reluctantly, to oppose uprisings in Egypt and Sudan; nevertheless, he was a notable opponent of imperialist expansion and warfare, denouncing the Turkish slaughter of the Bulgarians and later of the Armenians, the British war against the Zulu in South Africa, and the British invasion of Afghanistan. At the end of his career, he fought (although unsuccessfully) against the buildup of British naval power in competition with Germany, during his last term from 1892–1894.

The glass is falling [104] The weather vane and the barometer (glass) indicate a coming storm.

Cleopatra [104] For Woolf's English readers, Cleopatra would most likely stir memories of Shakespeare's *Antony and Cleopatra,* and Enobarbus's famous tribute beginning, "The barge she sat on, like a burnish'd throne"—a line echoed in T. S. Eliot's *The Waste Land* (line 77). The choice of Cleopatra as one of Lucy's buried selves makes an amusing but also profound statement about the multitudinous selves in our unconscious life, for Lucy's personal self is clearly at an extreme remove from her "unacted part" as Queen of Egypt: "Age cannot wither her, nor custom stale / Her infinite variety: other women cloy / The appetites they feed; but she makes hungry / Where most she satisfies" (II.ii).

a twitcher of individual strings [105] The image suggests the handler of string puppets but is perhaps even closer to the *sutradhar* in classical Sanskrit theater, literally "the one who holds the threads." Related to the strings (*sutra*) in early puppet theater (although scholars debate which came first), the *sutradhar* combines the roles of producer, director, narrator, and stage manager, and has the crucial function of linking together the performers, the performance, and the audience. Mulk Raj

Anand's *Conversations in Bloomsbury* ends with the translation of *sudtradhar* as "puller of strings," to which John Maynard Keynes replies, "I am already that!" (London: Wildwood House, 1981: 159). Images of threads and strings run throughout *Between the Acts*.

Unblowing, ungrowing are the roses [106]   Isa's poetry echoes the words and the mood of Algernon Charles Swinburne's poem "The Garden of Proserpine" (1866), with its longing for the quiet and peace of the underworld, and escape from the doubts and pressures of time: "But no such winds blow thither, / And no such things grow there" (lines 23–24). Proserpine (Persephone), the daughter of the earth mother Ceres (Demeter), was seized by Hades, the god of the underworld, and carried away by force, but when her mother grieved so much that the earth turned barren, Persephone was permitted to return to her mother for a portion of each year, thus explaining the cycle of the seasons.

the great pear tree [106]   The pear is an ancient symbol of fecundity and fertility possibly due to the correspondences between its shape and a rounded breast or pregnant womb. In Katherine Mansfield's "Bliss," another story about a woman who suspects her husband of adultery, the wife believes she shares a hallowed moment with the other woman, looking at a flowering pear tree. In T. S. Eliot's "The Hollow Men," spiritual sterility is instantiated in the obverse image: "Here we go round the prickly pear."

caravanserai [106]   Although Woolf confuses this word, taken from the Persian and referring to "a roadside inn," with the long procession of camels, mules, or wagons making up a traveling caravan, she evokes a powerful image—used in *Three Guineas* as well—for the long, arduous journey that is life. A caravanserai figures in FitzGerald's "Rubáiyát of Omar Khayyám" as a tavern that offers a brief hedonistic respite from the bleakness of the journey.

leaders who in that they seek to lead desert us [107]   As early as 1919, Woolf wrote in her diary, "And more & more I come to loathe any dominion of one over another; any leadership, any imposition of the will" (*Diary* 1: 256). Psychoanalysts like Gregory Zilboorg later argued that the isolation of even a normal leader results in emotional detachment from the people, so that power and a sense of responsibility are inversely correlated. (See Robert A. Clark, "Psychiatrists and Psychoanalysts on War," *American Journal of Psychotherapy* 19 [1965]: 540–58.)

London street cries [107]   Vendors and hawkers for centuries called out their wares in the London streets, and over time their calls gradually acquired distinctive pitches and sounds. The famous Cries of London inspired numerous paintings and musical works.

to skip two hundred years [107]   Woolf stretches historical time by placing two hundred years between the reigns of Queen Anne (1702–1714) and Queen Victoria (1837–1901).

What's history without the Army? [107]   Woolf records a conversation, in 1921, with Lytton Strachey: "History must be written all over again. Its all morality— / & battles, I added" (*Diary* 2: 115).

a Grand Ensemble, round the Union Jack [107]   Pageants of the time would traditionally end with a patriotic glorification of the British Empire. Conversely, "The Abinger Pageant," a collaboration between producer Tom Harrison and E. M. Forster, ends—one wonders how they did it—with a flock of sheep.

a hansom . . . a growler . . . runners [108]   Hansom and growler refer to two different kinds of horse-drawn carriages (two wheeled and four wheeled), and runners were porters who ran alongside hoping to be hired to unload luggage.

D'you remember [108]   The following memories mix London low life (thieves, cutthroats, prostitutes, the poor Irish) with the privileged upper classes. Benjamin Disraeli's novel *Sybil: or, the Two Nations* (1845) launched a stinging critique of Victorian society as divided into the separate worlds of the rich and the poor.

Knocked 'em in the old Kent Road [108]   Another well-known music-hall song reflecting the experiences of the Victorian working class and the urban poor. The Old Kent Road, in South London, was also the route taken by Chaucer's pilgrims on their way to Canterbury.

the Crystal Palace [108]   The song stirs memories in the audience of the contrast between the harsh conditions of servants' lives and the grand architectural and technological accomplishments of the Victorian age. The Crystal Palace, a marvel of modern design built out of iron and glass, was the site of the Great Exhibition of 1851, a world fair organized to celebrate and stimulate British manufacturing throughout the empire.

ring up the Stores [109]   Replacing the row of little Victorian specialty shops, the modern city brought the economical efficiency of the department store. The Army and Navy Store, or "the Stores," was initially a cooperative formed in the nineteenth century to provide goods to the officers and families of those in the higher ranks of the armed forces at reduced cost; after World War I "the Stores" made its reasonable prices available to a free and open membership.

'Yde Park [110]   Speaking like a Cockney, Budge drops the *H* in *Hyde Park, hansom cab,* and *horses.*

Shah of Persia; Sultan of Morocco [110]   Budge gestures to the growing cosmopolitan nature of London, which he interprets as a sign of Britain's predominance in the world. Persia and Morocco, however, were not part of the British Empire.

Cook's tourists [110]   The firm of Thomas Cook began to operate in the mid-nineteenth century specifically to facilitate middle-class travel by providing organized tours, passports, guidebooks, and currency exchange.

Mansion House [110]   The official residence of the lord mayor of London, located in the financial district and used for public functions and as a court of law. The following speech mixes government, finance, and religion in a satiric critique of Victorian hypocrisy.

Famine. Fenians [110]   During the nineteenth century, the Irish suffered intensely from famines, notably the Great Famine caused by the potato blight in 1845–1849 that lasted until 1852. In a rising independence movement, the Fenian Brotherhood was formed by immigrant Irish in the United States, mounting attacks on the British Empire first through physical force, and then through financial support for the Irish Republican Brotherhood, a forerunner of the Irish Republican Army. Although Home Rule was achieved in 1921, the division of Ireland and the continuing ties to Britain angered the revolutionary nationalists and in 1939, just before the outbreak of World War II, the IRA began a bombing campaign in English towns.

natives of Peru [111]   In the middle of the nineteenth century, Peru was at the height of its guano trade, experiencing a financial boom due to the value of dried bird excrement as a natural fertilizer. But as artificial fertilizers were developed and the supply of guano became depleted, Peru fought a financially disastrous war with Chile over possession of the guano coast—the Costaguana of Joseph Conrad's *Nostromo*. Britain, seemingly nonimperialist in its support of Peruvian independence against imperial Spain, nevertheless benefited from assuming Peru's foreign debts in return for concessions on Peruvian railroads and guano exports, although by this time Britain was primarily interested in Peru's silver.

wherever one or two . . . come together [111]   A phrase echoing "Where two or three are gathered together in my name, there am I in the midst of them" (Matthew 18:20), echoed in turn in the order for Morning Prayer in the Anglican service: "and dost promise that when two or three are gathered together in thy Name thou wilt grant their requests."

Cripplegate; St. Giles's; Whitechapel; the Minories [111]   Areas of London associated with poverty, crime, or Jewish immigrant settlement, and thus aspects of the city excluded from centers of power like Mansion House.

white man's burden [111]   A common expression, taken from Rudyard Kipling's poem "The White Man's Burden" (*McClure's Magazine*, February 1899), and referring to the duty of the white races to spread the benefits of their civilization to the undeveloped world. Whether Kipling's poem is interpreted as imperialist racism, moral exhortation, or ironic self-deprecation, in October the same magazine consolidated the popular understanding of the phrase through an ad for Pears Soap—possibly parodied in the words "THE SOAP" in the "Circe" chapter of James Joyce's *Ulysses*—which promoted the "virtues of cleanliness" as the "first step towards lightening THE WHITE MAN'S BURDEN" and "brightening the dark corners of the earth as civilization advances."

the basement [112]   A reference to *downstairs,* the partially below-ground area of the house where the servants would be located.

peg-top trousers [112]   Peg-leg or peg-top trousers, so called because they were wide and pleated at the top and narrow at the ankles, thus resembling the shape of a child's toy, a cone-shaped spinning top. See note to "pegged down" (13) for repetitions of peg as a rhyming homonym.

the best days of life are over [113]   In spirit, the nineteenth-century act resembles the light comic operas of Gilbert and Sullivan, with their satiric spoofs on Victorian institutions and behavior, and their parodic replications of melodramatic plots. Edgar's speech and the following dialogue make fun of Victorian moral earnestness, while pointing to the gap between such high-minded spirituality and the exploitative dimension of imperialist missionary zeal.

butterfly nets . . . botanical cases [113]   An amateur craze for science blossomed in the nineteenth century, inspired by such earlier works as Gilbert White's *Natural History and Antiquities of Selborne* (see note to pages 70–71). Collecting bugs, moths, and butterflies was a passion of Virginia Woolf's own childhood, when she and her siblings formed their own Entomological Society.

those skulls and things [114]   Fossil collecting was another avid pursuit of the amateur scientist—one that profoundly disturbed the Victorian mind, however, not only by exposing geological records that conflicted with the biblical account of creation but also by evidencing the disappearance of whole species. The challenge to religious faith posed by "quarried stone" is captured in the image of "Nature, red in tooth and claw" in Alfred Lord Tennyson's *In Memoriam* (LVI).

O has Mr. Sibthorp a wife? [115]   Repetitions resembling the reprise sung by the chorus in a Gilbert and Sullivan operetta.

"The Last Rose of Summer" [115]   The nineteenth-century scene includes a number of popular parlor songs, stories, and poems, evoking the sentimentality of the Victorians yet also testifying to the circulation of popular culture through quotation and mis-quotation in a range of other works. "The Last Rose of Sum-mer" (from Thomas Moore's *A Selection of Irish Melodies* 5, 1813) adapted the tune of an earlier song, "The Groves of Blarney," a comic burlesque on a still earlier song, "Castle Hyde," set to an old Irish folk melody. "The Last Rose of Summer" was itself in-terpolated into the German composer Friedrich von Flotow's opera *Martha* (1847), much loved by nineteenth-century London audiences. Numerous allusions to both the song and the opera weave their way through the "Sirens" chapter of James Joyce's *Ulysses*.

"I Never Loved a Dear Gazelle" [115]   The opening line of Lewis Carroll's satirical "Tema Con Variazioni" (1869), which parodies "I never nursed a dear gazelle," a poem from Thomas Moore's *Lalla Rookh: An Oriental Romance* (1817). Changing the meaning of *dear* from "loved" to "expensive," Carroll accompanies his parody with the argument that poetry, like music, should be sub-ject to "that process of Dilution" called by composers "setting," in which a few notes of a tune are woven into the new com-position, saving us from the transports of the original in its concentrated form. Carroll's misquotation is repeated but resen-timentalized by the character Leopold Bloom in the "Circe" chapter of James Joyce's *Ulysses*.

"I'd be a Butterfly" [115]   A song by Thomas Haynes Bayly, trans-lated solemnly into Latin by the Reverend Francis Wrangham, the archbishop of Cleveland, in 1828, but parodied by a young

William Makepeace Thackeray as "I'd be a tadpole" (*Gownsman*, November 12, 1829). Referenced ubiquitously throughout the nineteenth century, Bayly's song is described by Elizabeth Barrett Browning's Aurora Leigh, in the poem of that name, as "a paltry tune you never fairly liked" but that you cannot get out of your head (lines 960–65).

"Rule, Britannia." [116]   The patriotic poem by the Anglo-Scot James Thomson, set to music by Thomas Arne as part of the masque *Alfred* (1740), based on the life of Alfred the Great. In the nineteenth century, the exhortatory line "Britannia, rule the waves" was changed to "Britannia rules the waves," and the song came popularly to epitomize the idea of empire, accompanying, for example, along with the next song, "Home, Sweet Home," Queen Victoria's opening of the Colonial Exhibition in 1886.

time, gentlemen, time ladies [117]   The traditional closing call of the publican (and therefore appropriate for the actor playing Budge) but with the ominous sense of mortality in the similar call, "HURRY UP PLEASE IT'S TIME" in T. S. Eliot's *The Waste Land* (line 140 ff.)

'Ome, Sweet 'Ome [117]   A song from the operetta *Clari* (1823) with music by the English composer Henry Rowley Bishop and adapted from a play by the American poet John Howard Payne, in turn inspired by a Parisian ballet *Clari* (1820) with music by Rodolphe Kreutzer. Immortalized by Jenny Lind, "Home, Sweet Home" is referenced by Leopold Bloom while listening to the orchestra tuning up at the Gaiety Theatre in the "Sirens" chapter of James Joyce's *Ulysses*.

For here . . . comes the bread-winner, home from the city [117]   An inversion of "Home is the sailor, home from sea, / and the hunter home from the hill," the last lines of the poem "Requiem" by

Robert Louis Stevenson, which were engraved on Stevenson's tomb.

Sindbad the sailor [117]   The stories of Sindbad's seven fantastic voyages are narrated in the *Arabian Nights* (translated into English by Sir Richard Burton in 1850). There are references to "Sinbad" in both the "Eumaeus" and "Ithaca" chapters of Joyce's *Ulysses*, in which Sinbad acquires multiple reflections as "Tinbad the Tailor and Jinbad the Jailer," etc., and ultimately merges with Ulysses, the Flying Dutchman, and the Ancient Mariner.

mechanics' institute [117]   As part of the adult-education movement in the nineteenth century, mechanics' institutes were created to provide workers with technical training and scientific instruction in the evenings; as the education offered moved into areas of culture, however, the institutes became vulnerable to the charge that they were imposing middle-class values on the working class.

unhygienic [118]   Domestic hygiene was greatly promoted during the early twentieth century, as streamlined designs and developments in technology made possible a greater cleanliness than in the cluttered, unsanitary conditions of the nineteenth-century household. Hygienic concerns relating to physical health, however, expanded in metaphorical ways to include mental, spiritual, social, and ultimately racial hygiene. The quotation marks around the word thus imply that Woolf's satire cuts both ways.

You don't believe in history [118]   William's remark reflects the approach known as "historicism," which emphasizes the distinctiveness of past eras, regards time as change, and bases all understanding on historical context. Against the view that art is "immortal" and therefore "unprogressive," for example, Woolf's father, Leslie Stephen, posited the historicist view that the individual is "an organ of the society in which he has been brought up" and "dependent on what in the modern phrase we call his 'environment'" (*English Literature and Society in the Eighteenth Century* 8).

one-making [119]   Compare the comic attempts at such one-making as performed by Jinny Carslake in *Jacob's Room* (chapter 11), or by the Christian missionaries in Forster's *A Passage to India* (chapter 4); yet also, in Forster's novel, the more profound, humble, and generous attempt to encompass the whole performed, in the Hindu temple, by Professor Godbole (chapter 33).

Shakespeare and the musical glasses! [119]   An expression, originating in Oliver Goldsmith's *The Vicar of Wakefield* (1766), where it represents "fashionable" conversational topics in high society, not unlike T. S. Eliot's "In the room the women come and go / Talking of Michelangelo" ("The Love Song of J. Alfred Prufrock") Coming to signify high culture, the phrase entered the popular lexicon, quoted variously in Charles Dickens, *American Notes* (1842); Rhoda Broughton, *Cometh Up as a Flower: an Autobiography* (1867); Henry James, *The American* (1877) and *The Ambassadors* (1903); Rudyard Kipling, *The Story of the Gadsbys* (1888); Israel Zangwill, *Without Prejudice* (1896); William Archer, *America To-day, Observations and Reflections* (1899); Alice Muriel Williamson and Charles Norris Williamson, *The Princess Passes: A Romance of a Motor-Car* (1905); and G. K. Chesterton, *The Return of Don Quixote* (1927). "Musical glasses" refers to an instrument, highly popular in the eighteenth century, made from a set of wineglasses containing differing amounts of water. Benjamin Franklin perfected a version that in 1761 he named the "glass armonica," for which numerous composers, including Mozart, wrote. Due to its soft tones, the instrument did not survive the advent of the large concert hall in the nineteenth century.

a fund for installing electric light [120]   The production in 1934 of *The Rock*, a pageant for which T. S. Eliot wrote the choruses, was similarly in aid of fund-raising for the Forty-Five Churches Fund of the London Diocese. See also the note to page 123, "rebuilt (witness man with hod) by human effort."

Four and twenty blackbirds [121]   From another nursery song, "Sing a song of sixpence," where the first stanza ends, "The maid was in the garden hanging out the clothes, / When down came a blackbird and pecked off her nose!" Isa's shift to an eagle and the overtones of punishment recall the altered nursery rhyme in the opening section of James Joyce's *Portrait of the Artist as a Young Man*, following "the eagles will come and pull out his eyes" (4).

One window, looking east [122]   Directional symbolism in religious observance is ancient in origin, evident in pagan, Jewish, and Christian rituals. Facing in the direction of the rising sun traditionally signified resurrection, rebirth, and hope. In Mulk Raj Anand's *Untouchable* (1935; London: Penguin, 1940), however, the story is told of a Hindu saint, supposedly Gandhi, who was chastised for sleeping in the direction with the image of God at his feet, whereupon the saint replied that God is everywhere, and it was discovered that if the saint's body was turned, the image of the god moved as well (139).

ten mins. of present time [122]   This portion of the pageant presciently anticipates the American composer John Cage's stochastic or aleatoric composition *4'33"* (1952), in which the performer(s) sit silently on the stage for the duration of the piece, during which time the audience listens to the ambient sounds and the sounds that they make themselves. Cage's purpose was to have "no purpose": that is, to focus his audience's attention on awareness, rather than understanding, and on responsiveness to the random collective whole.

Tears. Tears. Tears. [122]   Echoing a poem by Walt Whitman, beginning and ending "Tears! Tears! Tears!" in which a storm at night is imaged as the tears of some mysterious "ghost," some "form in the dark" bent and huddled on the beach, weeping for the world. Compare Woolf's "Not a sound this evening to bring in the human tears. I remember the sudden profuse shower one night just before war wh. made me think of all men & women weeping" (*Diary* 5: 274).

rebuilt (witness man with hod) by human effort [123]   Compare the chorus of workmen in T. S. Eliot's *The Rock* who chant of building with "new bricks," "new stone," and "new speech" a "Church for all," and yet are reminded "We build in vain unless the LORD build with us." Woolf was unable to attend a performance of the play but, in reading it, she judged Eliot's writing as too full of priestly dogmatism (*Letters* 5: 315).

the League of . . . [123]   In popular Empire Day celebrations mounted by schools and local communities, the participants typically dressed up to represent the colonies. La Trobe's pageant goes beyond empire to represent the League of Nations. In the interwar years, the League of Nations pursued the goal of peace through international cooperation, but such efforts collapsed with Japan's invasion of Manchuria in 1931 and Italy's invasion of Ethiopia (Abyssinia) in 1935. Through its lay societies, however, like the League of Nations Society, of which Leonard Woolf was a founding member, the League successfully mobilized public support for disarmament and international goals. A week before her death, writing to Lady Cecil about Lord Robert Cecil's autobiography *A Great Experiment* (1941), Virginia Woolf wrote, "There wasnt, even for me, a non-politician, a word too much about the League" (*Letters* 6: 482). Leonard's review of Cecil's autobiography argued that a primary reason for the League's failure was its exclusion from the bodies determining foreign policy of the national states, which preserved their right to autonomy, and he praised Cecil's dedication to the establishment of a new international body for a postwar world (*New Statesman and Nation,* February 15, 1941: 163–64).

temple-haunting martins [124]   A reference to Banquo's speech welcoming Duncan to Macbeth's castle in Shakespeare's *Macbeth:* "This guest of summer, / The temple-haunting martlet, does approve / By his loved mansionry that the heaven's breath / Smells wooingly here" (I.vi.3–6). The martin is a species of swallow, but in Shakespeare's play, its augury of peace and prosperity functions ironically, since Duncan will be murdered in Macbeth's castle.

in the crannied wall [124]   A displaced image from Tennyson's poem "Flower in the Crannied Wall" (1869), in which the intense visualization of the flower moves the speaker to reflect, "*If* I could understand / What you are, root and all, and all in all, / I should know what God and man is." In the new hygienic vision, the refrigerator becomes the microcosm of macrocosmic design.

Jazz? [124]   In rhythm and rhyme, this paragraph imitates the syncopations of jazz (which at this time referred loosely to a range of popular music, including ragtime), but jazz was understood to alter the sequence and syntax of linear progression as well. In an early protest against such perceived iconoclasm, Clive Bell sounded the warning that Virginia Woolf "has lately developed a taste for playing tricks with traditional constructions. Certainly she 'leaves out' with the boldest of them: here is syncopation if you like it. I am not sure that I do" ("Plus de Jazz," *Since Cezanne* [New York: Harcourt, Brace, 1922]). T. S. Eliot shared gramophone recordings and talk about the popular dances the Grizzly Bear, the Chicken Strut, and the Memphis Shake with Virginia Woolf. (See Bonnie Kime Scott, 102–3.)

shiver into splinters [124]   The image of splinters runs throughout Woolf's writing, sometimes signifying the destruction of warfare, sometimes pain, sometimes a new complex beauty. In *Jacob's Room,* the target of the guns on a battleship "flames into splinters," and in *Between the Acts,* Giles has premonitions of German planes coming to "splinter Bolney Minster into smithereens and blast the Folly." In 1932, describing a neurasthenic attack, possibly heightened by thoughts about death, Woolf wrote in her diary of "pain, as of childbirth" and a gradual coming to consciousness until she "lay presiding, like a flickering light, like a most solicitous mother, over the shattered splintered fragments of [her] body" (*Diary* 4: 121). Yet in *The Waves,* Bernard speaks of a morning vision as "that sudden rush of wings, that exclamation, carol, and confusion; the riot and babble of voices; and all the drops are sparkling, trembling, as if the garden were a splintered mosaic, vanishing, twinkling, not yet formed into one whole" (182–83); and Woolf, as early as 1908, was writing of her attempt to achieve "a different kind of beauty ... a symmetry by means of infinite discords ... some kind of whole made of shivering fragments" with which to record "the flight of the mind" (*A Passionate Apprentice* 393). In a later (1940) essay, she wrote, "Yet it is the only way of getting at the truth—to have it broken into many splinters by many mirrors and so select" ("The Man at the Gate," *Collected Essays* 3 [New York: Harcourt, 1967]: 220).

Mopping, mowing, whisking, frisking [125]   Echoing Christina Rossetti's "Goblin Market." See note to page 59.

old man with a beard [125]   A ghostly figure, like William Blake's Urizen or Nobodaddy, who haunts *Between the Acts* either in the form of this actor or in the plant that Isa plucks at various times to sniff its bitter scent. See the note to page 77.

some phrase or fragment from their parts [125]   The pastiche of allusions
on page 126, which in turn draws on allusions in the words of
both actors and audience, recalls the androgynous Tiresias's line
in T. S. Eliot's *The Waste Land,* "These fragments I have shored
against my ruins." In the following citations, page numbers refer
to earlier occurrences in *Between the Acts: I am not in my perfect mind*
(page 59); *I'm the old top hat* (music hall song; page 83); *Home is
the hunter* (page 117); *the miner sweats* (page 85); *maiden faith is rudely
strumpeted* (adapted from Shakespeare's sonnet 66, see "strumpet" page 67); *Sweet and low* (song from Tennyson's "The
Princess," see page 64); *Is that a dagger* (*Macbeth,* II.i, see references to daggers throughout); *Lady I love* (page 81); *I'd be a butterfly* (page 115); *Hark, hark* (page 80). *"In thy will is our peace"* echoes
a line in T. S. Eliot's *Ash Wednesday,* "Our peace in His will," a
translation of "E'n la sua volontade è nostra pace," from
Dante's *Paradiso* (canto 3, line 85), which in turn alludes to a line
in the *Confessions* of Saint Augustine, which has been translated
as "In thy good pleasure is our peace" or "In a good will is our
peace" (book 13, chapter 9, section 10).

the audience saw themselves [126]   Reflected in numerous little mirrors
and shiny surfaces, the audience would see themselves in a manner possibly resembling Roger Fry's description of the art of
Henri Matisse: "By the magic of an intensely coherent style our
familiar every day world . . . has been broken to pieces as though
reflected in a broken mirror and then put together again into a
far more coherent unity in which all the visual values are mys-
teriously changed—in which plastic forms can be read as pattern and apparently flat patterns are read as diversely inclined
planes" (*Henri Matisse* [1930; London: A. Zwemmer, 1935]: 21).

orts, scraps and fragments [127]   Words from Shakespeare's
Troilus and Cressida, occurring in a speech where Troilus rages
against Cressida's infidelity: "The fractions of her faith, orts of

her love, / The fragments, scraps, the bits, and greasy relics, / Of her o'er-eaten faith, are bound to Diomed" (V.ii).

the warring battle-plumed warriors straining asunder [128]   The image echoes the final scene in E. M. Forster's *A Passage to India:* The Muslim Aziz and the Englishman Fielding come together in a violent "love" scene in which the riders strain to be together but the horses force them apart.

Must I be Thomas, you Jane? [129]   John Thomas and Lady Jane are common pet names for male and female genitalia, made famous by D. H. Lawrence's *Lady Chatterley's Lover,* a novel first published in Italy in 1928 but banned in England, and then published in expurgated form in England in 1932.

A few were chosen [130]   The Reverend Streatfield's talk is laced with obvious allusions: "For many are called, but few are chosen" (Matthew 22:14); "For Fools rush in where Angels fear to tread" (Alexander Pope, *An Essay on Criticism,* line 625); "Speak every man truth with his neighbour: for we are members one of another" (Ephesians 4:25). The latter phrase is reiterated as well in Winifred Holtby's *South Riding* (1936), another novel that ends with a village pageant in which a gramophone plays a strong role.

Oracles? [135]   In the ancient classical world, oracles (people or places) were consulted for prophetic utterances or "oracular wisdom," generally spiritual in nature. The Later Typescript more correctly reads: "Were the oracles a foretaste, if I'm not being irreverent, of our own religion?" (*PH* 417).

science . . . is making things . . . more spiritual [135]   James Jeans and Arthur Eddington were astrophysicists who wrote popularly accessible books on science (with which Woolf was familiar) and who both argued—although in radically different ways—that there was no incompatibility between science and religion. In a 1928 debate against the secularist Chapman Cohen, published as "Materialism: has it exploded?" C. E. M. Joad argued that physics had dissolved matter into a space-time continuum, citing Eddington as his authority. In Mulk Raj Anand's *Untouchable*, a young Indian poet says, "The word *maya* does not mean illusion, it means magic. That is the dictum of the latest Hindu translator of the *Vedanta*, Dr. Coomaraswamy. And in that signification the word approximates to the views on the nature of the physical world of your pet scientists, Eddington and Jeans" (London: Penguin, 1940: 152–53).

Ah, that's the question [135]   The opening line of Hamlet's famous soliloquy—"To be, or not to be: that is the question" (III.i)—and the question T. S. Eliot's Prufrock dares not ask.

playing bodkin [136]   A bodkin is a little dagger or a long pin; with the analogy of a long, thin object, to ride or sit bodkin is to travel squeezed between two people. The word appears in Hamlet's "To be, or not to be" speech, when he imagines that a man, "might his quietus make with a bare bodkin" (*Hamlet*, III.i).

Tears, tears, tears [136]   A poem by Walt Whitman. See note to page 122.

couldn't the blue thread settle [139]   The wording in the Early Typescript illuminates the compression of the final version: "Can't civilization—visible to her vision-haunted eyes as the blue thread or the dragon fly—light there? ... She was retrieving from sharks above [the aeroplanes] and sharks below [imagined] a foothold for new people, other people, the red-skinned or if you like the black, to settle on" (*PH* 171). The dragonfly–blue thread conflation appears in Dante Gabriel Rossetti's sonnet "Silent Noon," a poem that conveys an experience of unity in a suspended moment of inarticulate silence: "Deep in the sun-searched growths the dragon-fly / Hangs like a blue thread loosened from the sky" (from *The House of Life,* 1870).

her semblable [141]   A resonant word in the first line of Charles Baudelaire's "To the Reader," the opening poem in *Les fleurs du mal* (1857): "Hypocrite lecteur,—mon semblable,—mon frère!" (Hypocrite reader,—my double,—my brother!). Baudelaire's direct address to the reader is quoted in the last line of "The Burial of the Dead" section in T. S. Eliot's *The Waste Land* (76).

Old Man's Beard [141]   See notes to pages 77 and 125.

like Venus … to her prey [141]   A line from Jean Racine's *Phèdre,* "Venus toute entière à sa proie attaché" (Venus wholly fastened to her prey), depicting Phèdre as consumed by her guilty and unrequited love for her stepson, Hippolyte. Lytton Strachey praised the phrase as being as "compact as dynamite" (*Books and Characters,* 15) in representing "the furies of insensate passion" (*Landmarks in French Literature* ([1912; London: T. Butterworth, 1929]: 104). See also the note to page 97, "And so Racine."

a woman, veiled; or a man? [145]   Compare the hooded figure, "I do not know whether a man or a woman," in T. S. Eliot's *The Waste Land,* and the "veiled sister" in part 5 of his "Ash Wednesday." Eliot associated the hooded figure with the Hanged Man of the tarot, the Hanged God of Frazer's *The Golden Bough,* and the risen Christ (see his "Notes on 'The Waste Land.'")

beetle, rolling pebbles [147]   The ancient Egyptians held the dung beetle or scarab to be sacred, since it was thought to resemble the sun god rolling the sun across the sky, thus conveying ideas of transformation, renewal, and resurrection. The image is used by D. H. Lawrence.

Outline of History [147]   A simplified version of an early passage in G. M. Trevelyan's *History of England:* "For many centuries after

Britain became an island the untamed forest was king. Its moist and mossy floor was hidden from heaven's eye by a close-drawn curtain woven of innumerable tree-tops, which shivered in the breezes of summer dawn and broke into wild music of millions upon millions of wakening birds" (3–4). See also the note to page 6.

raised great stones [148]   G. M. Trevelyan refers to ancient monuments such as the Iron Age hill fort of Maiden Castle in Dorchester, and the prehistoric stone circle, likely of sacred significance, at Stonehenge in Wiltshire.

heart of darkness [148]   The central image in Joseph Conrad's *Heart of Darkness*, a novel that, like *Between the Acts*, opens by underwriting the present with evocations of the past when England was yet a swamp and wilderness, undergoing colonization by the Romans. See the note to page 4, "Romans."

Suggestions for Further Reading:
Virginia Woolf

Editions

The Complete Shorter Fiction. Edited by Susan Dick. 2nd ed. San Diego: Harcourt, 1989.

The Diary of Virginia Woolf. Edited by Anne Olivier Bell. 5 vols. New York: Harcourt, 1977–84.

The Essays of Virginia Woolf. Edited by Andrew McNeillie. 6 vols. [in progress]. San Diego: Harcourt Brace Jovanovich, 1986–.

The Letters of Virginia Woolf. Edited by Nigel Nicolson and Joanne Trautmann. 6 vols. New York: Harcourt Brace Jovanovich, 1975–80.

Moments of Being. Edited by Jeanne Schulkind. San Diego: Harcourt, 1985.

A Passionate Apprentice: The Early Journals, 1897–1909. Edited by Mitchell A. Leaska. San Diego: Harcourt, 1990.

Biographies and Reference Works

Briggs, Julia. *Virginia Woolf: An Inner Life.* San Diego: Harcourt, 2005.

Hussey, Mark. *Virginia Woolf A to Z: A Comprehensive Reference for Students, Teachers, and Common Readers to Her Life, Works, and Critical Reception.* New York: Facts on File, 1995.

Kirkpatrick, B. J., and Stuart N. Clarke. *A Bibliography of Virginia Woolf.* 4th ed. Oxford: Clarendon, 1997.

Lee, Hermione. *Virginia Woolf.* New York: Knopf, 1996.

Marder, Herbert. *The Measure of Life: Virginia Woolf's Last Years.* Ithaca, NY: Cornell University Press, 2000.

Poole, Roger. *The Unknown Virginia Woolf.* 4th ed. Cambridge: Cambridge University Press, 1995.

Reid, Panthea. *Art and Affection: A Life of Virginia Woolf.* New York: Oxford University Press, 1996.

General Criticism

Abel, Elizabeth. *Virginia Woolf and the Fictions of Psychoanalysis.* Chicago: University of Chicago Press, 1989.

Bazin, Nancy Topping. *Virginia Woolf and the Androgynous Vision.* New Brunswick, NJ: Rutgers University Press, 1973.

Beer, Gillian. *Virginia Woolf: The Common Ground.* Ann Arbor: University of Michigan Press, 1996.

Cuddy-Keane, Melba. *Virginia Woolf, the Intellectual, and the Public Sphere.* Cambridge: Cambridge University Press, 2003.

DiBattista, Maria. *Virginia Woolf's Major Novels: The Fables of Anon.* New Haven, CT: Yale University Press, 1980.

Fleishman, Avrom. *Virginia Woolf: A Critical Reading.* Baltimore: Johns Hopkins University Press, 1975.

Froula, Christine. *Virginia Woolf and the Bloomsbury Avant-Garde: War, Civilization, Modernity.* New York: Columbia University Press, 2005.

Guiguet, Jean. *Virginia Woolf and Her Works.* 1965. Reprint, New York: Harcourt Brace Jovanovich, 1976.

Harper, Howard. *Between Language and Silence: The Novels of Virginia Woolf.* Baton Rouge: Louisiana State University Press, 1982.

Hussey, Mark. *The Singing of the Real World: The Philosophy of Virginia Woolf's Fiction.* Columbus: Ohio State University Press, 1986.

———, ed. *Virginia Woolf and War: Fiction, Reality and Myth.* Syracuse, NY: Syracuse University Press, 1991.

Majumdar, Robin, and Allen McLaurin, eds. *Virginia Woolf: The Critical Heritage*. Boston: Routledge, 1975.

Marcus, Jane. *Art and Anger: Reading Like a Woman*. Columbus: Ohio State University Press, 1988.

———, ed. *New Feminist Essays on Virginia Woolf*. Lincoln: University of Nebraska Press, 1981.

———, ed. *Virginia Woolf: A Feminist Slant*. Lincoln: University of Nebraska Press, 1983.

———, ed. *Virginia Woolf and Bloomsbury: A Centenary Celebration*. Bloomington: Indiana University Press, 1987.

———. *Virginia Woolf and the Languages of Patriarchy*. Bloomington: Indiana University Press, 1987.

McLaurin, Allen. *Virginia Woolf: The Echoes Enslaved*. Cambridge: Cambridge University Press, 1973.

McNees, Eleanor, ed. *Virginia Woolf: Critical Assessments*. 4 vols. New York: Routledge, 1994.

Minow-Pinkney, Makiko. *Virginia Woolf and the Problem of the Subject: Feminine Writing in the Major Novels*. New Brunswick, NJ: Rutgers University Press, 1987.

Phillips, Kathy J. *Virginia Woolf Against Empire*. Knoxville: University of Tennessee Press, 1994.

Roe, Sue, and Susan Sellers, eds. *The Cambridge Companion to Virginia Woolf*. Cambridge: Cambridge University Press, 2000.

Ruotolo, Lucio. *The Interrupted Moment: A View of Virginia Woolf's Novels*. Stanford, CA: Stanford University Press, 1986.

Silver, Brenda R. *Virginia Woolf Icon*. Chicago: University of Chicago Press, 1999.

Zwerdling, Alex. *Virginia Woolf and the Real World*. Berkeley: University of California Press, 1986.

Suggestions for Further Reading:
Between the Acts

(in addition to the works cited in the introduction)

Ames, Christopher. "The Modernist Canon Narrative: Woolf's *Between the Acts* and Joyce's 'Oxen of the Sun.'" *Twentieth Century Literature* 37 (1991): 390–404.

Beer, Gillian. "*Between the Acts:* Resisting the End." In *Virginia Woolf: The Common Ground,* 125–48. Ann Arbor: University of Michigan Press, 1996.

———. "The Island and the Aeroplane: The Case of Virginia Woolf." In *Virginia Woolf: The Common Ground,* 149–78. Ann Arbor: University of Michigan Press, 1996.

———. "Virginia Woolf and Pre-History." In *Arguing with the Past: Essays in Narrative from Woolf to Sidney,* 159–82. New York: Routledge, 1989.

Busse, Kristina. "Reflecting the Subject in History: The Return of the Real in *Between the Acts.*" *Woolf Studies Annual* 7 (2001): 75–101.

Cuddy-Keane, Melba. "The Politics of Comic Modes in Virginia Woolf's *Between the Acts.*" *PMLA* 105 (1990): 273–85.

De Gay, Jane. "Bringing the Literary Past to Life in *Between the Acts.*" In *Virginia Woolf's Novels and the Literary Past,* 186–211. Edinburgh: Edinburgh University Press, 2006.

DuPlessis, Rachel Blau. "'"I" rejected; "We" substituted': The Later Novels of Woolf." In *Writing Beyond the Ending: Narrative Strategies of Twentieth-Century Women Writers,* 162–77. Bloomington: University of Indiana Press, 1985.

Esty, Joshua. "Insular Rites: Virginia Woolf and the Later Modernist Pageant-Play." In *A Shrinking Island: Modernism and National Culture in England*, 54–107. Princeton, NJ: Princeton University Press, 2004.

Herman, David. "Towards a Metapragmatics of Represented Discourse: Prague School Functionalism and Woolf's *Between the Acts*." In *Universal Grammar and Narrative Form*, 139–81. Durham and London: Duke University Press, 1995.

Hussey, Mark. "' "I" Rejected; "We" Substituted': Self and Society in *Between the Acts*." In *Reading and Writing Women's Lives: A Study of the Novel of Manners*. Edited by Bege K. Bowers and Barbara Brothers, 141–52. Ann Arbor: UMI Research Press, 1990.

———. "Reading and Ritual in *Between the Acts*." *Anima* 15.2 (Spring 1989): 89–99.

Joplin, Patricia Klindienst. "The Authority of Illusion: Feminism and Fascism in Virginia Woolf's *Between the Acts*." *South Central Review* 6.2 (Summer 1989): 88–104.

Marder, Herbert. *The Measure of Life: Virginia Woolf's Last Years*. Ithaca: Cornell University Press, 2000.

McIntire, Gabrielle. "Remembering what has almost already been forgotten: where memory touches history." In *Modernism, Memory, and Desire: T. S. Eliot and Virginia Woolf*, 180–209. Cambridge: Cambridge University Press, 2008.

McWhirter, David. "The Novel, the Play, and the Book: *Between the Acts* and the Tragicomedy of History." *ELH* 60.3 (1993): 787–812.

———. "Woolf, Eliot, and the Elizabethans: The Politics of Modernist Nostalgia." In *Virginia Woolf: Reading the Renaissance*. Edited by Sally Greene, 245–66. Athens: Ohio University Press, 1999.

Miller, Andrew John. "'Our Representative, Our Spokesman': Modernity, Professionalism, and Representation in Virginia Woolf's *Between the Acts*." *Studies in the Novel* 33.1 (2001): 34–50.

Miller, J. Hillis. "*Between the Acts*: Repetition as Extrapolation." In

Fiction and Repetition: Seven English Novels, 203–31. Cambridge, MA: Harvard University Press, 1982.

Miller, Marlowe A. "Unveiling 'the Dialectic of Culture and Barbarism' in British Pageantry: Virginia Woolf's *Between the Acts.*" *Papers on Language and Literature: A Journal for Scholars and Critics of Language and Literature* 34.2 (1998): 134–61.

Pridmore-Brown, Michele. "1939–40: Of Virginia Woolf, Gramophones, and Fascism." *PMLA* 113.3 (1998): 408–21.

Rosenfeld, Natania. "Monstrous Conjugations: Images of Dictatorship in the Anti-Fascist Writings of Virginia and Leonard Woolf." In *Virginia Woolf and Fascism: Resisting the Dictators' Seduction.* Edited by Merry M. Pawlowski, 122–36. Basingstoke, England: Palgrave, 2001.

Ruotolo, Lucio. "The Tyranny of Leadership: *Between the Acts.*" In *The Interrupted Moment: A View of Virginia Woolf's Novels,* 205–30. Stanford, CA: Stanford University Press, 1986.

Scott, Bonnie Kime. "The Subversive Mechanics of Woolf's Gramophone in *Between the Acts.*" In *Virginia Woolf in the Age of Mechanical Reproduction: Music, Cinema, Photography, and Popular Culture,* 97–113. Edited by Pamela L. Caughie. New York: Garland, 2000.

Southworth, Helen. "Virginia Woolf's 'Wild England': George Borrow, Autoethnography, and *Between the Acts.*" *Studies in the Novel* 39.2 (2007): 196–215.

Tratner, Michael. "Why Isn't *Between the Acts* a Movie?" In *Virginia Woolf in the Age of Mechanical Reproduction: Music, Cinema, Photography, and Popular Culture.* Edited by Pamela L. Caughie, 115–34. New York: Garland, 2000.

Westman, Karin E. "'For Her Generation the Newspaper Was a Book': Media, Mediation, and Oscillation in Virginia Woolf's *Between the Acts.*" *Journal of Modern Literature* 29.2 (2006): 1–18.

Wiley, Catherine. "Making History Unrepeatable in Virginia Woolf's *Between the Acts.*" *CLIO: A Journal of Literature, History, and the Philosophy of History* 25.1 (1995): 3–20.

Wirth-Nesher, Hana. "Final Curtain on the War: Figure and Ground in Virginia Woolf's *Between the Acts*." *Style* 28.2 (1994): 183–200.

Yoshino, Ayako. "*Between the Acts* and Louis Napoleon Parker—the Creator of the Modern English Pageant." *Critical Survey* 15.2 (2003): 49–62.

Virginia Woolf Annotated Editions

Top Woolf scholars provide valuable introductions, notes, suggestions for further reading, and critical analysis in this paperback series. Students reading these books will have the resources at hand to help them understand the text as well as the reasons and methods behind Woolf's writing.

Between the Acts
Annotated and with an introduction by Melba Cuddy-Keane
978-0-15-603473-9 • 0-15-603473-5

Jacob's Room
Annotated and with an introduction by Vara Neverow
978-0-15-603479-1 • 0-15-603479-4

Mrs. Dalloway
Annotated and with an introduction by Bonnie Kime Scott
978-0-15-603035-9 • 0-15-603035-7

Orlando: A Biography
Annotated and with an introduction by Maria DiBattista
978-0-15-603151-6 • 0-15-603151-5

A Room of One's Own
Annotated and with an introduction by Susan Gubar
978-0-15-603041-0 • 0-15-603041-1

Three Guineas
Annotated and with an introduction by Jane Marcus
978-0-15-603163-9 • 0-15-603163-9

To the Lighthouse
Annotated and with an introduction by Mark Hussey
978-0-15-603047-2 • 0-15-603047-0

The Waves
Annotated and with an introduction by Molly Hite
978-0-15-603157-8 • 0-15-603157-4

The Years
Annotated and with an introduction by Eleanor McNees
978-0-15-603485-2 • 0-15-603485-9

Each volume includes a preface by Mark Hussey, professor of English and women's and gender studies at Pace University, and editor of *Woolf Studies Annual*.

Harcourt | HARVEST BOOKS
www.HarcourtBooks.com

CPSIA information can be obtained
at www.ICGtesting.com
Printed in the USA
LVOW12s1507200118
563154LV00015B/4/P